PRAISE FOR
LAWRENCE C. CONNOLLY

"Sharp images . . . etching depictions of eerie scenes and telling analogies are this writer's forte."
—Jetse de Vries, *The Fix*

"Plain and simple, this guy can write."
—Thomas F. Monteleone, Bram Stoker Award winner

"One of the joys of my days at *Twilight Zone* was encountering the work of an extraordinarily subtle and imaginative writer, Lawrence C. Connolly, who brought enormous power to the shortest of stories."
—T.E.D. Klein, author of *The Ceremonies* and *Dark Gods*

"Lawrence C. Connolly writes with a purity of prose, his world not confined to the page, but breathing, soaring, sometimes kicking and cussing, but ever appealing to all the senses. Connolly is a writer to follow, and his work a thing to savor."
—Mary SanGiovanni, author of *The Hollower*

"[O]utstanding short stories."
—Robert Morrish, fiction editor of *Cemetery Dance*

"[A] captivating writer who crafts drum-tight plots, loaded with realistic characters and fantastic settings with great style and substance."
—Michael Arnzen, author of *100 Jolts*

"["The Others"] showcases Connelly's ability to cross the sub-genres from SF to horror and back."
—Colin Harvey, Suite101.com

PRAISE FOR
VEINS

"With . . . expert imagery, Lawrence C. Connolly takes a reader on a different kind of magical mystery tour . . . about what drives people to extremes, and how destiny ultimately intervenes."
—HellNotes.com

"[S]ubtly haunting, bringing together Native American Okwe myth with a crime thriller. The plot is fast and intense and the characters are wonderfully real."
—Laura Lehman, BellaOnline.com

"Feels like some of the best magic realism that's been written lately . . . highly readable."
—BookSpotCentral.com

"For years I've been an admirer of Lawrence C. Connolly's exquisite and deeply affecting short fiction—with VEINS he has done the impossible and surpassed his own high standards. This darkly wondrous novel held me under its spell for days, and haunts me even now, weeks later. I began the novel as an admirer of Connolly; I finished it as one in awe—and so will you."
—Gary A. Braunbeck, author of *Destinations Unknown*

"Much like the souped-up vintage Mustang that cuts through the heart of the story, VEINS starts fast, accelerates quickly, and finishes with a flourish, fulfilling all the promise at novel length that Lawrence C. Connolly has been flashing for years in his outstanding short stories."
—Robert Morrish, fiction editor of *Cemetery Dance*

LAWRENCE C. CONNOLLY
VISIONS
SHORT FANTASY & SF

Fantasist
Enterprises

WILMINGTON, DELAWARE

Text copyright © by Lawrence C. Connolly
except "Wayward Wilder" © by White Wolf Publishing

Artwork copyright © 2009 by Nathaniel G. Sawyers

Designed by
Nathaniel G. Sawyers
and
W. H. Horner Editorial & Design

Published by
Fantasist Enterprises
PO Box 9381
Wilmington, DE 19809
www.FantasistEnt.com
www.FEBooks.net

VISIONS: *Short Fantasy & SF*
ISBN 13: 978-1-934571-01-9
ISBN 10: 1-934571-01-6

FIRST EDITION
September 2009

10 9 8 7 6 5 4 3 2 1

"Aberrations," "Strands," and "Looking Back" are appearing here for the first time.

The other works originally appeared in the following publications.

"Beerwulf." *Bash Down the Door and Slice Open the Badguy*, edited by W. H. Horner. Fantasist Enterprises, 2007.

"Buckeye and Spitball." *Amazing Stories*, January 1981.

"Cockroaches." *Amazing Stories*, May 1980.

"Daughters of Prime." *The Magazine of Fantasy & Science Fiction*, July 2007.

"Great Heart Rising." *The Magazine of Fantasy & Science Fiction*, January 2002.

"Gwythurn the Slayer." *Castle Fantastic*, edited by John DeChancie & Martin H. Greenberg. DAW, 1996.

"Echoes." *Rod Serling's Twilight Zone Magazine*, Jan/Feb 1983.

"Errors." *Triangulations*, edited by Diane Turnsheck. Parsec Publishing, 2003.

"Flashback." *Thou Shalt Not*, edited by Lee Howard. Dark Cloud Press, 2006.

"Flow." *Beyond the Last Star*, edited by Sherwood Smith. SFFnet, 2001.

"Ghosts." *Sewickley Magazine*, October 1985.

"Horror by Sunlight." *Horrors: 365 Scary Stories*, edited by Stefan R. Dziemianowicz, Robert Weinberg & Martin H. Greenberg. Barnes & Noble, 1998.

"Julie of the Shadows." *Amazing Stories*, March 1982.

"Mercenary of Dreams." *Elf Fantastic*, edited by Martin H. Greenberg. DAW, 1997.

"On the Brink." *New Amazons*, edited by Margaret Weis. DAW, 2000.

"The Others." *The Magazine of Fantasy & Science Fiction*, August/ September 2009.

"Prime Time!" *The Magazine of Fantasy & Science Fiction*, July 2001.

"Rope the Hornet." *Fantastic Stories*, June 1980.

"Step on a Crack." *Pirate Writings 13*, Spring 1997.

"Wayward Wilder." *The Splendour Falls*, edited by Erin Kelley. White Wolf, 1995.

For
Lauren

CONTENTS

Vision is the art
of seeing things invisible.

Jonathan Swift

ILLUSION

ABERRATIONS

You are not reading these words.

This page is an illusion, concocted by you in an attempt to deal with something you cannot understand. Something uncanny is approaching, and you are in serious danger.

Turn around.

Do you see?

Perhaps you see only the trappings of your everyday existence, things that you expect to see—nothing strange, nothing dangerous, nothing but a veil of denial. You cannot accept what has happened, and what has happened is something so far beyond understanding that it has plunged you into a fugue.

But you cannot remain here. You cannot flee inward. Doing so will make you easy prey, and the hunters are coming. They are almost here. Your suppressed desire to see the truth has projected these words into your fantasy. Your unconscious is giving you these words to guide you back. And you must come back. You must regain your senses and run from this place before it is too late.

Try to remember how it began, how you turned to glimpse something that could not be: a visitor from another sphere that vanished when she realized you had seen her. And now she and her people are concerned. They know that the vision has thrown you into delusion, but they fear you will recover.

And when you do, you will recall everything. You will recall the gold of her face, the light of her arms, the iridescent pattern of her wings, and the barbed talons of her feet and hands. Even now, as your memory struggles to recover, your mind converts these words into images, and with the images the memory rises. This is what they fear. They cannot let it continue.

Your only hope is to flee.

They will not take you if you attract the attention of a crowd. They will not destroy you while others watch, but if you continue as you are—quietly staring at a page that does not exist—they will finish with you before the world knows you are gone.

Do you need more proof?

Look up! Make yourself see. They are coming.

But you remain blind. Your denial is strong.

You might as well keep reading. Maybe, if you are lucky, the illusion will persist while the creatures tear you apart. Perhaps the fantasies conveyed by these words will protect you from the true horror and pain of your impending obliteration.

You might as well keep reading, and pray the next fantasy holds your interest.

NIGHT VISIONS

ECHOES

Sometimes stories take on lives of their own. I wrote this one in the spring of 1981. By early summer it had sold to Rod Serling's Twilight Zone Magazine, *within a year it had resold to both Karl Edward Wagner's* Year's Best Horror Stories *and Isaac Asimov's* 100 Great Fantasy Short-Short Stories. *Since then it has seen print at least a dozen times, been translated into as many languages, and made into two short films, the most recent of which won Best Cinematography at the Fusion Film Festival in New York City. An audio version of it also appears as a bonus track on the CD* Veins: The Soundtrack, *currently available from Fantasist Enterprises. And to think, when I first wrote the story, I wasn't sure people were going to get it. Guess I had nothing to worry about.*

Marie stood in the kitchen, staring at the magnetic birds on the refrigerator door, and after a while Billy yelled in from the living room to tell her that Paul wanted some milk. She didn't answer.

Paul had been dead for three months.

"Mom?"

She looked around, trying to remember what she had come into the kitchen for.

"Mom! Paul wants some milk. Can he have some?"

It wasn't a game anymore, and it was starting to worry her. Billy was old enough to understand death. He was old enough to know that Paul couldn't be there in the living room, watching television. Billy was six.

Paul, had he lived, would have been five.

She turned, walking from the kitchen and feeling the awful stabbing pains in her back that the doctor said she would have for the rest of her life. Marie was twenty-nine; the rest of her life—if she died of old age and not another accident—would be a long time. She wondered if she would ever come to regard pain as a normal thing.

The living room was dark. She had tried opening the heavy blue drapes before breakfast, but Billy had wanted them closed. He had become an in-door child, preferring dark rooms to the world outside, preferring his dead brother's company to that of living children. He sat alone, leaning on the couch's arm, slouching with wonderful ease; it was amazing how his young body had recovered. His scars were gone. His broken bones were whole and straight. Looking at him, it was easy to forget that he, too, had been involved.

An uneaten doughnut sat on the coffee table. She pointed to it. "Don't you want that?"

He shook his head. "I'm leaving it for Paul, but he won't eat it without milk. He's mad because you wouldn't give him breakfast."

She looked at the television and asked, "What are you watching?"

"*Edge of Night*. Paul wants to know if—"

"Aren't there any kids' shows on?"

"Yeah, but you put this one on. Remember? You put it on, then you went to the kitchen. Paul says—"

"Well, let's at least turn it down. I have a headache, and—"

"Why are you doing that?"

"What?"

"Talking about other things when I talk about Paul."

"What would you like for lunch?"

"Mom!"

He looked near tears, and she almost gave in, almost turned to the empty spot beside Billy to say hello, almost went into the kitchen for milk. It would have been easy to play along. She knew. She had done it. And sometimes she had caught herself believing Paul was there. . . .

She turned away, knowing that if she continued the discussion it would go Billy's way. And she couldn't allow that. Last night Roger had come home early and caught the two of them talking to Paul. Roger had laid down the law then; he had told her it was no good pretending, no good for anyone.

She looked back at the couch, back at her older child who was once again an only child, and she said, "Later I might want you to go to the store for me. We're nearly out of butter."

Billy stared at the uneaten doughnut.

Marie wondered if she was getting through.

Later, when lunch was long gone and the empty afternoon became evening, Roger mixed a martini and asked about her day. She said it had been fine, and he took the chair across from her at the kitchen table. He no longer wore the neck brace, but she could see that his pain was no better. The doctor had been against him working full days, but Roger wasn't one for taking orders. He would probably have two more martinis before dinner.

The television was still on in the living room; Billy had spent the whole day in front of it, passively watching whatever Channel 4 threw at him. Now he was watching a *Leave it to Beaver* rerun. The sound was still too high. Roger looked over Marie's shoulder toward the noise, and something in his look roused her.

She realized dimly what was coming.

"Marie," he said, "why is the television on?"

Beaver and Wally laughed.

"Please, Roger, let the boy be." She had met the man halfway. Surely that was enough.

She looked away as he got up from the table. He moved into the living room. The television fell silent. "I don't like you doing that," he said, stepping back into the kitchen. "I don't like you playing that set to an empty room."

She cried after that. And after that she tried telling him about the talk she and Billy had had that morning. But every time she began he asked her about dinner, or about sewing, or about Mrs. Burke up the street.

After a while, when it seemed useless to insist, she put on her coat and went to the store for butter. It was five blocks. The walk was painful, but she didn't want to drive. She no longer felt safe in cars.

Roger stayed behind in the empty house.

He mixed a second martini. And he wondered if he was getting through.

GREAT HEART RISING

In a number of ways, this novelette is the precursor to my novel Veins, *which features a young man who goes on a journey of spiritual awakening with his great grandmother. Although "Great Heart Rising" stands entirely on its own, people who have read the book may recognize the seeds of the novel in this tale of self discovery and environmental responsibility.*

The Chevy cleared the corner, its squeal shattering the park's early-morning calm. Eli gripped the leash and pulled Coyote to the sidewalk. "Easy, boy!" He had come to the park to find peace in the long shadows of tall trees, but the speeding car was a reminder that the city was still there, eager to intrude.

The driver, a middle-aged African-American in a rumpled sports coat, glanced toward Eli and hit the brakes. The car swerved, jumped the curb, and plowed a strip of brittle turf before rocking to a stop.

Coyote barked, tugging the leash as the Chevy's doors clicked and swung wide.

The driver climbed out, slid a hand into his jacket, and said, "Your name Hayet?"

A kid climbed from the passenger side, his short hair lying like an air-brushed shadow against his scalp. Eli figured he was nineteen—twenty max.

The driver was older, the paunchy side of fifty. Flecks of gray silvered his temples. He produced a wallet, keeping his eyes on Eli as he rounded the car.

"Are you Eli Hayet?"

"Who are *you*?"

He opened the wallet, flashing a badge. "Police." He said it as if it were all the name anyone needed. Then, more forcefully, "Are you Eli Hayet?"

The kid held back, leaning against a fender, hands clenched in the pockets of his multicolored windbreaker.

"What's going on?" Eli asked.

A city cruiser rounded the bend, slowed, and pulled to a stop in front of the Chevy.

The first man folded his wallet. "Don't make me ask you again."

Eli glanced at the cruiser as its passenger door swung wide. "All right," Eli said.

Coyote barked louder.

"I'm Eli Hayet. What is this?"

A city officer stepped from the cruiser.

The first man pocketed his wallet. "We need your help, Mr. Hayet."

The city officer advanced, dropped to a squat, and extended a hand toward Coyote. "Hey, boy." Coyote sniffed the policeman's hand. "Good boy!" Then, to Eli: "I'll take your dog, sir."

"Take him?"

"Home. To your wife."

"We called her," the first man said. "She told us where to find you."

The officer took the leash.

The first man turned to the kid. "Maurice!"

Maurice straightened up.

"Get in the car. You're driving."

Maurice turned and darted around the grill.

The first man turned to Eli. "There isn't much time, Mr. Hayet." He walked to the Chevy's rear door, opened it, and stepped aside. "My name's Jones. I'll explain on the way."

Maurice glanced in the rearview as the Chevy thundered out of the park. "Eli Hayet!" His reflected eyes narrowed. "Didn't I see you on TV?"

"Did you?"

"Yeah! It was you," Maurice said. "You and that environment lady." His eyes darted back to the road. "She don't like you much, huh?"

"She has issues."

"What'd she call you? A heartless bastard?"

Eli winced.

The environment lady: Sara River, half Iroquois and full-time spokesperson for the Open Space Coalition. She had looked into Eli's past and decided that his lineage gave him responsibilities.

"Heartless bastard," Maurice said again. "Why'd she call you that?"

Eli turned to Jones. "Is this about the Trees Glen Development?"

"No," Jones said. "This got nothing to do with suburban sprawl." He lifted a fabric tote from the floor. Velcro rasped as he opened the flap.

"Is it about the Open Space Coalition?"

"No." Jones took out a cell phone. "It's about multiple murder and hostage taking." He opened the phone and turned the screen toward Eli, revealing the image of a single-level home on a parched, straw-covered lot. Yellow tape surrounded the property. In the background, skeletal homes formed an under-construction skyline.

"This house." Jones tapped the screen. "It's in the far-north suburbs, in a new community called Pleasant Springs. 134 Morningside Drive. Been there?"

"No."

"The family's named Driscol."

"I don't know them." Eli looked toward the front seat. Maurice's eyes kept darting to the mirror, watching.

"About forty minutes ago," Jones said, "Creek Township got a call from seventeen-year-old Brenda Driscol. She said that Woneesa had done something to her parents."

"Woneesa?"

"That's all she said."

"Woneesa did something to her parents?"

"Near as we can figure, the parents are dead."

Eli looked at the house on the screen. He felt as if he had missed something. "Who's Woneesa?"

"We were hoping you'd tell us."

"Why me?"

"Because," Jones said, "Woneesa is asking for you."

They drove north on 279, toward the sprawling fiberboard communities that had leveled the hills and supplanted the forests north of the city. They passed Wessex Glen, the plan where Eli had lived for a year during his nomadic teens, and proceeded along the border of Westgate, a newer division that Eli remembered seeing long ago, when it had been a mass of stripped earth and skeletal homes.

Lawns, driveways, and cookie-cutter Tudors raced beyond the side windows as Jones continued his story.

"Four minutes after Brenda Driscol's call, two Creek Township officers arrived at the house. They'd been there before. Seems Brenda has a minor drug record. They entered the house at 8:14."

Eli studied the picture: windows closed against the summer heat, front door leaning into a hall that stretched past a kitchen arch and toward a dim living room. Among the shadows lay something that might have been the body of a man.

"At 8:16, Creek Township got a second call from Brenda Driscol. Woneesa had stopped the officers and was prepared to do the same to anyone else who entered the house without permission."

"*Stopped* the officers?"

"That's what she said."

"But what does it mean?"

"It means they went in and didn't come out. One of them is lying in the hall. The other's face down in the kitchen. Basically it means the Township is in over its head, so they've called us."

"Who's 'us'?"

"Crisis Negotiation."

Maurice accelerated out of the end of the Westgate plan and veered left toward a bulldozed forest.

Jones turned toward his side window. "Look at this place." He scowled at the blur of splintered stumps and tread-gouged clay. "Everyone wants to live in the country, but the country keeps getting evicted." They passed a real estate office built in the split-level style that had become popular in the sixties, after choice lots became scarce and developers began exploiting sloping terrain. Fresh sod covered the yard. Beside the declining walk, a fiberboard sign read:

Your Next Move
PLEASANT SPRINGS
A Billingham Homes Development

Billingham Homes was the same company that would soon break ground on Trees Glen—the community for which Eli's firm had negotiated the purchase of a wide swatch of privately held forest along the Northwest Expressway. Like Pleasant Springs, Trees Glen would be composed entirely of single-family lots. No community parks. No significant reserves of free standing trees or flowing water. But unlike Pleasant Springs, which had been built on a landfill, Trees Glen would displace a dense second-growth forest. It was that point that had led Sara River to brand Eli a heartless bastard.

"We're talking *coexistence*," she told Eli, pumping the word with a 4/4 rhythm: "*Co-ex-zis-tense!*" She followed him as he walked from the Courthouse to a Second Avenue garage.

He pushed on, conscious of the pivoting microphones and Betacams. One thing about Sara River, she knew how to stage an event.

"We're talking open-space planning, Mr. Hayet!" She cut in front of him, walking backward, giving the Betacams her strong cheeks and flashing eyes. She held an oblong of corrugated board. Scored and folded like a large book, the oblong opened with a snap as she spread her arms. "I want people to *know* you've seen *this*!"

A painting clung to the placard: a landscape of multi-family homes positioned between thick swatches of forest. He had seen it before, but Ms. River was not so much showing it to him as she was showing it to the five-o'clock news. "We're talking communing *with* nature, not *against* it!"

He set his jaw and kept walking, knowing that if he tried explaining the other kind of nature—human nature and the fact that homeowners valued property over forests—Ms. River would be ready with a sound-bite rebuttal.

"We're talking working *with* the environment, Mr. Hayet. You of all people ought to understand!" She stepped aside, letting him pass as she shouted, "Don't act like you don't know what I'm saying, *Hayethwas*!" And then, for the waving microphones: "*Heartless bastard*!"

Two cruisers blocked the entrance to Morningside Drive. Behind them, empty asphalt stretched toward a courtyard of newly finished lots. In front of them, a crowd gathered. Some of the people wore the bewildered look of evacuees. These were evidently the Morningside residents. One of them, a jogging-suited woman with tied-back hair and flip-flops, turned toward the Chevy as it nosed into the crowd. She held an infant over a towel-draped shoulder, patting its butt as she made suspicious eye contact with Eli. He read her gaze and looked away. He knew about the territorial instincts of tract-home dwellers. Nowhere is an outsider less welcome than in the mazy heart of a housing plan. Certainly, if Woneesa had moved into the Driscol home, the neighbors would have seen him.

Maurice reached beneath the seat and placed a flashing light on the dashboard. He hit the siren, giving a quick WHOOP-WHOOP! as he eased forward. The crowd parted, and it was then that Eli saw the Eyewitness-News van.

Jones frowned. "Turning into a circus."

A reporter stood near the curb, positioned between the barricade and a shoulder-mounted Betacam. Behind her, neighborhood kids bounced in place, getting in frame for the morning news.

The barricade opened. Looking back, Eli saw the Betacam panning toward him. "I've made the news again." He glanced at Jones. "Next they'll offer me a series."

Jones ignored the joke.

Maurice smirked and gunned the engine.

They roared past the bare Tyvek faces of under-construction buildings and into the circular cul-de-sac rimmed with a dozen finished homes. The asphalt courtyard was a riot of vehicles: two cruisers, a Tri-Valley ambulance, and two vans—one black and ominous looking, the other white and sporting an array of antennas.

Along the road, construction equipment lay abandoned in the rising sun. In the courtyard, marksmen stood ready. Jones tapped the side window, pointing toward the brick- and-vinyl face of the Driscol's single-story home. "That's it," he said. "The place you can't get near without Woneesa's permission." The double-pane windows blazed with reflected sun. "Our negotiator asked Brenda Driscol what it takes to get permission, and she told him *nothing*. It takes *nothing*. No one can *get* it. Only one person *has* it."

"Who's that?"

"You."

"Me?"

"That's what she says."

Maurice squeezed into a space behind the white van.

Eli said, "But I don't know Brenda Driscol."

"No. And she doesn't know you." Jones reached for the door handle. "But Woneesa does." He popped the latch and stepped out into the white van's oblong shadow.

The van's interior was a riot of cables, reconditioned computers, and second-hand communication equipment. The cabinets and counters bore the not-quite-plumb look of low-bid labor. The air-conditioned breeze reeked of dirty coils.

A line of tinted windows overlooked the courtyard. Facing the windows, a young man spoke into the duct-taped mouthpiece of a reconditioned headset. He spoke slowly, as if reasoning with a child. Beside him, a woman with blue-black hair turned as Jones, Maurice, and Eli stepped through the doors. Her almond eyes glanced at Eli and then at Jones. "This is him?"

Jones nodded. "Eli, this is Shef."

She extended a hand. "That's Shef with an S—as in Shefali."

Maurice snorted. "Now we got like a Indian-American and a American-Indian."

Eli let the comment pass. He was only one-quarter Iroquois on his father's side, which in his eyes hardly qualified as Native. Nevertheless, his face gave him away. He was the image, if not the spirit, of his paternal grandfather.

Jones turned to the man with the duct-taped headset. "You talking to her, Walter? You got the kid on line?"

Walter touched a switch. An adolescent voice shrilled through a console speaker: "Woneesa's man has to come inside!"

"Woneesa's man," Walter said, cupping the mouthpiece as he turned to Eli. "That's *you*."

Eli frowned. "Woneesa's man?"

Walter took his hand from the mouthpiece. "That's good, Brenda. If Woneesa knows that Eli Hayet is here, Woneesa will let you go. That was the deal."

Silence.

"Brenda?"

"What's she doing?" Jones asked.

Walter shrugged. "Not sure. Sometimes she hangs up. Sometimes she just stops talking."

Jones stared at the house. "Where exactly is she?"

"Basement. Claims she's been down there all week."

"What have you learned about the parents?"

"Father, Tom Driscol, manufacturers rep. He made his own hours, worked out of the home. Mother, Anne Driscol, teacher. No work in the summer."

"So both parents were home when Woneesa arrived?"

Walter nodded. "That's when he killed them . . . six days ago . . . nearly a week before the kid called the Township."

Jones frowned. "Doesn't make sense. Even a self-employed rep and a vacationing teacher can't vanish for six days without being missed."

"Actually, they can," Walter said. "People do it all the time." He dialed the parents' phone and patched it through the speaker. Two rings, a click, and then a message—Brenda's voice, cheerful with an attitude: "Wassup? Dad's taking us to the beach—finally!" She stretched the last word into a nasal whine. "Back in six days. Want to talk? Tell the machine!" Walter broke the connection, sat back, and looked at Jones. "With the machine running interference, Brenda had plenty of time to bond with Woneesa."

"Excuse me?"

"That's what she called it—bonding with Woneesa."

"Sounds romantic."

"Gets better. She says Woneesa appeared in a dream. Told her to set up an apartment in the laundry room. She did, and they moved in together."

"And the parents?"

"The mother's in the kitchen." Walter turned his monitor toward Jones and Eli. The screen displayed the grainy enlargement of a kitchen window, apparently taken from the roof of the command van. It showed what appeared to be an outstretched arm lying on a patch of gray floor. The hand lay palm down, fingers curved around a dishtowel. The contours of the hand and towel seemed muted, as if coated in gray dust. The rest of the body lay out of frame, blocked by the windowsill. "We don't know about the father. He doesn't show in any of the window shots, but we assume he's in there."

Jones glanced at the evacuated homes. "Six days ago was Saturday. Did the neighbors see anyone enter the house?"

"No. But the houses are all new. No one knows anyone."

"Doesn't matter," Eli said, remembering the glare he'd taken from the woman at the entrance to Morningside Drive. "If a stranger came down this street, he'd have been noticed."

"Maybe," Jones said, staring at the Driscol home. "But what if he wasn't a stranger?" To Shef, he said, "What have you learned about Woneesa?"

"Not much." Shefali shrugged. "It'd help if we knew how to spell the name."

"The kid won't help?"

"No. And her pronunciation's all over the place." She keyed the name into her computer. "This is our best guess." The name hung on the screen. WONEESA. "Name, word, and language searches have turned up nothing."

Brenda came back on line, ranting: "Where's Hayet?" Her voice crackled in the speaker. "Woneesa wants to see him. *NOW!*"

Walter lowered the volume. "Listen, Brenda—"

The speaker clicked and went dead.

Eli faced the van's tinted windows and stared past the Driscol home, toward a line of far-off hills. His mind raced over the route he had taken with Jones and Maurice: Wessex Glen, Westgate, and the bulldozed forest. Though the terrain had changed over the years, he knew the area. He had been here, long ago, when the paved lot had been a shale-rimmed precipice. "Those hills." Eli pointed to the rounded hills. "Blaston's over there. Am I right?"

"Four miles north," Shef said. "You know you got serious expansion when one city's sprawl becomes another town's suburbs."

"If the Blaston coke ovens were operating, could you see the smoke from here?"

"Easily. But those mills closed ten . . . maybe fifteen years ago."

Eli leaned toward the window, stopping short of pressing his nose to the glass. "I've been here before," he said. "This very spot, when it was all forest." He looked at the house. "There used to be a waterfall . . . a stream—"

"Could have been diverted underground," Shef said. "This area's all landfill . . . riddled with culverts."

Eli leaned against the glass, bracing against a rush of memories.

He was seventeen and walking with the spirit of his grandfather.

"Is this a dream?" Eli asked.

"No. Your body's sleeping, but this isn't a dream."

They headed north along the fresh-asphalt streets of Wessex Glen, advancing toward the skeletal walls of Westgate. They moved with the speed of spirit walkers, covering furlongs with single steps.

"Why didn't you come south for my funeral?" Grandfather asked.

"Dad said I'd miss too much school."

"Was that the real reason?"

"No. I don't think he wanted me at the ceremony. He's a Christian. He doesn't like the old ways."

"Aren't Christian ways old ways?"

"Not to him."

Beneath their feet, a Westgate street became a field of broken stumps. Ahead loomed the edge of a sheared-off forest. Above the trees, a gibbous moon nuzzled a pocket of night.

"Where are we going?"

"To the heart of something old."

They entered the forest and followed a trail to the top of a moonlit waterfall. Beyond the cliff, empty sky stretched toward the glowing exhaust of a dying steel town. Everything in between, from falling water to rising smoke, was unbroken forest. No bricks. No asphalt. Just a shimmering ocean of wave-shaped pines.

Grandfather sat on the mossy shale beside the falling water. "That forest."

He pointed to the sea of conifers. "It isn't yours."

"Not *mine?*"

"It's the forest of your ancestors."

"What's the difference?"

"It's coniferous. The first forest was pine. Settlers killed it. When it grew back, it was deciduous—hickory, oak, walnut. . . ."

"Why'd it change?"

"It didn't."

"But you said—"

"It didn't change. It *was* changed. There's a difference." Grandfather leaned forward, angling his body toward the abyss. "Pay attention. Things are going to happen fast." He leaned until his center of gravity cleared the precipice. But he didn't fall. He held his ground, angled like a rooted trunk, pointing west with a gnarled limb. "Do you see it?"

Eli looked, following the line of Grandfather's finger. Across the valley a wedge of moonlight struck the back of an arched sapling. The tree had been bent until its branches became a second set of roots. Now it grew with its bowed trunk in the air, forming the entrance to a darkened room.

"You're inside that room," Grandfather said.

The world turned. The waterfall's roar receded, and Eli found himself sitting on the floor of a house made of bent trees.

Grandfather stood before him, gripping a decorated pole. Carved eyes gazed from the wood—human eyes in animal faces. Grandfather asked, "What will you do when you finish school?"

Eli shrugged. "College, I guess."

"What does this mean?" Grandfather rolled his shoulders, mimicking Eli's shrug.

"I don't know. I've been accepted. What else am I going to do?"

"What will you study?"

"Maybe law."

"White man's law?"

"What else?"

Grandfather gripped the carved pole. "Let me show you." He twisted the rough-hewn point from the floor and lifted it to reveal a hole filled with quivering darkness. "Come closer." He leaned the pole against a curved wall and dropped to his knees. "There are things I can't tell you. I'm only a seed spreader. You'll have to harvest your own answers." He peered into the hole and beckoned with a crooked hand. "Closer."

Eli approached. "What's down there?"

"Many things. And one of them is rising." Deep in the hole, something stirred. "It's a creature that eats stone."

"Nothing eats stone," Eli said.

"It also eats meat and leaves. And wood and bone."

A dusty stink rose from the hole. Eli jerked away, snorting.

"It has no stomach, no mouth, but it is always hungry."

Eli tried clearing the stink from his nostrils.

"It can also be eaten. It can give visions and induce death-like sleep."

Eli snorted again. "It stinks!" He felt lightheaded, as if he had inhaled a drug.

"And it burns. Our ancestors used it for tinder. Light a little, it burns. Light a lot, it explodes." His eyes glowed. "Do you know its name?"

Eli shook his head.

"You will."

"When?"

Something dark bubbled from the ground.

"You will know it the day it calls your name," Grandfather said. "You will know it the day you set it free."

Darkness filled the room, and suddenly Eli was lying in his bed, head pounding, afraid to move. . . .

The narcotic stink clung to his nostrils, filling his head with the echo of Grandfather's words. One day the thing in the hole would call his name.

He sat up and turned on the light beside his bed.

One day he would set it free.

He shivered. The dream made no sense, but somehow that made it all the more frightening.

"The kid's back!"

Walter patched Brenda's voice through the console's speaker.

"Woneesa is tired of waiting," she said. "Hayet has to come inside *now*!"

"We hear you, Brenda." Walter remained calm, focused. "We need you to stay on the line this time. We need you to tell us—"

"No!" Her voice shrilled. "I can't tell you anything else."

"We need you to ask Woneesa—"

"Hayet can ask questions when he comes inside."

"Can Hayet bring a friend?"

"No. He comes alone!" Her voice cracked, turning jagged. "No one else has permission!"

"I'll do it." Eli turned to Jones. "Let me go inside."

Walter turned off the speaker and adjusted his headset.

Jones studied Eli. "You're serious?"

"She says I'll be safe."

"You understand what you're doing? You're volunteering." He spoke slowly, making his point in the presence of witnesses. "I am not asking you to go into that house."

"I understand."

"Swell!" Walter said. "She did it again. She hung up."

"Get her back!" Jones said. "Tell her to come into the front hall. Tell her Hayet will meet her there." He stepped toward the door.

Eli followed, wincing against the blast of August heat as he left the air-conditioned van. But this time, when his feet touched the pavement, he knew exactly where he was. Even through the sheath of asphalt, he could feel the memories rising.

Three days after the spirit walk with Grandfather, Eli followed the paved roads of Wessex Glen until they gave way to dusty clay.

It took twenty minutes to reach Westgate and another quarter hour to reach the forest. The trail was as he remembered, stretching beneath tall trees and ending at a fast-moving stream. He followed the currents, heading north toward the sigh of falling water.

He stopped by the cliff overlooking the wooded valley. In the distance, beyond a line of glacial hills, dense smoke rose from the Blaston ovens.

The pines were gone, replaced by a wasteland of deciduous trunks. The second-growth forest had been cleared, and now, on a barren cliff 200 yards away, earthmoving trucks spewed dirt and rock from gaping chutes. The debris tumbled into the valley, smoking as it fanned over the spot where he had dreamed himself sitting in a house of bent trees. He stepped back, sat beside the tumbling water, and watched as the valley filled with the grit of leveled hills.

Jones's voice crackled in Eli's headset. "Can you hear me?"

Eli nodded.

Jones said, "Test your microphone. Say something."

"Something."

"Funny guy." Jones reached under Eli's arm and adjusted the transmitter. "Everything feel OK?"

"Good enough."

"All right. Now Kaminski's going to hook you up."

Jones moved back as a utility man approached with a coil of 7/16-inch rappelling line.

Kaminski was a stocky man with a jarhead haircut and steely eyes. He reached toward Eli's groin, where a rappelling harness formed an X across each thigh. A figure-8 ring hung from a central strap, dangling over Eli's crotch. He picked up the ring and looped the rappelling line through the harness. "Now we can pull you out if you get in trouble." He turned to Jones. "He's ready."

Jones stepped forward again. "Do it like we said: prop the screen and stay in sight. You'll see the basement stairs through the kitchen. If the girl's not there, call to her."

"If she doesn't come?"

"You leave." Jones said. "No heroics. Step out of sight and Kaminski's gonna haul you back. Understood?"

"Understood."

"Ready when you are," Jones said. "Take it slow."

Eli turned and started up the walk. Through the screen, he saw the arch that led to the kitchen, the open space that must have been the living room, and a heap of gray that was now clearly the prostrate form of a fallen officer. "Nothing's moving inside." He stepped onto the front stoop, opened the screen door, and paused. . . .

Dust spilled past his face, drifting close and then swirling back into the house.

"Something wrong, Hayet?"

"No. I'm all right." He adjusted the metal stop on the screen door's pneumatic hinge. "There's some kind of grit inside the doorframe." He reached up, slapped the aluminum molding, and watched as more grains sifted down, avoiding his face as they swirled into the house. "It looks like mold spores."

The sun tossed a blade of dusty light across the carpet. Beyond the swirling motes, the Creek officer lay with his arms folded beneath his chest. The dust had piled around him, drifting like gray sand.

Eli stepped inside, crouched, and set a hand against the officer's jaw. The flesh quivered. Eli turned toward the open screen, looking toward Jones and Kaminski. "There's a pulse."

Jones signaled the paramedics.

Kaminski said, "Don't move him, Hayet!"

But the fallen officer was already rousing, rolling onto his back and looking up with glazed eyes.

Eli held him steady. "Easy now."

The officer coughed, his breath misting in the low-angled light.

"Just take it easy."

The officer gripped Eli's arm, clinging fast as Eli helped him to his feet. Together, they moved down the hall, through the front door, and out to the waiting paramedics—none of whom seemed eager to enter the house without Woneesa's permission.

Eli returned to the hall and proceeded to the edge of the living room. "There's a man on the couch, slumped over, face down. He's covered with dust." He noticed other things, too: mold creeping from baseboards and webs sprouting from sockets and rheostats. The air shimmered with drifting spores, none of which came near him. It was as if each grain were aware of his presence, as if the dust were holding back—creating a breathing space that followed him through the house.

Jones asked, "Do you see the girl?"

Eli turned and stepped toward the kitchen. "No. The basement's closed." Thick dust covered the counter, muting the contours of a toaster, a microwave oven, and an assortment of knives in a butcher-block holder. Dust sifted over the counter's edge, falling onto the bodies that lay between hall and basement. "I see your second officer," Eli said. "And a woman, face down, early-to-mid forties. I assume it's Mrs. Driscol." Covered in gray dust, she looked almost like an unfinished statue.

"I need to get closer." Eli turned toward the front door, meeting the anxious stares of Jones and Kaminski. In the center of the courtyard, paramedics lifted the first officer into the back of a Tri-Valley ambulance. In the distance, sirens wailed. More vehicles were on their way. "I need to step out of the hall. I'll be out of sight for less than a minute."

A deliberating silence, and then: "All right, Hayet. Go for it. Stay in voice contact. Keep talking."

He entered the kitchen.

Nothing he had seen in the hall or the living room had prepared him for what spilled from the cabinets beneath the sink. There, five feet from Mrs. Driscol's spore-covered body, lay a mass of tendrils and fluttering webs. They stretched from the darkness, pushing the cabinet doors to reveal pipes overgrown with fungal twine. . . .

"Hayet! Talk to us!"

"I'm kneeling beside the woman." He reached for her. Spores fanned away from his hand, scrolling back in two feathery arcs as they left the body. The woman trembled. "Her eyes are open. Pupils dilated." Her skin was pale but unmarked, free of the plethoric tattoos that should have been evident in flesh that had lain for a week on hard linoleum. The spores had preserved her—knocked her out, but kept her whole.

He helped her to her feet. Together, they left the kitchen and stepped into the light of the rising morning.

The others were the same: not dead, merely unconscious, needing only his touch to bring them around. One by one, he led them into the light and delivered them to the waiting arms and gurneys of the Creek Township paramedics. And through it all, the girl remained silent. No more phone calls to the command van. No cries from the basement.

"The hall," Jones said, his voice buzzing in the headset. "Stay in the hall this time. Give her one more chance to come to you."

Something stirred beneath the floor as Eli reentered the hall. "I think I hear her."

She called out now, her voice rising through the boards, welling to a shriek.

"I need to go down for her."

The rappelling cord pulled at his waist, keeping him in the hall as he leaned into the kitchen. The cries coalesced, forming words: *"Down! Come down! Help me!"*

Eli tugged at the cord. "Let me go after her!" He turned toward the open screen.

A second black van had arrived in the courtyard. Jones stood in front of it, waving to Eli. "You're coming out, Hayet. We're moving in."

Kaminski tugged the line as a team of heavily armed men fell into position behind him.

Eli caught himself on the counter. Blades clattered in their butcher-block holder. "Wait!" He kept one hand out of sight, reaching for the counter. "Don't pull." He grabbed a knife. "I'm coming."

Kaminski relaxed.

Eli grabbed the line and brought out the knife.

Jones saw it. He barked a broken question, something Eli barely heard as Kaminski once again tugged the line—hard.

Eli flew forward, slammed the carpet with a bone-bruising thud. The knife rasped away from the cord. He rolled and brought the blade down again, struggling to hold it steady as Kaminski hauled him toward the door.

Filaments popped, snapping like tendons beneath the running blade. Eli looked up, squinting as he raced into the full flare of the sun. Another second and he'd be outside, skidding against the flagstones. . . .

He pivoted, angling his legs to catch the doorframe. WHAM! The knife slipped again, slicing his skin and drawing a ribbon of blood that curved across his forearm and onto the carpet.

Kaminski pulled harder.

Eli gave the cord a final slash.

The line broke and recoiled.

Eli dropped the knife, scrambled to his feet, and raced toward the kitchen.

The courtyard fell silent behind him. The SWAT officers stayed at ready. One gas grenade would stop him, but no one fired.

Eli stormed across the dusty linoleum, threw open the basement door, and raced headlong into a squall of spores.

Brenda shrieked louder—her voice rising from the foot of the stairs.

"She's right below me," Eli said. "I'm going down."

"What's happening? Describe the scene!"

"The air's thick with spores. Swirling around me. Keeping their distance." He looked up. "Ceiling's filthy. Mold hanging like rotting cloth. Webs covering everything." He continued his descent, walking on mycelium knots. The stairs creaked, sounding brittle, dried by the leaching of the fungal sheath.

"Do you see the girl?"

"No." He reached bottom and stepped out onto a carpet of webs.

"Where are you now?"

"Foot of the stairs." He turned. A pulsing membrane fluttered beside him. "There's something here. Something huge." The mass coalesced as he advanced, undulating like a floor-to-ceiling cocoon, and finally solidifying as his hand closed over it. His fingers tingled with the shock of recognition. "It's a sheet," he said, looking up to see a blackened clothesline stretching beneath the ceiling's pipes and beams. "A wall of hanging sheets." He found a point where two sheets overlapped, parted them, and looked in at the vacant eyes of a teenage girl. "I've found her!"

"Is she alone?"

Eli peered through the gale of spores. "I can't tell."

"Is she all right?"

Eli paused, trying to decipher the scene that sprawled before him. "No," he said, wanting to run, unable to move. "She is not all right." Then, more softly: "Oh my god!"

Brenda's eyes turned toward him, staring through the shifting dust. Her mouth opened. The void behind her teeth looked black and deep. Her voice emerged like a rising darkness. "Who you talking to?" she asked. "Who—?"

Her words faded beneath Jones's roar: "Is she alone? Talk to us, Hayet!"

He stared, taking in details as his mind adjusted to the horror. He saw ordinary things first: a coiled garden hose, a humming humidifier, and a simmering hotpot. Steam mingled with drifting spores. Brenda Driscol had done more than build an underground apartment. She had created an incubator.

"Talk to us, Hayet. Is she alone?"

"No." His gaze settled on the thing that sprawled behind her. "She's not alone."

Again, Brenda Driscol asked: "Who you talking to?"

She had positioned her incubator over a concave section of floor. In the center of the space, slime bubbled from a grate-covered drain. Fibrous tendrils grew from the slime, radiating across the concrete, over pipes, up walls, and onto the ceiling. . . .

A shattered cell phone lay in a corner. The girl's limp hand dangled above the receiver. Clinging filaments grew along her arm. . . .

"Hayet! Talk to us!"

She reclined on her back, her shoulders propped against massing tendrils, her body blanketed deep in a fungal cocoon. Thready creepers grew about her, clinging to her skin with hair-thin hooks.

"I'm going to try bringing her out."

The creepers shifted, tugging Brenda Driscol's cheek and temple, pulling her expression into a half grimace. In a voice as dusty as the air, she asked, "Is it *them*? Are you talking to *them* . . . the *others* . . . the *people outside*?"

"Yes." He pointed to the headset's microphone. "We're working to get you—"

Her hand blurred toward him, missing his nose and arcing away with a sound of cracking plastic and snapping wire.

"No one else," she said, gripping his detached microphone. "Later you can talk to the others. Now you talk to me."

She turned and tossed the microphone into a drift of spores. A ropy mass extended from the back of her head, flaring along the base of her scalp.

"Me," she said again, turning to face him. "Now you talk to me."

He realized that *me* was not Brenda Driscol. Her body had become a mouthpiece, a symbiotic extension of the thing that had grown through the grate in the floor. "What are you?" he asked.

"Ask your grandfather."

"He's dead."

"Then find the answers in—"

"Hayet!" Jones's voice boomed, drowning out the creature's words. "Who's with the girl? Talk to us!"

Eli looked into the creature's symbiotic eyes. "You used the girl to call me here?"

"Yes."

"You killed her to get to me?"

"No." The voice changed, deepening, becoming thicker. "I'm not ready to kill. Soon maybe. Not yet. All the people will recover if—"

"Hayet! Respond!"

"If what?"

Creepers quivered, pulling the girl's lips into an awkward grin. "Leave. Take the girl. Leave now, but remember me. Remember my power. Remember what—"

"Hayet! We're coming in!"

The girl's eyes rolled, seeming to glow as they looked around at the dangling fungus and swarming spores. "It burns." Her voice rasped, sounding old and masculine. "Our ancestors used it for tinder." It was Grandfather's voice. "Light a little, it burns. Light a lot—" She seemed to flinch as the tiny hooks pulled free of her skin. "It explodes!"

The ropy mass released her head. Her body slumped forward.

Eli caught her. She felt like a bundle of rags, her body shriveled from its week with Woneesa. He stood, holding her close as a kitchen window shattered. A grenade slammed the linoleum. Eli heard the hiss of incendiary teargas.

With Brenda in his arms, Eli turned and thundered up the stairs. More glass shattered as he rushed into the kitchen. The second grenade sputtered as it careened off the dishwasher and rebounded toward the basement.

He closed his eyes against the gas, not opening them until he reached the hall. Through acrid tears he saw the SWAT team storming up the walk. "No!" He rasped. "Get away!"

Something huge grabbed him from behind. His feet left the floor. He ran on air, hurling forward like a ball in a musket—propelled by a force so loud it registered only as pain. The SWAT team dropped, and he sailed over them, somersaulting with Brenda Driscol still in his arms. The world wheeled before his tumbling face. He saw the ground. He saw Jones and Kaminski. He saw the sky flecked with smoke and scattering debris. . . .

His head slammed the flagstone walk. The girl landed atop him and skidded away, arms and legs flailing like knotted cords.

And then—for a moment that transcended time—he felt nothing.

He lay on his back, gazing up at the blackening sky, watching the spores rise and scatter. Their shadow fell toward him . . . settled over him . . . slipped inside him.

He was with Grandfather's spirit.

"Is this a dream?" Eli asked.

"No," Grandfather said. "We are dreams. This is real."

They stood in the rear compartment of a speeding ambulance. Bags of fluid dangled from aluminum trees. Transparent tubes ran through pump boxes and into the arms of an unconscious man. Paramedics worked in hasty silence—cutting the front of a Hathaway shirt, peeling the cotton, and dotting the exposed chest with the colored disks of an EKG monitor.

Eli watched in bemusement.

There is nothing stranger to a man than the three-dimensional image of his own face. Throughout life he may see his features reversed in mirrors or pressed flat in the emulsion of photographs, but the face itself remains forever hidden behind his gaze. Looking at the battered man, Eli felt a strange twinge—a hazy sense that he knew the dying stranger.

He moved closer. The ambulance rocked as the road veered. Hanging bags swayed. A siren clicked on. Lights flashed beyond the windows, pulsing as Eli looked at the face on the blood-flecked pillow. His gaze dropped to the left arm, crusty with blood from a diagonal wound. He felt the ache of broken bones and lacerated flesh.

"It's me," he said.

Grandfather nodded as a paramedic turned and opened an overhead cabinet. The swinging door passed through Grandfather's face—in one side and out the other—as if Grandfather were nothing more than a plume of smoke. "You broke your neck on the front walk," Grandfather said. "The wound will add to the legend. By the time you regain consciousness, you will be a hero."

"Me?"

Grandfather took Eli's arm, pulling him away from the gurney, turning him toward the back of the ambulance. "I'll show you." They stepped toward the doors. "Walk with me."

A suburban street raced beyond the rear windows.

"Walk where?"

"You'll see."

The glass parted as Grandfather led Eli out into rushing air, across straw-covered lawns, and toward the smoke of a burning home. News reporters stood with their backs to the rising cloud.

"They will call it the Killer House," Grandfather said. "And when they interview Maurice, he'll tell them that its victims came alive when you touched them."

"But they weren't dead."

"People will believe otherwise."

"It was the spores. The spores kept the bodies sedated until—"

"People know what they see," Grandfather said. "And Kaminski saw you fly from the exploding home. He will tell his story over and over . . . and every time he does you will fly higher." Grandfather kept walking, down Morningside Drive and into the burning ruin of the Driscol home. In the flames, gritty flecks darted skyward, spreading out as they reached a ledge of cooling air.

Grandfather looked skyward, watching the plume as it feathered westward. "It will descend on new developments," he said.

"It?"

"The cloud of spores. Our ancestors called it *Unehsa*."

The name echoed in Eli's memory. "Woneesa," he said. "The Driscol girl called it Woneesa."

"The old tongue in a young mouth," Grandfather said.

"*Unehsa*." Eli spoke the name slowly.

"The last time it rose was in my father's time. He was *Unehsa's ha-tseest-atsi*."

"You're speaking Iroquois?"

"Iroquois-Mingo. It means missionary. It was your great grandfather who scattered the seeds of the second forest."

"By himself?"

Grandfather nodded. "*Unehsa* made him powerful, but his job was easy compared to yours. This time, *Unehsa* will need a greater hero."

They walked into a new scene. Timber rotted on lilting skids. Earthmovers sat mired on corroded tires. Workers lay prostrate on the naked earth. Everywhere, spores swarmed like locusts.

"You're saying I'll make this happen?" Eli asked. "I'll help *Unehsa* destroy construction sites?" The words tasted bitter. "What kind of hero—"

"A people's hero." Grandfather turned in place, regarding a landscape of crumbling hardware. "*Unehsa* will rain over new developments. Spores will clog engines, rot tires, devour supplies. Workers will have visions. But those things won't be enough. Someone will need to offer a solution, a plan for coexistence." Grandfather turned and started up a gentle rise, a mound of earth capped with a fringe of yellow grass.

Eli followed. "What plan?"

Grandfather paused at the top of the rise. He spoke without turning. "You lost your way, Grandson. *Unehsa* will help you find it again, provided you're strong enough to change."

Eli moved toward him, climbing into a cool breeze as he reached the top of the rise.

"Your father took his name from the Mingo," Grandfather said. "He thought *Hayet* sounded more American than *Yethwas*, but they are both part of the same word—*hayethwas*, one-who-plants."

A great valley stretched below them, lush and green.

"You will plant ideas." He turned to Eli. "If you are strong enough."

The air darkened with evening shadow.

"Are you up to the challenge?"

Soft lights winked through the valley trees, and Eli realized he was looking at Sara River's open-space- community—a landscape that developers had insisted could never be sold.

Grandfather said, "Sara River has the blueprint. If it succeeds, others will follow."

Eli stepped toward the valley's edge. He felt the wind on his face. Breathing deep, he smelled the scent of life.

"Are you up to the challenge, Grandson?"

Eli felt something rising—a quickening of suppressed spirit that sprang from the pit of his heart. He had been shown the way as a child, but it took the man to discover what had to be done. "I'm up to it," he said. "I'm ready."

The scene faded. He closed his eyes. And in the moment before he awoke to pain and wailing sirens, he sensed the strengthening pulse of the forest's heart . . . and he knew that he had reclaimed his soul.

BUCKEYE AND SPITBALL

We come now to one of the oldest tales in the book, a slightly autobiographical story that I wrote in the fall of 1979. Note that I say slightly autobiographical. My family did move east when I was in grade school, and I did, for a time, attend a crowded parochial school in the Philadelphia suburbs. That much is true. The rest, thankfully, is dark fantasy. At least, I think it is.

Had Timmy Baker's dad not been transferred east, Timmy might have spent his entire life in Clairton, Pennsylvania, growing up, growing out, and growing old in the shadow of the Clairton Works coke Ovens. As it was, he was uprooted and transplanted into a strange town full of people who breathed clean air and thought Coke was something you drank from a bottle.

Timmy's new home was in a place called West Fenton, a sprawling development where residents embraced a cookie-cutter American dream of the early 1960s. Each weekday morning, dads left for work in big-finned cars while moms got kids ready for school, which in Timmy's house meant donning a parochial-school blazer, white shirt, pressed slacks, and loafers. School was a short walk from home, but a kid had to be careful not to get lost, since the houses and streets were as indistinguishable from one another as the residents. In West Fenton, a person could get lost in the sameness.

But then there was Buckeye.

Buckeye was different. He was starting his second year in fifth grade, which made him bigger than his classmates. And he had a way of wearing his navy blazer and red tie that made them clash with his white shirt and brown loafers. And then there were his eyes. The right was blue and normal. But the left was a dead chestnut brown. The story around school was that he had once taken a dive on a garden rake, but the truth was anyone's guess. With Buckeye, anything was possible. He was an outcast, the sort of reject that only a new kid would hang out with, and Timmy was doing just that when Buckeye decided to show him the comic book.

"Is Sister looking?"

Timmy turned, wind blowing his tie from under his blazer as he looked around. Sister Peter Francis stood across the way, habit billowing, face turned toward the girls side of the school playground.

"No," Timmy said. "Not looking."

"Keep checking," Buckeye said. "I have to show you something." He reached beneath his tie and unbuttoned his shirt. "Look at this." Something tumbled out, smacking his hands, catching the wind with a clatter of rifled pages. It was a comic book, its colors seeming to catch fire in Buckeye's hands. He slapped the book, holding it closed so Timmy could see the image on the cover: a man with a narrow face, hooked nose, pointed fangs.

Timmy leaned closer. "Vampire?" He reached for the book.

"No." Buckeye pulled the book away. "No touchies." He pushed the comic back into his shirt. "I just wanted to show you, is all . . . so you'd know."

"Know what?"

"What to look for," Buckeye said. "What to *watch* for." He buttoned his shirt. Then he put his hands in his pockets and started walking as if he didn't have a horror comic stashed against his chest.

Timmy followed. "What to watch for where?" he asked.

"Here." Buckeye looked around, turning his good eye toward the school. "You're new. You don't know about this place. That's why I showed you."

"So I'll know what to look for?"

"That's right."

"Here at school?"

"Yeah." Buckeye glanced back at Sister. She was looking now, staring right at them, eyes glaring the way they did when she suspected trouble. "We've got them," Buckeye said. "Vampires. In the school."

"What do you mean?"

"Just what I said."

"I don't get it."

"Nothing to get. There's vampires. Lots of them." He snorted, cleared his throat, made like he was going to spit on the playground, then just swallowed. "I can show you," he said.

"Show me?"

Buckeye stopped walking. "Today." He shifted, turning in place. "But not now." He cut Sister another glance before fixing his good eye on Timmy. "After school. You'll see."

"A vampire?"

"Yeah. I'll show you his office."

"A real vampire?"

Buckeye nodded. "His name's Spitball."

Timmy laughed.

Buckeye's face remained stone still, as serious as his dead eye. "He's the leader, the vampire chief."

"Named Spitball?"

"Like I said."

"Why Spitball?"

"It's his name."

"I don't believe you."

"By the swings," Buckeye said. "After school. Meet me by the swings. I'll show you."

After school, Buckeye was right where he'd said he would be: sitting alone on a swing, waiting with his back toward the school. His shadow stretched behind him, staining the ground like an elongated skid.

Timmy started toward him, stopping twenty paces away, wondering if it might be better to go straight home instead. He didn't believe the vampire story, but whatever Buckeye's game was, it was sure to be more interesting than going home and doing chores. Besides, his parents wouldn't mind if he was a little late getting home. His mother would be glad to hear he'd made a friend. And his father, who seemed extra busy since the move, probably wouldn't miss him at all.

"Hello, Timmy." Buckeye spoke without turning. "I know you're there."

Timmy didn't answer.

"I hear you," Buckeye said. "Hear you breathing." Buckeye turned, shifting his feet against the ground, rotating the swing until the chains formed an X above his head. He looked at Timmy. "You were changing your mind, huh?"

"No."

"Don't lie. I know. I could hear it."

"Hear me changing my mind?"

"Sort of." Buckeye's bad eye narrowed, darkening beneath a furrowed brow. "My mom says blind people hear better than normal people. I'm half blind. So my ears are half better than yours."

"Half better means you can hear me *thinking?*"

"Yeah. Sometimes. It's weird, but it's true." Buckeye looked toward the school.

Timmy stepped forward, taking the swing beside him. For a moment they just sat there, watching the brick walls darken as the sun sank behind the convent.

"You going to show me Spitball?" Timmy asked.

"No," Buckeye said. "Not him. Just his office. He usually doesn't start till after dark."

"He *works* here?"

"Yeah."

"What kind of work?"

"Janitor work."

"A vampire janitor?"

Buckeye got up from the swing and started across the playground. "And he's not the only one. The other janitor's a vampire, too. And the cleaning ladies."

"All of them?"

"Yeah, all *two* of them."

"All right." Timmy paused as they neared the east-wing door. "So what's the joke?"

Buckeye frowned. "You." He snorted, cleared his throat, and spit on the pavement. "It's you for not believing." He paused as they reached the door. "But that'll change. You'll believe after I show you the office, after you see where he keeps the bodies. Then—" He paused, tilting his blindside ear toward the school's second floor. "Hear that?"

Timmy looked up at second floor window. Inside the room, someone was singing.

"That's one of them," Buckeye said. "One of the cleaning ladies."

"Vampire cleaning lady?"

"Yeah. They start before the janitors."

"While it's still light out?"

"Yeah. They can do that. That stuff about vampires and sunlight, it isn't really true. Sun doesn't kill them. It just makes them uncomfortable, like an allergy." It was clear Buckeye was winging it, making things up as he went along. "There's all kinds of stuff like that. Crosses are another. They're not really afraid of crosses."

"What about stakes?"

"Stakes?"

"Though the heart."

Buckeye blinked his good eye. "Don't know." He frowned, looking thoughtful. "Guess you'd need to find a sleeping vampire to test that one."

"Maybe not. What if you had, like, a stake sword?"

"A what?"

"You know, like a stake with a handle. You could run right up to Spitball and go like, 'Die, Vampire!'" He jerked his arms, thrusting upward. Then he laughed.

Buckeye just stared.

Timmy stopped laughing.

"A stake sword?" Buckeye looked thoughtful. "Yeah." For a moment, his voice came from a scary place, deep in his throat. "Could work. But you'd have to go after them one at a time." He blinked, coming back from the deep place, refocusing on Timmy. "You ever stab anybody like that?"

"Me? You mean, like, with a stake sword?"

"I mean, like, with anything."

"Heck no."

"Think you could?"

"No. No way. I was kidding, Buckeye."

"Yeah? Maybe you were. But it'd still work. If a person had to fight a vampire—one vampire at a time—a stake sword might just do it. But you'd need to be quick. They can turn into things . . . bats and smoke. How would you stab smoke?"

"I wasn't serious, Buckeye."

Buckeye blinked again, then he turned as if the discussion had ended. "Come on." He gripped the knob, opened the door, and slipped inside.

A flight of stairs led down into a basement hallway. Buckeye paused when he reached the bottom, touching a metal cabinet that extended from a cinder-block wall. Stenciled letters on the cabinet read:

DANGER
HIGH VOLTAGE

Buckeye opened the door and reached inside.

"What're you doing?" Timmy asked.

"Turning on a light." A circuit clicked.

Down the hall, a fluorescent glow flickered within an open room.

"That's it." Buckeye faced the lightened door. "That's Spitball's office." He hurried toward it, looked back to see if Timmy was coming, then slipped inside.

Timmy followed, pausing to see Buckeye standing beside a row of six metal lockers. Five were closed and secured with padlocks. The sixth stood open, empty.

"This is it?" Timmy asked.

"Yeah."

Timmy walked into the room, continuing past the lockers, and paused beside an ordinary-looking desk. Behind the desk was a tool cabinet with a piece of label tape on the top. The name on the tape read:

Nathan Spitzbaugh

"Hey, Buckeye." Timmy leaned on the cabinet. "I think—"

"No touchies," Buckeye said. "That's Spitball's."

"But—"

"Leave it alone. Safer that way. Remember, this is a vampire's office."

"You think?"

"I know."

Timmy looked around. "What's so *vampire* about it?"

"These lockers," Buckeye said. "Come here."

Buckeye stepped away from the desk.

"These lockers might look normal, but it's the stuff you can't see that matters." He studied one of the padlocked doors. "Over here." He gestured for Timmy to stand beside him. "This locker here. This is where he keeps the *fresh* ones."

Timmy stepped closer, noticing a ripeness in the air as he approached the lockers. "The *fresh* ones?"

"Yeah."

"Fresh what?"

"Victims."

Timmy caught the full force of the stink. "Phew!" He backed away.

"Believe me now?"

Old clothes, Timmy thought. *Dirty socks*. But he decided to quit resisting, play along with the game—whatever it was. "So what's Spitball do? Store bodies in the lockers?"

Buckeye turned suddenly, staring at the dark hall.

"Buckeye?"

"I hear something."

"What?"

"Spitball."

Timmy listened. "I don't hear—"

"I do. My ears are better, remember?" He looked around. "We have to hide."

Timmy looked toward the doorway. He heard it now. Footsteps descending the stairs.

"Hide!" Buckeye said.

"Where?"

"Anywhere!"

Timmy looked around, realizing it didn't matter if the person entering the basement wasn't really a vampire. What mattered was that kids did not belong in this place. If someone found them, they'd have some serious explaining to do.

"There!" Buckeye pointed across the room, toward a folding chair that leaned against one of the walls. "Hide behind that chair."

"What about you?"

Buckeye didn't answer. He just turned and squeezed into the open locker. Then he pulled the door behind him, leaving it open enough to keep the latches from catching.

Timmy hurried toward the chair.

The footsteps were right outside, close enough for Timmy to tell that it wasn't just one person. And now he heard their voices, too. One talking. The other laughing.

Timmy hurried along the wall, hunkered down, and crawled behind the leaning chair. It wasn't the perfect hiding place. He'd be seen if someone looked straight at him. Perhaps behind the desk would have been better, but it was too late. The men were already in the room, walking past the lockers, talking and laughing like ordinary men. He couldn't see their faces. The chair blocked his view of their heads and shoulders. But everything else was clear enough. One wore threadbare sneakers. The other wore work boots. Calluses covered their hands. One of them carried a combination lock, spinning it by the shackle, catching it in his palm.

"So I told him," he said, evidently finishing a story. "Blood is thicker. Know what I'm saying?"

"I hear you."

The man with the lock paused beside the slightly open locker, the one with Buckeye inside. He leaned on the door, pushing it until its latches engaged. Then he slid the lock's metal loop through the latch and—*click!*—sealed Buckeye inside.

"Hey!" the sneaker man said. "What's in there?"

"Nothing."

"So why lock it?"

"It's a locker, right?" The work boots stepped around the desk. A new sound followed. The wood-on-metal sigh of a drawer opening. "Lockers should be locked. Know what I'm saying?"

"Maybe."

"What's that supposed to mean?"

"Maybe? Maybe means maybe. Like *maybe* you got something you don't want to share."

"You talking about my Johnnie Walker?"

"You know I am."

Timmy didn't know anyone named Johnnie Walker, but there were lots of kids at the new school he didn't know. And exactly *who* the kid was didn't matter. The point was that sneaker man thought work-boot man might have someone stashed inside the locker.

"You think I'm holding out on you?"

"It's not that. Not exactly. I just hate to think of you drinking alone."

Drinking! Timmy's mind raced. *They're talking about drinking blood!*

"Seriously, Spitball. I'm just saying—"

Spitball. Work-boot man is Spitball.

Timmy shifted, watching Spitball as he moved behind the desk, catching a momentary glimpse of his face: wide forehead, dark eyes, hook nose.

Just like the face on the comic book!

Timmy felt dizzy. He tried bracing his arms against the wall, but that didn't help. He needed to get up, stretch his legs, flex his shoulders. Most of all, he needed to breathe. If he didn't breathe, he'd pass out. If he passed out, Spitball would see him and grab him and put him in one of those stinking lockers with Johnnie and Buckeye and whoever else they were saving for later.

Timmy closed his eyes. *Please let them be gone when I look again.*

Something banged.

Timmy opened his eyes to find Spitball lifting a tool belt from the metal cabinet. "We can drink later," Spitball said. "Right now, we've got that mess in the second floor lavatory." He put on the tool belt. "C'mon." He rounded the desk, moving past the lockers.

The other vampire turned, following Spitball out of the room. A moment later they were in the hall, moving away. Then the footsteps stopped. Something clicked—the metallic sound of a disengaging latch, a small door swinging open. And then, with the click of a master switch, the overhead light winked out, leaving Timmy in darkness.

And then the feet shuffled away, fading into silence as the vampires climbed the stairs.

"Timmy!" Buckeye called from the locker. "You out there, Timmy?"

Timmy tried standing. His knees buckled, giving way. He struck the leaning chair, knocking it over as he dropped to the floor.

"Timmy!"

"I'm all right."

Metal groaned, the sound of Buckeye pushing against the door. "Get me out of here, Timmy!"

Timmy got up. "I can't. They locked you in." He stumbled forward, set his hand on the tool cabinet, and felt along it until he found one of the drawers.

"Timmy!"

Timmy opened the drawer, running his hands over the hard-edged shapes inside, finding what he needed.

"Timmy!" Buckeye's voice trembled. "You still there!"

"Yeah." Timmy turned, put his hand against the edge of the desk, and moved toward the sound of Buckeye's voice. "Keep talking. I need to hear—"

"All right. OK. I'm talking. Jeez, Timmy! It stinks in here."

Timmy noticed the smell as he advanced. A stench like old socks. Only it wasn't socks. He knew that now. The lockers held nasty things. Dead bodies. He was sure of it.

"Timmy! *Get me out of here.*"

Timmy touched the padlock.

"What're you doing, Timmy?"

"They locked you in."

Buckeye made a tight little sound. "Timmy!" He sounded ready to cry. "Timmy! You heard what they said? Johnnie Walker?"

"I heard."

"He's been gone a long time. Police said he drowned, but they never found him . . . never found his body."

Timmy lifted the hacksaw blade, set it against the padlock.

"Timmy!"

He pushed the blade forward, making a notch in the shackle.

"What're you doing, Timmy?"

"Getting you out." The sound of sawing thundered through the lockers.

"They'll hear you, Timmy!"

Timmy worked faster, holding his breath against the stinking air, losing himself in the motion until the blade went limp. The lock turned. He pulled it free, flung it down, and opened the door.

Then they ran from the room, down the hall, up the stairs, and out into the fallen night.

"Now you know!" Buckeye said, gasping for breath as they crossed the parking lot. "Right? You believe me now?" He grabbed Timmy's sleeve as they stumbled down a slope that marked the end of school property.

"We need to tell someone," Timmy said.

"No." Buckeye's eyes widened, the dark one bulging from its socket. "I mean . . . who'd believe?"

"The police?"

"No way."

"Father Larkin."

"Forget it, Timmy! Its got to be us. You and me. We're the only ones."

"The only ones what?"

"Who can fix it."

Timmy looked back at the school.

A shadow appeared in a second-floor window, pivoting behind the glass, scanning the grounds.

Timmy and Buckeye ran.

But Timmy's fear was short lived.

In the days that followed, he began making sense of the things he'd heard and seen in the school's basement office. All except one. The kid in the locker. That one haunted Timmy until he saw an ad in a magazine, a picture of a tall bottle and a walking man. Johnnie Walker, the ad said. Twelve-year-old Scotch whisky.

But Buckeye wouldn't hear it.

"Johnnie Walker's a kid," Buckeye said. "*Was* a kid. He was twelve years old."

"But it's not a kid!"

"You saw them, Timmy! You saw their teeth."

"I didn't."

"You did. We both did."

"You were in the locker, Buckeye!"

"That was *after* I saw them. They didn't see us, but we saw them. Remember?"

"There are no vampires, Buckeye! I'm telling you—" He felt a hand on his shoulder, turned, and found himself looking up into the stone-cold face of Sister Peter Francis.

"You're yelling, Timothy." Her frown deepened. "No yelling on the playground."

He swallowed. "Sorry."

Her eyes narrowed. "Excuse me?"

He closed his eyes. Stupid! How could he be so stupid? "Sorry, *Sister*."

She withdrew her hand. "Now keep your voice down." She looked at Buckeye. "You too, Sean."

Buckeye nodded. "Yes, Sister."

She turned away.

The nuns and priests were being vigilant since the janitors had reported a hacksawed padlock in the basement. They claimed that someone had broken into a locker, and although nothing had been stolen, Sister had been reminding the children each morning about the sin of silence. A person could lie by saying nothing, and there were special places in hell for children who withheld criminal information.

"You want to tell her, don't you, Timmy?"

"No."

"You do. Don't lie. I heard you thinking it."

"I wasn't."

"You *were*. You *are*. Still *are*. I hear you." Buckeye's bad eye caught the sunlight.

"Buckeye! I swear."

"Cross your heart?"

"And hope to die."

"With a needle in your eye?"

"Yeah. You know—"

"I want to believe you," Buckeye said. "You can think about telling if you want. The important thing is not telling."

"I won't."

"And something else, Timmy. You have to swear—death-oath swear—you won't try stopping me."

"Stopping you?"

"Someone has to get rid of those things, Timmy. Someone has to do it. If you won't help, I'll have to do it alone."

A week passed, and all through it Timmy tried believing that Buckeye hadn't been serious. Then, two weeks after the incident in the janitor's office, he saw Buckeye stash a bag in the woods behind the school. *Stake sword*, Timmy thought. *He made one. He's going to do it.* He shivered, wondering if he were being like Buckeye now, imagining things that weren't real.

He watched Buckeye step from the trees, brushing his hands on his jacket as he stepped onto the playground. He tried intercepting him, but the bell rang, signaling the kids to line up. Ignoring the bell wasn't an option, especially with Sister staring at him from the main entrance.

Timmy got in line, moving forward with the other kids, watching Sister looming ever larger as he advanced toward her.

"Good afternoon, Sister."

"It's *morning*, Timothy."

He winced, walking past her and into the school's shadows, through the long institutional-green walls interspersed with classroom doors. Timmy had never thought about it before, but the school was like a cave. Perhaps it was the look of the place that had made Buckeye think of vampires. Then came the face on the comic book, with its uncanny resemblance to Nathan Spitzbaugh. After that, things must have fallen into place quickly for Buckeye, clinching with the encounter in the basement two weeks ago. Whatever the case, Timmy had the sense that things were about to go too far.

Timmy's class was in room 112. He went in, took his place, and heard nothing until lunchtime.

In the cafeteria, Buckeye seemed preoccupied. Timmy sat beside him, taking a seat on his right side—the side with the normal eye. But Buckeye got up, repositioning himself to Timmy's right.

"Why'd you move?" Timmy asked.

Buckeye tapped his blind-side ear to indicate he was listening to more than Timmy's words.

"What's in the bag, Buckeye?"

Buckeye opened his lunch, pulling out a ham sandwich. "Lunch," he said.

"Not *that* bag, Buckeye. The one in the woods."

Buckeye bit his sandwich, chewing slowly. His dead eye rocking in its socket. "Why aren't you talking?"

Buckeye jammed the rest of the sandwich into his mouth. "Mmmff ffflll."

"Jeez, Buckeye!"

A hand closed on his shoulder. He didn't need to look back to know whose it was.

"Not eating today, Timothy?"

Timmy glanced at his bagged lunch, the top still folded closed.

"Not hungry," he said.

The hand tightened. "Not hungry what, Timothy?"

Timmy closed his eyes. "Not hungry, *Sister*."

The hand slipped from his shoulder. "That's better." She started walking away, then paused. "Is there something on your mind, Timothy?"

"No, Sister."

"You're sure?"

Buckeye kept chewing, listening with his hear-all ear.

"You look like you want to tell me something," Sister said.

"No, Sister. Nothing. Honest."

She nodded. "All right, then. But if you're not going to eat, you can help in the kitchen. Give your lunch to the souls in Purgatory."

The souls in Purgatory were one of Sister's favorite causes. So on this day, Timmy got to serve the greater good by forgoing lunch and recess.

For his final chore, he carried a load of trash to the cans behind the school. He glanced at the woods as he lifted the lid, looking for the bag that Buckeye had stashed among the trees. He considered retrieving it, stashing it with the rest of the garbage. *There's time*, he told himself. *Go now!* He looked back toward the kitchen door. No one there. *I can do it! Do it now!* He stepped away from the cans, gauging the distance, hesitating until the bell rang. An instant later Sister appeared. "You'll be late, Timmy."

He followed her inside.

"We should talk," she said, walking him to room 112.

"About what, Sister?"

"Whatever you like. About how you're getting along here."

"I'm getting along fine, Sister."

"Making friends."

"Yes, Sister."

"I don't mean just Sean. I mean other friends."

"I'm OK, Sister."

"Do you miss your old home?"

"Sometimes, Sister."

"It can be difficult settling in at a new school, Timothy. A talk with Farther Larkin might help. Would you like that?"

Timmy hesitated.

"He's free after school."

"Today, Sister?"

"Yes."

His heart raced. "I can't, Sister." He swallowed. "Not today. I need—"

"I've telephoned your mother. She says it'll be fine."

They reached the classroom.

"So it's all decided," Sister said.

The other students were already in their seats.

Buckeye shifted in the second row. His good eye watching as Sister led Timmy inside.

"I'm glad we had this talk, Timothy."

Timmy took his seat, trying not to slump under the weight of Buckeye's one-eyed gaze.

Father Larkin had tired eyes and a ruddy blush that became spider veins up close. He spoke softly, but although Timmy seemed to listen, the truth was he heard nothing. His thoughts remained with the woods and the stake sword that Buckeye had stashed there.

"Timothy?" Father leaned nearer, so close that Timmy feared he might get caught in the red webbing of his face. "You're not listening, are you Timothy?"

Timmy tensed. "I am."

Father Larkin stared. Timmy expected him to say, *You are what, Timothy?* But he didn't. He sat back, crossed his legs. "You know, Timothy, I don't need to do all the talking here."

"I know, Father."

"If you have something to say, I'll listen."

"All right, Father."

"I'm a good listener. And I can be trusted. You believe that, don't you?"

"Yes, Father."

"Trust is important, Timothy. And this school, indeed our entire parish, operates on a system of mutual trust. That's why our doors are always open. A person can walk into our church any time. And this rectory, too. It's never locked. You know that, Timothy?"

"Yes, Father."

"We live in remarkable times, Timothy. Our country is safe. And our president . . . he's Catholic, you know?"

"Yes, Father."

"His people are Irish, like yours. Like mine. We're the same, you see. Almost members of the same family. And family members should feel free to speak their minds, don't you think?"

"Yes, Father."

"So is there anything on your mind, Timothy? Anything you'd like to say? Anything you'd like to tell me . . . or maybe ask me?"

"Yes, Father." Timmy swallowed. "If I can. There is something . . . something I need to ask you."

Father spread his hand. "Ask it, Timothy."

Timmy glanced toward the door of Father's office, out the narrow window at the end of the rectory's front hall, toward the long shadows of forest trees that were already dark with the colors of night.

"Ask it, Timothy. I promise to listen."

Timmy turned around. "Can I go?" His voice quivered.

"That's it? That's your question?"

Timmy nodded. "Can I please, *please* just go?"

There was nothing stashed in the woods behind the school. Timmy scoured the area, fruitlessly searching the deepening shadows, finally realizing that the lack of a hidden sword stake could only mean that Buckeye had already gone inside to wait for the vampires.

He looked toward the back of the school, toward the rear door and the soft light of the second floor window. Once again, he heard the sound of someone singing—a cleaning lady on the second floor. What if Buckeye were even now sneaking up on her, preparing to confront her before returning to the basement to lie in wait for Spitball?

I have to stop him.

Timmy left the woods and hurried across the playground. The door wasn't locked. He ran inside, pausing when he reached the stairs: one flight leading up toward the singing woman, the other descending toward the dim light of Nathan Spitzbaugh's office. Someone was down there. Was it Buckeye? Timmy started down the stairs, moving faster when he heard the rhythmic metal-on-metal rasp of a saw blade working through the shackle of a padlock:

kkkksssHHHHKKK . . . kkkksssHHHHKKK . . . kkkksssHHHHKKK!

The sound grew louder. The air thickened, reeking with the stink of dirty clothes, unwashed overalls and socks stashed inside closed lockers. And there was something else, an equally pungent but entirely different smell. He sniffed the air. What was it?

The rasping sound grew louder.

Timmy paused beside the lighted doorway, leaned back against the wall, and peered around. What he saw made no sense, but there it was—crazy, but undeniably there.

Buckeye stood with his back to the door, leaning against one of the lockers as he hacksawed a combination lock. And scattered around the office, apparently dumped from a large paper bag that now lay crumbled on the desk, were countless cloves of garlic—some mashed to a pungent slime on the cement floor.

So *that* was what had been in the bag. Garlic. Vampires were supposed to hate garlic, but what had made Buckeye think that garlic would work when crosses and sunlight didn't?

The sound of sawing stopped abruptly as Timmy entered the room.

"Timmy." Buckeye spoke without turning around. "I knew you'd come."

Timmy stepped on a piece of smashed garlic, slipping forward, catching himself on the desk. That was all he needed—to fall and be covered in garlic paste.

"Come here, Timmy. Hold this lock. My hand's tired."

Timmy stepped forward, his nose tingling from the ripe stink from the closed lockers. "What are you doing, Buckeye."

"Getting them out."

"Who?"

"The kids."

"No, Buckeye. There aren't any—"

"Don't say that, Timmy. Don't even think it!" He stepped away from the locker, letting Timmy see that he had nearly finished cutting the shackle. "You *know*. You were here. You heard! It's Johnnie Walker."

"That's not a person, Buckeye. I told you. It's the name of—"

"He's a person. *Was* a person." Buckeye pointed the hacksaw at Timmy, thrusting it like a sword. "And it's not just him. It's Paul Duffy. And Jamie Simpkins. And Kathy Evans. They went missing, and no one knows what happened. No one but us!"

Timmy took another step forward, foot sliding on smashed cloves. "This is crazy, Buckeye." He looked around. "This garlic. Where'd you get—"

"Stole it."

"All of it?"

"Not all at once. I picked up a few at a time down at the A&P." Half his face jerked into a smile. The other half stayed flat. "No one watches a kid in the vegetable section. I just picked them up and kept walking . . . kept going back till I had enough."

"But will it work? I mean, if crosses and sunlight—"

"Some of that stuff's got to be true, Timmy. Everything in the stories can't be wrong. Besides—" He bit his lip, then turned back to face the locker. "I didn't want to try your idea. *Stake swords!*" He shook his head. "Man, what kind of sicko thing—" He stopped abruptly, glancing toward the hall.

"Buckeye?"

Buckeye cocked his blind-side ear toward the stairs. "He's coming back."

"The janitor?"

"Yeah," Buckeye said. "Spitball."

Timmy heard footsteps on the stairs.

Buckeye looked around at the scattered cloves. "Hope this stuff works." He rubbed his nose. "I think it will." He grinned. "I sure got a mess of it, didn't I? I mean, if you put this many crosses in a room, I bet that'd do something. I bet—"

"Hey!" A man called from the hall. "Who's in there?" Footsteps quickened, coming nearer. "What the—" Nathan Spitzbaugh entered the room, stopping in his tracks. "What the hell are you kids doing?"

"We know," Buckeye said, his voice coming from deep in his throat. "We know about you, Spitball."

Nathan Spitzbaugh looked at the garlic-strewn floor. His face buckled, scowling. "No!" He gasped, staggered backward, bracing himself against the wall. It was clear he couldn't believe what he was seeing: his office smeared with garlic, two kids hacking into one of his lockers. Or maybe it was more than that. His hand went to his chest, pulling his collar, struggling for air.

"Timmy!" Buckeye shouted. "Look at him. Look at his mouth! His *teeth*!"

Spitball fell sideways, kicking with his feet, pushing backward into the hall. Then he raised his head, rolled his lips into a sneer, and roared toward the stairs.

Buckeye dropped the hacksaw. "Run, Timmy!"

"What?"

"He's calling the others. Run!"

Timmy didn't need to be told twice. He raced from the office and into the hall. The stairs loomed before him, growing brighter as a light came on in the second floor. Someone was running, coming down as Timmy raced up. He saw her through the banister bars. It was a cleaning lady, and she wasn't alone. Another woman moved beside her, pushing her cart to block the exit from the basement stairwell.

"Buckeye!" Timmy stopped. "What now, Buckeye?"

But Buckeye hadn't followed. He was still in the office, sawing through the latch on the locker door.

"Going somewhere?" The cleaning woman leaned over her cart, grinning at Buckeye, baring her fangs. "Come here. Let's get a look at you."

Timmy charged, plowing into the cleaning cart, spilling trash and soapy water out across the floor. The woman leaped back, then forward again—lunging as Timmy raced from the stairs. He skidded, slipping on the wet linoleum, falling toward the door as the vampire lady grabbed his leg. He rolled onto his back and kicked her, driving his heel against her forehead, staining her skin with a big smear of soapy water and smashed garlic.

The vampire lady reared back.

He kicked again, but this time she dodged the heel, feinting left, coming at him from the side. Her mouth opened, lower jaw dropping until it was almost parallel to her neck. Then she lunged, driving her fangs through his pants and into his calf. Pain shot through him, burning like acid.

He threw back his head, arching his back against the linoleum until he could see the door at the end of the hall. It swung open. A figure stepped in. Timmy couldn't see the face, only a pair of jeans and two threadbare sneakers.

"No!" Timmy realized he was surrounded. No way out. No escape. But still he struggled, kicking as the vampire lady gnawed his leg, feeling the strength bleed out of him as the second vampire lady bared her fangs and leaped forward. They'd kill him for sure. Tomorrow there'd be one more missing kid, another unsolved mystery. And just when he thought things couldn't get worse, down in the basement, Spitball stopped screaming.

The other vampires froze. The one that had hold of Timmy's leg looked toward the stairs.

FffhhhhrrrOOOOMMMM!

A muffled explosion shook the basement, echoing from the cinderblock walls as a wave of smoke burst from the stairwell, curled across the ceiling, and shot for the back door.

The sneaker-wearing vampire stepped aside, holding the door open.

The smoke curled out, and then—

FffhhhhrrrOOOOMMMM!

A second burst of shifting air rocked the hall. This time it came from the open door as the sneaker-wearing vampire vanished into a curl of oily smoke. Then, in rapid succession—

FffhhhhrrrOOOOMMMM!

FffhhhhrrrOOOOMMMM!

The vampire ladies vanished, disbursing into smoke that raced quickly out through the closing door.

Timmy struggled to his feet, limped forward, and leaned out into the night. The smoke was still there, four clouds blending as they cleared the trees, glowing in the haze from the road beyond. For a moment the look of it reminded Timmy of home, like smog rising from the Clairton Works. He shivered, feeling a sudden chill for all the things he had left behind . . . for all the things he could never reclaim. And then, from the basement, a new sound.

A metal door had banged open.

And now it was Buckeye's turn to scream.

The next morning Timmy Baker was in the hospital, suffering from a strange infection that had spread from a pair of puncture wounds in his leg. There was something wrong with his blood, forcing him to undergo three transfusions before he stabilized. Buckeye was in the same hospital, though Timmy never saw him again. When Timmy returned to school, it was to a private academy in Vermont. A year later his dad transferred again, this time to Davenport, Iowa. By the time Timmy finished middle school, memories of West Fenton, Buckeye, and Spitball had crawled to the back of his mind—never fully forgotten, but always there, coiled like copperheads, ready to bare fangs whenever his dreams soured and he woke shivering between sweat-soaked sheets.

Once, during that nondescript stage in life that is neither adulthood nor adolescence, Timmy tried finding Buckeye by calling every O'Rourke in eastern Pennsylvania. But no one had ever known a kid named Sean, let alone one who called himself Buckeye. And if they did, they weren't telling.

So Timmy came of age with only his own uncorroborated memories of what had happened that night. Of course, he had the official reports and bits of hearsay. He knew the school had been vandalized—a cleaning cart overturned, a basement office smeared with garlic, a locker door hacksawed open. No one knew who had done it, and the janitorial staff that should have been on duty that night was nowhere to be found. Nor did they report to work the next day. A week later, they were replaced with new people, or, more accurately, *real* people.

And there were other things.

The police found the first one inside the hacksawed locker. Then, one by one, they cut open the rest and found the others. Four of them in all.

The oldest had been missing for nearly a year.

HORROR BY SUNLIGHT

I was attending a party at World Fantasy in Baltimore when Larry Segriff, vice-president of Tekno Books, mentioned that Stephen Dziemianowicz was buying stories for a Barnes & Noble anthology entitled 356 Scary Stories. "Nothing longer than 750 words," Larry said. "Do you have anything like that?" I didn't, but I had an idea. A few minutes later, I left the party, rode the elevator back to my room, and wrote the following.

First Nelson saw the wolves.

They lay inside the front door, leering with yellow eyes and bared fangs.

Julie stepped over one of them. "Come on." She looked back, flashing a coy smile at Nelson. "These wolves won't bite."

She was right, of course. The wolves were nothing but skinned hides, wolf-skin rugs with the heads intact. But seeing them after a seemingly endless ride through the Pennsylvania night was enough to rattle Nelson's already shaky nerves. Julie had told Nelson that her stepfather was eccentric. Now, for the first time, he saw what she meant.

"Come on, silly," Julie said. "Bring those bags inside and shut the door. But be quiet. Daddy's already gone to his room, and we dare not disturb him till morning."

Nelson summoned his remaining strength and lugged a pair of suitcases (both hers) and a flight bag (his) through the foyer and into the wolf-carpeted hall.

Nelson had to bed down alone in the guest room. But he couldn't sleep. Exhausted as he was from the long drive, he lay awake while light from the full moon spilled across his bed. Somewhere a dog whimpered and whined. Nelson tried blocking the sound by wrapping a pillow around his head, but the sound soon escalated from whimpers to growls. Nelson couldn't stand it. The animal sounded as if it were trapped inside the house.

He got up and followed the sound to a room at the end of the hall. The whimpers came from behind a door. He knelt down and peered through the keyhole. On the other side, a wolf paced through slatted moonbeams.

In that instant, everything came together: the full moon, the locked room, the eccentric father with the mysterious condition that Julie had promised would be revealed during their weekend visit to his country estate. It was clear now— as clear as the moonlight that shimmered on the wolf's rippling shoulders.

Julie's father was a werewolf!

Nelson backed away from the keyhole. He stumbled backward down the hall and threw himself against the door of Julie's room.

Julie sat on the edge of her bed, apparently waiting for him.

He fell into her arms.

"Sorry," she said. "I had to let you see it for yourself. You would have thought me crazy if I'd told you."

She led Nelson back to the guest room and stayed with him until he drifted into an exhausted sleep.

He awoke to the chirp of birds and the warm smell of bacon and coffee. Sunlight streamed through the bedroom window.

Nelson dressed, telling himself that the madness from the night before had been a nightmare. Those rugs in the downstairs hall were enough to make anyone dream of monsters.

Feeling renewed, Nelson descended the stairs. He caught a glimpse of Julie sitting at a long, mahogany table. At the table's far end, a white-haired man with rosy cheeks chuckled and spoke to her over the rim of a steaming coffee cup. Yes, it had all been a crazy dream.

"Morning!" Nelson said as he reached the bottom of the stairs.

The white-haired man set down his cup and smiled at Nelson.

"You wouldn't believe the dream I had last night!" Nelson said as he stepped into the hall. "I dreamed—"

He stopped abruptly, gripping the banister to keep from falling. . . .

It wasn't the wolf skins in the hall that frightened him this time. The wolf skins were gone. In their place lay tan swatches of hairless skin, the human heads smiling at Nelson in the warm glow of the morning sun.

FLASHBACK

One of the most exciting graduate writing programs around is Seton Hill University's Writing Popular Fiction Program. In 2002, one of the program's founders, the author and poet Michael A. Arnzen, invited me to come on board as a resident writer, and I have been involved in the program ever since.

Among the program's graduates is Lee Howard, a truly gifted editor and writer who, in 2005, launched Dark Cloud Press. Their first book, Thou Shalt Not, which appeared in 2006, featured stories centering on the consequences of breaking the Ten Commandments. All right, I thought. Murder, adultery, false gods – those certainly lend themselves to dark fantasy. But what about the others? Intrigued by the challenge, I set to work on a story centering on the violation of the day of rest. The result is a locked-door mystery that quickly veers into the realm of dark fantasy.

She always slept through the night and awoke just before dawn. It was a routine that drove Harold nuts, but this morning he wasn't there to notice. The space beside her was empty. She touched it. It felt cool. He hadn't returned in the night.

She sat up, looking toward the closed door that she had left open before coming to bed. If Harold hadn't returned, who had closed the door?

A lamp stood beside the bed. She reached for it, feeling along its base until she found the switch.

Click!

Light struck her arm.

"Sweet Jesus!"

She drew back from the lamp, turning her hand in the light, trying to understand what she was seeing. And as she raised her other arm to verify that it was as filthy as the first, she became aware of the pungent smell of dead matter: wood, peat, leaves, and grass. The room reeked of compost, and her hands and arms were covered with loam.

What have I been doing?

The answer was obvious. The condition that Auntie Ariel had helped her overcome nine years earlier was out of remission and back with a vengeance.

She stood. Clumps of dirt fell from her nightgown. Her feet were clean, but her shoes (lying on their sides at the foot of the bed) were as filthy as her arms. She recognized the signs. She had been sleepwalking again.

Fully awake now, she hurried toward the door, following the tracks of her muddy shoes, stopping abruptly when she reached the far side of the bed.

A pile of wood lay between the bed and door. The pieces were familiar: twelve three-foot slats, two fifteen-foot stringers—the remains of the rickety basement stairs that she had ripped out and dumped in the landfill behind the tool shed.

I brought them back.

She had done such things before. In her early teens she would awake to find her room full of garbage: pizza boxes, milk cartons, coffee filters, all retrieved from alley dumpsters and arranged into patterns that defied reason.

Sometimes the piles came with notes, the writing always as cryptic as the garbage.

But that had been long ago. Auntie had cured her. But now Auntie was gone. And the condition was back.

A long strip of decorative wood sat atop one of the stringers. And there were other things, too: a power drill with a Philips-head bit, a box of screws, a crowbar.

Don't ask what it means! Auntie's voice came back to her as she stared at the pile. *Knowing what it means isn't as important as knowing how to stop it.*

Rachel turned and faced the door. She had evidently closed it herself after bringing the wood and tools into the room, and now, as she gripped the knob, she realized she had done something else, too.

The door was locked.

Two keys could open the door. One was a master that unlocked everything in the house. She kept that one in the kitchen. The second worked the bedroom door alone, and that key she kept in the top drawer of the nightstand.

She turned, retraced her steps, and opened the drawer.

The key was gone. In its place lay a dirt-smeared note:

THE KEY IS IN THE CROWN.
GET TO WORK!

Unlike the cryptic notes she had left herself in the past, this one seemed to mean something.

The bedroom occupied the top floor of a pentagonal tower on the house's northeast corner. High overhead, plaster gave way to a peaked ceiling of galvanized tin, and between the two, softening the transition, ran five strips of wood molding—*crown* molding.

THE KEY IS IN THE CROWN.

The key was up there. She could just make it out, jammed into the molding, shoved so deep that only its handle was visible. *The trim*, she thought, realizing how she had placed the key. She looked down at the long piece of decorative wood lying atop the disassembled stairs. A notch had been cut into one of its ends, perfect for holding a key and pushing it into place, useless for pulling it free. "You want me to work," she said, speaking to her compulsion. "It's Sunday morning, and you want me to build something."

She looked at the long planks of roughhewn pine, each tooled with a succession of right-angle cuts. Placed parallel, the stringers would support the planks, transforming them into a series of risers that would almost reach the key in the crown. She stepped back, trying to estimate the actual distance. With one end of each stringer wedged against the foot of the bed and the other elevated and pressed high against the wall, the reassembled stairs would get her close enough to hook the crowbar against the molding. She had no doubt she could dislodge the wood with a few well-placed tugs. But why had her sleeping mind felt a need to goad her into working on the Sabbath?

She sat on the bed, trying to understand, and it was then that she became aware of something new inside the room. It was silent, invisible, but definitely there—becoming more noticeable each time she took a breath.

Somewhere in the house, something was burning.

She returned to the door, dropped to her knees, and peered through the keyhole. The lamp was on in the hall, illuminating plumes of rising smoke.

Panicking now, she left the door and crossed to the window. It opened grudgingly, groaning as she forced it upward. There was no screen.

She leaned out, looked down along the wall, and realized the terrible risk of dropping to the ground below. Down there, right where Harold had left it, lay a menagerie of garden tools: hoe, shovel, pick, pitchfork, rake. She had asked him to clear the weeds from the foundation, and that simple request had started him shouting about the same things he'd been on her about since she had inherited Auntie's house. He didn't care that Auntie's memory was important to her. He couldn't understand why she didn't want to sell the place, and he was tired of watching her put effort and money into a renovation project that would never be finished.

"And besides," he had said, storming toward the house, "I'm tired. I'll clear the weeds tomorrow."

Perhaps, if she had been able to leave it at that, he would never have stormed out of her life, but instead she chased him, catching him on the porch where she explained that there would be no working on the house tomorrow. "Auntie's rule," she explained. "No work on Sundays."

That was the last straw. He went ballistic. Five minutes later he was gone.

The smell of smoke grew stronger after she shut the window and returned to the center of the room. She understood that the fire was her doing. After lighting it somewhere on the first floor, she had returned to bed, leaving her conscious self to wake and contend with it. And now it completed the message, combining with the wood, tools, and note to convey the fears of her unconscious mind: her commitment to Auntie's memory was destroying her life. The old woman's house was not worth keeping, and her rules no longer applied.

But the message missed a crucial point. It was as if her unconscious failed to grasp that the rule wasn't Auntie's alone. It predated her by over three thousand years, and its importance had as much to do with Rachel's mental health as it did with Auntie's religious devotion.

Rachel remembered how Auntie had explained it.

"You sleepwalk because you don't know how to rest. You collect garbage because you don't know how to work. Rest and work need to be purposeful, with times set aside for each. Do you understand, Rachel? Are you listening?" Auntie took Rachel's hand, pulling it down against the table. Only then did

Rachel realize that she had been using that hand to pull her hair, plucking out individual strands and wrapping them around her fingers.

"The work you do should always be purposeful, never compulsive." Auntie leaned closer. "Six days for purposeful activity. One day for contemplative rest. Learn these things, Rachel. Learn them and understand that your problem extends far beyond sleepwalking."

Rachel's hand jerked in Auntie's grip. The fingers wanted to go back to pulling hair.

But Auntie was strong. She held firm a moment longer. "Do you understand, Rachel?"

"Yeah. You're like saying it's Sunday. I can't do stuff because it's Sunday." She slipped her hand from Auntie's grip, but she did not go back to pulling her hair. "You're saying I can't do nothing on Sunday."

Auntie frowned. "You can. Sometimes emergencies arise. Some things can't be put off. That's where sound judgment comes in. Not only on Sunday, but every day. Your actions must always serve a greater good." Again, she took Rachel's hand, this time to stop it from drumming the table. "Do you understand me, Rachel?"

"What's a greater good?"

Auntie leaned close, looking deep into Rachel's eyes.

"For the moment," she said, "it's your health."

"We gonna work on that?"

"That's right."

"That why Mom brought me here to live with you?"

"Yes."

"So when do we start?"

Auntie gripped Rachel's hand, squeezing tight. "We've already started."

But even if her unconscious didn't grasp it, and even if her long-overdue breakup with Harold had caused a return of her sleepwalking, Rachel still understood what Auntie had told her about the greater good. Auntie would not want her to sit in the house and burn. *Sometimes emergencies arise. . . .*

Rachel rose from the bed, lifted one of the fifteen-foot stringers, and wedged it between bed and wall. She did the same with the other, positioning it parallel to the first. When the two were aligned, she secured them by screwing a single tread into position about five feet from the floor. Then she pushed on the tread, testing it. The stringers groaned. The left one shifted, angling outward. She let go and grabbed another tread, but this one she positioned beneath the first, creating a brace. The drill whirred, anchoring the wood. Then, again, she tested the structure with her weight. It held.

She threw down the drill and picked up an armload of treads. There was neither time nor need to secure them. She simply laid them down as needed, sliding them into every other position as she climbed. Then she returned to the floor, grabbed the crowbar, and hurried back up the creaking stairs.

The height looked much more precarious from the top and, as she stood on the top step, the left stringer shifted again, skidding out of alignment and digging into the plaster wall. But she couldn't stop to secure it. The smell of smoke was stronger than ever. She had to act now, get the key, get out of the room.

She swung the crowbar, driving it hard against the molding. She pulled. Nails groaned. Mahogany splintered. The key dropped, pinging against the hardwood floor.

The left stringer shifted again as she descended, the top planks falling away as she reached the secured tread in the middle position. From there she jumped, landed on the bed, and bounded down to the floor to retrieve the key.

She crossed the room, disengaged the lock, and opened the door.

Smoke poured in, breaking over her like a soundless wave. She raced forward. Three strides brought her to the balustrade. She gripped it and turned, stumbling down into thickening smoke.

She lost her balance near the bottom, falling backward to crack her head against the chair rail that extended along the front hall and into the foyer. She started to pull herself up, but stopped when she realized that the air was clearer near the floor. She could see the length of the hall, past the door that led to the living room, all the way to the foyer and the closed front door. Smoke billowed from the living room arch. Dark smoke. No hint of flame. What kind of fire was this, anyway?

She hurried forward, crawling beneath the smoke, keeping her head low. And then something stepped in front of her. She saw it through the smoke, a creature with the face of a pig and the body of. . . .

He reached for her. She recognized his hand.

"See!" he said. "You don't have to follow her rules!" He grabbed her and pulled her down the hall.

She leaned against him, blinking back the stinging smoke as she saw Harold's eyes peering through the Plexiglas goggles of a pig-nose gasmask. And behind him, barely visible as they passed the living room, she glimpsed the fireplace piled high with smoldering peat. He had ignited the stuff and closed the flue. Then he had donned a breathing mask and waited for her to work herself out of the bedroom.

"I did this for you," he said, pulling her to the foyer. "Teach you a lesson!" His voice came muffled through the gasmask, adding to the strangeness of the moment. She felt confused, disoriented, as if the churning smoke had entered her head, and yet now she understood that she'd been too quick to blame herself, too willing to believe that her old compulsions had returned. The mind game had been Harold's, not hers. And as was often the case, his game was all about blaming her.

She looked into his crazy eyes as he headed for the door. She wanted to scream at him, but suddenly a shape in the smoke struck her dumb. A face had formed behind Harold: gaunt cheeks, sunken temples, strong eyes. It was Auntie, her features advancing as Harold entered the foyer.

Am I dreaming this?

Auntie extended a smoky arm, reaching out as Harold opened the front door. Rachel felt a gust of inrushing air. Cool and sweet with misting rain, it broke against her shoulders, tousling her hair and stirring the smoke. Auntie became a whirlwind, a soot-black cyclone with an extended arm that touched Harold's neck, brightened, started to crackle, and then ignited. . . .

BLAM!

The wind was no longer at Rachel's back. It slammed hot against her face, throwing her out of the house, through the door and onto the porch . . . and all the while her eyes remained open and staring as Harold and the whirlwind melded into a fiery tongue that split against the ceiling. And then, as suddenly as it flared, the flame died, falling in on itself as Rachel scrambled off the porch and into the mist of a sweet-smelling rain.

The house went dark. But the rain was brightening.

She turned, looking east to see a sliver of sun clearing the slope behind the shed.

She found Harold's remains stretched across the front hall. There wasn't much, just ashes on the carpet, the charred shadow of a man in flight that scattered with the wind as she reentered the house.

The fire marshal talked about flashbacks as he inspected the damage. "You had the flue closed," he said, looking at the fireplace. "That starved the fire, but didn't put it out." He stirred the peat ashes with a blackened poker. "That's why your house filled with smoke. And that's why you got that flash when you opened the door. You was lucky."

"Guess I could've been incinerated."

He looked at her. "Not likely. Not if you was opening the door. The flash you saw was back here, in the fireplace. When I said you was lucky, I meant on account of the smoke. Smoke kills more people than fire. You was lucky you made it to the door."

"But the flash was in the hall," she said.

"No." He grinned. "It might've looked that way. A flash in a darkened house can seem closer than it is. But it was back here." He pointed at the fireplace. "So what the hell kind of fire were you trying to build here, anyway?"

The police helped her put the rest of it together.

Harold had waited until she was asleep before reentering the house. He carted the wood to her room, sprinkled her with dirt, and jammed the key into place. Then he locked her door with the master key, lit the fireplace, and closed the flue when he heard her footsteps on the floor above.

It all made sense, but naturally she didn't tell them about the part where Auntie came out of the smoke and set Harold aflame. As far as they were concerned he had fled the scene.

"We'll find him," they said, but she knew otherwise. After all, it had been Harold who had violated the commandment by engaging in malicious work on the Sabbath.

And Auntie had always understood the importance of working for the greater good.

STEP ON A CRACK

Consider this one a cautionary tale about the willing suspension of disbelief.

Chaz was different. All the kids knew that. He believed things. When Billy Jacob told him that there were ghosts in the attic, Chaz nodded as if Billy's lie had been the gospel truth. Then Chaz went about his business, which involved things like staring at the swirls in plaster walls or the grain patterns in strips of plywood. When I asked him what he was doing, he said that he was thinking about the ghosts in the attic. "Oh, Chaz!" I said. "Billy was kidding." But Chaz shook his head and said, "No. There's ghosts up there. Go check. You'll see." And damn if I didn't believe him. See, Chaz had a knack for turning lies into truth.

I'll never forget when Judy Hendershot told him about cracks and lines. By then, most kids knew better than to fill Chaz's head with lies. But Judy was new on the street, and she thought that Chaz needed to be messed with. She ran up behind him as he walked along the sidewalk. "Hey, boy!" she said. "Be careful!"

Chaz turned real slow. He blinked at Judy, giving her that squint-eye expression that made him look like he was peeking through a keyhole. He didn't say anything, so Judy pointed to his shoes.

"Look," she said.

And when Chaz looked he saw that his left heel was an inch away from one of the sidewalk's tar-filled seams, and his right toe was nearly touching a crack in the concrete. We all saw it coming, but, before we could stop her, Judy said, "Step on a crack, break a grown-up's back. Step on a line, break a person's spine." And then, in a burst of poetic inventiveness that for a moment made us forget the terrible implications of planting lies in Chaz's mind, Judy added, "Jump over a crack, break a daddy's sacroiliac." Not that we knew what a sacroiliac was. We thought it was a butt-hole, which conjured some comical images in our prepubescent minds.

Chaz stood there, staring at Judy. Then he looked along the sidewalk, nodding slowly as his squinty eyes saw all those cracks and lines. We could tell that he believed Judy's lie, and when Chaz believed something the world adjusted accordingly. See, his mind was sort of a transformer; a thought would get inside him, and his brain would transform the world.

Sometimes things scared Chaz. Like those ghosts in the attic. Chaz never went near the attic on account of those ghosts. (And it was a good thing too, since once he started believing in them, the ghosts were really there!) But other times Chaz liked what he heard, and I guess Chaz liked Judy's crack-and-line poem because, before anyone could stop him, he took off down the sidewalk—stepping on cracks and lines like they were bugs and worms. Sometimes he would land on a line with both heels and then leap forward over a crack. And all along the street people collapsed in pain.

We chased him, but of course that only made him run faster. It was me that caught him. I dove and grabbed his legs. He fell forward. To this day I don't know why he didn't put his hands out to break his fall. His freckled face slammed the sidewalk, and his head made this wet, splitting sound that vibrated right through his legs and into my hands.

After that everything changed. All those people with broken backs and sacroiliacs rose up like they'd been cured by Jesus. Everybody was fine—everybody, that is, but Chaz. Chaz just lay on the sidewalk, dead as a bug on a windshield.

I don't know how Chaz was able to turn lies into truth, but I want to learn. I spend a lot of time staring at plaster swirls and wood grains. I try believing that Chaz isn't dead. I try believing that he's standing beside me. I try believing that everything's the same as it was before Judy Hendershot told him that crazy crack-and-line poem. And sometimes, when I squint my eyes just right, I can almost see him smiling at me from the wood-grain patterns in the attic door.

GHOSTS

Although all of the other stories and novelettes in this collection first appeared in genre magazines and anthologies, the following story appeared in a slick publication titled Sewickley Magazine. *For that reason, it is perhaps the most mainstream story in this book. It is also one of the most personal.*

She looks at me and says, "You're kidding," which is Amy's way of saying, "Act your age." She never comes right out and accuses me of being immature; she does not have to; I know when she is telling me to grow up, even when all that she is saying is: "You're kidding, Jerry. Please tell me you're kidding."

We are creeping through an intersection in downtown Pittsburgh. Our Buick's windows are up. An air-conditioned breeze whispers from the dash. Outside, people cross the street, lumbering along in shorts and tank-tops. Some of them are developing their first serious burns of the summer. Mick says their arms look like hot dogs, and he should know. He eats enough of them.

Mick is our two-year-old son. He rides behind Amy and me, sitting in his travel-seat, staring out the windows as I ease through the intersection and pull to the curb.

Amy is meeting old friends for lunch, people from her college days that she has not seen since we moved to New York. She opens the passenger door, and the hot summer day rushes in. She leans toward the backseat and kisses Mick. "Make d] Daddy take you to a playground, pumpkin. Make him take you someplace nice."

She finishes with him. Then she leans across the front seat, kissing me while people pass on the sidewalk. "You take him someplace nice, Jerry."

"All right."

"The museum."

"That's second on my list."

"What's first?"

"The Spiegel house."

"You weren't kidding?"

"No. I'm serious. We'll drive by it on the way to the museum, and we won't stay long. Only a moment. Only long enough to see if it's still there. It'd be a shame to be back here a week without at least taking a drive by. I'll tell Mick the story."

"Don't scare him, Jerry. OK?"

A cab has pulled behind the Buick. Traffic is heavy. The cabbie can't go. He leans on his horn and shouts at me to move it.

Amy kisses me once more in spite before slipping away.

I ease the Buick forward, and for a moment we are moving together—Amy on the sidewalk, me in the car. We move side-by-side for a few dozen feet. Then she turns away, sinking into a sea of strangers. And I think of how alone and how different I had been before Amy came to walk beside me for the first time.

I first saw the Spiegel house when I was seventeen. That was the year my grandmother, who had been my guardian for longer than anyone else, decided that I needed someone capable of commanding my attention. She felt that I ignored her. I still remember her telling me how attentive my father had been when he was seventeen. She wanted to know why I couldn't be more like him, though I suppose the answer was obvious.

I spent a lot of time thinking about my parents back then, brooding on their half-remembered faces. They had died when I was four, and I was certain that they were the only people who had ever given a damn about me.

My godparents took me in after the accident, but after a few months they turned me over to an aunt who lived on the city's south side. After that I was given to another aunt who lived along the north shore. And after that it was someone else. I was always in motion, always packing and unpacking while relatives pawned me off on one another for reasons that were never as compassionate as they sounded.

I had lived in nearly a dozen neighborhoods before I reached my uncle's, and by then the memories of my dead parents had become a persistent presence in my mind. No matter who I was with, the only family that mattered was inside me, and I grew with my memories into a tall, lean loaner—a blank-eyed seventeen-year-old who walked with no one but the shadows of his own mind. It frightened me to be that way, but the harder I tried anchoring my thoughts in the real world, the more I realized how little there was for me to hold on to.

"Those blank stares won't work in my house, Jerry. You understand? You listening to me?"

My uncle had pulled his car into his driveway, and now the engine was off. We sat in the long front seat, my suitcase a battered wall between us. I turned. My uncle looked angry. "You haven't heard a word I've said, have you?"

I didn't look at him. My gaze had settled on a house at the street's dead end, standing alone in a weed-filled yard, tall and narrow—as if emptiness had caused its walls to shrink inward. Boards covered the windows. No-trespassing signs covered the boards. I had never seen a place look so forgotten.

"That was Joe Spiegel's place," my uncle said. "He and his wife lived there a while back. They're gone now."

"Gone where?"

"Don't act stupid, Jerry. I don't like people acting stupid."

"You mean they're dead?"

He did, but he wouldn't say it. Instead he told me that he wasn't about to spend all day in the car. So we got out and moved up the steps that led to his front door. He showed me inside. But I didn't care about his place. My thoughts were elsewhere, drifting toward the empty house up the street.

That night, before the moon rose, when gaslights punched holes in the darkness and wind sighed through the trees, I wrote a note that said I was running off to California and left it on the guestroom bed.

And then I left the room that would never be my room.

And I slipped into a night that belonged only to me.

There was a 7-Eleven a few blocks away. I went there first, buying a Coke and stealing a flashlight before doubling back. I avoided the sidewalk that led past my uncle's home, moving instead through backyards—climbing fences and shoving through hedges—trying not to get lost in the shadows. And then, finally, after pushing through a wall of tangled hedges, I was there.

I pushed forward through the weeds, waiting until I was up against the back of the place and hidden from the street before snapping on my stolen flashlight. The beam cut the darkness and flattened against a wall, forming an eye-like circle on the mossy brick. I swung the light, moving the eye onto the boards that covered the windows. The wood was warped, held in place by rusty nails. I grabbed a splintered corner and tugged.

The board shifted.

I pulled harder. Wood splintered. I gave another tug, forcing the board until it dangled on a single nail. The window beneath was closed. I pressed against the glass and panned my flashlight over the room's walls. The place looked empty at first. But then the beam struck the shadow of a high-backed chair. I stared, holding the beam steady, noticing a small end table beside the armrest. And atop the table—resting on the polished walnut—was a hand.

I stood, too surprised to move, staring at those fingers and realizing that they belonged to a chair-sitting woman. She had her back to me, all but her head and hand hidden by the chair's high back.

A man sat across from her, his shape barely visible in the shadows. He was speaking to the woman, his voice a wordless murmur through the glass.

I moved the flashlight, swinging the beam onto his face, and it was then that I noticed the eye on the room's far wall. It was the same circular eye that I had seen on the outside of the house. The light passed through everything: chair, table, man, woman. . . .

I did not go into the Spiegel house that night, nor did I linger at the uncovered window any longer than it took to realize that the people in the room had no more substance than the pale light that had passed through them.

I dropped the flashlight and ran from the weed-filled yard, not stopping until I reached my uncle's house.

He wanted to know where I had been.

"Nowhere," I said, trembling, waiting to see what he would do.

He stared a moment, then turned away, shaking his head and muttered something about it being too late to make me better than I was. Days later, catching him in a good mood, I asked him to describe Mr. Spiegel, and ever since I have believed that I once looked through a locked window and into the eyes of a ghost.

I've changed.

Knowing that I was not the world's only haunted orphan made a difference. I was already a better person when I met Amy a few months later. We met in Oakland, where she was a freshman at Pitt. She was from Staten Island and knew nothing about Pittsburgh or the string of neighborhoods I had tried calling home. She knew nothing about me that I did not want her to know. She offered a clean slate. We filled it together.

Amy's father is a realtor. I work for him now. He calls me son. And when

Mick was born he helped Amy and me with the down payment for a place of our own. My family is outside me now.

Sometimes, however, I still find myself wondering about what has become of that other orphan.

The neighbors do not recognize me.

I stand with my son, leaning back against the Buick's door, looking across the green lawn that stretches toward what was once called the Spiegel house. The no-trespassing signs are gone. Boards no longer cover the windows. A child peers at us through lace curtains, exchanging peek-a-boo grins with Mick.

Someone touches my shoulder.

I turn.

My uncle stands behind me. "Damn, Jerry! It *is* you. For a second I thought it was your father out here."

He wants to know why I did not tell him that I was in town, but we both know the answer. Living together did not bring us closer, and we have not stayed in touch since I moved away.

I introduce him to Mick, and we exchange small talk before turning our attention back toward the house.

"They're from Michigan," he tells me, speaking of the people who have bought the place. "They didn't know any better, I guess. No one told them. I felt bad for them until I saw what they were able to do with it." He pauses. "You're looking pretty good, Jerry. Darn good."

"Thanks."

"Who'd have thought?"

I turn away.

"Sorry, Jerry. Don't take me wrong. I mean it as a compliment."

He doesn't understand. I haven't turned away from him. I'm just looking at the house.

"You were a lot different back then," he says.

"I know," I tell him. "We both were."

The house's front door flies open. The peek-a-boo boy races out into the yard. I take a step back, turning toward my uncle. "You want to hear a story?"

"Sure," he says. "So long as it's good. I'll always listen to a good story."

I look again at the wide windows, lace curtains, painted shutters, and clean brick walls. The house is brilliant in the aging morning. Shadows fade with the rising light. I look at it all while the children play in the weedless yard, and I tell my uncle the only ghost story I know.

PROPHECY

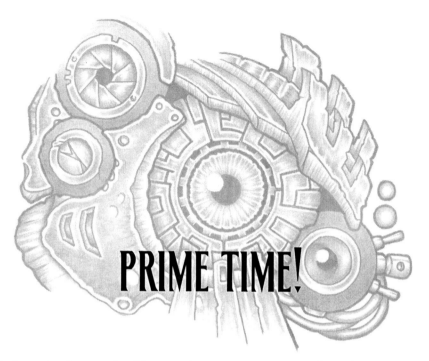

PRIME TIME!

My introduction to the SF magazines came in 1966, when the junior high school that I was attending took part in a magazine fundraiser. Among such mundane offerings as Newsweek, Redbook, *and* Home and Garden *was something called* The Magazine of Fantasy & Science Fiction, *for which I purchased a year's subscription for $5.00. During that first year I encountered the work of F&SF regulars Robert F. Young, Ron Goulart, and Bob Leman. The latter would, many years hence, become my mentor when I learned he lived within a short drive of my home. Also years later, when I started writing seriously, F&SF became the publication that I most wanted to sell to, a desire that became a reality when Gordon Van Gelder purchased the story you are about to read.*

Will you take the job, Mr. Underwood?"

Underwood looked around at the rows of telephone solicitors. Some faced computer screens and spoke into headsets. Others were at their desks. A few ambled sluggishly toward a door marked "Employee Rest Area."

The office looked like a decent place to work, but Underwood, who really wanted to begin his professional life as something better than a telemarketer, still had questions. "Did you say that your people place calls to all fifty states?"

Mr. Singleton gave a balding nod. He was a bird-like man—beaked nose, diminutive chin, and wide eyes that filled the concave lenses of his glasses. "Also Puerto Rico, Mexico, and Canada," he added.

"And—" Underwood hesitated. This was the one detail of Singleton's operation that he still had trouble grasping. "Your computer system allows you to place calls on a time delay?"

"More than that. It allows us to place calls at any time and still reach prospective customers at six in the evening."

"Dinner time?"

"Prime time!" Singleton said. "At Singleton Marketing, it's always prime time!"

"So if I come to work in the morning at eight—"

"Nine. You can arrive earlier, but we only require our workers to be here from nine to five."

"So I come in at nine in the morning, I place a call, and someone answers at six in the evening?"

"Precisely! Prime time! Dinner hour! Best time to reach two-income families."

"So I have a conversation with someone who's not going to hear my voice for nine hours?"

"Exactly!"

"I hear them and they hear me?"

"Just so!" Singleton beamed. Then, softly, he added, "Of course, all employees sign a contract prohibiting them from using the system for personal gain." He chuckled. "Now, if you're interested, you can start tomorrow." He gestured toward an empty desk. "We try to retain good people, but when someone feels he has a better future elsewhere, we let him go. Fortunately, most choose to stay."

To the right of the empty desk sat a silver-haired man with tired eyes. To the left was a woman with blond hair and a face that looked as if it had been hung out to dry.

"Your neighbors will be Mr. Royal and Ms. Corona."

Underwood glanced at his watch. It was 5:02. "Shouldn't they be going home?"

"Some of our people put in extra time," Singleton explained. "No reason not to. We have excellent facilities." He gestured toward the rest-area door. "And remember, whenever a Singleton solicitor places a call, it's prime time!"

Underwood soon discovered that telephone solicitation was hopelessly boring work, and after a week of sitting between the tired-eyed Mr. Royal and the sagging-faced Ms. Corona, he began hatching a scheme to make the system work for him.

His plan was simple. At 9:00 A.M., using the Singleton lines, he telephoned his own apartment. He hoped to reach his future self and get the day's closing stock reports. Instead, he got Singleton.

"What's going on?" Underwood asked. "What're you doing in my apartment?"

"Taking care of business, Mr. Underwood."

"Where am I?"

"Why, Mr. Underwood, you're at your desk placing a call—"

"I mean, where am I *there*? If you're in my apartment, where am—"

"I'm afraid you're not here, Mr. Underwood. In fact—" A pause, and then. "I'm afraid you're dead."

Underwood realized that the tired-eyed Mr. Royal was staring at him from the next desk.

"You're dead," Singleton said again. "Not dead on your end, of course. But here, in the six o'clock world of final stock reports, you have become the *late* Mr. Underwood."

Underwood leaned forward. He felt dizzy.

"We can't have people making time-shifting calls for personal gain," Singleton said. "It would wreak havoc with the system, not to mention the space-time continuum. I'm sorry, Mr. Underwood. If it's any consolation, there's still a place for you at Singleton Marketing."

Now Ms. Corona was staring at him too.

Singleton's voice crackled in the headset. "By placing a call to your future self, you forced us to take corrective action. You were—or should I say *will be*—killed after leaving the office. The death will be painless and swift. You didn't—that is you won't—see it coming. However, if you choose to never leave the office—"

Royal and Corona continued to stare.

Underwood choked. "Mr. Singleton, please—"

"Cheer up," Singleton said. "Think of all the people who work for companies in which they have no future. You, on the other hand, have no future except with the company. Welcome to the family, Mr. Underwood!"

The line went dead.

"They monitor our calls," Mr. Royal said.

Underwood's computer scrolled to a new account. Auto dialing kicked back on. A ringing line purred in Underwood's earpiece.

"They had nine hours to get to your apartment before your call went through," Ms. Corona said.

"Cheer up," Mr. Royal said. "Life here isn't as bad as you might think." Then, with a dry chuckle, he delivered the punch: "It's worse."

The line stopped ringing. A voice answered: "Hello." Dinner dishes clattered.

Prime time!

FLOW

And now for the strangest story in this collection, a narrative that takes place so far in the future that the human race is all but forgotten. The challenge was to build a world that was both accessible and alien. Early on, I decided that the characters would communicate via scent, heat, and aural patterns. They would live in organic cities and use machines that were genetically designed organisms. And before the story was over, they would discover a predator older than time, a form of fluid life that resides deep beneath the surface of their dying world.

To make the narrative accessible, I gave the characters recognizable emotions and desires—feelings that we might expect to find in sentient, social creatures of any era.

I wrote the story for myself as a kind of writing workout and was delighted when Sherwood Smith purchased it a few months later for the anthology Beyond the Last Star.

I awoke to the slap of breaking waves. Beyond the edge of my driftwood raft, across a rippling stretch of reflected sky, an approaching leviathan plowed the glassy ocean. Its forward eyes glared down, fixing me in its sights as I blazed with terrified heat.

The leviathan raised its flukes, slowed its approach, and bellowed three long blasts from its dorsal throat. The crew responded. I heard broad feet slapping the fleshy deck, and braided tendons angled over the gunwales, curling toward me as smooth-skinned amphibians plunged into the water.

By the time they lifted me on board, I was burning with warnings about the killer wave.

The crew tried calming me. One of them leaned close, fixing me with black eyes that flashed behind milky lids. Smooth skin shimmered, speaking with yellows and greens:

"There are no waves. The sea is calm all the way to the mainland. You're safe."

I lashed out, blazing with heat:

"The wave isn't from the sea. It's from the island!"

I sat up, looking toward the receding beach. Reduced by distance, the island's forest of gnarled trees had dwindled to a haze, dim branches against a sanguine sky. Somewhere in those shadows, cloaked in the jungle's brume, stood an enigmatic collection of spires and domes—the eroded puzzle that the islanders called the Temples of Rain: home of the fluid beast that had lured me with false light.

Passengers milled behind me. Among their murmurs, a familiar whisper: uneasy redolence bearing the scent of my name.

Turning, I saw my former mates, Ov and Spur, their faces black and confused. Last night I had told them to sail without me, now I had returned, plucked from the sea, once again blazing in their midst.

I had to tell them what had happened. They needed to understand. Everyone needed to know. The danger might not be over. It might pursue me. If it did, no one was safe.

My skin flashed, ranting:

"It came from the ground. Hungry fluid. A living wave!"

I stumbled.

An amphibian caught me. Its skin flashed, speaking with reds:

"We need to get you to a chamber."

I slumped, giving into the weight of my exhaustion, plunging into a heat of frightening dreams. . . .

I awoke within the leviathan, somewhere down the baleen corridors that ran beneath the dorsal ridge. The air hummed with the pulse of machined muscles and the thud of pounding flukes. We plowed the open sea, accelerating into the rusty dawn: another day of dwindling sunlight, one sunrise closer to permanent darkness.

My former mates glowed before me. Leaning close, they whispered with scented warmth:

"Your skin burns with terrible dreams."

I tried getting up, but they pushed me back. Ov's touch tingled with forgiveness:

"The amphibians say you must have been towed by the tide, but how could that happen if you had gone to live among the ruins?"

I responded with feeble light, telling them about the wave: how it had erupted from conduits in the temple streets and rained over the sunken pavements. . . .

To them, it was the stuff of madness, delirious ravings. They believed none of it, but they attended with soft scent until I slipped back into my private heat, and there I stayed until the leviathan reached the docks of the mainland city.

I spoke with scent as Spur and Ov helped me cross the crowded docks:

"I abandoned you last night, and now I've returned, raving like a rustic. I wouldn't blame you if you ascended without me."

They kept moving, holding me between them as we angled past the blistered skin of seaside walls, toward the peristaltic tubes that would carry us to the edge of the Port of Ascension.

Despite the large segment of the population that had already ascended to the higher sphere, the arteries of the old city were as crowded as ever. Rustics had immigrated from the forests and hills. Soon the city would belong to the unskilled masses. Machines would roam free. High towers would sicken from lack of maintenance. In time, the walls would topple. Between the closing of the Spheral Eye and the falling of the darkness, chaos would reign.

We left the tubes and pushed along a tractway crowded with soldiers and rustics. The former stood at ready, legs flexed, mandibles raised. The latter, held at bay, called to us as we advanced toward the Port of Ascension. With wan light, they begged us to take them along. Ov glanced toward them, offering weak apologies as Spur hurried us through the tricuspid door and into a rotunda of living bone.

Though not a specialist, I have perused the recorded lights of the great metaphysicians. From them I have learned that the universe is a mass of concentric spheres, each remaining viable until a new one forms around it. The image serves as a workable metaphor, one that might one day be replaced by another, but it is a good illustration for our time. Without it, our scholars might never have divined a means of escaping this dying world, and our fleshwrights would never have grown the transspheral gate that came to be called the Spheral Eye.

Within the Port of Ascension, standing on an amber dais and powered by nerves as thick as tendons, the Eye provided a conduit to a new world—a planet in a universe where the future loomed as large as the past did in ours.

The Eye's lids were as large as leviathan fins. Retracted and anchored to hooks of living bone, the lids framed an oval sclera, which in turn encased a ring of swirling blackness—the void between the spheres. Within the void, looking all the more beautiful for being surrounded by blackness, a world of yellow light blazed through a window of curved energy. The light emanated from a yellow sun; in its glow, a young city rose from a rocky desert.

Encased in amber scaffolds, the city's young towers still had the downy look of hatchling skin. Fleshwrights walked upon the scaffolds, leaning into the young walls as they cauterized seams, sutured joints, and hydrated tracts of thirsty veins.

There was water on that young planet, but it lay deep underground, necessitating a network of shafts and tunnels for the city's roots. Behind the city, a mountain of displaced rock lay beneath the sky's warm glow. Our ancestors had constructed cities with such material, but the days of building with blocks were behind us. The ages of stone had given way to the age of flesh.

The only inorganic substance used in the raising of the new city came from a pit of molten amber. Headless machines, guided by muscle memory, carried the amber in bone casks and shaped it into lattice scaffolds that hardened as they cooled. These shells supported the city's delicate walls until the subcutaneous supports ossified into bone.

Encouraged by the sight of that glowing city, I felt a healthy heat returning to my face and limbs as my mates and I reached the aural judges.

To be approved for ascension, an individual needed to possess skills that would benefit the growing city. Exceptions were made for those individuals who had formed long-term relationships with skilled mates. Fortunately for me, Spur and Ov were fleshwrights. The new city needed them.

Alone, I advanced toward the judge's scanning glow. Grown for a single task, the judge stood anchored to the floor. It spoke with impartial light:

"You have no skill. No trade."

I didn't answer. Direct responses were pointless. The judge saw all of my thoughts, past and present.

It continued:

"You study stones . . . ancient ruins . . . but there are no ancient ruins in the young sphere beyond the Eye."

I steadied myself, knowing what was coming.

"You will serve no good purpose in the new world, but, since your mates are fleshwrights, you feel that your passage is secure."

A nervous blush flickered on my hands. I resisted the urge to hide them.

"But how secure is your union with your mates? You abandoned them once. You might abandon them again after you have ascended."

I focused my mind, filling it with things that I knew to be true. I had a restless spirit, given to wild dreams and rash decisions, but last night's actions had been partly beyond my control. Were it not for the cruel influence of the luring wave, I never would have deserted my mates.

"There is something in your memory. A terrible thing, a fragmented dream, but your mind has stored it as if it were real. It could be madness."

For an instant, the light dimmed in the carapace eyes. Then, welling once again:

"But it is not madness."

The light brightened still more:

"I sense greatness in you. I do not think you will abandon your mates a second time."

The glow swung away.

I had been approved for passage.

As Ov stepped forward into the judging light, I angled toward the bone ramp that led to the base of the Spheral Eye.

Up close, the gate's white sclera proved to be a field of pulsing energy, crackling plasma that curved inward against a maelstrom of star-streaked blackness. Only the retracted flaps and glowing core remained as before, larger but nonetheless recognizable as the lids and pupil of an enormous eye.

Holding back as I reached the front of the queue, I stood gazing into the pupil, admiring the yellow light of the glowing city until Ov stepped behind me.

With a soft touch, she asked:

"Shall I go first?"

I stepped aside, letting her advance with confident light. She looked back, tossing me a gentle glow as she vanished into the void.

A moment later I felt Spur's hand on my back, giving me assurance as I followed Ov.

The bone ramp disappeared. I fell through darkness, angling sideways into a swirl of stars. Then the light returned, and within it, glowing so bright that I wondered how I could have ever left her, Ov reappeared. Rocky ground rose to meet me. I fell into Ov's embrace, steadying myself as we waited for Spur to appear.

Then, together, we advanced toward the quickening sarcopolis—the city of flesh growing from a bed of stone.

What followed was a strange variation of the routine we had followed on the island. Whereas before I had busied myself among the ruins of a lost culture, here I spent my days among the uprooted rocks that had been cleared from the foundation of the new city. Even young stones have stories, and I often lost myself in their strata and veins. Other times I sat among the lines of cleaved sediment and tried making sense of what had happened to me on the island.

Long ago, one of my stonemaster teachers told me about the island ruins:

"They stand in the heart of the forest, hidden in trees, half-swallowed by subsiding earth. The islanders have abandoned them, calling them unclean without remembering why. Someone should study those ruins before the ascension begins. Their secret might be worth knowing."

The stonemaster's light stayed with me. Years later, when the Spheral Eye opened and the slow exodus began, I convinced my mates to join me on a visit to the island. They agreed. There was, after all, no point in being among the first fleshwrights in the New World. Better to wait until the heavy work was done. Growing spires was easier than planting roots.

So we sailed to the island, pushed through queues of departing natives, and camped on the edge of the tangled forest.

The next morning, as my mates slept, I went to explore on my own.

An ancient berm wound through the trees. Graceful bridges, assembled without mortar, spanned ravines of jagged water. Following directions given by an island child, I turned left at each fork until I glimpsed stone spires through thinning trees.

I spent my first day walking along concave streets that wound between ruined walls. Fluted ramps and oval doorways seemed to have been shaped for liquid inhabitants. Within the rounded temples, inlays of colored stone depicted scenes of spewing fountains, racing rivers, and supine bathers. With foreshortened torsos and blunted limbs, the bathers bore little resemblance to their descendants—the fragile folk who now inhabited the island's shores. The ancient likenesses, rendered in colored stone upon the temple walls, were of a stone-wielding people: strong, rugged, and possibly incapable of speaking in hues.

I followed the succession of stone-carved scenes, trying to read the expressions on the primitive faces as they sank into what appeared to be the wavy lines of a rippling pool. Facial muscles are poor communicators. A curve can mean so many things, all of them vague.

Perhaps, given time, I would have divined the agony in their blunted features, but before long I sensed something stirring outside. A triad of wild machines huddled on the concave pavement, their low carriages and flattened backs suggesting that their ancestors had been used for hauling loads. Like most wild things, their eyes had lost the dim submissiveness of machined intellect. Brightly aware, they turned as I approached, studied me a moment, and then darted into the forest. I pushed forward, stepping down into the bowed pavement to find a conduit that whispered with gentle heat.

Bending low, I gazed through the opening and into a funneled darkness. Far below, my reflection floated on a rippling pool. A seductive scent rose through the darkness, telling me that the liquid was alive.

With light, I asked:

"What are you?"

The pool responded in the universal language of light and scent:

"Something old."

"Are these ruins yours?"

"Yes. They were fashioned in my honor. The builders were an artful race, full of dreams, like you."

Kneeling before that conduit, looking down at that pool of liquid flesh, I felt a strange, unhealthy longing. I wanted to touch that silver skin. I wanted to delve beneath its surface and sound its depths. I wanted to drown in its boneless embrace.

Sensing my desires, the pool promised to rise:

"This evening, after the sun has warmed the stones and I have gathered my strength, come back to this spot. I will rise for you. We will flow together."

Drugged with light, I returned to my mates and told them to leave the island without me. I blazed hurtful things, and we argued until our lights darkened and a stunned chill hung between us. Then I turned and vanished back into the forest.

They did not follow. They did not know the way, and I had made it clear that I wanted no more of their hard-edged couplings.

Alone, I returned to the ruins, stepping down into the bowed streets as the evening sun poured between the spires. Shadows streaked the pavement. And the ground quivered with a strange pressure, as if the stones themselves were waiting to exhale.

Up ahead, I saw more wild machines gathered in a sunken courtyard. They didn't dart as I approached, but instead kept their faces pressed to a line of grated holes. And then it happened. The ground heaved, and with a silver roar the conduits erupted. Liquid pillars spewed and rained over the pavement. Rills formed. Currents converged, becoming waves . . . and still the machines held their ground, eyes flashing with dull submission as currents crashed with bone-rending roars. . . .

I stepped back, suddenly afraid.

The fluid had changed. Gone was the alluring light. In its place, savage forces buckled and swirled, thickening as the machines were torn to pieces by the liquid's churning craw.

I screamed, my voice flashing against the trees.

The fluid turned, following the light of my scream, and then it surged, coming toward me as I fled into the forest.

I ran.

The fluid followed.

Ahead, a stone bridge arced over a jagged river. Waves crashed in the ravine, and I decided, as I climbed the arch of interlocking stone, that it would be better to die in those indifferent rapids than give myself to the flowing beast. Feeling the creature's misty breath on my shoulders, I turned and threw myself from the stone arch. Tumbling, looking skyward as I fell, I glimpsed a wave collecting on the bridge's center. It pivoted, curled, then plunged after me.

My back slammed the river. Water parted and folded back, pulling me down into racing darkness. For a moment I felt safe, weightless, suspended. . . .

And then, with a misty blast, I broke the surface to find the monster gone. The stone bridge veered from sight, vanishing as the river carried me over a ledge of rounded rocks. And that's when I saw it once again, a fist of black fluid rising from the rapids. It grabbed the rocks, curled into a column, and lifted itself from the sheeting water. Then, stretching like a shadow, it shot back into the forest, gathered itself into a wedge, and angled back toward the Temples of Rain.

I hurtled onward, riding the currents, wondering how long I could survive in the cold water.

Skeletal trees overhung the banks. I reached for them, caught one, and held on until the roots lost their grip and we tumbled together. Folded in the branches, I drifted as the river widened. Currents slowed. My thoughts flickered, sputtering out as I plunged into a dreamless sleep . . .

. . . only to be awakened by the pounding flukes of an approaching leviathan.

I worked through the memories as I lay among the stones at the city's edge. In time, I reached an understanding, an insight that, even if wrong, allowed me to drape the horror in a shroud of logic.

The flowing creature had told me it was old, and yet the islanders had never spoken of it. Except for a vague sense that something unclean lurked among the ruins, the islanders had given no hint of the thing's existence.

I realized, then, that the temples had probably been built as a reminder, a shrine to warn of a danger that might one day return. The architects had understood the softness of memory, how it erodes faster than stone. And for a while, before the island culture declined, the Temples had warned of the danger that slept beneath them. But the fluid beast was immortal. It could outlast stone memories, waiting until the monuments eroded to dust and new victims came to inhabit the land. . . .

I shivered, sensing that the creature might be nearly as old as the dying earth. How wise it must be! I tingled as I contemplated the things it must have learned from my light as I stood before it, and from my movements as I raced along the forest path. Perhaps it had sensed the nearness of my mates and the waiting leviathan. Perhaps it had even divined the existence of the Spheral Eye and the terminal state of our dying world?

Were these idle thoughts? Were they the fears of an unengaged mind? I tried dismissing them. What did I have to be afraid of now that I had passed through the Spheral Eye? The creature was far behind me, part of another sphere. To get to me it would have to breach the transspheral gate, and it could not approach that gate without first swimming to the mainland. And yet. . . .

It *could* swim. I had seen it pull itself from the island river. And if it could navigate rapids, what could keep it from crossing a waveless sea?

I had given up discussing such things with Spur and Ov. They were convinced that I had simply fallen from the stone bridge. In their opinion, the evil wave was the product of frightened dreams, a color of imagination. They made it sound convincing. I tried believing them, but the trying ended on the day that a frantic Spur came and pulled me from my retreat among the rocks.

Spur blazed, ranting with light as he directed my gaze past the city and toward the new world's side of the Spheral Eye. The transspheral migration had continued nonstop since we had passed through, an endless stream of fleshwrights, scholars, amberworkers, and machines—all emerging onto the parched ground beside the pit of molten amber. But now the queue was gone, and through the Eye's swirling pupil I saw the liquid beast crash against the Port of Ascension's bone walls. The beast was there, thrashing wildly as it made its way toward the Eye. And all the while, fleshwrights struggled to close the tricuspid lids.

I gripped Spur's arm, pulling him along as he stumbled beside me. My hands spoke with heat:

"It's followed me."

I knew this for certain.

It would cross the gate, devour everything in its path, and then plunge into the deep cavities that the rootworkers had dug beneath the city. And there it would sleep while the city's survivors braced for its second attack. But the attack would never come, and in time, fearful that future generations might lower their guard, the survivors would assemble crystal warnings. Perhaps they would even erect stone reminders on the city's edge, but none of it would matter. The creature's bloated sleep would outlive all memory. The terrible cycle would continue through the ages of this bright new world.

A crowd met us as we reached the city. They knew my story, some having read the glow of my so-called delusions, others having learned of my private madness by second light. Only now they knew that I was not mad. In their frightened eyes I had become an authority, the only one among them who knew what we were facing. And I, having devoted so much time to musings among the stones, had an intimation of what to do.

I climbed onto a scaffold. Newly fashioned, the ledge tingled with the lingering heat of molten amber. Gripping the hot lattice, I looked toward the Eye and saw that the fleshwrights had secured the gate's tricuspid lids. Perhaps those lids would buy us time. With light, I screamed:

"The creature dissolves flesh. If it enters the gate, the lids will not hold it. If it enters the city, we're doomed."

They blinded me with protests. Surely there was something they could do.

I blazed against their fears:

"It flows. And if it flows, it will boil. If we can catch it as it breaches the gate . . . if we can direct it into the amber pit. . . ."

The crowed crackled with heat. A mob of fleshwrights pushed forward, offering to graft a tube onto the tricuspid lids. I dimmed them back with blazing light:

"A tube is no good. The creature devours living matter!"

The amber guild advanced, insisting that their machines could assemble a modified scaffold, a half-pipe chute to direct the beast into the molten pit. Again, I blazed back:

"Amber alone won't hold it. We need something strong, something it can't dissolve. We need stone!"

For a moment they flickered as if I had resumed my madness. But the flickers gave way to flashing acceptance. They would trust me. I had seen the wave in action, and I understood the art of stonecraft. It was enough. If I would lead, they would follow.

I organized a chain of amberworkers, fleshwrights, scholars, and machines— all arranged in a stone-passing line that stretched from the rubble pile to the sealed lids of the Spheral Eye. Another chain assembled the stones, arranging them into a chute that curved toward the pit of molten amber. I had studied ancient walls and bridges built with interlocking seams, and I understood the principles that had allowed the ancients to build arches and domes without mortar. But such art took time and skill, and we had neither.

As the tricuspid lids bulged with the force of the breaching wave, I ordered the workers to seal the misaligned stones with molten amber. Hardening quickly, the amber would fill the gaps, creating a fluid-tight chute.

Spur raced up beside me. He wiped the dust from his hands and face, speaking with uneasy light:

"What if it avoids the trap and comes for us?"

I considered his fears and then rounded up the amber workers, breaking them into two groups: one to position their broad-shouldered machines in a line along the base of the ramp, the others to cover the molten pit with sheets of brittle amber. And then, when the trap was set, I turned and blazed:

"Find shelter! Hide your lights!"

The amber sheeting buckled as the workers retreated from the pit, and as I followed the crowd back to the city, I feared that the stuff would not hold long enough to conceal the danger. Would that be our undoing, the one miscalculation in an otherwise workable plan?

Something exploded behind me. Still running, I looked back to see the Eye's tricuspid lids give way. The wave burst through, its head flattened into a silver fist. The flue buckled, the ground shook, but the stonework held.

Light flashed at my side. It was Ov, and she wasn't alone. A crowd stood behind her. In spite of my orders, no one had hidden. All stood in plain sight, watching as the wave hurtled downward. At any moment it might read the truth in our communal glow, but still it surged on, seemingly fixed on the easy prey, the line of dim-witted machines with nothing in their lights to betray their purpose. The beast was taking the bait, and why wouldn't it? In its ageless existence, the only traps it had ever known were the ones it had laid for others.

Its head rose as it neared the machines. Flying now, spewing with the combined force of gravity and its own hunger, it curled into a wave, engulfed the machines, and crashed down toward what it must have thought was a sheet of sun-heated rock.

Ov flashed, unable to contain her excitement:

"It's working!"

But once again, I felt my own doubts tingling. I had tried to think of everything, but now I realized that I had indeed made a terrible mistake.

As the amber sheet gave way beneath the falling wave I turned and blazed to the crowd, once again telling them to run.

Seeing the terror in my light, they turned and fled, racing along fleshy streets as the amber pit exploded behind us. It was over. I'd tried killing the wave, but instead I had unleashed something worse. The creature would explode into steam, and the steam would condense, forming rain. I had seen the beast rain over the island ruins before engulfing the herd of wild machines. What was to stop it from doing the same here?

I stopped running as the explosion faded behind me. I realized that everyone else had already stopped, most of them looking back toward the pit. More than a few, all of them amberworkers, were retracing their steps. One of them looked at me, his light full of amazement:

"Brilliant! A brilliant plan! How did you think of it?"

Another grabbed me, pulling me around to show me the ground littered with shards of amber, rock-hard diamonds blazing in the heat of the bright, young sun.

I picked one up, turning it over in the light, peering through its translucent sides to gaze at its quivering heart, a fragment of trapped fluid.

The amberworker blazed his approval:

"A million drops! A million tiny prisons!"

Another approached, carrying one of the fist-sized lumps, looking at the piece of liquid flesh trapped within.

"The amber condensed around it . . . turning to rock."

He raised the trophy—a yellow rock with a liquid center, one of many that now littered the ground around the ruined pit. His face flickered with new respect:

"The perfect trap for a fluid beast! Amberworkers should have thought of it. But it was you! How did you know?"

But I hadn't known. With modest light I said:

"I intended to cook it . . . to boil it away. But boiling alone wouldn't have worked. The creature would have survived and fallen as rain."

The amberworker blazed on:

"And so it did. It rained! Rain encased in amber. Beautiful!"

The others closed around me, each holding an ambered drop of liquid flesh. Not one of them acknowledged my modest protests. To them, I was a hero who had foreseen everything.

I turned, scanning their close-set faces, seeking a gap through which I might escape the heat of unmerited praise. And then I saw them, Ov and Spur, angling toward me. I pushed toward them, fighting against the currents, swimming through the crowd until I plunged into the blue glow of Ov's embrace. Spur enveloped us, holding fast with sweet warmth.

Their acceptance was the only reward I needed.

At last, I'd come home.

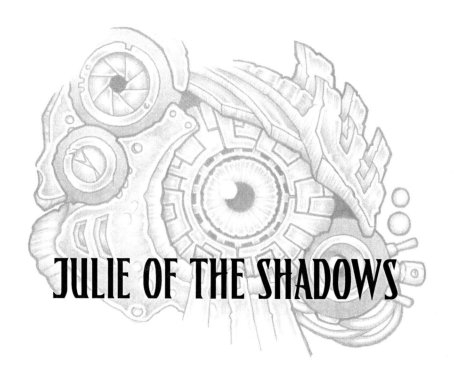

JULIE OF THE SHADOWS

"Julie of the Shadows" was my fourth sale to Elinor Mavor at Amazing Stories. *Written in the early winter of 1980, it finally came out two years later, in the March 1982 issue. After the story's publication, I lost touch with Elinor until the winter of 1987, when she telephoned to tell me that a film production company was interested in optioning the story. I suppose the noirish narrative style and near-future setting (which had by then made the Ridley Scott film* Blade Runner *a cult favorite) appealed to the producers. In any event, although the contract was inked and signed a few months later, the film was never made.*

The near-future setting was some sixty years away when I wrote the story, and although some of its depictions of a post-industrial America may still ring true, the near-space elements are still the stuff of SF.

If old men could buy tickets to the moon for spare change, Walt and Orville Stacy would not have had enough to get off the ground. They didn't have much. But what they did have was four walls and heat in the winter, and that beat living on the street. Government subsidies covered the rent, and with help from a lot of community-store pasta and public-works water, they manage to finish each month just about even.

I was still on my first week of official leave when I took the apartment next to theirs. Spartan accommodations suit me fine. I'm a Belter, asteroid belt miner. I'll be working the asteroids till I'm fifty. By then I'll either be dead or rich. Either way, I won't be poor.

Counting the five-month round trip, Belt work keeps a man off earth nearly seventeen months at a time, and when vacation rolls around most guys spend it in the high-rent tropics, trying to wash away the asteroid grit with rum and women. Those guys go back to the Belt soft. They're the ones who don't make it. Me, I plan to be kicking around when I'm as old as Orville and Walt. And I do not plan on being poor.

Orville and Walt both turned seventy on the same day, but they're not twins. They're what you'd call two-thirds of a triplet. Their brother Jess died of pneumonia seven months back. Now Walt and Orville sit around, watching each other, scared silly that the other's going to die next and leave him alone. Funny thing is, for all their worrying about loneliness, Walt and Orville had developed a reputation for never reaching out to anyone. Because of that, when the diode over my door started flashing, the last person I expected to see on the other side was Walt Stacy.

Walt stood there in the narrow hall, his dead-pan face staring down at me. Like most Belters, I'm a little guy. These days, spacework favors people under five-ten. I looked up at Walt and stepped back. He looked troubled.

"Your name's Cheever?" he asked.

I acknowledged that it was.

"We heard about you."

"What'd you hear?"

"Mind if I come in, Mr. Cheever?"

When a seventy-year-old man calls you mister, you're older than you think.

"Call me Ben." I took another step back, making room. "You're one of the Stacy brothers, right?"

"Yeah. Sorry, Ben. I'm forgetting my manners. I'm Walt, from next door." He pushed off the door jamb and stepped inside. "Guess I'm a little distracted. See, we've got a problem—" He looked toward my apartment's tiny kitchen, not much more than a closet with a stove. "Smells like cooking," he said. "Like meat."

"Some of it's meat," I said. "Most of it's soy. Soy, rice, piece of shank bone."

"So it's true," he said. "You're a Belter. I mean, if you can afford shank—"

"I'm a Belter," I said. "But I don't have a lot of cash. Most of what I make goes into an annuity, long term investments. I don't even look at the statements."

"But you can afford meat."

"Sometimes. Enough to flavor a pot. That's it. But that's not why you're here."

"No. Not exactly. But if you're a Belter, you maybe can help me." He followed me into the apartment's main room, a narrow space with a sleeping tube, chair, and three-legged stool. The former tenants had left a digital window taped to the wall across from the kitchen, but I never turned it on. I'm not much for illusions. Bare walls suit me fine.

"Take the chair," I said, sitting on the stool. "And let me get a few things out front right away." I waited for him to sit before continuing. "I'm a Belter, but I'm not rich. In twenty years I might be close to that, but right now I'm just scraping by. And that other stuff you might have heard, about Belters being super-human strong? You can forget about that, too. You're forty years too late. Monster building went out with Harrison Adams."

Walter shook his head. "That's not it."

"So what is?"

He hesitated, seemed to consider what he had to say, then said it. "It takes a smart man to stay alive on the Belt."

"Really?"

"That's the way I heard tell it." He looked at his shoes. "And tonight I need a smart man. A problem solver."

"You got a problem?"

"Yeah," he said. "Big one." He stared into the distance. "Orville's caught something. Seemed like a bad cold until this morning. Now it's looking like it might be *ammonia*."

That's what he called it. *Ammonia*. I didn't bother telling him otherwise.

"His chest is filling up, Ben. It's getting so he can't hardly breathe."

"Maybe you should get him to a hospital."

"Orville don't need a hospital, Ben. When folks get old they get a feel for these things. Jess knew when it was his time. Now Orville says his is coming. He wants me to get Julie. Says he's got to see her before he moves on."

"Then shouldn't you be out getting her?" I suppose I might have been a little short when I said that, but I was hungry, and the conversation was getting long. What did any of this have to do with me, anyway?

But Walt didn't take offence. He just shrugged. "That'd be fine if I knew where she was. Orville used to say she worked at a noodle bar down around the old tracks, somewhere in Panther Hollow. He never got more specific than that."

"Sounds like you don't know much about her."

"No, not much at all. But she and Orville were pretty close once. That was forty years back."

"Either you or Orville seen her recently?"

"No. She and Orville called it quits after going together six months. I never got to meet her. Never even seen her. I was working an Arctic drill rig when they were going hot and heavy. By the time I got back, things had cooled, she was history."

"So what makes you think she's still around?"

"Orville. Orville thinks so. She was nineteen when they were dating. That'd put her about fifty now. And Orville's sure she wouldn't leave the city."

"You could try the public network, search for her name."

"Could," Orville said. "But I don't know it, not all of it. Orville just calls her Julie."

"*Just* Julie?"

"That's how I know he means *this* Julie. If he'd meant another, he'd have said a last name."

I stood there a moment, my dinner cooking down over a low flame, my appetite drilling a hole in my stomach. I was hoping Walt might comprehend my silence and say, *Never mind, Ben. Go eat.* But he didn't. He just stood there, waiting for an answer. Old people are good at waiting. I think time flows differently for them.

"What do you want me to do?" I said at last.

"Come with me."

"Where?"

"The Hollow."

"To find Julie?"

"That's right."

"The Hollow's a big place, Walt."

"That's right. And you're a Belter. Way I see it, if you can find ore in asteroids, you can find one woman in Panther Hollow."

His reasoning didn't make sense, but people have crazy ideas about Belters. We're like the cowboy in the American West, or the Lunies during the early days of the satellite frontier. Most Belter myths go back to the mid-twenties, back when building workers seemed like a better idea than training them. Bio-mechs were the big thing then, and there were plenty of specialists who could tear you down and build you back to where you'd never recognize yourself. Those were the days when Belters worked sixteen-hour shifts and retired after thirty months. Even after paying to get your old body back (or a better one if you didn't like the old one) you'd still have enough cash left to keep you in heat and soy for a long time.

Under better economic conditions, the arrangement might never have worked. But those were depression years. People were desperate. Looking back, you can see how it all turned ugly. Mining companies had never gotten involved in monster building. As far as they were concerned, bio-mech was dirty business—dirtier than mining. But if you showed up at a recruitment center wired for space, they sure weren't about to turn you down. It was a bad set up, and I suppose there were more than a few broken dreams when Harrison Adams had his day. Harrison Adams threw on the brakes without looking to see who'd get crushed. We know all about that now.

I looked at Walt's roadmap face, his eyes standing out like a pair of blood-shot cities in a network of wrinkled roads. If I've got one flaw, it's my curiosity. That's what sent me to the Belt when I was nineteen, as soon as I had reached work age. It's also what made me decide to find out what was so special about Julie that it would make Orville want to see her one more time rather than go to the hospital.

I glanced toward the kitchen and the large pot I had simmering on the stove. "I've got to eat," I said. "You tell Orville we'll look for his Julie. I'll meet you in the hall."

But Walt didn't leave. He just got up and stood there a moment, following my gaze into the kitchen. "Been a long time since Orville and me tasted proper meat," he said.

"It's just a soup bone, Walt. More marrow than meat." But I got his point. Lots of people still haven't recovered from the rolling depression that rocked the world in the teens and twenties. I can't usually get too worked up about the suffering of the masses, but that one hungry man standing in my apartment was getting to me.

"All right," I said. "Let's eat." I took the pot from the stove and followed Walt to his apartment next door.

Orville was worse than I could have imagined. He sat in the corner, scared to lie down for fear of drowning from the fluid in his lungs. Walt gave him a cup of broth. He drank some. Not much, though. Just enough to let me know he appreciated the offer.

I asked him about Julie.

He nodded, or maybe it was just a tight little shiver. "Yeah," he said. "Julie. Go get her." He swallowed. "I'll wait."

He'd wait? I wasn't so sure. The life in his eyes looked ready to check out, and I still had no idea who this Julie was or how to find her.

"Where's she live, Orville?"

"The Hollow." He wheezed. "Last I saw her, that was it. In the Hollow."

"Where in the Hollow?"

He stared.

"What's her last name, Orville?"

He licked his lips. "Ask around," he said. "Tell them 'Julie.' Tell them you're looking for 'Julie of the Shadows.'"

The Panther Hollow District lies in a steep valley east of the city and north of what was once one of the largest steel production plants in the world. Local legend says panthers used to live in the valley, back in the days before settlers moved in and pushed them out. Then came heavy industry, hot-metal plants spewing soot and flames. But those plants didn't last either. When they closed, the valley became a squatter district of disposed workers living in scrap-wood homes. It's a little more respectable now, with prefab structures of resin and steel. But it's still no place to go without a good reason.

The Shadows had gone down like kindling in the winter of 2023, but memories of the place still lingered in the Hollow. Orville had been right. The long-time residents knew all about the place, but Walt had been a little off about thinking Julie had worked at a noodle bar. The Shadows Brothel hadn't been a place for noodles, not in the usual sense anyway. The locals were quick to point that out. But when it came to memories of Julie of the Shadows, the residents couldn't help us. It seemed there'd been a lot of nineteen-year-old girls at the Shadows before it burned down. Nevertheless, Walt figured a visit to the former site couldn't hurt.

So we pushed on.

Wind blew hard off the river as we walked south along Boundary Street. The air smelled of dead fish from the co-op canneries along the wharf. The Monongahela River, a one-time industrial sewer, was alive again, revived by the economic changes that had begun sweeping the region in the 1980s and 90s. You can't produce twenty-first century alloys with twentieth century technology, and rust-Belt economies had already been in serious decline when heavy industry began moving into space. Around the turn of the century, the few earthbound mills that had survived the waves of third-world *out*sourcing found themselves contending with twenty-first century *up*sourcing. Rolling depressions began, and young people with the right resources found work in earth's oldest profession.

Walt and I walked until we came to a prefab structure that crouched on the former site of the Shadows. It was a rooming house. The woman at the desk looked like a bulldog. She laughed when I asked about the old establishment. It was a hard and dry laugh—like sandpaper on iron.

"Things are tough when a young man goes looking for old skin workers." She glanced at Walt, then back at me. "Is he your daddy?"

"Friend."

"An *old* friend." She laughed again, as if she had said something clever. Then her eyes narrowed. She leaned forward. "You're a Belter."

Working the Belt makes a person move differently when he's at the bottom of a G-well. Most people spot us without looking twice.

"I guess that excuses you." She set a balled fist to her fat chin, leaning forward. "This spot's been clean for years. You want skin trade, you've got to head farther south. I don't recommend it, though. Things get rough there after dark. Know what I'm saying?" She looked at Walt. "Folks there is crazy."

"How far south you talking?"

She thought a moment. "I wouldn't go under the last bridge after dark," she said. "If you get close enough to see the old foundry, it's time to turn around."

"There's a foundry?"

"What's left of one. It's a rowdy place. Mind you, I've never seen firsthand, but when folks talk about certain things, I listen."

"What kind of things?"

"There's some old-style Belters out there what never got changed back to human." She reached into a drawer. "If I were you, I'd stay here till morning." She took out a scanner. "It'll be a lot safer then. You'll be rested too." She glanced at Walt. "Your old friend looks like he could use a night's sleep."

I told her we didn't have till daylight. Then we thanked her and left.

She called to us once, her voice slicing off as the door closed. "Old-style Belters," she said. "You watch out for them old-style—"

The dead-fish wind caught us as we reached the sidewalk. Then we turned right, heading farther south, our shadows rising and falling in the streetlights as we headed into the valley of old-style monsters.

I'd heard stories of early Belters who had refused the operations that would make them human again. I remember hearing about the clinics when I was a kid. Folks called them monster shops. Their front offices might have told you otherwise, but their reason for being was to turn a profit cranking out organic mining machines. If you were nineteen, or willing to lie and say that you were, they'd tear you down, reassemble you, and direct you to the nearest recruitment center. Some of those young people were little guys, the kind who used to send for Charles Atlas Body Building kits in the twentieth century. When those kids came back from the Belt, some of them decided they liked being 100 kilos of armored muscle. They skipped the second operation and retired as monsters.

But there were also economic reasons for opting out. The initial operation, the one that made a person ready for off-world labor, was entirely free. It had to be. People with money didn't need to look for work among the stroids. So the monster shops charged an exorbitant fee for the second procedure. Sometimes Belters stayed as they were and pocketed the difference. Other times, the money just wasn't available—good old Harrison Adams.

I thought about these things as I walked on, following the road until it veered beneath a steel-arch bridge. Beyond the rusty rainbow, a mass of brick and girders glowed with the yellow haze of chemical lights.

"That'd be the foundry," Walt said. "Used to be a smelting plant, worker-owned, independently run. It's residential now."

I heard music: loud, thumping, and coming from the shadows of an old blast furnace. I remembered what Ms. Bulldog had said about going too far.

"What do you think?" Walt said.

"Want to turn back?"

"Don't suppose we can," he said. "Come this far. Might as well see it through."

"Could get rough."

Walt shrugged, pretending like he didn't care.

So we kept walking.

The foundry had been re-scavenged, taken apart and put back together to suit the needs of a squatter community. We passed bars, shops, apartments, and dim nooks whose purposes I didn't even want to think about. We glanced at them all as we walked along, wondering where to begin.

A few of the bars had holosigns, poorly calibrated and sputtering like spastic ghosts. Others had recycled neon. One place had no sign at all, just a handprint on the door, as if an old-style Belter had palmed some dayglo and slapped the entrance. It looked promising.

We went inside.

"You say you're looking for *her*?" The woman filled her chair like old laundry, rolling flesh lumping within the folds of her clothes. Her eyes were the color of bad teeth. She looked at me, then at Walt. "That kind of news don't come cheap," she said. "What're you offering?"

I kept thinking I didn't know the Stacys from Cain and Abel and here I was being weaseled by a woman who looked like a bag of hammers. "You want me to pay for what you know?"

"That's a start," she said. "And I don't take those paper presidents. Coin only."

No one trusted paper money. Coins with traces of silver and gold were seen as having value beyond the bankrupt institution that backed them. While on Earth, I always carried a few with me.

I took out a pair of smiling Reagans and held them up for her to see.

"That all you got?"

"It's all I'm offering."

She seemed ready to hustle us, hold out for more. But then she just reached for it. "Good enough." She flicked her wrist, and the coins were out of my fingers and in her palm.

"Good reflexes," I said.

"You should've seen me in my day, in my prime." She stood up. "Come on. It's not far."

We followed her from the bar and back into the street. Half a block later we veered down an alley that weaved between windowless walls and high fences. She moved ahead of us, cloak fluttering behind her, hands finding the way in places where it was too dark to see. In those places, we just followed her voice.

"You boys will want to stay close," she said. "Watch your step . . . and stay away from the edge."

I saw that we had come to a flight of eroded steps, a mass of concrete and metal that rose along the valley wall. She started up. We followed, moving past hillside shacks with doors that opened onto ledge trails. Between the structures, vines grew thick from weedy trees, sometimes forming a canopy over the stairs.

I heard Walt wheezing, struggling to keep up.

"We should rest," I said.

But the woman kept moving.

I was beginning to think we'd been hustled, that her game was to take my cash and then lose us in the dark, but then the steps ended at a path lined with giant ferns.

"What is this place?"

She just kept moving, leading us through an arch and into a vast area with a trellis ceiling. "The old botanical gardens," I said. "Is that where we are?"

My answer came as our path veered through a second arch. Looking back, I saw the ruins of a vast, overgrown greenhouse. The glass panels were gone, leaving only the open frame of the building, and the plants—the ones that had been hardy enough to survive, had overrun the place.

A larger building stood in front of us, rising like a tombstone. A moment later we were inside it, moving toward a stairwell that reeked of urine and garbage. *Not that way*, I thought. *Please, don't go that way.*

But a moment later we were walking through the stink, clanging up along a flight of corrugated stairs.

We came out on the seventh floor. Dark windows tossed weak light over a pair of empty elevator shafts, gaping doors filled with deep darkness. She moved away from these, turned to open a door, and then vanished into a pitch-black room. We went after her, following the thud of her feet. Ahead, another door opened and slammed. We reached it, opening it in time to hear another slamming somewhere in the distance. We were in an old office suite, a maze of cubicles, offices, and meeting rooms.

She was trying to lose us.

"Hey, Ben!" Walt grabbed his arm. "Hold up. Stop." His voice was raw, breathless. "I have to stop." He leaned forward, grabbing his knees. He'd probably run out of breath a long way back. It was only his determination to help Orville that had kept him going. But now he was done in, and the woman was getting away, ditching us in the abandoned building.

I turned in place, listening as she circled back toward the stairs.

"We've been set up," I said.

Something moved to my left. An ambush? Thugs waiting in the dark? There's something about the dark that makes a person assume the worst, and now I was thinking about the woman in the rooming house saying: "There's some old-style Belters out there what never got changed back to human."

There've been two times in my life when I've been absolutely terrified. Once was when my straw boss sent me inside a primed mass driver to check a jam. The second was on that dark seventh floor.

I grabbed Walt's arm. "We got to get out of here." I started walking fast as I could, heading toward a patch of deep darkness that I was sure led back to the stairs. But I didn't get far. A few steps later something slammed me hard across the face. My brain flamed out. I went down, falling into darkness, feeling nothing until I awoke to the glow of a chemical lamp. Huge arms held me in a gentle grip, rocking me beneath a pair of burning eyes.

And that is how I came face-to-face with Julie of the Shadows.

"Funny thing," she said. "I used to dream of a day when Orville'd come looking for me. Forty years gives a person lots of time for plotting revenge. I must have killed that bum a thousand times in my dreams."

I was sitting across from her now, probing the damage to my swelling cheek and eye. "So you took it out on me?"

She looked confused. At least, I think it was confusion. Her face was so twisted it was hard to be sure.

Then Walt said. "It wasn't Julie that hit you. We told you that."

"Told me?" My memory seemed to be lagging behind. "Told me what?"

"You ran into a beam," Walt said. "A low beam. You hit it edge on."

"A *beam*?" I rubbed my eye, making it hurt. The pain was easier to take than the irony of what had happened. "I've done seven tours of Belt work, and I get nearly killed by a beam?"

"Not nearly killed," Julie said. "Knocked silly is all. Serves you right for running." She leaned forward, raising the glow on the lamp, backing away as the light found the ridges of her cheek and jaw. Massive and heavy boned, it was a face built to hold up in a vacuum. Old-style Belters weren't built for looks, but they'll live through anything.

"So it wasn't you?" I said. "You didn't slug me?"

"I'd never hurt anyone," she said, her voice softening, settling into a whisper. "Even Orville never had anything to fear. I might have dreamed of getting even, but in real life I forgave him long ago. Now it seems as if he's finally no longer afraid to face me." She swung her massive head. "Mother Time's a real peacemaker, isn't she? I mean, here it is, forty years later, and all my hate's gone up in daydreams." She glanced at Walt. "Exactly how bad is your brother?"

"Pretty bad. Can't hardly breathe. Sounds like he's sucking air through a sponge."

"He on meds?"

"No. No meds. Things are tight."

"The things we could be if we had money." She looked at me. "But you wouldn't know, would you?"

"I do all right," I said. "Money's good, but it's nothing like Belters made in your day."

"Who are you calling a Belter?" she snapped.

Now that threw me. Who was she trying to kid? I know my history, and no one got to look as bad as she did without having gone under the knife for a Belt assignment. I started to tell her that, but she stopped me.

"Sorry," she said. "I suppose there're some things that Orville didn't tell you." She shifted, shadows pooling in the hollows of her face. Then, slowly at first, she told us the story that started when both she and Orville had been less hard on the eyes.

When she finished talking, the three of us headed crosstown for a long over-due reunion with Orville. Julie went on to the Stacy place alone while Walt and I headed next door to finish what was left of my stew. Half an hour later, Walt went to check on them. When he wasn't back after a few minutes, I went to check for myself.

I found Walt sitting by the window, looking out at the night. On the sofa, Orville's body lay like a set of old clothes. I touched his jaw. No pulse. He felt cold.

Julie was gone.

I sat with Walt for a while, saying nothing. Then I headed off to bed. But I couldn't sleep. I kept thinking of Julie and Harrison Adams and the awful twists that life puts us through if we don't play a few moves ahead of the game.

Orville and Julie thought they had found a way to beat the system. They'd met at the Shadows, but things soon went beyond customer relations. Julie hated the skin trade, and she must have done too much talking the night she met Orville. Over time, their plan grew as easy as their love for each other. Orville must have been quite a talker, telling her that he had a plan to get her out of the Shadows and into a life where the two of them could get a fresh start. Then he told her about Belt work. Even after paying for the second op-eration, a worker would still have enough money to get out of poverty's dead end and onto a road that led somewhere better. That was the story, anyway. Lots of people believed it, and Julie was one of them. She embraced the plan, remaining committed to it even after Orville told her that he himself was too old for Belt work, that she would have to be the one to go under the knife.

So Julie went.

After a year in the Shadows, being a monster for a few years didn't seem so bad, not with the future it offered.

So they bet on the spinning wheel between Mars and Jupiter—rocky bits of promise that should have paid off. They thought they had planned for everything.

Orville had never used a last name when talking about Julie. That had to have been a touchy area. Forty years ago, Orville hadn't been about to let

Julie take her first step toward the new American dream without insuring his place within it. He married her the day before she went under the knife, making her Julie Stacy—for better or worse. They hadn't counted on the worst.

As the gaps in Julie's newly toughened hide were healing, a young senator was busy making a name for himself in Washington. Harrison Adams was a wave maker. Building monsters didn't sit right with him. His reforms passed the day Julie showed up at the recruiting office.

She first heard of Harrison Adams while sitting in a chair under a recruitment sign. The mines were no longer allowed to hire bio-meched workers. If she wanted to work, they told her, she'd have to return to the monster shop for degrafting and report in a month for testing. The days of monster labor were over.

She never saw Orville again until I brought them back together forty years later. In the meantime, she was lost. The only thing she knew was working in the Shadows, and they weren't hiring monsters either.

Lost, confused, and burning with anger, Julie went back to the Hollow, poured gasoline over the Shadows' west wall, and burned it to the ground, watching it go up in smoke like so many glowing dreams.

Then she killed Orville Stacy—every night for forty years, up in the dark seventh floor of an abandoned building. In time, revenge's bitter dreams replaced the better dreams that should have been.

It all went together like a mad jig-saw puzzle. All but the end—where Orville tore open the scar that had taken so long to heal.

The diode over my door flashed.

I checked the clock. It was near dawn. I figured it was Walt wanting to talk. I was wrong.

It was Julie.

"How's the head, Ben?"

I touched the swelling over my eye. "It'll heal," I said. "Where've you been?"

She shrugged, shoulders like rolling hills. "Walking," she said. "Mind if I come in?"

I didn't.

She squeezed through the door, looked at my human-size chair and three-legged stool, and decided to sit on the floor.

I took the stool.

"I tried Walt's door," she said. "He didn't answer. Guess he's got a lot to think about."

"When I left him he was looking out at the river."

She nodded, keeping silent for a long time. I knew she still had a few un-shared troubles.

"If there's one thing I've learned," she said at last, "it's that right and wrong only work for politicians and lawyers." She started to say something else, seemed to think better of it, then bowed her head.

I heard boats on the river.

She looked at me. "How well did the Stacy's live, Ben?"

"They paid the rent," I said. "Not sure what they ate, though—or how often. I made beef-bone stew tonight. Walt almost went apoplectic over the smell."

"That's what I was afraid of."

"How do you mean?"

She pulled out a scancard and held it out for me to see. "It was Orville's," she said. "He told me it's good for twenty grand."

"Where'd he get that kind of money?"

She didn't answer right away. Instead, she fell back into silence, staring at the card before filling in one last piece of her story, a little detail that went a long way toward redeeming the memory of Orville Stacy.

Orville should have been around to help Julie when the recruitment center sent her packing. But he wasn't. Instead he skipped town, leaving neither a forwarding address nor word of when he expected to return. Over the years she had imagined all kinds of selfish reasons as to why he had run out on her, but now she knew the truth.

While she was torching the Shadows, Orville was fleeing south across the leveled hills of West Virginia, hitching rides until he came to a place where there were still mountains to be mined. He worked the mines for three years, gutting mountains and extracting one of the few commodities that had not yet been upsourced, not going back home until he heard that Walt had returned from working the Arctic platforms.

Orville banked his mine wages and took a job at a Monongahela fishery. And there he worked until his back gave out, forcing him to retire and move in with brothers Jesse and Walt. After that, the three of them managed to make ends meet while Orville's modest savings earned interest in an off-world bank.

"You believe that?" Julie stared at the scancard. She seemed afraid to look away from it, as if it might vanish if she did. "All along he'd been working and scrimping, doing what he could to get the funds to put me right." She shook her head. "But I don't feel right taking it. I mean, there's still Walt to think of. He and Orville were supposed to have been splitting everything fifty-fifty."

"You're asking my advice?"

She closed her hand, gripping the card, looking at me.

I held her gaze. It occurred to me then that her eyes were all wrong. They didn't go with her face. She'd been pretty once. She still was if you only looked at her eyes.

"I guess that's what I'm looking for," she said. "Advice. I could use some advice."

"Get the operation."

"You sure?"

"If Walt needs anything, I'll see that he gets it," I said. "After tonight, I feel like we're old friends . . . almost brothers."

"When do you leave?" she asked. "For the Belt, I mean?"

"Seven weeks. Why?"

She stood up, easing for the door. "Because I'm coming back after I heal. I'll have those surgeons give me the youngest, finest body and face money can buy. Then I'm coming back to thank you." She turned in the doorway. "That's a promise, Ben."

I looked up at her hazel eyes, at the woman trapped within that monstrous form. "Good night, Julie."

"It's morning, Ben."

"Almost."

"I'll be back."

"I'll be here."

She left.

I went back to watching the boats on the river, and after a few minutes I saw Julie leave the building's lower lobby and skip across the street, her massive shoulders swaying with odd grace. The sun was coming up, yellow over the river, sending golden rays over the banks. Julie moved into the shadows on the street's far side and was gone.

It was the last time I ever saw Julie of the Shadows.

The day my vacation ended, Walt and I went to the pound to get a dog. I wanted him to get a puppy, but he fell in love with a runny-eyed bitch with arthritis. Love is strange. We laughed all the way back to the apartment, telling lies about women we'd never known while the dog moped along at Walt's side.

Back at the apartment, the dog curled up on Walt's favorite chair and went to sleep. It was the start of a fine relationship.

Walt didn't want the account I'd set up for him, but I made him take the scancard. Then I paused at the door, turned, and promised to return in seventeen months. Funny thing, saying that made me think of Julie, and I left before the irony got too strong.

A person leaving for more than a day shouldn't make promises like that. Life isn't static enough. People only return when it's convenient or if they have to. We can only try to do what we think is right at the time and hope for enough strength to finish the important things.

Orville Stacy was the strongest man I ever knew.

COCKROACHES

Although I had been pondering it for some time, I began writing fiction seriously in the summer of 1978. It was then that I hammered out the following story on an old electric typewriter and sent it off to George Scithers at Isaac Asimov's Science Fiction Magazine. Scithers didn't take it, but he suggested that Ed Ferman at F&SF might. But he didn't. Nevertheless, I kept the story in the mail, and three submissions later, in the spring of 1979, Elinor Mavor purchased it for Amazing Stories.

Everyone starts somewhere. For me, this is it.

Sam was the super in a tired little apartment building in a forgotten part of the city. A simple man with few aspirations beyond his chosen profession, Sam could always be seen making his rounds, a row of tools clanking at his hip, through the building's narrow halls, repairing the unending chain of leaks, clogs, and assorted apartment maladies.

He and Myrtle, his wife of twenty-four years, had two children in community college, a third in the Peace Corps, two-thousand dollars in the bank (not counting an additional sum set aside for Arthur when he returned to the States), a rent-free apartment in the basement, and cockroaches.

"Sam!" Myrtle called from the kitchen, voice shrilling over the sound of running water. "You've got to do something about these things. I told you once this morning, and I'm telling you once again." Pipes banged as she shut off the water. "Sam! Are you listening to me?"

He wasn't. He was in the bathroom trying to toe-kick a cockroach that had wedged itself into a corner beside the sink.

Myrtle's face appeared in the mirror. "Why, Sam? Why is it my husband can't get rid of cockroaches?"

He'd tried, of course. For twenty-seven years he'd tried, and for twenty-seven years the cockroaches tried just a little harder. Spray, powder, gels, traps—nothing worked.

"Sam!"

He turned, looking down the fourth-floor hall to see Mrs. Goodman leaning out from her apartment. She wore an orange bathrobe, green slippers, and a wide swatch of maroon lipstick. The latter overflowed onto her teeth, flashing as she spoke. "I've got bugs again. Big as kiwi fruit. They're all over the kitchen!"

Sam stepped inside.

"When I was a girl, you never got crawly bugs if you lived above the third floor."

Sam entered the kitchen, approached the sink, and looked down into a jumble of dishes. "Having a banquet, aren't they?"

"And on the fourth floor! How do they do that? How do they get up here?"

"Maybe they take the elevator." He looked under the sink. "You got roach spray?"

"Roach spray? You kidding? They shower in spray!"

Sam stood up, gave the sink a final look, and turned to go. "You going out today? I could fumigate."

"But you fumigated Thursday."

"So I'll hit them again. A one-two punch."

Sam fumigated three other apartments, and when he returned home that afternoon he smelled so bad that Myrtle made him get undressed in the hall. She washed his clothes three times to get the smell out and once more to get them clean. Meanwhile, Sam sat in the bedroom watching television.

More than once he heard Myrtle in the pantry getting more soap, and more than once he heard her complaining about the stink.

"What happened to that sweet-smelling stuff you used to use, Sam?"

"Roaches like sweet-smelling stuff. This stuff's stronger."

"They didn't used to like that sweet-smelling stuff. It used to kill them real good, Sam."

Sam turned up the sound on the TV. There was a man with a big haircut holding a can of what could have been Raid or Black Flag (a big X covered the brand). The man was talking about roaches, and the woman next to him kept interrupting, saying things like, "That's amazing!" and "That's for sure!" And all the while the man kept talking, going on and on about some new kind of roach killer that didn't smell bad, required no repeated applications, and was one-hundred percent effective in clinical trials.

A number flashed on the screen.

Sam grabbed a pencil.

Sam had just finished fumigating four more apartments and was coming through the first-floor hall smelling of roach death when he saw the UPS man carrying a big box into the lobby.

"That box for me?"

The UPS man checked the label. "Got your name on it."

Sam entered the lobby.

"Whew!" the UPS man said. "You smell like roach death."

"The roaches should think so." Sam turned and carried the box downstairs, opened it, and looked beneath the packing to find a plastic jar containing what looked like a hundred black medicine capsules.

"Pills?" Myrtle said. "So you give the roach a glass of water and a poison pill? You spent $99.99 for that?"

"And a book." Sam rummaged around in the packing. "I ordered within fifteen minutes, so they sent me a book." He fished out a saddle-stitched pamphlet.

"That's a book?"

"And it's money back if not delighted."

"Well I'm not." She turned, took her shopping cart from the closet, and left.

Sam switched on a light and read the book, which explained that the tiny black capsules were actually little cars. Not that they looked like cars, but that was what the book called them. Each had a long-life power cell, tiny motor, and three little wheels.

Scatter them wherever you see roaches, the book said. *Then stand back and wait for the ZAP!*

"Zap?"

Sam put one of the cars on the floor near the baseboard. It spun about, accelerated across the floor, and fishtailed beneath the sink.

ZAP!

Three roaches raced out from under the sink, scurrying pell-mell across the linoleum. The little black car was right behind, shooting sparks from its nose.

ZAP—ZAP—ZAP!!!

One zap each was all it took. The bugs died on the spot. Legs in the air, bellies smoking, burning inside.

Sam went back to reading the book.

The next three pages explained how cockroaches became immune to man-made forms of pest control due to something called genetics. A strong poison might kill a million roaches, but a few would always survive. And when those survivors reproduced, all of the baby roaches would be immune to the poison. Before you knew it, you had a million super roaches. So people made super poisons, but the same thing happened. A few survived. A vicious cycle.

Sam looked at the floor. The little car was gone. He reached into the jar, lifted out another car, and set it on the floor. This one raced beneath the sofa.

ZAP!

Sam went back to reading. The rest of the book was about printed memory chips and the wonders of miniaturization. Just the thing to put a super to sleep.

"Sam!"

He turned to see Mrs. Goodman's orange robe flowing behind her as she ran from her apartment.

"Three weeks, Sam!" She grabbed him. "Three weeks and not a single cockroach!"

Her lips slid like a wet crayon against his cheek.

"You're a wonder, Sam!"

Sam smiled his Gene Autrey smile, the one he hadn't used since he'd been a kid. Then he turned and walked down the hall, tool belt jingling like six-guns as he looked back over his shoulder. "It's nothing, Mrs. Goodman. It's nothing at all."

Soon the building was roach free. A month passed. Sam wondered about the little cars. Where were they? Had they run out of power, or were they parked among the wall cracks, ready to spring into action should the roaches return?

Not wishing to take unnecessary chances, Sam got out the book, filled out the reorder form in the back, and dropped it in the mail along with another check for $99.99.

Two weeks passed. The replacement cars never came. Instead, Sam received a letter from the company along with his uncashed check. The letter explained that, although the new method of roach control had proven successful in clinical trials, a few unexpected drawbacks had arisen since the product's release. It was, of course, nothing to worry about. For the time being, however, no orders would be filled until a full investigation was completed.

"Sam!"

Myrtle ran water in the sink while Sam lay on the couch in the living room.

"Sam! There's a roach in the sink!"

"So drown him!"

The water stopped. "I tried. He ran up the sink and behind the counter. How come we have roaches again when you've still got those smart little cars?"

"Maybe the roaches are getting smarter."

"You have to do something, Sam! If they're coming back, you have to do something. Sam? You hear me, Sam?"

He got up and left the apartment. He wasn't leaving so he could do something about the roaches. He just wanted to get away. It was quieter in the halls.

He walked along, thinking about cars and roaches and unexpected drawbacks. And then something caught his eye, movement along the baseboard, three roaches scurrying away to vanish behind a radiator. And there was something else. He stopped, bending down to find a tiny black object lying near a crack in the baseboard. It was one of the little cars. He picked it up.

The insides had been torn out.

No . . . not torn out. Laid out! The plastic skin of the car had been cut open and the circuitry inside removed in nice, orderly fashion. And there were two more disassembled cars just like it a little farther on. No, not two. There were three . . . four . . . a half dozen. He picked them up and raced back to the apartment. He opened the door and snapped on the light.

"Myrtle?"

No answer.

A huge cockroach stared back at him from the wall above the kitchen sink.

He dropped the broken cars on the kitchen table and walked to the sofa for a roll of newspaper.

From the wall, two antennae waved in mute defiance. Two? No, there were six. . . .

Eight . . . ten . . . dozens!

He turned with the rolled up newspaper in his hand. The wall was covered with cockroaches. He moved toward the door. Something blocked his way. It was one of the cars. No, not one. Two . . . four . . . more. They drove in formation, forming a black perforation on the floor between him and the only way out of the basement apartment.

The situation was clear.

The little black cars were no longer working for Sam.

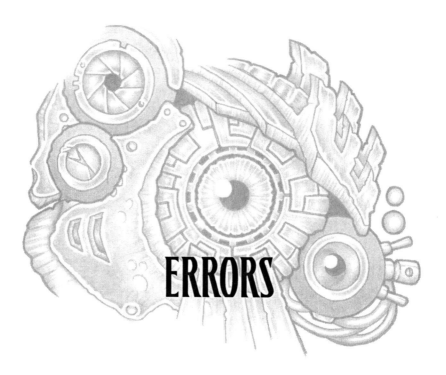

ERRORS

One of the friendliest and most efficiently run regional SF organizations I know of is PARSEC, which bills itself as "Pittsburgh's Premier Science Fiction Organization." Getting its start in the early days of the Internet, the organization first considered its name as an acronym for "Pittsburgh Area Realtime Scientifiction Enthusiasts Club." It has since become a nonprofit consortium devoted to the promotion of all things SF.

In 2002, the organization began its own imprint, Parsec Publishing. The following year, it launched the anthology series Triangulations. *Edited by Diane Turnshek,* Triangulations 2003 *included the following story about alien occupation and (possibly) the resilience of the human spirit.*

Even as Greg deactivated the alarm, he sensed that someone had broken into the cottage.

He passed through the foyer and smelled the scent of the closed house. His wedding ring lay atop a folded note on the coffee table, just as he had left it a week ago. Nothing appeared to be missing, but the place had been invaded.

Beth watched him silently from a frame above the fireplace. The picture was old, circa 1991. Her hair had been red then, her face not yet creased by the weight of a husband's chronic depression. She was a different person now—drawn, tense as piano wire.

Greg took the picture from the mantle and held it to the light that slanted in through a bay window. The frame bore the waxy print of an unfamiliar hand. Someone had handled it: taken it down, looked at it, and returned it to the mantle. Who? He studied the smudge.

Who's been here?

Sound drifted from outside, a grating noise—the sigh of shifting macadam. He turned toward the door. Long shadows covered the ground. One of the shadows drifted, as if someone were running toward the mountain road.

The wise thing would be to let the intruder flee. Insurance would cover any theft (though there appeared to be nothing taken), and there was always a chance the thief might be armed. But Greg didn't consider these things until he reached the center of the driveway . . . and then it didn't matter.

He stopped running. The gravel stretched before him, clear and empty. He stood alone, just himself and the setting sun.

He gripped the back of his neck, flexed his shoulders, drew a breath. Nearby, the engine of his BMW clicked as it cooled from its uphill climb through the Pennsylvania mountains. Farther off, crickets buzzed in the darkening woods. Farther still, toads grunted in the ditch behind the generator shed. The rest was silence.

Then, once again, he heard the crunch of gravel. And this time, a voice: "Hey! Behind you!"

He turned to find Beth walking down the drive.

"Beth?" She wasn't due to arrive before nightfall. "What's going on?"

The figure kept walking. It wasn't Beth. He saw that now. The face was too young, the hair too red, and the blouse was one that she had not worn since a lazy afternoon in 1991.

The figure drew nearer. "What's wrong, Greg?" It reached for him.

He leaned away, arching against the BMW's fender as the thing touched his shoulder. He felt a cold tingle. The hairs on his nape stood on end as the hand pulled him closer to the face that wasn't entirely human.

He tried pulling away, but the creature's hand had fused to his skin. "Don't fight me," it said. Its hair blanched from red to highlighted silver. Its eyes darkened. Bones shifted and flared beneath its skin. Greg wanted to look away. He couldn't. "Don't fight me, Greg. We want the same things."

Tingles shot along his spine. The world blurred, and suddenly he was no longer looking at a near-perfect replica of Beth. Instead, he was looking at himself through the creature's eyes, seeing himself as the other saw him: troubled gaze, nervous lips, furrowed brow. He saw sweat blooming in the creases of his Polo shirt. He saw heat rising in orange waves from the BMW's hood.

His mind raced, but the mind wasn't his. The creature was inside him, accessing his mind: installing, overwriting, rebooting. . . .

Greg's vision blurred. When it cleared, he found himself staring at a perfected replica of Beth.

"I'll help you," the replica said. "Then you'll help me. OK?"

"Help how?" Greg asked, though he already sensed the answer.

"I'll help you finish what you started last week." The smile was perfectly Beth, down to the faint imprint of long-gone braces. "Go inside, Greg. Go upstairs." Its hand gave a wet sigh as it left his spine. "Go upstairs," it said. "Get the gun."

The sun set, sinking into the mountains like a burrowing worm. The world dimmed. Shadows deepened.

In blue darkness, Greg left the driveway and returned to the house.

He saw the fireplace, the mantle, and a twilight glow beyond the bay window. Beth's photograph, dimmed to shades of gray, watched from its colorless frame.

He walked on.

Shadows filled the upstairs. He groped for the wall switch.

Click.

Darkness remained.

No power. Of course. What had he expected? He still needed to start the generator.

Sliding his hand along the wall, he walked through darkness until he reached the door to his study. It was a simple room. No shelves. No cabinets. His life's work required only a desk, a satellite dish, and a power source. A laptop workstation supplied the rest, but tonight, at Beth's request, he had come alone.

"We need to talk," Beth had told him, her voice buzzing through the telephone as she tried convincing him to give the marriage one more chance. "No computer. No work. Just you, me, and the twins. We'll meet at the cabin. And we'll talk."

"We're talking now, Beth."

"I mean face to face."

They had covered this ground before. Talking never got them anywhere. Or worse, it festered into arguments because Beth refused to believe that depression was not a lifestyle of choice.

"Why can't you be happy, Greg?"

"I'll try." It was a lie, but he wanted to believe it.

"And can you try to forget about work?" It always came down to that question. She could not understand why a man with a substantial inheritance had to busy himself writing computer software.

"Meet us at the cottage, Greg."

He had two choices. He could tell her no and let the marriage die from neglect, or he could agree. Two choices. Always two choices. Such was life. Binary code.

"Tomorrow, Greg. Meet us tomorrow."

The plastic handset creaked from the tension of his grip. "All right." He rubbed his eyes. "I'll get there early and start the generator." To himself he added: And I'll get rid of the note I left in the living room.

Red light from the setting sun spilled into his office as he raised the shade on a west-facing window.

He opened the desk, grabbed the pistol, and returned to the first floor.

The creature stood facing the china cabinet. The doors hung open like glass wings. "We haven't much time," it said. "Beth and the twins are nearly here." It turned slowly. "I called her, Greg. Hope you don't mind." It wore a Polo shirt. Its eyes looked troubled.

Greg realized he was seeing an effigy of himself.

"This is a nice place," the creature said. "Nicely appointed. I like these." It took a Calcedonia wineglass from the open cabinet. "Wedding gift," it said. "From Beth's mother."

"Aunt," Greg corrected. "Her aunt gave us those."

"No." The creature put the glass back on the shelf. "The cobalt dishes were from her aunt."

Greg realized the creature was right. Its recall was better than his own.

"Don't feel bad." The creature closed the cabinet doors. "A man can't remember everything." It turned and touched Greg's hand—the hand with the gun. "At least you remembered this."

Greg tightened his grip, afraid the creature would try taking the pistol. But instead it released his hand and started toward the foyer.

"Come on," it said. "Walk with me. I need to start the generator."

Gun in hand, Greg waited outside the shed while the creature went in and pulled the starter cord. "You write code," the creature said, raising its voice above the generator's roar. "Code for software!"

A light came on inside the shed. Through the trees, another bulb flickered in the cottage's second-floor hall.

The creature passed through the shed's lighted doorway and stepped out onto a patch of oblong light. "You're good at what you do. Some say brilliant. But brilliance has a price."

"What are you saying?"

"I'm setting up an argument." It stepped forward.

Greg raised the pistol, taking aim.

"No, Greg. That's not the plan."

"It is now."

"We're working together, Greg. You help me. I help you."

Greg held the gun steady.

"All right, Greg. Point the gun, but hear me out."

Greg racked the slide, chambering the first round with a metallic slap.

"For over a year," the creature continued, "you've been working on a new operating system. Very ambitious. But the code contains errors."

"I'm correcting them," Greg said.

"But the corrected code seems bland. It's reliable, but you—"

"Get to the point."

"You know it, Greg. You know the point. It's inside you with everything else."

Greg felt the tactile echo of the creature's hand on the back of his neck.

"I'm giving you an opportunity, Greg. You can die tonight, and no one will suffer. I'll bury your body. I'll move in with Beth and the twins. I'll give them the life that was beyond you. I'll mend what's broken, and everyone wins. What do you say?"

"You sound so sure."

"Yes. It's a proven system."

Greg shivered.

"You know what I'm saying, don't you, Greg?"

The world seemed to blur. Greg knew the feeling. *Déjà vu.* But it wasn't that. Not exactly. *Jamis vi.* That was the better term. *Never seen.* The creature had placed things in his head, and now those things were opening, entering his consciousness, laying out an alien agenda in a single burst of insight. . . .

The creature had not come to earth alone. It was one of many, part of an osmotic invasion that sought out destructive personalities. They replaced melancholia with contentment, and because the lives they conquered were better for the conquest, no one questioned the changes.

"Think about it, Greg." The creature stepped forward. "It'll be for the best." It reached for the gun. "If you like, I can help you do it." And then, with a blur of shadows, it changed. Its arm rippled, enveloping Greg's hand, pouring over him like a fibrous wave.

He fell backward. The earth caught him with a hard thump. He struggled, looking up while the creature's face bubbled between amorphous shoulders. Greg met its gaze, and for a moment he lost himself, unable to tell where his vision ended and the creature's began.

To his left, approaching headlights fanned through the trees. The ground hummed with the crunch of tires. "They're here," he said—or was it the creature speaking? "Beth and the twins."

The car turned. Headlights angled toward the cottage, leaving Greg to struggle in darkness. . . .

He raised his hand, felt the weight of the gun, swung the barrel around and pulled the trigger.

The barrel flashed.

Beyond the trees, Beth's Lexus fell silent.

The gun slipped from his hand as he wiggled free of the dead weight. He clawed out of the ditch and gathered himself at the base of a gnarled pine. Staring into the night, blinking away the tattoo that the muzzle flash had left in his eyes, he realized that Beth and the twins were out of the car. He heard footsteps walking away, heading for the cottage.

"He must be working," Beth said, her voice ringing taut and clear through the quiet night. "The light's on upstairs. Go tell him we're here."

He had to hurry. He had to get to them before they entered the house— before they saw the week-old note on the coffee table.

"Hey!" He called through the trees as he pulled himself from the shadows. "Behind you!" He had to hurry. "Beth! Wait up!" He leaped across the ditch. The body was in there, hidden by the night, buried in darkness. He would have to slip out later, bury it deeper.

Beth turned to peer at his shadow through the trees. "That you, Greg?"

He stepped into the glow from the cottage window.

She frowned as if she didn't know him. "You're filthy!"

He looked down. Humus and leaves covered his clothes. How was he going to explain that?

The twins saved him. "Dad!" They called together, running back from the porch.

He watched them run, Bryan in the lead, Mark holding back—but only a little. He caught them one after the other in a wide-armed hug.

"Mom said you were working upstairs."

"No!" He picked them up and turned toward Beth. "No more work. Boss's orders."

"Boss's?" Beth asked.

"Yours," he said. He stepped toward her. "Things have changed, Beth. I promise." And then he was hugging her . . . hugging them all . . . nuzzling their faces with dirty hands that no one seemed to mind.

He marveled at the sudden change in himself. Facing the creature had short-circuited his depression. By facing the prospect of losing everything, he had come to realize what mattered.

Together they walked toward the porch. "Listen, Beth. I want you to know—"

Something stirred behind them.

He turned as an updraft rustled the pines. "Listen," he said.

The wind rose, and amid the clatter of branches he thought he heard the departing flap of fibrous wings.

"Something wrong?" Beth asked.

The sound dwindled.

"You hear that?" he asked.

"Wind in the pines," she said.

But it no longer sounded like wind or even wings. Listening carefully, he thought he heard the forlorn sigh of a conquered soul.

ROPE THE HORNET

I wrote most of my earliest stories in the back of a printing office, and it was there that I spent a few weeks in the fall of 1979, wrestling with an alien cat-and-mouse story that took place entirely in a convenience store. I liked the concept, but the writing was going slowly, and the story kept getting longer. Eventually I gave up and tossed it in the trash, and that might have been the end of it if my brother hadn't pulled it out and started reading. I considered telling him to mind his business, but he seemed engrossed, so I let him go. And he kept reading, page after page, until he finally looked around, nodded, and said: "This is good!" He dragged out the last word, tugging his scruffy beard as he spoke—the way he did when he really meant something.

A few months later, the story sold to Fantastic Science Fiction. *It was my second sale.*

It was late.

Marty slid two cartridges into his shotgun.

It was time to make some money.

The Observer had been on Earth three weeks. He found it backward, but he didn't mind. His home while on earth was in a small control center in the bowels of a massive simulacrum, an organic machine that would have dwarfed him if he were to climb out and stand beside it. But there was never cause to do that. He was the simulacrum's brain. His job required him to remain inside, plugged into the sensory interface that made the machine's biotronic body a virtual extension of his own.

Sometimes he lost himself within the machine, inhabiting the simulacrum's senses so fully that he began to think like a native of the backward planet he had been sent to study. Such lapses were not a problem. Indeed, they rendered the simulacrum's behavior all the more convincing.

The paths crossed shortly after 2 AM—just within the city limits of Carson, Pennsylvania.

Marty and Rick sped through a flashing red light at the intersection of Cedar and Hamilton Avenue. Two thousand feet ahead, another intersection waited, unmarked by flashing lights or road signs, identified only by a red-and-green sign:

Day & Night Mini-Mart
Always Open.

Marty held the sawed-off shotgun against his hip, its metal warming in his hands. The gray eyes across the counter stared at the hack-sawed barrel while Rick searched behind the counter for the night safe.

Marty wished he would hurry.

There were things in life more important than money. Marty realized that even if Rick didn't, and Rick's procrastination was adding to an already disastrous headache.

It had been a rough day, the kind that made patience a scarce commodity come night. It had started early that afternoon at breakfast, when the blond waitress at Delany's Diner forgot the extra sugar for the coffee. The pain started then, beginning in Marty's temples and spreading into a throbbing ring. It was so bad now that he had trouble moving his eyes. They seemed to squeak when he blinked, as if internal pressure were pushing them against his lids. Rick claimed that the pain was all in Marty's head, which was true enough—although the way Rick said it implied that Marty was just pretending, as if anyone could pretend pain.

Rick never understood such things.

"All right, old man." Rick gave up looking for the store's safe and stood up behind the counter. "Where's it at?"

The old man's mouth clicked when he opened it. "It?" he said.

Marty watched the man's lips. There was something odd about them, the way they just got dryer when the man ran his tongue over them.

"The safe," Rick said.

The man licked his lips. "There isn't a safe."

Rick looked at Marty, glanced at the shotgun, then stepped out from behind the counter, moving past a display of sunglasses that stood between the register and the storefront windows. Hand-lettered signs covered the glass, some of them advertising specials, the others announcing that the place was under new management. One of the latter faced inward. Rick glanced at it as he moved along Marty's side of the counter. It read:

Thank You for Shopping
TOMMY'S DAY & NITE
Did We Tell You About Our
Grand Opening Specials?

Rick faced the old man. "You Tommy?"

The old man nodded.

Rick grinned. "Well, look here, Tommy. When you open an all-nighter in Carson, you've got to have a safe."

"Let's just clean out the register and beat it," Marty said.

"You in a hurry?" Rick asked.

Marty blinked, wincing at the pain. "Yeah. I want to go."

Rick crossed behind Marty, set a hand on his shoulder, and looked at the old man. "My partner lacks patience," he said.

The old man just stared at the barrel.

Rick leaned against a bread display, ran his fingers through his hair, and gave an exasperated sigh. "All right," he said. "Empty the register."

The old man rang No Sale and pulled the tray from the drawer. The money hit the counter like scattering leaves, fluttering in the AC wind from above the door.

"That's a lot of cash to keep in a register," Rick said.

"It's like I told you," the man said. "I don't have a safe."

"Keep it all in that drawer?"

"That's right."

"That's not very smart."

"Sorry."

Rick smirked. "Bag it," he said.

The old man cracked a bag in the air while Rick crossed to the glass door that opened onto the parking lot. With all the paper plastered across the storefront, there wasn't much chance of passersby getting a look inside. Not that there was ever much late-night traffic out there. The old man had certainly set himself up as easy prey. Folks said he was from out of town. He had to be.

Rick pushed against the door, letting the hot August air mix with the AC cool. The small parking lot stretched away toward its Cedar Road entrance. Yellow light from overhead lamps cut the smog from the coke ovens by the river. By the door, Rick's red Ford sat rusting on bald tires.

Marty caught a glimpse of the car as he looked over Rick's shoulders. Another minute or two, and that car would be taking them home. That would be good. Marty blinked and turned his squeaking eyes back toward the old man. *Home. Eat some aspirin. Put my headache to bed*. He blinked. The old man had finished emptying the register. The full bag sat on the counter, its top folded down, ready to go.

"That's it," the man said. "All of it."

Rick turned from the door, grabbed the bag, and stepped aside. "Do it, Marty." Rick tucked the bag beneath his arm. "I don't think he's going to tell us about the safe."

The man licked his lips. "Honest, boys. It's like I told you. I don't *have* a safe."

"I'm thinking you do," Rick said. "It don't make sense not to. And if you've got this much in the register—"

"I swear."

"In my experience," Rick said, "a safe always has like ten times as much as the register. Sometimes more."

The man looked at Marty.

"What're you looking at?" Marty asked.

"You," the man said. "You believe me, right?"

"Don't look at me!" Marty said.

Rick shifted. The bag crinkled under his arm. "No witnesses, Marty."

The man glanced at Rick.

"Do it," Rick said.

The man looked back at Marty.

"Turn around," Marty said.

"Excuse me?"

"Don't make him say it twice," Rick said. "Turn around, Tommy."

The old man turned, facing a cigarette display, an indifferent wall of surgeon-general warnings.

"You don't have to worry about me talking," the old man said.

Marty could almost hear the man's tongue clicking against those dry lips, rasping across them, making them dryer.

"I won't say anything to nobody," the man said. "I won't call the police, won't even report the robbery to insurance. It'll be like you boys were never here."

"That's the idea," Rick said. "Do it, Marty."

Marty closed his eyes. The pain was there, pounding harder, drowning out everything in the room.

When he pulled the trigger, he didn't even hear the gun.

The double-barrel blast tore through the simulacrum, throwing it forward against the cigarettes, then down to the floor with a convincing thud.

Below the wound, safe within the machine's pelvic control center, the observer pulled his head and arms from the sensor sheaths. He was himself again, enveloped in darkness, untouched by the blast. And yet his thorax throbbed with sympathetic pain. With the simulacrum's eyes, he had looked down the barrel of the sawed-off shotgun and dreaded the impending pain of the blast—dreaded it as if it would be his own. And now it was.

He rolled into a ball, probing his body, touching it to be sure all was well. But the pain continued. And in his mind's eye, he once again saw the gunman regarding him with cold, indifference.

He tried thinking of home, hoping it would calm him.

In the cooler, behind the soft-drink racks, a transfer point waited. He needed only to wait until the robbers were gone. Then he could force the simulacrum back to its feet, ambulate it into the cooler and through the transfer point. Once he did that, he'd be a thousand light years away, faster than a creature named Marty could fire a shotgun.

Do it, he thought. *Lie still till they leave. Then go home.* He shivered, realizing he was still thinking in the native tongue—the *human* tongue. *Do it!* The voice in his mind wasn't his own. *Do it, Marty.* It was the voice of the robber. *I don't think he's going to tell us about the safe.*

Recalling the voice, the Observer felt a wave of fire surge through him. Terrible urges. Dark and alien. Their power shocked him. He tried resisting them, knowing that he couldn't let what had just happened jeopardize the mission. The penalties for breaking the Observer's Code were severe. If the Elders found out—

But they won't. Not if I'm careful. If I do it right.

The plan formed quickly.

He could jam the recorder, say it had been damaged. He could make it look convincing, so convincing that they'd never question it. And if they did, could any penalty they metered out be worse than what he'd experienced when that gun had discharged into the simulacrum's chest?

But it was wrong.

Do it!

It would jeopardize the mission.

Do it, Marty. The human's voice echoed in his mind, growing louder, filling him. *Do it, Marty.*

He unfurled his arms, drawing them away from the phantom pain and back into the sensor sheaths. His awareness shifted, out of himself, back into the artificial man with the blasted chest. . . .

At first he noticed only a heavy numbness in the simulacrum's left arm. He knew there would be other things, damaged functions that he wouldn't notice until he needed them. If he was going to get up and settle the score, he was going to have to be quick about it.

Marty stared at the blasted cigarette display behind the counter. The old man was down, dead on the floor, but something was wrong. He couldn't tell what it was at first, but the cigarette display looked wrong. Something was missing.

Blood.

Marty squinted.

There's no blood.

He heard Rick moving behind him, the paper bag crackling beneath his arm as he walked toward the back of the store.

Marty turned. "Where're you going?"

Rick kept walking.

"Aren't we leaving?"

"Not yet."

"You still thinking about that safe?"

"That's right."

The store was small, four aisles on each side of the counter. The back wall was a large refrigerated section, glass doors that opened onto racks of soft drinks, dairy goods, and fruit juice. Rick paused at one of the doors, pressing his face to the glass. "There's a lot of space behind these racks," he said.

"You think the safe's back there? In the cooler?"

"Could be." Rick pushed away, his face and hands leaving haloes on the glass. "There's a walk-in door." He pointed to the side of the display. "Take a look."

"You want me to look in the cooler?"

"Yeah." Rick turned, heading toward a closet-sized office near the ice machine. "You look there. I'll check the office."

Marty didn't feel like protesting, but he wasn't in the mood for being Rick's gofer either. He watched Rick step into the office, waited for him to start rummaging, and then went in after him.

Rick crouched in the tiny office, his back to the door. Boxes and crates were stacked against the walls. A bare bulb hung from the ceiling. A night deposit bag lay open on a metal desk. The bag was empty. No money in sight, and there was Rick, peering behind a stack of boxes for a night safe that they wouldn't be able to open anyway. Marty was about to protest, tell Rick that they were wasting time, when he heard something moving behind the counter. He turned, and there was the old man, pulling himself up on the cigarette display.

"Hey, Rick," Marty said.

The old man shuffled toward the paper-covered entrance, raised a twitching arm toward the deadbolt latch, and locked the door.

"Rick!"

The old man turned from the door.

No blood, Marty thought, his eyes squeaking in their sockets as he looked from the old man's too-dry lips to the gaping wound in his chest. There was no blood anywhere on the man. Instead, the hole in his chest seemed to be packed with some kind of padding, like foam insulation.

Rick came up behind Marty, setting a hand on his shoulder. "Did you check the cooler?"

Marty didn't answer. He just waited for Rick to notice the old man.

It didn't take but a second.

"What the—"

"He's alive."

"The hell!" Rick said. "Can't be."

"Look at him, man."

"Maybe it's like nerves, or something."

The old man slumped against the glass, his right arm twitching, spazzing like a shorting cable.

"What?" Marty said. "You're saying he's, like, what? Not really alive."

The paper bag crinkled under Rick's arm. "Let's get out of here."

"Are we done looking for the safe?"

"Yeah, we're done." Rick kept walking. "Did you check the cooler?"

"No." Marty said, too unnerved to lie.

Rick didn't comment, he just kept walking, advancing toward the door.

Marty followed, still carrying the shotgun, trying to look like he was loaded for bear even though both barrels had already been discharged. He had more shells, but they were outside, in the Ford's glove compartment. He hadn't planned on needing a reload.

"We're out of here!" Rick shouted.

The man just stared, gripping the door handle, holding himself steady with his good arm while his knees threatened to give way.

"Out of the way!" Rick reached for the deadbolt.

And that's when it happened.

A tremor shot through the old man's knees, and suddenly his posture went from slump to crouch. He leaned forward, lowered his head, and lunged.

POW!

He slammed headfirst into Rick's gut, driving him back against the counter. Marty tried leaping away, but the old man pivoted, grabbing Marty with his good hand. A moment later, Marty's feet were off the floor. He saw the water-stained ceiling, then felt himself spinning, flying past soap and cereal boxes to collide with a display of toilet paper and paper towels. The rack collapsed. Marty went down hard, cracking his head on the floor.

The world vanished.

He fell into himself, into dreams that were really memories, back to a time when he had learned the importance of power.

He dreamed of parochial school.

And hornets.

Each spring, hornets set up residence in the eaves of the school, and for a while—in the stretch of time that it took the janitors to get rid of the big papery nest—there was no shortage of excitement in the schoolyard of Mother of Christ Elementary.

Afternoon recess took place on a large asphalt playground along the highway side of the school. A painted line divided the lot: uniformed girls on one side, jacketed boys on the other. And everywhere, throngs of Saint Joseph nuns, habits billowing like death-angel wings in the spring wind, moved in silent patrol.

Running was forbidden. A child unfortunate enough to get caught moving faster than a dull walk got a swat across the knuckles with a ruler.

Shouting or laughing was likewise prohibited.

All winter the children had kept to the proper sides of the boy-girl line. They had not run, shouted, or laughed. They had suffered the cold like good pilgrims, but now it was spring. Almost summer. And there were hornets in the eaves.

"Hey, guys! Look what Marty's got."

"Something in a jar?"

"Don't let Sister see."

"Is that what I think it is?"

"Sure is a big one!"

"Hey, guys. Keep it down. Sister's looking."

On a hot June morning, with only a week of recesses before the freedom of summer, a boy with a hornet in a jar was king. All winter he'd dodged his classmates' iceballs, but anyone could make an iceball. It took someone special to catch a hornet in a jar.

"Are you letting him out, Marty?"

He loved teasing them, unscrewing the lid, lifting it, and then slapping it back before the buzzing madness flew out and started stinging. He laughed at them as they backed away. He could see they wanted to run, but they didn't dare. So he shook the jar, getting the hornet good and mad. And then, once again, he unscrewed the lid.

But it was all just warm up—cartoons before the movie, and he waited until they were all just about peeing themselves before bringing out the big surprise.

He carried a thread in his pocket, its end tied into a noose: a miniature lasso. Facing the highway, his back to the patrolling nuns, he slipped the thread through the air hole in the metal lid. He bobbed the loop up and down, waiting to catch the hornet at rest on the bottom of the jar. He took his time. No need to hurry. Marty was the best hornet roper in Carson.

He waited until the hornet was calm before unscrewing the lid, and this time he let it fly out, pulling the long thread after it. Then, gripping the thread, he led his hornet across the line that divided the playgrounds.

Those uniformed girls could sure move when they had to, goaded into forbidden motion, screaming bloody murder.

And even Mother Sebastian, principal of the school, wouldn't lay hands on him so long as he held that thread. But he didn't hold it for long. Pretty soon the hornet figured things out, and then it was time to release the thread and run like hell. First from the hornet. Then from Mother Sebastian.

When she finally caught him, she led him to her office—a dark cell with a desk, two chairs, and lots of pictures depicting the suffering of St. Sebastian, a martyr who had been tied to a tree and shot through with arrows.

"Do you know the story of St. Sebastian?" Mother asked, standing besides one of the larger pictures—one in which the saint's eyes seemed to look directly at Marty. "Do you, Martin?"

He shrugged.

"Is that an answer?"

"No, Mother."

"You're defiant, Martin."

Another shrug.

"St. Sebastian was defiant, too. But his defiance was to a purpose. It was holy defiance. And it helped change the world. Changed it for the good." She crossed to her desk, opened a drawer, took out a ruler. "What will your defiance accomplish, Martin?" She tapped the ruler against her palm. "Will it leave a mark on the world, change it for the good?"

"No, Mother."

"For the bad?"

Marty shrugged. He found it hard to believe that anything he did would change the world one way or another.

"You might be surprised, Martin." She said this almost as if she were reading his thoughts. "You might be surprised what one person's actions can do. And I hope, as you go through life, that the surprises will be good ones." She raised the ruler. "Now put out your hand."

He didn't move.

She smacked the back of his head.

"Your hand, Martin!"

His head throbbed. Looking back, Marty was pretty sure that the headaches had started then, with Mother Sebastian's ruler.

"Your *hand*, Martin." She smacked his head again. "Put out your *hand*."

Eventually, he did as she said.

Then, when it was over, she called his home. And then, when Marty got home, his foster father beat him up.

The next day the hornets were gone. Marty went back to being just a dumb punk kid. After school, the other boys beat him up.

And so Marty learned the lesson that was to define his life.

So long as you were dangerous, nobody hurt you.

━━━━━━   ━━━━━━

Marty regained his senses to find himself sitting on the floor of Tommy's Day & Nite. The old man stood nearby, facing away with feet apart, back hunched, one hand gripping Marty's shotgun like a club.

Rick lay at the man's feet, trying to get up, pressing his hands against the floor. But each time Rick moved, the old man swung the gun, slamming the butt hard against Rick's shoulders, the small of his back, the back of his head. . . .

Wham!

Wham!

WHAM!

And each time Rick let out a heaving sound, as if each impact were driving the life out of him.

Marty had to do something. "Stop!" He tried getting up, leaning back against the cooler as he rose—first crouching, then standing. "Just let us go, all right?"

The old man turned, looking back at Marty. He grimaced: lips clenching, eyes staring empty and dead. Then he sighed, a hollow sound that blew some of the packing from the hole in this chest.

"What are you?" Marty said.

The man didn't answer. He just extended his arm, holding out the gun as if he wanted Marty to take it. *Come on*, the gesture said. *You want it? Come get it.*

Rick moaned and started crawling for the door. The exit wasn't far, but it was still locked, bolted from inside.

"Let us go." Marty stepped forward, hands out, imploring.

The old man just stared, gripping the gun in one hand while his other arm went back to twitching like a live wire. It was clear he couldn't control it. He was a mess, but not a mess in any way that had to do with flesh and blood. *Like a machine.* Marty looked at the chest wound. The hole went clear through. And there were metal plates in there, wafer thin and arranged like battery cells. And there was something else about them, a detail that Marty saw for an instant when the panels caught the light. The plates were etched with swirling patterns that changed with the rhythm of the twitching arm.

"We'll leave," Marty said. "OK? Just let us go. You'll never see us again." He took another step, then another, cautiously making his way to the door. And then. . . .

WHAM!

The thing let him have it, spinning on one foot and driving the butt of the gun against the back of Marty's head.

Marty recoiled, careening into a candy display. Brackets snapped. Shelves gave way. Marty went down in a shower of Zagnuts and Mars Bars, landing on his back, looking up as the gun came at him again. Marty rolled. The gun missed, cutting the air at the side of his face. Then it swung again, coming at him from the other direction. This time Marty grabbed it, bracing against a force that nearly tore off his hand. But he held on, sliding over the scattered candy bars to slam the side of the counter.

"Let go!" Marty gripped the stock tighter, both hands now, pulling the man-thing toward him. They were close now, so close that Marty should have been able to smell the thing's breath. But it wasn't breathing. And its eyes looked strange—glassy, illuminated from within. "What the hell are you?"

The thing just made a low, twittering sound—as if some of the loose foam from its chest had gotten blown up into its throat. And all the while it kept tugging the gun, pulling with the slow and constant force of a machine.

Not a man, Marty thought. *No breath. No blood. Not a man!* He felt the gun slipping from his fingers. "Just let me walk out of here, OK? I'll let go of the gun if you just—"

A face appeared over the thing's shoulder. It was Rick: forehead bleeding, left eye swelling. He had something in his hand, a piece of twisted metal that flashed between the fingers of his raised fist. It looked like a corkscrew, evidently lifted from the hardware aisle.

The thing must have noticed a change in Marty's expression. Or maybe it heard the nearly inaudible shifting of Rick's feet as he crept nearer. Whatever the case, it turned, looking back while Rick drove the corkscrew deep into its neck. And then, with the swiftness of a jump cut, the thing released the gun, grabbed Rick's throat, and forced him back against the coolers.

And now Marty had the gun. He jumped up, lunged, and swung at the thing's head.

WHAM!

He hit it broadside.

Something snapped. The head lolled, rocking down onto the left shoulder, rolling forward like a ball on a short tether. The thing lost its balance, fell against the counter. Marty swung again . . . then again . . . pummeling the thing until Rick grabbed him from behind.

"Stop! Marty! You got him man. It's cool. You got him."

Marty stopped swinging to find himself standing in a cloud of linty foam. Between his feet, trailing an array of cables, the thing's body lay like a headless mannequin.

"You got him, Marty. Got him good!"

Marty blinked and leaned closer. A large gray eye dangled from one of the cables. It didn't look organic, more like a large diode. And the head, now completely detached from the neck, lay broken among the scattered candy bars, staring with one inhuman eye and one empty socket.

"You got him *real* good!" Rick's voice trembled. "Man! Look at him!"

"Not a him." Marty shivered. "Some kind of thing."

"Killed him real good, Marty!" Rick didn't seem to notice the threads and wires.

"I want to get out of here," Marty said. "This place . . . this isn't a store." He looked around. "It's, like, all wrong." He looked back at the thing at his feet. "And this . . . I don't even want to know what this is."

But Rick was already turning away, scooping spilled money from the floor, stuffing it back into the bag.

"I want to go, Rick. Now!"

Rick dropped to his knees, grabbing bills from under the bread display.

The front door banged, shaking in its frame.

Marty turned to find a pair of eyes peeking between the paper signs. They were there for an instant, staring in. Then they vanished.

Rick looked back, saw nothing, returned to stuffing bills into the bag.

"Someone's out there!" Marty crossed toward the door, put his face to the glass, peering out between the signs. "She saw us, Rick."

Outside, a car door slammed.

Marty twisted the deadbolt and opened the door.

A few yards away, under the glow of the parking lot's lights, a woman looked out through the side window of a wood-paneled station wagon. Again, she stared right at him, then she locked the door, fumbling with her keys.

Marty didn't go after her, not directly. Instead he ran to Rick's car, opened the passenger side, and stabbed the stud on the glove compartment.

The woman cranked her engine.

The glove compartment opened. A box tumbled out, spilling shells across the seat, onto the floor, over the pavement.

The woman's engine sputtered, changed pitch, ignited. Exhaust wafted past Marty as he slammed the gun across his knee to open the chamber. The spent shells slipped out. He tossed them away, grabbed two replacements, and loaded the gun.

Behind him, the woman's car reversed into the lot, tires smoking as she spun to face Cedar Road. Her backup lights winked off. The transmission clicked.

The car shot forward, burning rubber and oil as it careened out of range.

"Marty!"

Marty looked back at the store.

"What're you doing, Marty?" Rick's voice came muffled from the paper-covered glass. He was slurring his words, talking like a drunk.

Brain damage, Marty thought. *All those cracks on the head. He's got to have brain damage.*

"Get in here, Marty!"

Marty stepped away from the car and looked at the shells on the pavement. *What a mess!*

A car passed on Cedar Road, heading south toward town. It didn't slow down, didn't stop. But there would be more cars. Sooner or later, one of them was bound to stop.

We have to leave.

"Marty! Get in here! You've got to see this!"

Marty pushed away from the car and reentered the store to find Rick standing with his face pressed against the cooler door. He held the money bag tucked under his arm. All the bills were off the floor.

"Look at this." Rick spoke without looking around, his breath fogging on the glass. "There's something in there, behind the bottles. Might be a safe."

Marty walked past the counter, stopping when he saw nothing more than the creature's smashed head lying among the scattered candy bars. The headless body was gone. And something was moving behind him.

Rick turned.

Marty did the same, and there it was—the machine-man's body, cables dangling from its neck.

The thing raised its good hand, took hold of the diode that hung from one of its neck cables, and lifted it between thumb and index finger. It glowed as the hand turned it toward Marty, then toward Rick, and then finally toward the walk-in door on the far end of the cooler.

"Marty!" Rick's voice caught in his throat. "The hell is it?"

The thing started walking, heading for the cooler.

"Blast it, Marty!"

The thing no longer seemed interested in fighting. It walked past Marty like he wasn't there, shuffling through the fallen candy bars, picking up speed.

"*Blast it, Marty!*"

Marty stepped back, braced the gun against his hip, and fired both barrels.

The Observer, whose race had evolved beyond primitive reflexes, was not supposed to feel pain. But now, once again, as the double-barrel blast struck the simulacrum's chest, he recoiled. His body spasmed. He curled into a ball. And although he possessed no more than the vestigial folds of the spiracle glottis that had served his feral ancestors, he screamed. Not a loud scream. Little more than a hiss of constricted breath. But in the tight confines of the control chamber, the breath registered louder than the double-barrel report of the human's gun.

Revenge now seemed less important than getting out of the simulacrum and into the cooler where the transfer point waited. It would all be behind him then. That's what he needed to do, put the madness behind him.

Pulling himself from the sensor sheaths, he turned toward the escape hatch. How long could he survive in the thin air beyond the chamber? Could he even function without blacking out?

He hesitated, considering his options. The simulacrum was dead. There would be no driving it to the transfer point. But he couldn't just leave it behind. The rules for such things were clear. Leave nothing. No witnesses. No artifacts.

There's a way. Can't take the machine. Can't leave it behind. But there's a way. He was thinking clearly once again. Focusing on protocol. Considering the mission. *No trace. No witnesses. Complete erasure. Annihilation!*

He turned form the hatch, reaching out to touch the destruct mechanism—the simple safeguard that would fuse the simulacrum to a hunk of silicone and carbon while doing little damage to the immediate surroundings. He tapped in the code, setting the timer, and then—

"*No witnesses!*"

He froze.

"*No witnesses, Marty.*"

The recorded voice emanated from the malfunctioning database, thundering from one of the sensor sheaths.

"*Don't look at me! Turn around.*"

The voice brought it all back.

"*Do it, Marty!*"

And then—

BLAM!

He kept his hand on the timer, contemplating ways to enlarge the area of destruction. Not all Observers knew those ways, but he was a member of the Guild. And he was good with his hands.

It only took a moment.

When he had finished, he popped the hatch, braced against the inrush of foul air, and raced out along the simulacrum's leg.

A few yards away, the cooler waited. He had no idea how he would open one of its doors without the simulacrum's massive hands, but he would deal with that when he got there.

There was no turning back.

"You got him, Marty! Got him good!"

But Marty didn't care about shooting the machine.

Other things were happening. Bigger things. He felt them when he closed his eyes, felt them pounding in the darkness behind his lids. The discomfort had been building for a long time, possibly all his life, and now it seemed to be burning through his skull, melting his skin, leaking into the space around him until it filled the store. And still it grew, radiating through the windows, seeping through the cracks beneath the door, blowing out into the night to overrun the world.

The whole world is hurting, and I'm the center of its pain.

Then, far away, sirens screamed.

"Marty!"

He felt Rick's hand on his arm.

"Marty! *Lesssh go!*" He was still slurring, worse than ever now.

But Marty stayed where he was, in his private darkness, enveloped in pain.

"Marty! C'mon. That woman must have called the cops!"

Marty clenched his eyes.

"The hell's wrong with you, Marty?"

The pain carried him back to a time when he was small enough to wear an empty box of Mother's Oats like a helmet. He used to push the box down over his head, blocking out the world with the dusty smell of grain and cardboard. It used to drive his foster parents nuts, but wearing that box on his head had seemed like a good way of getting away, retreating from the madness of the world. Sometimes he'd leave the box on so long that his head would swell, filling the tight space so completely that he couldn't tell where his face ended and the cardboard began. When that happened, he would imagine he was the boy pictured on the front of the box: a happy kid being fed by a mother in a red dress. The illusion usually lasted until his foster mother started yelling.

"Get out of there! You'll suffocate!"

But by then the box was so tight that it had become an extension of his skin. He couldn't take it off. The best he could do was jab scissors through the cardboard, punch holes near his nose so he could breath. Sometimes he'd jab himself, rip skin, draw blood. But none of that mattered. The real pain was still outside.

"You hear me, Marty? Get your head out of there!"

But those days were gone, and now the person calling to him beyond the darkness wasn't his foster mother. It was Rick.

"Marty! Fercrysake, Marty!"

Marty opened his eyes, not all the way—just enough so that the world appeared beyond a pair of curved slits.

Rick stood by the door, hand on papered glass. "Let's go!" His hair blew back in the hot wind as he pushed the door open. "Come on!"

That's when Marty glimpsed something moving on the floor beyond the counter. He opened his eyes wider, seeing it as it shot along the baseboard. "Hornet!" Marty shouted.

Outside, the sirens wailed louder.

"There's a hornet!"

Rick looked back. "A what?"

Marty sidestepped along the counter, watching the thing as it ran.

"We got to go, Marty."

Marty rounded the counter, moving away from the door.

"Marty. Come on! I'm leaving."

Marty ignored him.

The door swung closed, biting off the sound of the wailing sirens as Rick left the store. Marty didn't care. His attention stayed with the dark shape that crouched at the edge of the counter. He studied it: triangular head, elongated thorax, pinched waist. The thorax pulsed, flaps opening on its sides, dilating like tiny lips. And its legs—it had six of them, each ending in a hand with three barbs: two small ones curling upward, one large one extending down to the linoleum.

It had no wings. And it was big, perhaps a foot long and six inches high, but there was no mistaking its shape. It was the biggest hornet Marty had ever seen.

Outside, Rick's Ford revved and backfired, the sound thumping like a shotgun blast. Tires squealed, pulling away as the giant hornet looked at Marty, staring with slit-pupil eyes.

The siren blared louder, swelling with the squeal of cornering tires, racing closer as the Ford roared away. A horn blared, followed instantly by the thunder of crunching metal.

Marty glanced toward the windows, eyes wide open now, head suddenly clear. He saw the red and green of the grand-opening signs backlit by the blue strobe of emergency flashers. And he heard voices, hard-edged and shouting.

"Stop! Stay in the vehicle!"

Sound of running.

Pop!

The flash of the handgun strobed against the paper-covered glass.

Pop! Pop-pop-pop!

And then, as if reacting to the sound, the hornet bolted away from the counter, out onto the open floor.

The Observer ran until he reached the cooler. He paused beneath one of the glass doors, probing the seal along the bottom, working his fingers in first, then two of his arms. He pushed. The door clicked open. Cold air tumbled over him, bristling the hairs along his head and shoulders.

Need to be careful.

The door was heavy. It could crush him.

Slow and steady. Take your time.

But even as he prepared to lift himself through, he heard the thump of the human approaching. He glanced back to see the giant coming on fast.

Marty ripped off his jacket and threw it over the hornet.

"Got you!"

The hornet's body clattered between lining and linoleum, struggling as Marty slid the jacket out onto the floor. The thing pulsed beneath the leather, trying to get out. Marty clamped the jacket's waist with his knees and leaned forward to press his arms against the lapels, working quickly to secure all the sides. The hornet kept moving, twitching beneath the leather, backing away from the waist, racing toward a gap near the collar.

Marty shifted, bringing his hand down hard to secure the collar, only to realize he had forgotten about the sleeves. The hornet was already inside the left one, racing toward the elastic cuff. Marty reached for it.

Too late.

The hornet shot from the cuff and scurried away, claws clacking like sputtering grease as it fled into the cereal aisle.

Marty followed, rounding the bend in time to see the hornet leap onto a low shelf. An instant later it was gone, its abdomen wiggling between the brightly colored boxes, vanishing with a rasp of skittering legs.

The darkness behind the boxes gave the illusion of safety. It was like being back inside the simulacrum, hidden where no one could touch him.

Except that he wasn't safe.

The sprint from cooler to cereal aisle had left him gasping, on the verge of passing out. And all the while, the timer in the simulacrum was cycling down, approaching zero. He needed to get to the transfer point, but now he had to hide, wait for the man to get away from the cooler doors.

He kicked against the cereal boxes, scurrying back along the shelf until his arm hairs bristled with the scent of moldy cheese.

He recoiled from the smell, looked around, and saw the source: wooden slab, wire jaws, cheese-smeared trigger. It was one of the rodent traps that the simulacrum had placed around the store a few weeks earlier. And this one was one of the big traps. A rat trap. He needed to keep his distance. The spring loaded jaws packed enough force to snap him in two. He tried backing away, but then something slammed into the boxes in front of him. The dimness parted, pushed aside by a massive hand. Fingers shot toward him, spreading wide, coming down hard.

"Got you!"

This time he had the hornet for sure, its hard-shell grating against his palm as he tightened his grip, squeezing hard. He didn't care if it stung him. He'd been stung before, many times. A hornet wrangler needed to be impervious to such things. Power did not come without a price. And right now, with the police outside, he needed all the power he could get.

ThwaACK!

He recoiled as something slammed his fingers, hard and narrow like the metal edge of Mother Sebastian's ruler. Only worse. A million times worse.

He screamed, drawing back his hand as the pain shot through his knuckles and into his arm. He saw it then. The thing on his hand. It wasn't the hornet. It was a rat trap, steel bar clamped tight over three fingers. Two of those fingers looked broken, bent at terrible angles between the first and second knuckles. The third had been severed at the second joint, spattering blood across the cereal boxes as he pried the hand free, threw the trap onto the floor, and looked around to see the hornet leaping from behind the boxes, racing down the aisle.

And then the front door swung open. A cop stepped in, shouting into the store.

"Police!"

Marty stepped to the end of the aisle as a second officer entered. Then a third. All had guns drawn, swinging them toward Marty. "Drop the weapon, mister."

Marty glanced left. The hornet was back at the cooler, opening one of the doors, squeezing through.

"Now, mister. Put it down!"

Marty couldn't tell which one was speaking. They all looked the same with their thin lips and anthracite eyes, staring at him with envy and hate, waiting for the hornet to get away so they could rush in and beat on him.

The cops eased forward, spreading out, coming closer.

"The weapon, mister. Put it down. No one gets hurt. Just put it down."

Marty stared at them—down the aisle, through the years, across the pain that was once again closing in.

He turned and ran toward the cooler.

A pistol fired.

The shot hit him in the shoulder, knocking him off balance. He fell forward, arms out, still holding the shotgun. Another shot struck the center of his back, numbing his legs. He slammed the cooler door. A third shot whizzed past his ear, shattering the glass. A liter bottle of Cherry Coke sprung a leak, spurting into his face. . . .

He went down hard, slipping on wet linoleum, landing in crunching glass.

The last thing he saw before the darkness closed in were a pair of slit pupils looking up at him from the shadows beneath the counter. The hornet was still in the store. And now it was coming toward him.

The Observer raced forward, over the bits of glass and fizzing cola, up onto the bleeding shoulder of the maniac who had been bent on killing him, and then through the shattered door and into the cooler.

The officer's voices rose behind him, spilling through the shattered glass.

"You see that?"

"What was it?"

"Hey! *Did you see that thing?*"

The voices faded as he ran to the transfer point, a swirling eye that opened as he approached, a vortex that seemed to rise out of the door of a small padlocked safe that had been bolted to the cooler's floor. He leaped toward it, passing through.

Behind him, in the ruined simulacrum, the timer cycled down.

Eight miles east, in the Mother of Christ Retirement Convent, Mother Sebastian awoke at 2:37 AM to see the sun rising through her western window.

She sat up.

"A miracle."

She had been waiting all her life for a sign to show her that the powers of light were still alive in this world of pain.

"So beautiful!"

And then it was gone.

She closed her eyes and dreamed she was young again, walking through a playground full of good children, all of whom seemed to understand that one misdeed—a single act of disorder—could change the world. And so they respected her rules. No yelling. No running. No acting out.

But then, from somewhere, the sound of buzzing. . . .

DAUGHTERS OF PRIME

Though written and published as standalone works, the next two novelettes can actually be read as a single novella, a heroic adventure that takes place over the course of five days. Based loosely on the first two agons of Beowulf, the stories recast the hero as a woman and transplant the adventure to a planet 100 light years from Earth.

"Sorry to bother you, Sister." Alpha's voice rose from the audile implants in Cara's ears, breaking her concentration as she finished calibrating the integration chamber. "We've got a problem."

Cara turned, climbed from the chamber, and stepped out into the long shadows of cliff-side trees. The hatch closed behind her, hissing to an air-tight seal. "Go ahead, Alpha." An implant in Cara's hyoid conveyed her voice to a transmitter in the back of her head. From there her words traveled straight up to the mission orbiter. "Break it to me gently."

Despite the 35,000 kilometers that separated orbiter and base, the answer when it came sounded as close as Cara's own thoughts. "The surveillance flier's gone down."

Cara winced as she turned toward a stand of trees that grew along the edge of her cliff-top base. "Tell me what happened." She eased toward the preci-pice. Below the ridge, a forest canopy extended unbroken toward a plowed field. Beyond the field stood a wall of woven wood and pointed stakes.

The field lay empty and silent, shadows pooling in the furrows while villagers rested behind the wall. This was their communal hour, a time that Cara usually spent eavesdropping, watching the natives with the help of a tiny drone that could hover undetected above the settlement. But this evening the camp's integrator had required attention, forcing Cara to leave Alpha in charge of monitoring the flier.

"I can't figure it," Alpha said. "It was functioning fine. Take a look."

A window appeared in Cara's cyberoptic field, an ineye projection from corneal implants, powered by cybernetic neurons that ran from the back of her head to the interior of her eyes. The window displayed the drone's last few seconds of visuals: an aerial view of villagers lounging between huts of woven reeds. Everything appeared normal. But then, abruptly, the image pitched: the village slid from view, replaced by a green blur that rose to fill the digital frame. After that, the window vanished.

"So the drone went down in the trees." Cara felt relieved that the flier's arc had carried it away from the village.

"Yes," Alpha said. "It's in the forest. That's the good news." A new window opened, framing an orbital shot of the jungle canopy. Dimmed by distance and atmospheric distortion, the visual lacked the clarity of the flier's image. "It went down here." A circle appeared, highlighting the site.

"Is the homing beacon operating?"

"Yes. For now."

Cara knew she had to retrieve the machine while the natives were at home.

She turned, looking toward the integration chamber, newly calibrated and primed to receive the orbital beams that would transmute the packets of raw matter she had placed within the central kiln. Mission protocol required her to maintain the chamber in a state of readiness, thus allowing for short-notice transmissions of emergency equipment or, in the event that she became incapacitated, the teleportation of a new field observer.

Alpha said, "If you leave now, you'll be back before dark."

Cara checked the sky: deep blue at zenith, golden yellow beyond the village. "All right. I'm going." She walked through the clearing, continuing until she reached the geodesic tent that served as her home. From the front door, she saw the grave of her predecessor, the daughter of Prime who had piloted the lander on its one-way flight from the orbiter. "I'd better make a statement for Mission Command."

"Go ahead. Recording."

Following procedure, Cara stated her designation and position: "Cara Gamma. Durgan Outpost." She readied her excursion pack as she spoke, folding her portable rover, lashing it to her shoulder harness. "I'm going to the forest to retrieve a downed flier. Projected off-base time: sixty minutes." She donned the pack and tightened the straps. "Required safeguards are in place. Integrator is primed and calibrated. Alpha will transmit a replacement if I'm out of contact for more than twelve hours. End statement."

Alpha said, "Want a playback?"

"No. Send it. It's fine."

"Sending now."

The statement was a formality, a document for clerics who would one day manage the estate of Prime. Cara did not wait for a reply. The Ministry was over thirty parsecs away. Even if all went well, she would be dead before her words crossed the galactic arm.

Cara descended the cliff's eastern face, keeping the crag between her and the village until she reached the forest floor. There, enveloped in long shadows and the drone of insects, she removed the rover from its harness and extended the control shaft. Nearby, a cloud of flies swarmed above the carcass of a large slug. The flies ignored her. They hunted by smell, and her scent lacked the chemical triggers that attracted them. Working in peace, she kicked down the rover's pedals, locking them into place on either side of a single gyro-balanced wheel. Then she climbed on, leaned forward, and took off—stirring the swarm with the wind of her passing.

The rover cruised at 40 klicks, its proprioception sensors maintaining stability as she leaned forward on the pedals. Gripping the control shaft, she bounded through the forest, over a carpet of brittle vegetation, and up onto the remnant of an ancient road that extended for nearly a kilometer before vanishing back into the forest loam.

The ruined roads were evidence that the jungle had once been more heavily traveled than it was now. And the other villages, abandoned and overgrown, presented a conundrum that she hoped to understand better before revealing herself to the inhabitants of the island's last remaining settlement.

The jungle thinned as Cara reached a swift-moving stream. Spreading branches rose above her, framing a patch of clear sky as she dismounted at the water's edge. Then, with the rover once again folded against her back, she stepped across a makeshift bridge of stones and emerged onto the far bank.

The flier was close, broadcasting its location from a tangled hollow. She hurried toward it, following the signal into the shadows of a brushwood cove. Then she stopped, recoiling as she saw what waited within.

She wanted to run, but it was too late.

A short figure stood before her, meeting her gaze with nictitating eyes. It was a villager. On his chest, swinging from a neckband of braided reeds, hung a twelve-centimeter disk of carbon fiber and molded plastic. She recognized the pendant. It was her fallen flier.

For a moment, Cara and the creature stood eyeing each other through the shadows: the villager hunching his shoulders in a posture of respect, Cara leaning back, stunned by the realization that her days of detached observation were over.

This time, it was Cara's turn to voice the alarm. To Alpha, she said: "Sister, we've got a problem."

The creature opened his jaws, silencing her with a loud click. Other sounds followed, shrill warbles from spiracle nostrils, clicks and chirps from a triangular mouth. There was nothing like it in human speech, except perhaps the self harmonies of Tibetan throat singers or the glottal clicking of the ancient Khoikhoins of South Africa. Nevertheless, after months of eavesdropping, Cara had become familiar with the sounds. Now, standing before the creature, she listened carefully, getting the gist of his words: "*I am Long-Eyes,*" he said. "*You are a* X-ooh. *Sent by* X-ah."

She knew the word *X-ah*, a throaty click followed by a mid-vowel sigh, but its meaning could be tricky. Depending on inflection, it could mean either *fate* or *spirit*. The other word, *X-ooh*, was more mysterious. She had heard it before, spoken in reverent whispers. She had assumed it was a deity.

Long-Eyes stared, waiting.

Alpha said, "You need to answer him."

Cara hesitated.

Alpha sent a prompt, keying it directly into Cara's view. It was a simple greeting, augmented with symbols for alien phonemes: X for glottal click, Ñ for nasalized whistle.

"Talk to him, Sister!"

Cara gave it her best, wishing she had been endowed with forehead nostrils to fill in the higher sounds: "*Greetings, Long-Eyes. I am Cara.*"

Long-Eyes raised his hands, fingers clenched in amazement. "*X-aha.*" He pronounced the *C* as a click, giving the name an intonation similar to *X-ah*.

Alpha said, "I think you just told him you're a *spirit*."

But Long-Eyes seemed more delighted than afraid. He lowered his head, clicking: "*You are* X-aha, *the* X-ooh *from* X-ah!" He bowed lower, removing the braided twine that held the flier to his chest. "*Yours,*" he said, handing her the broken drone.

She took it, wondering at his bland acceptance of the tiny machine. He could not have seen it before it fell, and yet he handled it as if he had known about it for some time. "*They fell,*" he said, gesturing toward the drone. "*I retrieved them.*"

"*Them?*" She didn't understand. "*You retrieved them?*"

He spoke again, repeating himself, and this time she discerned the subtle inflection that rendered the pronoun singular. This time, she understood. He had said *it*, not *them*: "*It fell. I retrieved it. For you.*"

All right. One question answered. But she was still confused. "*How did you know?*" She gestured, compensating for her uneven diction. "*How did you know about me?*"

"*Know?*" He considered the question. "*We have always known . . . for long times . . . ever since your sister came to the hills.*" He turned, facing the cliffs that stood beyond the wall of trees. "*She came at night, flying quiet and dark. But we knew. I knew. Long-Eyes saw.*"

Cara shivered. *Quiet and dark* was an apt description of the lander. It flew on ionic wind, without visible exhaust or guiding lights. Until now, she had never considered that the villagers might have seen it. Indeed, her months of eavesdropping had turned up no indication that the villagers knew they were being observed. Yet, here was Long-Eyes telling her differently. "*You knew?*" she asked. "*You knew about my predecessor?*"

"*Yes. First about her. Then about you. When we heard the clear-sky thunder, we knew that you had come to take her place.*"

Teleportation was far from silent. The power beams that accompanied orbit-to-ground transmission gave off thunderous roars that, loud as they were, should not have attracted attention on an island of frequent storms.

But evidently they had.

Long-Eyes said, "X-ah *brought you here to help us. It put you on the cliff, and now it has brought you to me.*"

"*No. That's not the way it is. I'm—*"

He turned away as she struggled with the words. "*We need to go now,*" he said. "X-ah *promised to protect me until you came. But now that you are here—*" He paused, cocking his head, listening to the forest. "*We must hurry before it comes.*"

"*Before what comes?*"

He glanced at her. Softly, he muttered: "*X-eeÑa.*"

Cara covered her mouth, subvocing to Alpha: "What'd he say?"

"No idea."

"Check."

"Doing it now." A pause, and then: "Not in our database. We're hearing the word for the first time." She played it back, letting Cara hear it again: *X-eeÑa.*

To Long-Eyes, Cara said, "*I don't know that word.*"

"*Yes. I understand. The* X-ooh *is as ignorant as it is powerful.*"

"*Ignorant?*"

He gestured toward her flier. "*You studied our voices. You listened, but some things are best not spoken aloud.*"

"*But you're speaking them now.*"

"*Yes. Because you are asking.*" He turned, moving toward the remnant of a forest road.

She hurried after him. "*I'm not—*" she struggled for the words. "*I'm not . . . what you think.*"

He walked faster, his muscular feet slapping the hard-packed clay.

She broke into a jog, keeping pace. "*I'm not a* X-ooh," she said. "*Whatever a* X-ooh *is, I'm not—*"

He stopped walking, gesturing for silence.

In the distance, beyond the forest brume, something stirred—a sound like the thumping of massive feet. Softly, Long-Eyes muttered: "*It's awake.*"

"*It?*"

The sound changed course.

She turned, following his gaze. To the south, beyond the point where distant trees merged to form a wall of trunks and shadows, the sound began moving away, heading toward the village.

Long-Eyes gestured to her shoulder pack. "*The running wheel,*" he said. "*You need to hurry.*"

Cara reached around, unhitching the rover from its stays. "*You want me to use this?*"

"*Yes!*" His nostrils flared. "*Hurry!*"

"*Hurry where?*"

"*To the village.*"

She gripped the rover, swinging it by its handle to extend the control shaft. "*But it can only carry me.*"

"*Yes! You go!*"

She kicked the pedals into place.

"*Go to the field,*" Long-Eyes said. "*Use your power. Kill the* X-eeÑa!"

"*Kill it?*"

"*We will help. We will distract it. We will make it an easy target for your power. Then you will kill it.*"

She turned from Long-Eyes, trying to remain calm as she called to Alpha. "What do I do?" She spoke aloud, no longer subvocing. "Tell me what to do!"

Long-Eyes stared, apparently intrigued by the cadence of human speech.

Alpha said, "Go to the field."

"And do what?"

"What you're there for. Observe. Record what happens." It was the advice of someone who had nothing to lose. If Cara were killed in action, the mission would continue with a fresh fieldworker, teleported from the orbiter's files, integrated within the chamber that Cara had primed and calibrated before leaving the base. The replacement would take possession of the outpost, review the records, and continue the study.

Long-Eyes said, "*You need to hurry. Go to the field. Use your power. Kill the* X-eeÑa!"

Cara leaped onto the rover, leaned forward, and accelerated toward the village.

She veered west, cutting a beeline toward the field, not decelerating until the trees thinned and the ground angled upward. Straight ahead, coalescing through the ferns and hanging fungi, the village stood backlit by evening sun. She changed course, turning left, steering beneath a cover of low-hanging branches. . . .

The gyros cut out as she hopped from the pedals. She dropped to her knees, coming to rest behind a clump of ferns. Before her, the field stretched toward the village wall. Above the gate, lookouts peered between fire-hardened stakes, listening as the approaching thumps grew louder, coming closer. . . .

A flock of leather-winged slugs leaped from the trees, soaring over the field on jets of vented air, scattering into the dusky sky as a massive head emerged from the jungle. It hovered two meters from the ground, gliding outward on the end of a powerful neck.

Alpha said, "I'm recording your visuals, but the Ministry's still going to want your impressions. Better start talking."

Cara swallowed, watching the thing as it stepped onto the field, its profile so unnervingly alien that it seemed to shift before her—altering as her mind wrestled with the contours of its strangeness. "First impression?" She glanced at the misshapen head, shielding her eyes as it passed before the sun. "It's hideous!"

The creature turned, cutting the sunlight into flaring rays.

"Its head is as big as I am."

It pivoted, surveying the field.

"Its jaws are misaligned, with the mandible extending beyond the snout." She squinted, trying to comprehend. "It's got a face like a deep-sea predator . . . a viperfish . . . that's the closest—"

The beast roared, rearing its head, opening its jaws.

She saw it then. The lower jaw was not a jaw at all. Rather than swinging downward, it split vertically—cleaving at the chin, becoming a pair of muscular limbs, each anchored beneath the head and sporting fanglike claws. And now, with those limbs flexing wide, she saw the beast's true mouth—an orifice near the top of the throat, chinless as the maw of a shark. She saw it for a second, and then the monster turned again, staring at the wall.

It seemed to be waiting.

Cara studied its profile. "I'm trying to get a handle on the physiology, but I keep getting lost. It has avian hips, but it's wingless—no forward appendages other than the ones that cover its mouth. The head is counterbalanced by a gigantic tail. It's obviously warm-blooded, agile, swift. I'm going to need months to review these visuals, Alpha. This thing's like nothing I've—"

A tremor moved through the village wall.

The animal leaned forward, lowering its head as the palisade gate stuttered back along wooden runners, cracking open to form a gap barely wide enough for a villager to squeeze through.

"Something's happening." She saw movement within the gap. A shadow emerged, coalescing into a village child. Another followed. Then another. They walked with halting steps, heads bowed, shoulders hunched—goslings with pear-shaped bodies. Their arms, folded like wings, shivered beneath capes of woven reeds—the handiwork of village artisans.

Then the gate skidded back, closing tight while the procession hurried across the field.

The animal watched, its tail twitching like a sputtering cable.

Cara muttered, "I don't believe what I'm seeing."

The beast moved forward.

"This looks like a sacrifice."

The children gathered in a tight huddle, heads together, shoulders locked. Cara stiffened. "I can't watch this."

Alpha said nothing. The scene's horror had taken her voice.

The beast crouched, folding its long legs, lowering the arch of its hips until the mandible arms touched the ground. Cara tried turning away. But she couldn't. It was her duty to watch, record, understand. And when it was over, when the beast had lopped the pear-shaped bodies into its crescent mouth and lumbered back into the forest, when all that remained of the children was an oval depression in the furrowed ground, then she finally mustered the strength to turn away. And when she did, she found that she was no longer alone amid the ferns.

Long-Eyes stood behind her, panting from his race through the forest. "*You did not kill it!*" He stood erect, shoulders stiff, hands clenched—an angry pose. "*The beast stayed in place. We gave you an easy mark. But you did not kill it!*"

Wailing voices rose from the village. The gate opened, scraping back once more. Cara tried watching to see if more villagers were coming out, but Long-Eyes stepped in front of her, standing close, blocking her view. "*You did not use your power,*" he said.

"*Power?*"

"*You are a* X-ooh." His faced darkened, turning sanguine near the spiracle ridge above his eyes. "*The* X-ah *delivered you to help us. The* X-ah *provided and you did not—*"

"*No!*" she shouted back. "*Not me. I'm—*" She paused. How could she even begin to explain what she truly was?

Long-Eyes spared her the effort. "*Your version of who you are doesn't matter. For us you are a* X-ooh." He reached out, grasping her shoulders, his hands hot with anger.

She pulled away. To Alpha, she muttered, "What do I do?"

"Return to base."

"But he's asking for help."

"Not your job, Sister. Return to base."

Long-Eyes watched, cocking his head as Cara spoke to empty air. And then, feeling overwhelmed, Cara mounted her rover and whirred away, racing for the trees, not looking back, not even thinking about what she would do if she met the *X-eeÑa* in the forest. For the moment, all that mattered was getting back to the illusion of objective study, away from the problem that was not hers.

The camp was as Cara had left it, but the setting sun had deepened its contours, bathing everything with low-angled light. Her shadow followed her, extending from her heels like an elongated skid, pivoting to move beside her as she turned toward the grave of her predecessor: a cairn of rocks with an auger drill serving as a marker. Her predecessor had used the drill to draw core samples from the forest floor. Now the tool tossed a cruciform silhouette across the grave.

Cara looked left and doubleblinked, disengaging streaming interface with the orbiter, opting for five minutes of privacy as she addressed the spirit of the woman within the cairn. "What should we do?" she asked, sitting by the grave, leaning back to search her own thoughts for an answer.

Her mind calmed. She closed her eyes, recalling the life of another Cara—an athlete with an aptitude for language and science, a twenty-three-year-old protégé named Cara Randall. . . .

As the inheritor of Randall's memories, Cara Gamma carried impressions of places that she herself had never been: the Ministry's cloistered lectoria, flight simulators, and exercise chambers.

She recalled the joys of study, accessing the cybernetic wisdom of a hundred years of theoretical xenthropology. And when the call went out for volunteers to serve as fieldworkers on the Ministry's growing catalogue of unexplored worlds, she took the vows and passed through the one-way doors that led to the chamber of scanning and deconstruction.

She remembered the hiss of the closing seal and the dim pause that preceded the blinding light. Randall's memories ended with that flash, but Cara Gamma did not need inherited recollections to know what happened next. The facts were all matters of procedure.

The deconstructing flash transferred Randall's essence to a pair of identical crystals—one went into the Ministry vaults, the other into the AI system of an unwomanned vessel bound for a point of perturbation in the orbit of a fifth-magnitude star. Thus, the digitized Cara Randall became Cara Prime, the template for a series of lone observers who would study a planet that no human had ever seen.

The first reintegration of Prime occurred when the vessel drew close enough to verify the planet's existence. The shipboard computer activated the kiln, igniting the blocks of compacted matter that provided the substance for Cara Alpha—the first daughter of Prime.

After climbing from the chamber, Alpha assumed the role of orbiting commander, and her first job after checking herself for defects and wiggling into the piezoelectric unitard that powered her cybernetic system, was to verify the computer's assessment of the planet.

What she found was a world inhabited by a sentient species that had migrated from its point of origin to occupy a vast triangular continent. Along the opposing shores of an inland sea, two protocities had settled into a state of protracted aggression. Likewise, in the hinterlands, warring tribes slaughtered each other for possession of fertile deltas and valleys. These were not good places to initiate ground-based observation, but looking elsewhere she found isolated settlements dotting the forests of coastal islands. It was on one of these islands that she found a village of docile agrarians who had moved beyond the study of war. They lived inland, away from beaches that would have left them vulnerable to attacks from the sea. There, Alpha began the study.

After selecting the site, Alpha recalibrated the shipboard integrator and primed the kiln. Then she closed the hatch, activated the system, and gave life to Cara Beta.

It was Beta's job to pilot the lander to the planet's surface. Once there, she set up camp and began the first phase of observation. Two days passed without incident, and then, suddenly, Beta awoke to find herself facedown in the center of camp. She had blacked out.

A day later, it happened again, only this time when she regained her senses she found herself lying dangerously close to the edge of the cliff.

The next day, she blacked out twice in the morning, then once again in the afternoon. Each time, Alpha's voice brought her back, calling to her in tones that grew more anxious with each recurring fugue. Beta tried attributing the seizures to defects in her cybernetic interfaces, but when checks of those systems revealed nothing unusual, she and Alpha had no choice but to contemplate the grim alternative.

The process of deconstruction and integration had a failure rate of point-four percent. Sometimes there were errors in the scans. Other times, data became corrupted during imprinting. Beyond that, with each repeated integration, there was a chance that fluctuations in power or disruptions of the data stream could result in a defective copy—a functioning integration that soon lost its physiological integrity.

Not wanting to jeopardize the mission, Cara Beta instructed Alpha to send a replacement. Then, with her interfaces disengaged, Beta self-administered a lethal injection of morphine sulfate, stretched back beneath the lander's shadow, and entered a final blackout.

Within the hour, Cara Gamma arrived to bury the remains.

Cara leaned toward the grave, whispering to the stones. "What do we do, Sister?"

The stones lay still, cooling in the fading light.

Cara stood, turning toward the village as she felt Alpha coming back online. She stared through the veil of camouflaged netting, into the distance to see what appeared to be a lone figure standing outside the village wall. "Alpha, you online?"

"Here, Sister."

"Give me your view of the village field."

Alpha complied, dropping an orbital shot into an ineye window.

Cara closed her eyes. The image expanded, filling her head. There, amid blocky pixels and the wavy distortions of evening air, she saw a villager standing on the furrowed ground. She wondered if it was Long-Eyes waiting for her to return. "The villagers knew about us from the beginning, Sister."

"Yes," Alpha said. "So Long-Eyes claims."

"He says I am a *X-ooh*, sent by *X-ah*."

"But you are Cara Gamma, the third integration of Cara Prime. The Ministry sent you. A starship brought you. These things you know for certain."

"So it seems." She turned, looking back at the lander, its sides open to reveal the outer hull of the integration chamber.

"Long-Eyes said I have power."

"You do, although it is not the kind that kills monsters."

Atop the integration chamber, a heat exchanger sat like a steel lily, waiting to catch the next energy beam from the orbiting gun.

"But what if it is?" Cara said. "What if my power *is* that kind?" She approached the chamber, climbing onto its hull to inspect the reflector—the fist-sized cube that ensured a direct hit from the power beam. In some ways, the little single-use block of anodized metal was the integrator's most vital component—so vital that each supply transmission included a set of spares. . . .

It came to her then. She knew what she had to do.

Long-Eyes stood alone in the field, staring at Cara as she emerged from the forest. He did not seem surprised. Something in his expression told her that he had known she was coming. "*You are a strange* X-ooh," he said.

"*No. Not a* X-ooh." She lifted a heavy strap from her shoulder, unslinging the improvised weapon that hung across her back. She held it so he could see it: a fearsome graft of steel and aluminum—shaped like a cross, wielded like a sword with a spiral blade. "*I am not a X-ooh. But maybe I can help.*"

Long-Eyes studied the weapon.

Cara said, "*If that beast comes again—*"

"*There is no question,*" Long-Eyes said. "X-eeÑa *will come.*"

Cara swung the weapon, checking the bindings that held the spare reflector to the auger's handle.

Long-Eyes said, "*You have brought your power this time.*"

"No." She stopped swinging. "*My power comes from the sky.*" She spoke more fluently now, having taken time to practice the things she needed to say. "*This is only a tool to guide the power.*"

Long-Eyes leaned closer, looking at himself in the reflector's right-angled mirrors.

She glanced toward the wall. The gate remained closed. Silence hung in the darkening air. She asked, "*Why are you standing here?*"

"*Waiting,*" he said. "*Waiting for you or the* X-eeÑa. *I am glad you came first.*"

He was standing on the spot where the children had offered themselves to the beast. Dried blood stained the dirt.

"*I offered to stand here,*" he said. "*It was the only thing to do. I had promised the children that you would not let them die. Their task was to distract the beast, to give you time to use your power. I promised them that they would not die if they did as they were told.*"

"*You promised them?*"

"*Yes. They were not supposed to die. That was your doing . . . and my undoing.*" He looked toward the forest. "*Still, I am glad you have come back.*" He cocked his head, listening with dilated ears.

Something stirred within the trees.

"*It is coming,*" Long-Eyes said. "*It hears our voices. It will not pass up an easy meal.*"

The rumble came again, closer.

Cara turned away, speaking to Alpha: "Stand by to power up."

"Standing by."

The gun took nearly two minutes to charge, and once armed it had to be fired quickly to avoid damaging the capacitors. Cara's plan was simple. First, she had to plant the marker in the animal's side. After that, she needed to keep the thing out in the open, in clear sight of the marking laser that aimed the gun, away from the village where a direct hit would risk collateral damage. As for herself, if she were unable to get clear of the blast, there was a good chance that Alpha would soon be sending a replacement to the cliff-top base. For that reason, Cara had used one of the spare reflectors from her cache of supplies, leaving the original cube affixed to the top of the camp's integration chamber. One way or the other, whether she succeeded or failed, the study would continue.

The thump of the creature's long strides drew closer, the noise coming faster and louder as a cloud of slugs jetted from the trees. Then, seconds later, the *X-eeÑa* emerged, spreading its mandible arms.

Cara mounted the rover. "This is it, Sister. Power the gun!"

"It's powering."

Cara turned to Long-Eyes. *"I will do what I can. No promises."*

He raised his hands, folding them in a show of thanks.

She turned away, leaned forward, and took off across the field.

"Gun is charging, Sister. Full power in one-one-eight seconds."

Cara continued straight until she was sure she had attracted the animal's attention. Then she leaned left, veering parallel to the village wall.

The animal followed, coming on fast, its long strides easily matching the speed of the rover.

Cara looked back, saw the mandible arms coming toward her, and leaned into a tight turn that carried her back through the veil of her own dust.

The beast swung around, tracking her as she cut a tight arc around its legs. The ground shook as it turned in place. She moved with it, staying ahead of the arms only to find her course blocked by the whip-like tail. She veered again, ducked down, and hurtled between its legs.

Alpha called to her as she emerged from beneath its hips: "Did you do it? Did you plant the reflector?"

"No." She steadied the auger against her shoulder. "I'll get it this time." She leaned again, giving the beast a wide berth as she swung around for another go.

"Fifty seconds, Sister."

The animal lunged, reaching for her, forcing her into a one-eighty spin that sent her skidding back the way she had come. The claws closed behind her, shearing the empty air.

This time she kept moving straight, speeding toward the edge of the forest before looking back to find that the animal had given up the chase.

She pulled on her control shaft, decelerating, spinning to a stop. She stared back at the creature's mandible arms. Its crescent mouth quivered, pulsing in the shadow of its face.

It leered.

She returned the stare.

"Thirty seconds, Sister."

What had she been thinking? The plan was impossible. There was no way she was going to plant the marker, and now the clock was running out.

"Sister? You all right?"

She didn't bother to answer. There was nothing to say. She had failed again. But then, from across the field, the sound of clicking: Long-Eyes calling to the X-eeÑa.

The beast turned.

Cara leveled her weapon. "All right. One more try." She leaned forward, picking up speed.

She wondered what Long-Eyes thought of her now—a one-wheeled knight with a corkscrew javelin. Was this the sort of thing a X-ooh was supposed to do? Surely, there was nothing like this in the village legends.

"Twenty seconds, Sister! Place that marker and get out of range!"

Cara focused on the target, staying the course, holding the shaft steady, watching the flexing mass of the animal's right hip. She dodged the tail and raced toward the leg. And then, with a jolt that nearly threw her from the pedals, the auger struck its target, plunging deep, not stopping until the shaft hit bone and the beast roared like a klaxon.

She spun, bounding away, losing control. Something clipped the rover, knocking the wheel from under her. She never saw what it was. It could have been the animal's tail, or its leg, or even a ridge in the furrowed ground. Whatever it was, it sent her into a tumble—feet slipping across the sky, head plowing the dust. . .

. . . and somewhere, a voice: "Ten seconds!"

Cara rolled, careening across the ground, coming to rest with the animal's terrible head lunging for her. "Alpha! Fire the gun!"

The mandible arms swung wide.

Cara scrambled, crawling like a crab. "Do it now!"

The sky brightened, sparking with light from the orbiter. It was not the high-energy bolt—the one that would ignite the animal's blood and send its pieces scattering over the field. This first light was only the marking laser, the low-energy beam to illuminate the reflector and guarantee a direct hit.

The cool flash backlit the creature's body. Cara braced herself. And then. . . .

The night exploded.

Her suit ignited, melting her piezoelectric unitard, searing her flesh as she flew into the air. Furrows raced beneath her, streaked with her leaping shadow—a cruciform silhouette that swelled as it rose to slam against her outthrust hands. *BAM!* No pain. The agony would come later—after the shock had left her bones, after her flesh realized how badly it had been maimed.

A woman screamed, a voice like hers but not hers, a distant call that Cara could not answer. She could barely breathe, and it was all she could do to remain conscious as she once again pulled her face from the dust and looked back at the cleaved remains of the *X-eeÑa*.

The creature's torso had exploded, leaving the head and tail convulsing on the ground. The eyes glared, staring at her, burning with numb rage as the mandible arms clawed the dirt. And still the distant voice shrilled inside her. "Respond, Sister! Are you receiving?"

Cara coughed, finding her voice. "Receiving." She looked down at her arms, the left one bare and bloody, her cybernetic unitard ruined. "I hear you, Alpha."

"Your bios are offline, visuals full of noise."

"But you hear me?"

"Yes. Hear you. What's your condition?"

Cara tried lifting her arm. It responded. Still no pain. "Can't tell. I'm alive. But everything's . . . fuzzy."

Long-Eyes raced toward her.

She tried to rise. The world spun as the village gate slid open. Villagers hurried out. Not children this time, but tall males with heavy legs, kicking dusty clouds.

"I've got company." She tried focusing on the running males. "Can you see them?"

"Orbital image only. You're still not streaming."

Cara slumped to her knees.

Long-Eyes caught her, grabbing her beneath the shoulders, helping her to her feet. She fell against him, smearing his pelt with blood as the males gathered around her, pressing close, their faces taut with admiration. She kept her eyes open, returning their stares, hoping her vision would go back online so Alpha could see what she was seeing.

Long-Eyes said, *"The Elders will want to meet you. They will want to hear what you have done."* He walked forward, guiding her toward the open gate.

The crowd walked with them, and it was then that Cara glimpsed a shadow rising over the heads of the males. She turned, stumbling as she saw the *X-eeÑa* rearing high into the night sky. Her breath caught, and then she saw the hands that held the monster's neck and arms. The head swayed, dead eyes gleaming as the villagers carried their trophy through the gate and onto the narrow lanes that wound toward the dome in the center of the village.

They took her to a hut beside the great wooden dome, and there they peeled away the remnants of her ruined suit, clicking and whistling at the maze of cybernetic conductors that lay between her skin and unitard. She was hurting now. Pain thundered as the villagers dressed her wounds.

"Sister!" She called to the orbiter as she lay on her back, staring at a ceiling of bent poles and cured bark. Smoke from a central fire gathered between the beams, swirling through an oval vent. "I'm in the village, Sister. I wish you could see. I wish we were recording."

They brought her a steaming bowl that smelled of roots and grass. The drink tingled, warming her throat and stomach as she forced it down. Almost instantly, her burns stopped hurting, and soon she found herself standing under her own power as artisans draped a woven tunic about her shoulders. She raised her good arm, marveling at how the cloth followed the contours of her frame.

"They're giving me clothes. The fit is almost perfect. And the top's embroidered with—" She paused as she made sense of the pattern: dark threads depicting a warrior battling a beast with mandible arms. It was a stylized design, limited by the texture and color of the materials; nevertheless, the stick-figure warrior seemed to stand upon a rounded foot—a shape that resembled a rover's wheel.

She turned to Long-Eyes. "*When?*" She pressed a fist against the garment. "*When . . . you make this?*"

His features tightened. "*I did not make it. The cloth is old.*"

"*How old?*"

"X-eeo *days.* X-eeo *nights.*"

X-eeo. She knew that word. It was not so much a number as a concept—an expression used when speaking of things too vast for counting, such as seeds in the field or trees in the forest.

"X-eeo *nights ago?*" The words baffled her. "*How could you have known?*"

He leaned close, uttering only a single syllable—a word whose significance she still did not fully understand: "*X-ah.*"

"*X-ah?*" She said it back to him. "*What is X-ah?*"

"*It is what brings the* X-ooh."

"*What is X-ooh?*"

He opened his arms, reaching to embrace her. "*The* X-ooh," he said, "*is* X-aha."

Long-Eyes took her to see the Elders, processing into a great chamber that glowed with blazing fire. Ribs hung from spits, dripping fat into the flames, filling the air with the smoke of *X-eeÑa* flesh. And near the flames, impaled on blackened stakes, the beast's vacant eyes glowed in the firelight.

The Elders welcomed her, and she sat with them, drinking from their bowls and listening as Long-Eyes clicked and whistled an improvised song about the power of *X-aha*.

Again she shivered, thinking about how rapidly things had changed. For a scientist who had planned to devote a large part of her life to the impartial gathering of data, here was a new kind of accomplishment. She had become a warrior hero, a champion—the *X-ooh* from *X-ah*. To Alpha she said, "I could get used to this."

"No reason why you shouldn't. You're one of them now. It's an incredible opportunity. If only we could get your vision back online."

Long-Eyes returned to Cara's side as a young song-singer launched into a whistling lyric about the power of the *X-ooh*.

Long-Eyes said, "*Your wounds are deep.*"

"*Are they?*" She slurred the words. She didn't care. She was *X-aha*, the *X-ooh* from *X-ah*. If she couldn't slur her words, who could? "*I don't feel them.*"

"*You are strong.*"

"*Yes.*" She raised her bowl. "*And so is this.*" She drank.

"*It is good you are strong.*"

"*Yes. It is all good.*"

"*And your things. They are strong, too.*"

"*My things?*"

He did not have a word for *weapons*, so he resorted to pidgin, using gestures to describe the auger that had directed the power beam.

"*No,*" she said. "*No more.*" She raised her good hand, opening her fingers in a sign of letting go. "*Gone!*" Eventually, she was going to have to return to her base. She would get Alpha to send her fresh supplies: another rover, a new unitard. But all that could wait for now.

She leaned toward Long-Eyes. "*But I have other things for you. Better things.*" The words flowed, no longer impeded by doubt. "*I will teach you. You will learn my ways, and I will master yours. We will become each other's students. You and I will—*"

He tensed, drawing his shoulders together, leaning back in a troubled gesture.
She asked, "*What is wrong?*"

"*When will we find time for such idle things? What of the* X-eeÑa?"

She glanced at the severed head. "*What do you mean?*"

He looked confused. "*You must help us fight it.*"

She froze, wondering if she had heard him correctly. Again she stared at
the severed head.

"*It,*" he said. "*You must help us fight it.*"

But the word he used was not *it*.

In the native language, barely a half tone separated singular from plural.
To human ears, even to gifted ones that had spent months studying the inflec-
tions, the difference was barely discernable.

Cara drew an uneasy breath, letting it out in a constricted sigh: "Oh my
god!" She looked at Long-Eyes, holding his gaze as she spoke the pronoun
again, giving it the proper inflection—the slightly higher tone that made all
the difference. "*Them,*" she said. "Oh my god!" She reached out, grasping his
arm. "*How many?*" She swallowed. "*How many of those monsters are there?*"

He answered with a single word. "*X-eeo.*"

She released his arm, sitting back as the expression quaked through her:
X-eeo—the number beyond counting.

He leaned closer. "*At first they will come one at a time. But soon there
will be many, then more—rising from the forest like a deadly crop. It is not
always this way. They sleep underground for many seasons and seldom wake
together. Most winters it is only one . . . or a few. Most seasons we can
appease them with offerings—sometimes the elderly and sick, sometimes our
children. But* X-ah *tells us that this will be a winter of* X-eeo X-eeÑa—*a
winter like the one that destroyed the other villages. That is why we celebrate.
That is why we are glad that* X-ah *has sent you to us. We are glad to have
such a powerful* X-ooh."

Nearby, the young story-singer paused in his narrative. He turned to
Long-Eyes, raised his hands, and echoed the phrase: "X-ah *has sent us a
powerful* X-ooh!"

Others joined in, repeating the words, and soon the great dome reverber-
ated with joyful praise.

Long-Eyes leaned close. "*Lookouts stand watch by the wall. They will
let us know when the* X-eeÑa *return. Until then, you must rest, collect your
strength for the next battle.*"

Cara turned away, looking again at the beast's head. "Alpha," she said.

"I'm going to need some supplies." She stood, testing the strength in her legs and discovering she could stand on her own.

The room fell silent.

"You hear me, Sister? I need a transmission—supplies *and* personnel."

"Personnel?"

"I can't handle this alone. Send me Delta."

"No," Alpha said. "Can't do that. No multiples in the field. You know the rules."

"Forget the rules. I need Delta . . . and rovers . . . and all the core samplers and reflectors you can send."

"No Delta. It's a breach of protocol."

"So breach it."

"You can't make that call." Alpha's voice rose, bordering on indignation. "I'm the commander. Who do you think you are?"

Cara looked down at the pattern on her tunic: a lithe warrior riding a speeding wheel. When she answered, it was in the native tongue. "*I am* X-aha *the* X-ooh."

"You can't be serious."

"I can't be otherwise. Transmit Delta. Have her bring the supplies to the village."

Alpha did not respond. Cara gave up on her, took her seat, and tried thinking of another way. A minute passed. Then another. And then, in the distance, muffled thunder split the night.

The villagers looked toward the dissipating roar, hands raised in amazement, nostrils flaring. They knew the sound. And Cara, although she had never heard it from so far away, recognized it too. She closed her eyes, listening to the echo of what Long-Eyes had called clear-sky thunder.

"Thank you, Alpha."

"I guess this makes me your *X-ah*."

"Yes, I suppose it does."

"Just one question. If I'm the *X-ah* and you're the *X-ooh*, what's Delta going to be?"

"I don't know, but I'd better let them know she's coming." Cara looked up to find Long-Eyes staring at her.

He asked, "*You are talking to your* X-ah?"

"*Yes.*"

"*You are making a plan to face the* X-eeo X-eeÑa?"

"*Yes.*" She considered the supply of raw-matter packets that Beta had brought in the lander. The supply was limited, but if she and her sisters began relying on the village to provide food and shelter, the packets could be used exclusively for personnel, rovers, and reflectors.

She looked at Long-Eyes. "*I need to explain. I need to tell you what I'm going to do.*"

"*No need for that. My own* X-ah *has told me.*" He leaned closer, his nostrils flaring. He pressed his hands to his chest. "*There is only one way to fight* X-eeo X-eeÑa." He paused.

She knew what he was going to say.

They spoke it together: "*X-eeo X-aha*!"

THE OTHERS

And now, with the protagonist's exploits taking on the qualities of heroic fantasy, we continue Cara's adventure with her second agon—a story that serves as an apt transition between the realms of science fiction and those of pure fantasy.

A predawn downpour pelted the thatch roof, soaking the support beams and seeping down the walls. Aching dampness radiated from the floor, and even the fire, burning in a stone-rimmed pit in the center of the room, seemed to cramp beneath the chill.

Long-Eyes sat before the flames, neck arching from the raised collar of his tunic. He looked like a goose in a loose-fitting robe, but with arms in place of wings. He glanced at the dripping skylight, clucking idly at the drops falling through the smoke. Then he turned, abruptly swinging his head around to look at the damp cloth that hung across the door. *"They're coming,"* he said, speaking in the native tongue—all clicks and whistles.

"They?" Cara asked, trying to get the inflection right. This was only her third day of using the language without prompts from the orbiting database, and pronouns could be tricky. *"Who is coming?"*

"The others."

"My sisters?" Cara listened for the sound of approaching rovers but heard only the falling rain and crackling fire. *"Are you sure?"*

Long-Eyes raised a three-fingered fist, a sign of affirmation. *"The first one is already inside the village wall.*"

Cara stretched her wounded leg and climbed from the bed of dried grass and matted leaves. Her ankle twinged as it took her weight, flexing stiffly.

Long-Eyes turned a dilated ear toward the door. "*She is riding faster than the others.*" He paused, listening. "*Almost here.*"

Cara heard it now, the hum of an engine racing toward the hut, the splash of a single wheel braking outside the door.

"*It is the tall one,*" Long-Eyes said. "*She is carrying something heavy.*" He lowered his face, listened carefully, then added: "*She is carrying you to it.*"

"*Carrying me?*" Cara asked. "*Carrying me to what?*"

Long-Eyes sometimes spoke in riddles. Was this one of them, or had she misunderstood?

"*Not you to it,*" he said, speaking more slowly, letting her hear the glottal tones that trumped word order. "*I said that the tall one is bringing something to you. I do not know what it is. But you will see for yourself in a moment. She is almost—*"

The damp cloth swung back, sending a misty spray into the hut as Epsilon stepped into view. She carried a full load on her back, a bundle of field supplies that included a spare uniwheel rover in latch-down position. The rover weighted nine kilos. The pack added another two. But Epsilon stood tall, assuming the straight-backed posture that always made her appear larger than she was. "You're up," she said, lowering her hood. Her face was identical to Cara's: square jaw, narrow cheeks, wide-set eyes. But Cara barely noticed such things. It was the differences that put her on edge.

Epsilon gestured toward Long-Eyes. "Is he still taking care of you?"

"More or less," Cara said. "Mostly he just keeps me company."

Epsilon stepped away from the door. "I was afraid you might be sleeping."

"Can't sleep," Cara said.

"Pain keeping you awake? Is it your leg?"

"No. Not really." Cara stepped into the light, trying to appear strong.

"Your arm, then? Those bandages look loose." Epsilon rounded the fire, dragging her rover by its control shaft, its single wheel leaving a muddy streak on the clay floor.

Long-Eyes stepped aside, making room.

"I thought I'd wrapped those bandages tighter than that."

"Too tight," Cara said. "I had to take them off, reapply them on my own. I think—"

Epsilon raised a finger. "One moment." She cupped her ear and turned away. "Go ahead, Alpha. I'm listening."

Three days earlier, Cara would have listened as well, but she was now completely offline, her audio links having failed shortly after the other cybernetic systems went down. As a result, she waited in silence.

"All right," Epsilon said. "I'll ask her." She turned to Cara. "Alpha wants to know if you think the wound's infected."

"No. I gave the burns a good look before replacing the bandages. The scabs appear healthy. No abnormal discharge. And I don't feel warm. I think I'm fine." She realized that such observations were less reliable than a full-system diagnostic, but they were all she had.

Epsilon nodded. "Guess we'll have to take your word for it." She unslung the pack from her shoulders, dropping it and the spare rover onto the floor at Cara's feet. "This gear is for you."

Cara frowned. "The rover, too?"

"Yes. Provided you're strong enough to ride it."

"And the pack?"

"It's standard issue: rations, meds, field suit. Alpha transmitted it an hour ago. You need to get out of that native tunic, come back into service."

"But I'm offline."

"Right, but it's your experience that matters . . . provided you can ride."

Two more rovers splashed outside the door.

"Where are we going?" Cara asked.

"I'll tell you, just as soon as—"

The door cover slapped back, making way for Delta and Zeta, each identical to Epsilon in form but different in manner.

Delta's gait conveyed tension as she rounded the fire, turning her head just enough to make eye contact with Cara. *We need to talk*, the eyes said. *But not here.* She glanced at Epsilon, then Zeta. *Not around them.*

Zeta was less guarded. She drew up next to Epsilon, standing close enough to be her shadow. "Everything OK?"

"Yes," Epsilon said. "She says she can ride. I guess you could have stayed at the base after all."

"No problem," Zeta said. "I wanted to come." She peeled back her hood to reveal a fresh abrasion on her forehead: a wide, scabby streak that might have come from a swinging branch, as if at some point she had been following Epsilon too closely through the forest. "Did you tell her what we're doing?"

"Not yet," Epsilon said, keeping her eyes on Cara. "I want her to start suiting up first."

Cara glanced at the others, reading their expressions, intuiting the reason for their predawn return to the village. "You've found it, haven't you?" she said. "It's the nesting site, isn't it? You've found it."

Delta nodded.

Cara turned away. "*Long-Eyes!*" She called his name in the native tongue, looking back to where he had been squatting by the fire. "*My sisters have—*"

Long-Eyes was no longer in the room.

Cara looked toward Delta. "Did he leave?"

Delta shrugged. "I wasn't watching him."

Cara looked toward the door, the cloth cover swaying in the predawn wind.

"Maybe he went to wake the Elders," Epsilon said. "He probably wants them to know we've come back."

"But I have to tell him—"

"What you have to do is get ready. Alpha's predicting a break in the weather, clear skies at dawn. If you're going to help us, it has to be this morning."

Cara glanced once more at the door, then knelt beside the fresh gear, favoring her wounded leg as she lifted the new rover from its harness. She set it aside and broke the seal on the field pack. The contents were all newly integrated, form-fitted into a near-solid mass of plastic shells and folded fabric. She lifted out one of the latter, a compressed cybernetic unitard. "What I need is information." She set the unitard on the floor and removed her tunic. Her skin, imprinted with cybernetic conductors, flashed in the firelight. "Tell me about the nests. Where are they?"

"Eastern shore," Epsilon said. "There's a ledge overhanging the sea. The wall beneath it is honeycombed with caves. Access is through a pit that opens near the edge of the forest. I climbed down it yesterday morning. The fang-claws are there. Hundred of them. When the young hatch there'll be thousands."

"*X-eeÑa,*" Cara muttered, using the native name for the animals. Pronounced as a glottal click followed by a nasalized whistle, the name could be tonally inflected to be either singular or plural. Roughly translated, it meant *fang-claw*. Like most native words and names, it was aptly descriptive. "Thousands of *X-eeÑa?*"

"They'll decimate the island," Epsilon said. "It'll set this mission back a year if we don't do something."

Cara unfolded the unitard, opening its dorsal seam to reveal a lining embroidered with micro-circuitry. "You've got a plan for dealing with thousands of those things?"

"I do." Epsilon turned to Delta. "Show her the markers."

Delta unslung a field pack from her shoulders, reached inside, and pulled out four transmitters, each mounted to a spring-loaded rock anchor.

"Delta's going to mark the target with those," Epsilon said. "Then the two of you are going to stay on site, making sure the target stays marked until Zeta takes out the nests."

Delta returned the transmitters to her pack. "You get the picture?" she asked.

Cara's mind raced, putting the details together, filling in the blanks as she slipped her arms and legs into the unitard. "You're talking about using the lander, aren't you?" The unitard's lining tingled as it slid along her skin. For a moment she thought she felt the rush of cybernetic current, the heat of her personal system powering on, but it was only the residual warmth of the fabric, still fresh from integration. Her circuits remained dead. The unitard would keep her warm and dry, but her senses would remain offline. "You're going to crash the lander into the nests?"

Delta grinned at Epsilon. "I told you she'd figure it out. She might be offline, but she's still one of us."

Cara frowned. "Let me get this straight—"

"You're getting it just fine," Zeta said, furrows forming behind the scratches on her brow. "We've moved the lander's remaining fuel into the forward tanks and primed it to ignite after I power dive into the nests. The collapsing fuselage will seal the opening, forcing the energy down into the caves." She spoke softly but forcefully, with the stoicism of a disposable field-worker, someone trained to serve a brief term on the planet before yielding to a freshly integrated copy from the orbiter's digital files. That was the way things were supposed to work: one fieldworker at a time. "When it's all over," Zeta said, "the mission goes back to following protocol."

"You're saying all but one of us will be retiring this morning?"

"It makes sense," Epsilon said. "There'll be no need for multiples once we take out the nests."

"So it'll be you then?" Cara said, speaking to Epsilon. "The rest of us re-tire. You continue the mission. May I ask who made that decision?"

"No one." Epsilon extended a hand to help Cara to her feet. "We drew lots back at base camp."

"The luck of the draw?"

"No. Not luck. Duty. This mission was never about a single worker." She squeezed Cara's hand, but the pressure was anything but reassuring. "We're all in this together . . . and we're all expendable. You know that, Gamma."

Cara winced. *Gamma.* She wasn't used to hearing that name spoken aloud, but there it was, her sequential designation, the label that identified her as one in a series of identical fieldworkers, each transmitted from the orbiter to the base camp's integration chamber.

"Something wrong?" Epsilon asked.

Before the additional fieldworkers had arrived, Cara had found it easy to think of herself as unique. But now—in the presence of Caras Delta, Epsilon, and Zeta—everything was changing.

"You look tense," Epsilon said.

"It's nothing." Cara reached down with her good arm and lifted the field pack from the floor. "Just a little stiff, is all. I'll be fine." She didn't dare say otherwise. Among the field-pack's standard-issue supplies was a retirement kit containing a lethal dose of morphine sulfate. Any fieldworker who found herself unable to advance the mission was expected to inject that dose, retire herself, and make room for a replacement.

Epsilon was right about one thing. Retiring in action would be better than overdosing on a bed of matted leaves.

"So you want me and Delta to stay on site, make sure nothing comes along to dislodge those markers?"

"That's right," Epsilon said. "But the local wildlife tends to steer clear of the nests, and most of the fang-claws will already be underground after sunrise. At most, you'll only have to worry about a straggler or two."

"In which case, you'll want me to distract them."

Epsilon shrugged. "Nothing you haven't done before." She grinned. "You know their moves. You wrangled one and lived to tell about it." Her grin broadened. "But this time staying alive isn't a concern. The stragglers can catch you once Zeta locks in on the signal."

Cara nodded, turned away, and reached into the pack once again, this time lifting out a field jacket and a pair of lightweight boots. She put them on, then realized she might be needing one more thing before the morning ended.

The pack's medical compartment held a mix of supplies—some chemical-based, others cybernetic. Among the latter was a piece of hardware known innocuously as a dorsal plug. Sealed in a hard-shell container and emblazoned with a code-red label, the plug was as potentially lethal as a dose of morphine. "I might need this," Cara said, slipping the case into her pocket.

Epsilon frowned. "I thought you said you were feeling better."

"I am." She lifted the field pack over her shoulders. "Better than I was." She tightened the straps and picked up the rover. It was still in latch-down position: riding shaft collapsed into the chassis, wheel locked on its gyro-balanced hub. She held the handgrip, extending the shaft and freeing the wheel with a swing of her arm. "I'm ready." She turned to the door, realizing as she did that she no longer heard the patter of rain. The room seemed oddly still. "Maybe we should find Long-Eyes, tell him the plan."

Epsilon glanced left, checking her ineye clock. "No time," she said. "You need to go."

"But the Elders will want to—"

"I'll take care of the Elders," Epsilon said. "This is my post now." She stepped toward the fire, making a show of warming her hands over the flames. "The database will prompt me with the language. Alpha will advise me on the customs." She spoke with the authority of one who had already claimed the field as her own.

Not like me, Cara thought. *My face, my body, my training—but the arrogance is all hers.*

"Something wrong?" Epsilon asked.

Delta rounded the fire, stepping toward Cara. "We need to go," she said, her eyes once again conveying the dark weight of things unsaid. "The nests won't keep. We do this now or not at all."

Epsilon grinned. "You need to trust me." The flames played across her face, pooling in the hollows of her cheeks. "Trust me, Gamma." She turned away. "It should be as easy as trusting yourself."

A palisade surrounded the village. Within it stood a mass of densely-packed huts interspersed with dirt trails and clay courtyards. At the center of everything, on a rounded hump of land, a great hall spewed smoke from dormer vents.

"Something's going on," Cara said. "They're lighting fires, getting ready for something."

Zeta nodded. "So are we." She mounted her rover and took off toward the palisade.

Cara and Delta followed, their running lights cutting the predawn darkness.

The villagers seldom left their huts before sunrise, especially during the cool, rainy mornings that followed the harvest. Still, Cara couldn't shake the impression that the hovels looked unoccupied: no billowing smoke, no faces peering from cloth-draped doors as the rovers raced by. She wondered if everyone had gone to the great hall, leaving their homes as abruptly as Long-Eyes had left his—the entire village responding to some unspoken cue to convene with the Elders. She shivered, realizing yet again how much there was to learn about these people. . . .

The path remained clear until they reached the palisade. Here they found the resident gatekeeper standing beneath a thatch awning. The villagers called him Always-Ready.

Cara waved to him as they approached, giving him the formal greeting: a clenched fist with the thumb tucked beneath the fingers.

He returned the gesture, hunched his neck, and walked out to where a sliding gate rested in wooden runners.

"*The huts are quiet this morning,*" Cara said.

Always-Ready lowered his fist and reached for the gate.

"*They're lighting fires in the great hall. Is something—*" Her words gave way to the rasp of the gate sliding in its runners, moving back to reveal a narrow pass between overlapping sections of wall.

Zeta and Delta rode through.

Cara held back a moment. She considered asking Always-Ready for more information, but he seemed anxious for her to leave, as if he had something to do . . . someplace to be. She raised her fist and leaned on her control shaft, speeding out onto the harvested field that stretched between the palisade and the tall, dark face of the surrounding forest.

The rain had stopped, but low clouds still churned overhead, flickering with lightning, riding a stiff wind toward the eastern shore. And there was something else, a strange glow flashing above a familiar sheer-walled mountain to the northeast.

The mission's base camp occupied a ledge near the top of that mountain, hidden in a clearing behind cliff-side trees and camouflage netting. Until three days ago, the camp had been Cara's home. She had worked there alone, studying the village, eavesdropping with powerful microphones, learning the ways of the natives. Through it all, she had been careful to keep the camp dark. Evidently, her sisters no longer considered that a concern.

"What's going on up there?" Cara asked.

"Modifications to the lander," Delta said. "Epsilon had Alpha send us another worker."

"Eta?"

"That's right. Integrated yesterday afternoon. She's up there now, getting things ready. When she's done, she'll serve as Zeta's copilot."

"Two in the cockpit?" Cara tried picturing that. The lander, designed for the sole purpose of ferrying the mission's integration chamber from the orbiter, had a cockpit barely large enough for a single pilot.

"We've modified the design," Delta said. "Taken out some hardware, made room. Crashing the lander means flying with the higher functions disengaged. No fail safes. No autopilot. Epsilon says that kind of flying is going to take two pilots."

"Epsilon says a lot of things, doesn't she?"

Delta leaned forward, speeding away as if she hadn't heard the comment, hurrying after Zeta who had already reached the wall of trees.

The forest rang with invertebrate songs—the whistles of worms, squids, and carrion moths—all clearing the way as the uniwheels hurtled forward.

The sisters rode together until Zeta's course veered toward base camp. After that, Cara and Delta continued on, finally slowing their pace near the remnants of a deserted village. Here the forest became a riot of creepers, vines, and weeds—all contending for dominance among a jumble of leaning poles. But something had recently cut through the site, leaving a wide swath of sheared-off stubble that glistened with the mucous of grazing pseudopods.

Delta followed the stubble, wheeling along a curve of rising ground to pause beside the doorframe of a fallen hall. Cara pulled alongside her, looking east to where the trail widened along a stretch of level ground, finally ending at a stand of trees. And there, at trail's end, a line of grassy hillocks rose from a band of silver mist.

"Snails?" Delta pointed toward the hillocks. "That's what they are, right? Giant snails."

Cara nodded. "The villagers call them moving-hills. You've seen them before?"

"A couple times. At first we thought they were natural formations."

"It's the camouflage. They cover their shells with grass and moss, glue it on with spit that hardens like glass." Cara raised a hand, showing a scar on her thumb. "I touched one once. Not a good idea."

"What about going through them?" Delta asked. "Because that's the direction we need to go." She pointed toward a section of forest beyond the center of the herd. "Can we do that? Is it safe?"

"Safe enough if we don't startle them," Cara said. "When they sense danger they close ranks, lock shells, stay that way until the threat passes."

"Should we go on foot?"

"That'd be my suggestion, provided we have time."

Delta looked left, consulting her ineye display. "I planned on stopping here anyway, waiting a few minutes before moving on." She stepped from her rover. "If we start walking now, we'll be fine." She pushed her riding shaft into the chassis, latched it down, and fastened the collapsed rover into her shoulder harness. Then she turned away, cupped her ear, and spoke to the orbiter. "Alpha, I need five minutes offline." A pause, and then: "Yes, Alpha. Right now. I'm taking five minutes." Then she blinked, straightened up, and looked at Cara. "We need to talk." She started walking. "It's about Epsilon. I've got concerns. I need to know if you share them." She drew closer to Cara, speaking softly as they entered a band of mist at the foot of the rise. "We've got five minutes, Sister. Talk to me."

Cara frowned. "You want to know if I have concerns about Epsilon taking over the mission?" Her voice sounded flat within the mist, more like thoughts than spoken words. "I guess I don't feel all that good about it. I mean, she doesn't seem to have the temperament for fieldwork . . . and she's not particularly good with the villagers. Long-Eyes calls her the tall one. Did you know that? He thinks she's prideful."

"So even Long-Eyes sees it?"

"I think so."

"So that's three opinions," Delta said. "All agreeing that Epsilon is different."

Cara winced.

"Something wrong?"

"Maybe." Cara sighed. "Listen . . . it might be easier if I didn't say this, but we need to consider it." She turned toward Delta, looking into eyes that were partly her own, partly those of a stranger. "What if it isn't just Epsilon who's different? What if it's all of us?"

"I don't follow."

"No? Surely you've noticed we're not identical. Maybe we were at first. At the moment of integration we were perfect copies of Cara Prime, but work¬ing together has changed us. To function within our group, each of us has assumed a role. You turned quiet, secretive. Zeta became a devoted follower. Epsilon became—"

"Arrogant and devious."

Cara frowned. "That's harsh."

"It's true."

"Maybe," Cara said. "You've been with her since she integrated. I'm sure you know her better than I."

"That's right. I've seen things." Delta looked away, though this time she did not seem to be consulting her ineye display. Apparently she was weighing her words carefully. "Did you know she rigged the drawing we did back at base camp? She hid the short straw in her palm. I saw her do it. I would have said something then, but I figured it best to play along: deal with the nests, then deal with her."

"You saw her palm the straw?"

"I did," Delta said. "And I don't think behavior like that has anything to do with healthy social order. Her differences are deeper than ours, more troubling. What do you think?"

"What do *I* think?" Cara slowed her pace, lowering her voice as she and Delta moved among the grazing snails. "I think you're begging the question. You want me to say that Epsilon's differences are ingrained, that perhaps something went wrong during her transmission from the orbiter's data files."

"All right," Delta said. "You think that's possible?"

Cara shrugged. "Maybe. It might be, but the odds are against it."

"Forget the odds," Delta said. "Consider the evidence. You see it and I see it." She stepped ahead of Cara, moving away from a pivoting snail.

Cara moved with her. "You need to talk to Alpha about this, not me."

"I plan to," Delta said. "But not yet. We have work to do. I'll talk to Alpha *after* we place the markers. Then, once the nests are gone, I'll head back to the village." Her expression turned stern in the moonlight. "I have no intention of retiring, Sister. I'll leave you on site and tell Alpha I need a private link, just her and me."

"That's going to make Epsilon suspicious."

"There's no preventing that. The important thing is that Alpha hears our concerns."

"They are your concerns, Sister."

"And yours, too. And those of Long-Eyes. You've just confirmed it. Epsilon's not fit to assume control of the field. And I'm thinking maybe Alpha's got the same suspicions. When I lay it out, she'll understand."

"And then what? You'll go back to the village? Confront Epsilon?"

"That's right, confront her and hope she listens to reason. Best case scenario, she retires voluntarily and leaves me in charge."

"And worst case?"

"That could be—" Delta flinched, averting her eyes, looking left. "Yes . . . yes, Alpha. I'm here." Delta stopped walking. "Say again, Alpha. Are you sure?"

Cara looked up, noticing a clear patch of sky overhead. The orbiter hung at zenith, a bright speck among the predawn stars.

"Show it to me, Alpha." Delta's gaze turned inward. "Show me what you're seeing."

Cara heard something moving behind them: a shifting of the forest canopy, the rhythmic thump of heavy footsteps.

"Delta," Cara said. "We should—"

Delta raised a hand, gesturing for Cara to wait a moment. "Show me infrared, Alpha. Zoom in."

The thumping grew louder, reverberating through the ground, alarming the snails.

Cara turned in place, shifting on her good leg, looking back at the forest behind them.

"All right," Delta said, glancing down, still focusing on the view from the orbiter. "I see it! I'll tell Gamma!" Then she turned, blinking to clear the ineye image.

But Cara didn't need to be told. She already saw it for herself. Fifty meters behind them, above the jagged backs of the snails, a cloud of flying slugs jetted from high branches on the edge of the field. A moment later, a head emerged from the trees, three meters above the ground, staring at Cara with cold, milky eyes. It was one of the fang-claws, a straggler returning from the central forest.

"What now?" Delta asked.

The fang-claw reared back, brushing the trees with its reptilian head. But unlike a reptile, it had no lower jaw. Instead, a pair of arms sprouted from the base of its skull, thrusting forward along the face so that the claws curved like fangs across the snout: fang-claws.

"What now?" Delta asked again, reaching for her rover. "Do we ride out of here?"

The snails were closing in.

"No," Cara said. "Hold your ground." She flexed her knees, hoping her bad leg wouldn't fail. "We have to climb."

"Climb?" Delta turned in place. "The shells?"

"Get on top, but watch out for those jags."

The glass-like projections flashed in the moonlight, poking from tufts of camouflaging grass and moss.

"Climb!" Cara pointed. "That one! Go!"

Delta responded, scuttling up along one of the shells as Cara turned to find herself standing a step away from a pair of pulsing eyestalks. She pivoted on her bad leg, dodging the sweeping arc of the snail's razor-sharp tongue. The snails were still feeding, scraping up anything that came in reach. Flesh or grass, it was all the same to them.

Cara sidestepped, away from the snail's head, toward the grass-covered spiral at the side of its shell. Then she climbed, pulling herself up, reaching the top as the phalanx closed. Shells collided. She felt the impact through her hands and knees: hollow thumps followed by the grind of meshing jags.

Delta knelt a few meters away, hands bleeding, eyes going wide as two more fang-claws emerged from the trees. They came up behind the first, then the three of them raced forward, approached like wingless birds: bodies cantilevered across pulsing hips, heads counterbalanced by ridged tails.

"Find the center," Cara said, looking along the shells. "There!" She pointed. "Go there!"

Delta stood and started running, bounding across the shells. The closest fang-claw tracked her, head swinging like a derrick, mandible arms spreading wide, exposing the toothless mouth at the top of its throat.

"Stay put," Cara shouted. "You're out of reach. Just stay—"

Something moved to Cara's left, a second fang-claw reaching for her, talons splayed. She leaped back, rolled, and dropped into a gap between shifting shells. The talons clicked above her, closed on empty air, and drew away.

Delta called to her, voice shrilling.

Cara didn't answer. It was all she could do to cling to the jags, fingers slipping as blood bubbled from her palms, cuts deepening as she pulled herself up to peer across the shells.

The fang-claws circled, focusing on Delta.

"Hold on!" Cara unslung her harness, removed her rover. "You brought me along to wrangle these animals." She crouched, ready to sprint along the shells. "Here goes." She took off, powered by panic and adrenalin.

The fang-claws pivoted, tracking her as she leaped toward the ground, landed on her good foot, and yanked her rover out of latch-down. Then she mounted the pedals, snapped on her headlamp, and took off so fast that she nearly overpowered the stabilizers. Gyros whined, correcting her balance as she hurtled along at a forty-degree angle, wheeling away in a tight arc that carried her back toward the nearest fang-claw.

The animal's eyes flashed in her headlamp, then went dark as she shot between its hips. Clawed feet shifted, turning, nearly clipping her before she sailed out beneath a swinging tail. A moment later she was racing away, crashing through grass that whipped around her knees. The forest lay dead ahead, a dark wall of trunks and leaves. Above her, a school of flying squids reeled in jetting arcs, flocking toward high branches to await the inevitable kill. . . .

Cara cut her speed and turned to see Delta stumbling atop the shells. But the snails kept shifting beneath her. She lost balance and fell—first to her knees, then to her hands, and then sideways to vanish between the shells.

"Delta!" Cara raced back through the high grass, watching the locked phalanx of shells until a hand emerged, bloody and groping, climbing up along the jags. A moment later Delta was back on top, crawling now, slicing open the legs of her unitard as she reached the outer edge of the herd. Then she fell, slammed the ground, and tried getting up. She almost made it, rising on one foot, but falling again when she tried putting her weight on a leg that now ended in a bloody stump. One of the snails had taken her foot.

The fang-claws raced toward her, converging so fast that Cara barely made it past them in time to grab Delta by her shoulder pack. She held on, riding full throttle, trying to drag Delta clear as the beasts closed in.

Something popped, the sensation reverberating through Cara's wrist like a snapping tendon, and suddenly she was moving faster, overtaxing the gyros and crashing into a sideways skid. She looked up, expecting to see one of the fang-claws reaching for her. But the animals weren't there. Nor was Delta. The pop she had felt was the pack's straps letting go. She had dragged the pack to safety. Delta had remained among the fang-claws.

Across the field, the animals fed, heads together, tails waving in the air until one turned away. A piece of field jacket fluttered like a tattered flag from its mandible claws. An instant later the beast was running, coming toward Cara as she got up, lashed Delta's battered pack across her shoulders, and accelerated out of the field and into the forest.

The ground angled downward. She took the descent at full speed, crashing onto a level stretch that might have been the remnants of an ancient road. Here, still riding full tilt, she unclipped the rover's headlamp and held it high, letting the fang-claw fix on it. She didn't look back. Didn't need to. She felt its head looming behind her, angling forward, closing for the kill. . . .

She threw the lamp and pulled her feet from the pedals. The light shot away, streaking like a meteor as her rover's gyros cut out. She crashed to the ground. The animal kept moving, following the streak as it curved into a stand of weeds. She waited until she heard the animal thrashing through the leaves, digging for the light. Then she got up, leaped onto the rover, and rode into darkness.

Dawn broke in the distance, appearing as an indigo haze beyond the trees. She rode toward it, bracing herself against the control shaft as the aching thunder of her wounded leg, bandaged arm, and lacerated hands intensified. She needed to rest. "Soon," she told herself, and kept moving.

The ground angled upward. She followed it, accelerating until a ledge came into view beyond a stand of ferns. And then, too late, she saw the pit.

She pulled back, trying to stop as her wheel skidded over the edge. Gyros whined, cutting out as she slipped into empty air. Nerves took over. She released the shaft, threw out her arms, and spun around to grab the edge of the hole. Her hands slapped hard against the rock. She stopped with a jolt, chest and knees slamming the pit wall. Something popped in her shoulder, but she held on, legs dangling as her rover landed below her with an echoing thump. She looked down. Saw nothing. Only darkness. The rover was lost. She couldn't get it back. What mattered now was climbing out of the pit and back onto level ground.

The pack that she had taken from Delta shifted on her back, dangling from where she had lashed it to her rover's harness. The weight put her off balance, and her hands kept sliding on the shale, leaving bloody streaks until her fingers grabbed a break in the rock. She pulled . . . a moment later she was crawling . . . a moment after that she was face down amid the ferns, panting, almost too weak to move.

She slipped both packs from her shoulders and tried sitting up. No good. The best she could do was prop herself on a throbbing elbow.

Something sharp dug into her hip. It was the hard-shell case, the one she had placed in her pocket before leaving the village.

"Get it out," she muttered. "Use it."

On the back of her neck, beneath the no-longer functioning transmitter in the base of her skull, a pressure-release cover protected a slot in her C-3 vertebrae. Her good arm twinged as she reached for the cover, pinched it, and pulled it free. It slipped from her fingers, falling down into the bed of ferns. She didn't bother looking for it. Odds were she'd never need it again.

Then she pulled the case from her pocket and broke its code-red seal. Inside lay a dorsal plug, dermal pad, and wristband monitor. She hesitated, wondering one last time if she could get through the next quarter hour without using them. Perhaps she should try standing, take a few steps, see if things loosened up. But her back flared as she moved. "I'm wasting time." She looked at the contents of the open case. "Just do it!"

She picked up the plug, careful not to touch its gold-plated end. Then, using one arm to steady the other, she inserted the plug into the slot.

Next she took the dermal pad, pinched it to activate the adhesions, and pressed it into place over the plug.

The monitor came last. She lifted it from the case, wrapped it around her wrist, and remotely activated the plug by pressing a sensor on the monitor's side. Relief came at once, washing over her so fast that she fell sideways, landing hard on her bad arm. She felt the impact, sensed the cold hardness of the ground, but not the pain of collision.

All pain was gone.

She was halfway there.

Among her pack's cache of chemical meds was an injector with a code-orange seal. She pulled it out, uncapped it with her teeth, and jammed the needle into her thigh.

Then she waited, giving the first wave of time-release catecholamines time to burn through her, holding herself steady as exhaustion yielded to a rush of power. She leaned forward, hugging her knees, holding herself in place as she considered the dangers of what she had just done to herself. Energized and freed from pain, she could now harm her body in ways that would have been impossible a few moments earlier. Muscles and bones could now be pushed to catastrophic failure. She would need to be careful, keep her eyes on the wrist-band monitor, and remember that her euphoric sense of power had nothing to do with her true condition.

She stood up and turned in place among the ferns. Her knee popped pain-lessly as she gave it her wait. Bones shifted in her lower back. Nevertheless, she was ready.

Delta's pack lay at her feet. She opened it, pulled out the markers, and jammed the first one into the rim. Her shoulder creaked. She kept moving, placing the other markers, realizing that she could now see her rover lying in the bottom of the pit. A few minutes ago it had landed in darkness. Now it lay in a pool of golden light.

She crouched on the edge. The glow looked like sunlight, but the sun was still too low on the horizon to be shining into the pit. The light had to be coming from another source—from a cave that opened on the seawall below the ledge.

And if that light came from a cave, and if she climbed into it, she would probably be able to glimpse the nests.

Her thoughts raced.

Somewhere, deep inside herself, in a dark space that still lurked beneath her catecholamine-induced high, she feared her newfound sense of reckless cour-age. A few moments ago she had nearly fallen into the pit. Now she believed she could climb to its floor and back again. And why not? There were plenty of handholds among the rocks. And even if the climb entailed risk, the fact remained that there were at least three fang-claws in the forest. If they arrived before the lander, she'd find it hard to wrangle them without a uniwheel.

She turned, pulled the rover's harness from the back of her field pack, and strapped it over her shoulders. Then she returned to the pit, gripped the edge, and started down.

A moment later she entered the glow. It was indeed sunlight, warming her as she turned to find herself peering through the oval entrance of a long, funneling cave. The sun was there, rising out of the ocean, shining through a break in the seawall.

She shielded her eyes and looked at the sides of the cave. The walls seemed to be covered with blisters, translucent sores that quivered in the light. She moved closer, her eyes adjusting. The blisters were gelatinous sacks, hammock-like nests full of twisting shadows. The young had hatched.

And all through the cave, moving like giant birds, the adults went about the business of tending the nests and feeding the young. Some worked at repairing the sacks, reinforcing them with saliva that they drew into threads with their mandible hands. These saliva weavers were smaller and grayer than the hunters, with fingers that ended in pads rather than claws.

And the hunters worked too, disgorging meat that they dangled above the nests, encouraging the young to leap and grab. . . .

The hatchlings were strong, agile, perhaps only days away from leaving the nests.

Cara grabbed the rover, latched it down, and lashed it to the harness. Then she climbed out, her legs and hips filling with stiffness by the time she reached the top. She checked the monitor on her wrist, flinched, and looked away. Something was wrong with her lower back. A pulled muscle? A cramp? The bar graphs didn't specify. They merely showed that the pain was nearly off the chart. Now that she had the rover, the best thing to do would be to sit and wait, rest her limbs until one of the fang-claws arrived . . . or until the lander came to blast her into retirement.

But she couldn't rest, not with the catecholamines coursing through her. She was buzzing. She needed to move.

Turning toward the sound of crashing waves, she walked along the ledge until sandstone gave way to misting air. Looking straight down, she realized the extent to which the ledge overhung the wall beneath. Even leaning out as far as she dared, she could not see the vertical face below.

To her left, however, the view was different. There the slope of a partially collapsed wall curved beyond a narrow channel of mist and waves. Weeds grew along the slope, angling down to a hanging forest of windswept trees about thirty meters below.

Nowhere on the adjacent mass of rock were there signs of caves like the ones that riddled the wall beneath her. Was it possible that the *X-eeÑa* nests were to be found only in one place on the entire island? Long-Eyes had assured her that it was so. But why? And where did the *X-eeÑa* come from? And where did they go when their spawning period ended? So many questions. So much to learn.

"I want to learn it," she said, speaking aloud, almost shouting.

The pounding surf shouted back, echoing up from the inlet between the seawalls.

"I'm still capable," she said, speaking louder. "I know this island. I know its people. They know me." Her mind raced. Perhaps she should walk some more, burn off the endorphins. But she stayed put, her thoughts flashing to things Delta had said about Epsilon. A moment later, she came to a conclusion that crashed louder than the waves: "I have to go back!"

Echoes thundered in the narrow inlet, rising between the seawalls, reverberating through her. She lifted her face to the orbiter, its amorphous hull appearing as a point of fading light in the brightening sky. "I need to go back!" She exaggerated the words, enunciating them in hopes that Alpha might read them on her lips. "Tell Epsilon. Tell her I'm not retiring. I need to talk to her, and you need to listen in."

There had been times, before the age of cybernetics, when people had carried handheld communicators. In those days, hardware, not people, had been expendable. When a device failed, it was discarded for a new one. Life was easier, simpler. Perhaps, if Alpha transmitted the parts, Cara could assemble an external communicator that would enable her to resume control of the mission—provided she had not by then damaged her body beyond repair.

She glanced at her wrist. Pain had spread to her good leg. What did that mean? Nerve damage? And if that were the case, could she even make it back to the village? "I'll take it slow," she said, resolving to head into the forest and keep watch from there. That way, when the lander arrived, she would be clear of the blast. It was a good plan, but again she hesitated, realizing deep inside herself—in a level beneath her energized confidence—that she was in no condition to make such a plan. "I need to stay the course," she muttered, not believing a word of it.

Behind her, a shrill whistle rose from the trees, the sound of squids jetting from high branches. Their bodies shimmered in the sunlight, banking overhead, gliding down to a hanging forest on the adjacent wall. They flew like arrows, piercing the treetops, vanishing beneath the leaves. She recognized the behavior. Danger was coming. She heard it, too. The predators that had killed Delta were returning home. And something else. Another sound from farther away. She cocked her head, listening.

"The lander!"

She unslung her rover, extended the riding shaft, and mounted the pedals as the first fang-claw emerged from the forest. Sun struck its face, reflecting in its eyes. She suspected it was the one that had chased her into the forest. But it looked different. Sunlight revealed sagging skin, scarred flanks, and broken claws that had not been visible in the darkness. And its eyes looked dead, milky with cataracts, thickened with age. She wondered if this old male had a nest to care for in the caves below. Or did it live alone, going through the motions of a life that no longer mattered?

She rolled toward it.

The animal stopped, watching her as its two companions appeared behind it.

She accelerated, jumped the pit, and kept moving—weaving between their legs as she headed for the forest.

They turned with her, crashing together, giving chase.

She would lead them into the trees and lose them there. They would survive the explosion, but that wasn't a problem. A few confirmed survivors would work to her benefit once she returned to the village. She was the *X-eeÑa* wrangler, the person who knew their moves better than anyone, the logical choice for assuming control of the mission.

The plan flashed through her. It felt like destiny. But then a fang-claw leaped in front of her, cutting her off. She changed course. Another came at her. She swerved again. Claws swung. She ducked and turned once more, and suddenly she was racing out along the southeastern side of the ledge—the side that rose above a hanging forest of gnarled trees.

The animals followed.

The lander roared closer, changing pitch, entering its dive.

She pogoed, throwing her weight upward and spinning through a 180-degree turn. Her wheel smoked as it hurtled her back the way she had come, but this time one of the fang-claws caught her, clipping her with a swinging leg and throwing her sideways—first across level rock, then out into empty air.

She flew over the inlet, arcing down to crash into cliff-side weeds on the adjacent wall. Then she slid, down to where the slope ended above the hanging forest. Leaves spread beneath her. She struck them hard, crashing through. Boughs snapped. Or was it bones? She rolled, grabbing at branches, finally holding on to one as the lander hit its mark. She felt the explosion more than heard it, a deep concussive shifting in her bones. She gripped the tree, looked toward the adjacent seawall, and waited for the landslide. . . .

Nothing happened.

Something had gone wrong.

She scuttled back along the branch, then down the trunk to level ground. In that instant, as she collapsed among the cliff-side trees, the lander finally exploded.

The wall shivered. Dust flew from the caves, followed by swarming animals who raced out along the vertical rock. She watched them, amazed by their movements—as agile on the vertical wall as they were on level ground. And then, with a roar loud enough to drive her breath from her lungs, the wall calved, belched dust, and folded into the sea. And when the air stopped ringing, when the haze of airborne grit gave way to cleansing mist, she found herself looking down toward the remnants of the fallen wall. Dark shapes lay amid the rubble. On one of the rocks, a hatchling stood on spindly legs, stretching mandible arms toward empty sky.

Cara's legs finally failed as she neared the village. Her back cracked a final time, and she went down, falling onto a wedge of sloping ground.

Then she crawled.

The village came into view, dark beneath heavy clouds. Thunder roared, reverberating as a figure emerged from the gate. It waddled like a goose in a knee-length tunic.

It was Long-Eyes.

He was alone.

She reached for him. "*The tall one?*" she asked, garbling the words. "*I need to see her.*"

He cocked his head. "*The other?*" he said. "*You are asking about the one you left behind?*"

She raised her fist.

"*In the great hall,*" he said. "*I will bring you to her.*" He gripped her arm, swung it around his shoulders, and started walking.

"*The X-eeÑa,*" she said. "*They're gone . . . maybe not all of them . . . but enough. You'll be safe now.*"

"*We know,*" he said, holding her tighter as they slipped through the gate, past rows of silent huts, and toward the sound of chanting voices.

"*Everyone is in the great hall,*" Long-Eyes said. "*We received the signal before dawn, when you were meeting with your sisters.*" He swung his long neck around, looking deep into her eyes. "*The signal came from X-ah.*"

He pronounced the last word as a glottal click followed by a breathy sigh. A simple enough word, but one that Cara had not yet been able to translate. It seemed to refer to some kind of higher power, probably a deity, possibly a kind of collective consciousness.

They walked on, following a muddy trail until the great hall appeared before them, smoke rising from roof vents, voices chanting within. She tried making out the words, and realized she was hearing a single word being chanted over and over—the same word that Long-Eyes had just spoken: *X-ah!*

Higher power . . . deity . . . collective consciousness?

The entrance to the great hall lay through a passage that curved back on itself before opening into a wide fire-lit room. The air reeked of burning wood, boiled meat, and steeping tea. The latter produced a strong narcotic effect that would serve her well when her dorsal plug stopped functioning. For now, however, she resolved to have none of it. She would need her wits when she confronted Epsilon.

The crowd parted as Long-Eyes led her through the center of the hall, toward a raised dais that held a wooden chair, its height and depth contoured to accommodate the human form. Colored stones adorned its sides. Atop its backrest, a bright jewel flashed in the firelight.

Was it Epsilon's chair? Her throne? Cara shivered. "What has she done?" She spoke the question in her own language, muttering it aloud as if addressing Alpha. And then she blacked out.

A three-fingered hand gripped the back of her head, lifting her up, pressing her lips to a steaming bowl.

"*No!*" Cara pulled back. "*No tea!*" She opened her eyes to see Long-Eyes staring at her.

"*It is not tea.*" He pushed the bowl toward her, letting her smell the brothy steam. "*You're weak,*" he said. "*You need this. You—*"

She didn't need to be told again. Instinct took over. She was famished. She drank, gripping the bowl.

"*You haven't eaten since last night, and then hardly anything at all. You need your strength.*"

She finished and eased back, realizing that a figure now sat in the jeweled chair. Cara glimpsed an embroidered shoulder, the edge of a tall form in an ornate robe.

"*I need to talk to her,*" Cara said. "*Take me to her . . . now . . . please. Take me to her!*"

Long-Eyes arched his neck, a sign of confusion. *"Take you? What do you mean?"*

"You said you would take me to her."

"No." He gripped her hands, pulling her to her feet. *"I never said that."* He stepped aside, giving her a clear view of the gleaming chair and the robe she had glimpsed earlier. But Epsilon was not wearing the robe. No one was. Its broad shoulders draped the back of the chair. Its sides hung open, waiting.

It dawned on her then. She grabbed Long-Eyes' arm, holding on. *"What did you say?"* She squeezed his hand. *"In the field, what did you tell me? Say it slowly."*

He did, and this time she heard it—the glottal declension that trumped word order.

Her gut knotted, heaving weakly, producing only a dry cough as two strong-armed males pulled her to her feet.

"I brought her to you," Long-Eyes said. *"And now she is being brought to everyone."*

Looking around the great hall, Cara saw bowls being passed hand to hand.

"It is a wondrous morning." Long-Eyes said. *"You die but live. We consume you, and yet you remain. You consume yourself . . . and become stronger."*

Cara glanced at the bowl in her hand.

Long-Eyes stepped back, raising his voice. *"The great champion. The immortal champion!"* He held the bowl higher. *"X-aha ö X-ooh ee-ö X-ah!"*

The final exclamation went through her like a thunderbolt.

"X-aha ö X-ooh ee-ö X-ah!"

The first word wasn't a native word. It was her name rendered in native phonemes: *X-aha*. In sound and tone, it was nearly identical to the final word in Long-Eye's statement, the elusive *X-ah*.

The crowd chanted it with him, louder, stirring the smoky air as they walked Cara toward the robe-draped throne.

"Cara!" they chanted. *"Cara the champion from* X-ah!"

"You can't do this!" She dug in her heels, trying to stop them from leading her onto the dais. *"My commander won't let this happen."* There was no native word for *commander*, so she spoke it in her own language, the strange consonants reverberating like a feral roar.

How could she explain to these people what would happen now? They stood no chance of grasping it. And yet it was real, as real as the force that had blasted the *X-eeÑa* into the sea.

Alpha would now have no recourse but to transmit a new Cara—Cara

Theta, eighth integration of Cara Prime. But unlike the others, Theta would never set foot in the village. She would remain at base camp, studying from the safety of that sheer-walled mountain.

"*Do you realize what you've done?*" Cara roared. "*You've destroyed a great opportunity.*"

"*No,*" Long-Eyes said, leaning close as she mounted the dais. He peered into her eyes, gazing deep as if reading her thoughts. "*No more Caras will come. You are the last.*" He backed away, gesturing toward the glowing jewel atop the throne.

She blinked at it, noting how it caught the firelight, reflecting the flames on its mirrored surface.

"*Our X-ah told us where to find it,*" he said. "*We climbed the steep mountain after your sisters flew away. We took it and brought it here. For you. For all of us.*" He lifted the robe from the chair. "*Please trust us, Cara. Believe in us. It is better that way.*"

She felt herself moving again, yielding to the hands that gripped her arms. Then they released her. She teetered forward, catching herself on the arm rests and staring at the shining object that crowned the chair. It was the optical guide from the base camp's integration chamber—the piece of hardware that made it possible for Alpha to transmit supplies and personnel to the planet's surface.

"*It is the best way,*" Long-Eyes said. "*The best way to make sure you are our final champion.*"

"*But I'm crippled.*"

"*We will heal you.*"

"*No! You don't understand! We need someone here who can communicate with—*" Once again, she found herself groping for words that did not exist in their language. "*We need someone here who can communicate with my X-ah.*" She pointed upward. "*Do you understand? I need—*"

"*That isn't necessary,*" Long-Eyes said. "*Now that your voice is dead to your X-ah, we will teach you to communicate with ours. You will see. You are blinded now, cut off from the truth—but that is the way to realize who you are . . . why you are here . . . what you must do.*"

"What I must do?" She spoke the words in her own language, considering them as she gripped the throne. What she needed to do was heal, gather her strength, and then return to base camp. She would take the optical marker from the back of the throne and reattach it to the integration chamber. Then her replacement would come. And then, at last, she would retire.

She leaned forward, staring at her image reflected in the marker's right-angled mirrors. Multiple reflections stared back, gazing with the eyes of many Caras—Caras beyond number. But she could not take the marker now. She needed to heal before the dorsal plug's power supply ran dry and she found herself paralyzed with pain.

Something hissed along her back, pressing down, warming her. It was the robe. Long-Eyes hooked it into place as she collapsed into the chair. And now the storytellers launched into a synchronized song, one that sounded rehearsed even though it detailed the destruction of the nests on the eastern shore.

She looked upward, toward the smoky ceiling and the vent that stood open to a gathering storm. She couldn't see the orbiter, but it was up there.

"I can fix this!" She mouthed the words, wishing Alpha could see her through the skylight, through the smoke and gathering clouds. "I can fix this. Trust me." And so she prayed in silence to her other self in the sky, mouthing the promise as the song of her exploits rose around her.

DREAMS

WAYWARD WILDER

Written for The Spendour Falls, *an anthology based on* White Wolf's
Changeling: The Dreaming *game, "Wayward Wilder" is a bit of YA urban
fantasy that takes its inspiration from a poem by William Butler Yeats.*

It's coming up the stairs," Granny Fae said. "Do you hear it?"

Autumn turned toward the apartment's closed door. Something massive was
climbing the stairs, growling like a revving engine as it approached the landing. "I hear it," Autumn said. "But it never made that sound before."

"This time's different," Granny Fae said. "This time it wants a fight."

Autumn pulled her bare feet onto the sagging couch. She hugged her knees
and sat forward, trying not to tremble as she glanced toward the light that
seeped beneath the door.

"I could tell you it'll be all right," Granny Fae said. "But it's not for me to
say. This is your challenge. How it turns out is up to you."

Autumn wished Granny Fae would come closer, join her on the couch. For
the past three hours, the crazy old woman with the heart-shaped face and
hair like braided tinsel had become the friend and protector that the sixteen-
year-old runaway had always longed for. "Call me Fae," the woman had said
when she found Autumn in the alley below her window. "It's not my name,
but it'll do." Adding *Granny* to the name was Autumn's idea. Autumn had
always wanted a grandmother.

The rumbling on the stairs drew nearer. Then, suddenly, it vanished—overpowered by a crashing sound that rose from the basement. Autumn flinched.

"The band," Granny Fae said. "Only the band."

Of course, Autumn knew that. She recognized the thundering drums, grinding guitars, screaming voices. It was only the suddenness of the music that had startled her.

"Redcaps," Autumn said.

"Excuse me?"

"That's what they call themselves, The Redcaps."

"And I suppose they call that noise music."

"I don't know. I suppose." Autumn had never talked to the boys. But she had seen them: a trio of milk-white kids with pierced faces and slashed jeans. It had been their playing that had first drawn her to Granny Fae's tenement of crumbling brick and sooty glass. Their singing called to her, spoke to her:

Drifting aimless in the sea,
A battered child who seems to be
Drifting with the I and We—
The flotsam of identity.

Those words had drawn Autumn to a sooty basement window, and there, crouching on the sidewalk, she had peered through underground shadows to see the throbbing skin of a bass drum, across which had been painted:

The Redcaps

The name had seemed familiar, though she was certain she had never encountered it before. Indeed, she seemed to know the name in the same strange way that she sometimes knew other things: spontaneously, effortlessly, inexplicably.

"Pay attention!" Granny Fae said. "This is no time for daydreams."

"Sorry." Autumn shook her head, returning to the moment. "Sometimes I tune out when I'm scared." She wiped her nose. "The guidance counselor back home, she said I was A.D.D.—attention deficit dis-something."

"It's not that," Granny Fae said. "It's not a *deficit*. It's an *advantage*. Your mind's a gem, honey—an uncut diamond."

A shadow cut the light beneath the door.

"You see that?" Granny Fae asked.

"Yes."

"The monster's shadow." Granny Fae's eyes narrowed. "It's in the hall now."

Although the rock music still thundered from the basement, Autumn again sensed the rumble of the beast. The growling sound drew nearer, and with it came the pained creak of floorboards shifting beneath incredible weight. And then, with an abruptness that caused Autumn to catch her breath, the monster's shadow completely obliterated the narrow patch of light.

Instantly, the band stopped playing.

Silence.

Granny Fae rose from the table where Autumn had been sitting before moving to the couch. The table still bore the remains of a simple supper—an empty milk carton and a plate of stew that Autumn had wiped clean with a piece of crusty bread—a fine meal for a wandering waif who had spent the night on a train and the day wandering the cold streets of New York.

Granny Fae stepped toward the couch. Her sandaled feet peeking beneath the waves of her floor-length dress. Autumn knew about that dress, how in the 60s such things had been called granny dresses, how they had come into vogue along with wire-rim glasses and hairbuns, all of which had made the twenty-somethings of the 60s look like the sixty-somethings of the 20s. Granny Fae had told Autumn all about those days. It amused Autumn to think that, but for a flurry of wrinkles and a bloom of gray, Granny Fae had probably changed little in the last three decades.

Couch springs groaned as Granny Fae sat beside Autumn.

"The band," Autumn said. "Why'd they stop playing? Did that thing—"

"No," Granny Fae said. "That thing can't hurt them. Now if they were real redcaps, and not just a band of boys with a fancy name, maybe then that thing in the hall could do them some harm. But since they're only human, that thing out there could walk right through them and they wouldn't feel more than a tingle on their skin."

"Why?"

"The beast isn't part of their world."

"But it's part of mine."

"Yes."

"Am I a redcap?"

"No. Redcaps are hideous things. You're hardly hideous."

"What am I?"

"I can't tell you that."

"Why?"

"You have to figure it out on your own."

From the next room came the soft *thwack! thwack!* of paint striking a wall-size canvas. Mad Hieronymo, Granny Fae's paint-spattered roommate, was flinging paint in a Jackson Pollock frenzy to create art out of chaos. Autumn had met Mad Hieronymo only briefly when entering the apartment. He was a skinny man, a stick figure with a cotton-ball mane of paint-flecked beard and hair. He had been walking toward his studio when Granny Fae first led Autumn into the apartment. "Is that her?" Mad Hieronymo asked, nodding his bushy face at Autumn. Granny Fae didn't answer. She waved him on and said, "Go on. Mind your business. Paint something." She didn't have to tell him twice. He slipped into his studio without another word.

Now Autumn glanced toward the *thwack! thwack!* that echoed beyond the studio's darkened doorway. (According to Granny Fae, the man always painted in the dark.)

"What about Mad Hieronymo?" Autumn asked. "Is he in danger?"

"No," Granny Fae said. "He's like the band. The chimera can't touch Hieronymo, and Hieronymo can't help us if the chimera gives us trouble."

A ripple passed through the solid door, rising from the wood grain to slide down along the panels. It was a claw—a barbed talon that passed through the door without leaving so much as a mark in the wood.

"The door doesn't matter," Granny Fae said. "Even the stone walls of this place are like so much air to the chimera."

"You mean it can walk right in here?"

"If it wants to."

"Then why doesn't it?"

"It doesn't *want* to," Granny Fae said. "Not yet. It's playing with you."

"Why?"

A thundering guitar split the air. Drums exploded. Power chords launched another song from the basement:

She can see with her ears
And make lost things appear,
But she can't hide from the dream
That she's dreaming.

As was the case with many of the songs that the Redcaps had been singing since Autumn had arrived, the song seemed to be about her.

She can see with her ears . . .

Maybe the lyrics were intended to mean nothing. Maybe they were only meant to sound arty and spacey. Autumn had no idea what had gone through the writer's mind when he wrote those lyrics. What she did know, however, was that since the early days of her childhood, when the chrysalis of her self-awareness had crawled from the rocks of her being and began hardening in the glare of other people's eyes, she had known that she was different from other children. She remembered how her mother's frowns of confusion used to deepen to scowls of disapproval whenever Autumn said things like "That dog has a yellow bark" and "The phone is greening!" By the ripe age of six, she learned not to talk about the colors that she heard. By the age of eight, she managed to suppress her audio perception of colors so well that now—eight years later—she seldom heard anything but sounds.

. . . make lost things appear . . .

There were, however, a few wondrous skills that she had not suppressed. She was, for example, adept at finding things. A classmate would lose a pencil, and Autumn would spin on the balls of her feet, bend over, lift a flat rock from a patch of ground, and there (pressed into the earth among the worms and ants) would be the lost pencil. Or a neighbor might stand in his yard, calling the name of a lost dog, and Autumn would walk into the evergreen thicket behind her home, clap her hands, and step back as the lost dog leaped into her arms. She did not know how things like spinning on her feet and clapping her hands worked, she only knew that they did not work if she thought too much about them. The gestures had to be spontaneous. Equally important, the gestures needed to look as if they were nothing more than the twitches and ticks of a fidgety child. She dared not let anyone suspect what she herself believed—that the gestures were a form of magic.

. . . she can't hide from the dream
That she's dreaming.

But perhaps the strangest thing—the most secret thing that she dared not share with anyone—was the feeling that she was being watched. She would be alone in her room, and she would sense a presence under the bed or in the closet or just outside the curtains of her second-story bedroom. Or she would be in the woods behind her house, and she would notice a shifting of the leaves that didn't jibe with the swaying of the trees. But as skilled as she was at finding things, she could never locate the thing that seemed to be forever on the edge of her perception. She knew it was there, though. Its general presence was as certain as its precise location was elusive. And the thing followed her everywhere. Even when she cashed in a year's worth of hoarded lunch money for a ticket on the late-night train to New York City, the presence followed her.

And now, in the darkness of Granny Fae's Greenwich Village apartment, that thing—the stalker that Granny Fae called the chimera—was preparing to reveal itself.

"Autumn!" Granny Fae touched Autumn's shoulder. "Get ready, honey!"

The voice pulled Autumn out of her daze. It was a bad habit, this falling into herself whenever the world became too troublesome to face. For years she had been using the technique to tune out her parents, teachers, guidance counselors, and peers. Now, shaking her head as Granny Fae's voice pulled her back, Autumn found herself staring again at the glow beneath the apartment door.

A strange silence filled the room as the band in the basement slipped back into an interval of silence. From the studio in the next room came the soft whisper of a spray bottle—Mad Hieronymo applying spritzes of paint in the dark. Across the room, a new ripple passed through the door. A crumpled mass rose from the wood grain; this time it rose like the knobby hump of a surfacing whale . . . vanished back into the wood . . . surfaced . . . vanished.

"It's taunting you," Granny Fae said. "It wants to see if you'll run again."

"Again?"

"Like you ran when it came to you in the woods behind your home."

"I didn't run from it then," Autumn said. "I told you what happened." She had motor-mouthed the story between mouthfuls of supper. "I told you—I didn't run from it!"

"No?"

"No," Autumn said. She stared at the surface of the door. Nothing moved. "I ran away from home, is all. I couldn't stand being bored and not fitting in. My dad wanted me to start trade school, and my mom wanted me to learn about computers. My teachers wanted me to go for more tests so they could figure out how to deal with me. My counselor wanted me to consider beautician training. And the other kids . . . all they ever cared about were VCRs and TVs and IBMs and BMWs and the NFL and all kinds of . . . of . . . "

"Banality," Granny Fae said.

"What?"

"The banality of human existence—it was getting to you. You were hemmed in by banality, so you ran."

"Yeah," Autumn said. "The banality was getting to me." She knew the word. She had never heard it before, never used it, but it was part of her. She felt a chill begin in her neck and spread across her shoulders and head. It was the same chill that always touched her when knowledge surfaced from deep in her mind.

"I didn't run from the chimera," Autumn said. "I ran from banality."

"Same thing."

"How can they be the same thing?"

"Think about it," Granny Fae said. "The answer's inside you."

Autumn tried running through her thoughts as she stared at the door. She thought about that pivotal moment, less than thirty hours earlier, when she had walked away from home for the last time.

Her parents had been inside the house arguing. One of them (she didn't know which one; she could never tell them apart when they started yelling) was saying, "I told her to vacuum her room, and look at this mess. She'll never amount to anything. She's worthless. What's she going to do when she has to fend for herself?"

And as the voices rose inside the house, Autumn sat in the evergreen thicket at the end of the driveway and closed herself into a ball. "I'm invisible," she thought, clicking her tongue. "My clicking makes me the color of air. I can stay here all night and they'll never find me."

But something had already found her. She felt its gaze on the back of her head. She felt it leaning toward her. And as it watched her, her parents yelled louder. And somewhere in another home a blaring TV rattled with canned laughter. And on the street a car engine revved and fell back in a show of adolescent machismo. And somewhere else, a boombox roared with sampled music—old R&B compositions patched together by composers who had forgotten how to compose. That's when she knew she had to run away.

She took her money from its hiding place between the roots of a dying pine tree, and she walked to the train station where steel tracks waited to carry her from the shoals of Levittown to the mythical island of Manhattan. She'd heard there was a village there—a place where artists painted and poets wrote and musicians played, a place where people who didn't fit in fit in. With no more than a hunch that these things were true, Autumn set off in search of the Elysian Fields of lower Manhattan.

A day later—cold, hungry, and soaked with rain—Autumn crouched by a basement window and listened to the melodic throbbings of a band named The

Redcaps. It was there that Granny Fae found her. And there was a funny thing about the way Granny Fae smiled as she helped Autumn through the door of her apartment; it was almost as if the old woman's smile were saying, "What took you so long? I've been waiting!"

That had been two hours ago . . . a lifetime ago. So much had changed since darkness had fallen.

"Maybe," Autumn said, "maybe I wasn't running away *from* anything." She turned and looked at the gentle silhouette that Granny Fae's face made against the glow of the rain-dappled window. "Maybe I was running *to* you. Maybe part of me knew I would find you if I ran."

"But *I* found *you*."

"But not before I found your home."

A new sound rose from the basement. The soft hum of a synthesizer mingled with the echoing twang of a tremolo guitar. The singer whispered softly beneath the drone. The lyrics weren't original. Autumn remembered them from school. She had read them in an English textbook, and she had liked them before her teacher spent a day and a half talking about them:

Come away, O human child!
To the waters and the wild
With a faerie, hand in hand,
For the world's more full of weeping
than you can understand.

"I know those words," Autumn said. "They're by a poet—William Butler Yeats. They're about a baby being stolen by faeries . . . stolen so that a faerie baby can take its place in the human world."

"Yes," Granny Fae said. "But listen. The singer changes the words."
Autumn listened:

Now come away, O faerie girl!
To the trappings of the world
With a husband, hand in hand,
For the glens that you are leaving
you will never see again.

"There's a piece of you in that song," Granny Fae said. "A piece of you . . . and a piece of me."

"What do you mean?" Autumn said. "The singer doesn't know me."

"No," Granny Fae said. "But I do. And I'm giving him the words."

"How?"

"The same way I give him the words to all his songs. The same way I made him call his band The Redcaps."

"How?"

"Cantrips," Granny Fae said.

Autumn shivered. She rubbed the slow tingle in the back of her neck and said, "What are cantrips?"

"Don't make me explain things you already know, Autumn. Quit asking questions. Start finding—" Granny Fae's voice caught in her throat. Her eyes widened. "It's here," she said. "It's in the room!" She spun around to look toward the door.

Autumn turned with her.

And suddenly there it was, standing inside the apartment, watching them with a monstrous, rotating eye.

"Go!" Granny Fae threw her hand against Autumn's back, shoving her from the couch.

At first Autumn thought Granny Fae wanted her to hide, but when she tried running toward Hieronymo's studio, Granny Fae grabbed her arm. "No, Autumn! Face the chimera. You have to fight it!"

Autumn froze. She looked at the monstrosity that stood just inside the door. Was Granny Fae serious? The thing unfolded its massive arms in a gesture that seemed to say, "Look at me! Fear me!"

And Autumn, both feet frozen to the floor, her nape hairs turning to ice, looked at the chimera. The thing made no sense. It couldn't possibly exist. It was a collection of junk, an impossible beast whose head was a tangle of stripped wires, aluminum foil, and computer ribbons. A square window of glass lay imbedded in its forehead. Beneath the forehead, a zoom lens leered at Autumn with a cyclops-like stare. Beneath the lens, a vacuum-cleaner hose dangled like an expandable trunk. As she stared at the thing, the hose stretched toward her. Something clicked inside the creature's head—a soft, muted click, like the closing of a tiny switch—and with the sound, the hose started hissing, sucking the room's air with a long, sustained sniff.

Autumn backed away as the hose came toward her.

"No!" Granny Fae yelled. "Don't back away! You have to fight it!"

Fight it? The words thundered in Autumn's head. Fight it how? The hose-nose kept coming. Autumn glanced at Granny Fae who had not moved from the couch. "What do I do?" She backed away again, but the hose-nose kept coming. She could feel the whoosh of its one-way breath. The thing was smelling her, drawing her scent into its disgusting head.

"Fight it!" Granny Fae said.

Autumn raised her hand and slapped the side of the hose-nose. Instantly the sucking ceased. The hose-nose curled back, coiling in on itself like an elephant's trunk. For a moment the thing just stood there, staring at her with its camcorder eye. Autumn's hand throbbed. Her nostrils stung with the scent of something sharp and hot—the thick smell of smoking grease and scorched skin. She looked at her hand. Blisters bubbled on her fingers. The hand looked as if it had smacked a red-hot iron. She looked at Granny Fae. "What happened?" She winced as she tried bending the fingers.

"You tell me," Granny Fae said.

"But I don't know!" Autumn's voice cracked.

The chimera made a rustling sound.

Autumn looked back to find the thing leaning toward her. Its body was a heap of crumpled newspapers, aptitude tests, broken curling irons, old spray bottles, and dead batteries scabbed over with crusty acid. In its pelvis, a four-cylinder engine kicked on and started to throb; the engine's spinning fan rattled the crumpled papers of its groin, and a stream of smoky exhaust blew from a rusty pipe near the base of its spine. Autumn backed away as the engine revved. The chimera raised a shock-absorber leg and stepped toward her.

"What do I do?" she shrieked.

Granny Fae sat on the couch, watching, saying nothing.

A half-dozen backward steps later, Autumn felt her shoulders flatten against the unyielding plaster of the apartment wall. She tried darting sideways, but the chimera spread its arms. Garbage-bag tendons creaked and groaned beneath its paper flesh. Razor-blade and fish-hook claws clicked as the beast reached for her. Autumn froze. She looked up at the beast's face and saw its camcorder eye rotating, zooming outward as the glass square in its forehead crackled and hissed with phosphorescent snow. The glass was a picture tube, a tiny monitor in which snow coalesced into a face. Autumn recognized the face. It was her own. Looking up, she saw herself as the beast saw her—a frightened waif with limp brown hair and frightened eyes. And it was then that the sudden chills unfurled like icy wings across her shoulders, neck, and head. A word flashed in her mind—cantrip! Suddenly she knew what it meant. Magic! In an instant, she knew what to do. She raised her hand, looked at her charred fingers, blew on them and whispered "Enog nrub!" The scorched flesh vanished. She wiggled the fingers, brought them together, cupped them, and then clapped them hard against the cupped palm of her other hand. The air ignited. A shaft of light rose from her palms. The light hardened and dimmed, becoming a three-foot blade as the air between her hands gelled into a hilt of bronze and braided leather.

Across the room, Granny Fae let out a piercing squeal, a sound midway between a laugh and a gasp. With the corner of her eye, Autumn saw the woman leap to her feet and begin bouncing on the couch. "Go for it!" Granny Fae shook her arms in a two-fisted swing. "Go for it, Autumn!"

Autumn went for it. Her hands seemed to be on autopilot, rising unbidden over her shoulder and cocking at the elbows while the engine in the beast's belly revved and its pneumatic legs took a step back. Aiming for the head, Autumn swung. The sword's weight moved with the swing, flowing up from the grip and out along the blade, pulling Autumn forward as the shaft slammed the chimera's forehead. The TV screen imploded with a shattering thud. Autumn's video image collapsed in a shower of sparks as the blade cleaved the screen and uprooted the zoom-lens eye. Autumn stumbled forward as the blade ripped through the mass of papers and plastic and tape and debris. And then, as the sword struck the engine in the belly of the beast, the chimera exploded.

"Yes!" Granny Fae did a jubilant tarantella on the heaving couch. "Sweet!"

But Autumn kept falling, stumbling into the mass of flaming garbage. She braced herself for the sting of the fire, but suddenly the room was dark and her hands were empty. The chimera vanished with the sword. Autumn's face slammed the floor with a dull red thump! She rolled onto her back. Granny Fae, still standing on the couch, hovered over her. Beyond the old woman, standing in the shadow of a darkened doorway, a mad Q-tip looked out at them with a perplexed scowl. "What're you two doing?" Mad Hieronymo asked.

Autumn sat up. A fine powder covered the floor. Was it common dust or the ashes of the incinerated chimera? She looked down at her hands. Her palms bore the imprint of braided leather. "Jeez!" she gasped. She looked at Granny Fae, hoping for answers.

Granny Fae turned the other way, toward Mad Hieronymo. "Why don't you go finish your painting?"

"Cause I'm done," he said.

"Yeah?" Granny Fae said. "Well, is it any good?"

"Dunno," Mad Hieronymo said. "Haven't looked at it yet."

"Well go turn on the lights!" Granny Fae said. "We'll be right in."

Mad Hieronymo slipped back into his dark studio.

Granny Fae climbed down from the couch. "Come on." She took Autumn's hand. "Let's see what the ol' man painted today."

Autumn's face throbbed from slamming the floor. Her cheek tingled. She felt a prickly rash of splinters in her chin. But the pain was secondary to the strange awareness that stirred between her beating temples. It was as if for sixteen years her real self had slept like a tuber . . . and now the tuber was sprouting, unfurling petals of identity and understanding. "I'm a change-ling!" She looked at Granny Fae. "And so are you." She looked at the dust on the floor. "And the chimera . . . it came from my mind, didn't it?"

"Yes," Granny Fae said. "It was all the things that kept you from seeing the truth."

"And those things are gone now?"

A frown pinched Granny Fae's lips. "No. They're still with you, but you're starting to see beyond them. Now come on, Mad Hieronymo doesn't like waiting. We have to keep him happy. No Glamour, no cantrips. Understand?"

Autumn shivered as a rash of chills raced along her back. "Yes," she said. Glamour was a byproduct of creative energy. Glamour was the power that fueled faerie magic. "I understand," she said as she recalled yet another piece of her forgotten self.

Pale light glowed beyond the studio door. Through the doorway, Autumn saw a paint-spattered drop cloth and a dozen cans of acrylic paint. Mad Hieronymo and his giant canvas were out of sight, somewhere beyond the frame of the door.

"But there's something I don't know," Autumn said, holding back as Granny Fae tried guiding her to the studio. "My family back in Levittown, the people that I thought were my mother and father, if I took the place of their child when I left Arcadia, what happened to their real baby?"

Granny Fae frowned, her eyes peering deep into Autumn's. "What makes you think you came from Arcadia?"

"Isn't that where changelings come from?"

"Some," Granny Fae said. "Not all." She took hold of Autumn's arm. "You'll understand everything soon. For now you have to be patient with yourself. If you remembered everything at once it would knock you out. Give the memories time to surface."

They entered the studio, and there the paint-spattered artist stood staring at a monstrous canvas. Autumn's breath caught in her throat. She had expected the painting to be an abstract. But here, on the massive wall of canvas, she saw a beautiful landscape of pink-blossomed trees and yellow flowers. In the distance, green hills supported the oval redness of a rising sun.

In the foreground, beside a marble fountain, sat a girl with a narrow face and heather-brown hair. Autumn shivered, folding her arms as she shook against the chill of remembrance. "It's me," she whispered.

"No," Granny Fae said.

The chills deepened. Realization bloomed. The painted face belonged to the woman that Autumn had left behind in Levittown. "It's my mother before she left Arcadia."

Mad Hieronymo turned. "What're you two whispering about?"

"Your painting," Granny Fae said. "We like it."

"Yeah?" Mad Hieronymo tugged his beard. "It's okay." He kicked off his paint-spattered shoes and walked to the studio door. "I'm going to cook some oatmeal, make some tea. Want some?"

"No," Granny Fae said. "We ate."

Mad Hieronymo looked at Autumn as he shuffled past. "Your name's Autumn, right?"

"Yes."

"Glad you finally made it," he said. "The ol' lady's been talking about you for years. What took you so long?"

"I don't know," Autumn said. "Guess I got lost."

Mad Hieronymo nodded and padded through the door.

"Does he know you're a changeling?" Autumn asked.

"No," Granny Fae said. "He just thinks I'm eccentric. Believe me, it's better that way."

Together they turned back to the painting.

"You made this painting happen, didn't you?" Autumn said. "Just like you made The Redcaps sing those songs."

"Yes. I pulled out all the stops getting you to come here; I didn't want you to leave without discovering the truth."

Again, Autumn looked at the woman in the painting.

"Your mother and I left Arcadia together," Granny Fae said. "But after we arrived in this world she became enamored with the trappings of banality. She ran off with a man who sold annuities, and by the time you were born she had forgotten her changeling ways. Still, her fae nature lived on, lying dormant in the mind of her child, waiting to be rediscovered."

Autumn looked at the old woman's narrow face and wide eyes. "So you really are my Granny Fae?"

"Yes." She put her arms around Autumn. "Welcome home, my wayward wilder."

GWYTHURN THE SLAYER

For most of the 1980s and 90s, I made my home in Pittsburgh's South Hills, a part of the city that was also home to writers William Tenn, Bob Leman, and John DeChancie.

In the mid 90s, riding the success of a series of humorous fantasy novels centering on a place called Castle Perilous, John began editing an all-new anthology of castle stories for DAW Books. The book, entitled Castle Fantastic, *was released in 1996, and included the following story.*

The beast's tower stood on the horizon, cutting like a blackened tusk into the dusk-red lip of the sky. Gwythurn sat on the shivering back of her bone-white mare. Mist rose from the horse's nostrils as a chill wind hissed through autumn-thinned pines. Gwythurn shifted on the creaking saddle, tightened her grip on the reins, and gave a fast kick with her booted heels. Horse and rider thundered forward, out of the forest, onto the wasteland of rock and weeds, and toward the horizon where the setting sun bled behind the solitary tower.

Wind whistled as she rode, becoming a voice, calling her name.

"Gwyn!"

Gwythurn reined hard. Hooves clattered to a stop. The horse turned, stirring a cloud of dust as Gwythurn scanned the wasteland. She saw no one. But the voice was there, riding the wind like a demon's whisper.

"Slow down," the voice said.

Gwythurn reached for her sword. Bronze rasped from the scabbard as the blade slid free. She couldn't see the demon, but at least she could show it she was willing to fight.

And then the wind whispered another name.

"Virg."

She gripped the reins.

The wind brushed her face, and with that touch she sensed another reality. For a moment, though she remained in the saddle, she felt as though she were lying on cushions. The wind touched her again. This time taking her hand, squeezing it.

"You're talking too fast, Gwyn. Who is Virg?"

The sky crackled, lightning flashed, and then horse, tower, and blood-red sky vanished into plaster patterns in an off-white ceiling.

Gwyn sat up. Cushions creaked beneath her. She leaned forward, looking into the tired gray eyes of Carol Langland.

"You all right?" Carol asked.

Gwyn lay back down, placed a hand across her face, and covered her eyes. "Another one," she said. "It just happened again."

"The daydream?"

Gwyn nodded. "But it's hardly a daydream. It's too strong. Too real." She gazed up across the dark horizon of her hand. Her thumb was a dark tower rising from a fleshy plain. "Have I been talking?"

"Don't you know?"

"No. I was zoned. Totally gone."

Wrinkles deepened around Carol's eyes. "Gone?" The word lingered in the silent office. "What do you mean *gone*? Where did you *go*?"

"Not sure." Gwyn remembered entering Carol's office, but she had only the vaguest recollection of lying on the couch. "Was I talking long?"

"About ten minutes."

"About what?"

"About a lot of things," Carol said. "About Drake, for one. He's your ex-husband, right?"

"Sort of," Gwyn said. "The divorce is on hold. His idea." She rubbed her eyes. "What did I say about him?"

"That he's putting you through school."

Gwyn frowned. "Sounds generous, doesn't it. But it's not. It's just his way of possessing me from a distance, keeping me too busy to find someone else while he's free to do as he pleases."

"You sound angry."

"That's because . . ." She swallowed. "I don't like it that he's still calling my shots. He might be fifty miles away, but he's still sitting on my life."

"Are there things you'd rather be doing?"

"Yes."

"Why don't you do them?"

"I don't know. I mean, I don't mind being back in school. I like the program. Medieval studies was my major before I married Drake. I could be happy spending my life buried in books . . . if it weren't for . . ." She held her breath, listening.

"Gwyn?"

Her pulse raced, throbbing like drumming hooves.

"If it weren't for what, Gwyn? Were you going to say, 'If it weren't for Virg?'"

Gwyn shivered.

Virg.

The name sounded like a gust of wind.

"Did I talk about him, too?"

"Yes."

"What did I say?"

"A lot of things. But you were talking fast, mumbling. I didn't catch it all. I asked you to slow down, but you kept on. I think you said he asked you to visit him in Philadelphia. You said part of you wants to break away and go."

"But I can't," Gwyn said.

"Why not?"

"I've been burned once."

"All the more reason—"

"No." Gwyn rubbed her throbbing head, wondering if she were making a mistake sharing her problems with a woman who was little more than a campus counselor—a psychologist who spent most of her time listening to undergrads. Carol probably didn't get too many middle-aged teaching fellows with runaway daydreams.

"So where did you go?" Carol asked. "In the dream, where did—"

"I told you. It isn't a dream."

"All right. But tell me about it."

Gwyn closed her eyes, thinking. "There's a woman." She shifted, the couch creaking like a leather saddle. "She's on a horse. And she's searching . . . for someone . . . someone who's been imprisoned by a dragon." Her pulse throbbed like racing hooves. "She stopped riding a moment ago . . . but now . . . now she's riding again . . ."

The tower loomed before her, thrusting high into a tangle of crepuscular clouds. Dirt clung to the mortared seams. The base fanned outward, as if bulging from the weight of the worm that lived within.

Gwythurn stopped her horse, dismounted, and walked to the tower's base. She extended a hand, pressed her fingers to a door that had been bolted from the inside. The planks felt warm. She flattened her hand. The wood quivered. "I feel you," she said, speaking to the thing behind the door.

Her horse snorted and lowered its head, searching for grass among the weeds, indifferent to the danger.

Gwythurn pressed her face to the planks. "Can you feel me?"

The wood creaked.

"Do you know why I've come?"

A low rumble shook the tower.

Gwythurn stepped back. *It knows.* She studied the wall. No windows. No way in but the bolted door. *It thinks it's safe.* But she knew otherwise. *There's another way . . . always another way.*

Raising her hands high, she felt along the seams of protruding stones. A mixture of sand and lime flaked away as she forced her fingers into the gap. Then she held on and started to climb. . . .

The wind stirred.

"Gwyn."

For a moment, she kept climbing.

"Come on, Gwyn. You've zoned out again."

Gwyn sat up. "That time was stronger." She put her feet on the cushions, knees to her chest. "It's getting stronger." She ran her hands along the faded knees of her jeans, trying to rub away the gritty feel of the wall. "It's still in my hands. I can feel the tower in my hands."

"What tower?"

Gwyn's arms quivered with phantom motion. Sitting on the couch, legs folded, feet a scant eighteen inches from the carpeted floor, Gwyn feared falling to her death. "I'm . . . I mean she . . . she's climbing the dragon's tower."

"Who is?"

"Gwythurn," she said. "The woman in the dream. Her name is—" Her breath hitched in her throat as a foot slipped from the edge of the couch.

For a moment, as she drew the foot back to the cushions, the carpet's fibers looked like the stones of a distant desert.

"She's climbing," Gwyn said. "I feel her hands digging between the stones. I feel her legs pushing upward."

"You're feeling this now?"

"Yes. Now."

Someone knocked at the office door. Carol ignored the sound, keeping her eyes on Gwyn. "How long have you been zoning out like this?"

"I don't know," Gwyn said. "A few days. Maybe a week." She looked at the deepening knots around Carol's eyes. "You know what scares me?" she said. "You know what the worst part of all this is? It's that I've probably been doing things that I can't remember. I'll be zoned out, and I'll do things, and later I won't remember what I've done."

Again, someone knocked. Carol turned. "One minute!"

"You can answer it," Gwyn said.

Carol forced a smile. "It's probably my son. He borrowed the car. I told him to drop off the keys." She stood. "This'll only take a minute."

"It's OK."

Carol turned, crossed the room, and opened the door.

Cool wind struck Gwythurn's face. She stood atop the tower, perched on the splintered end of a broken beam that had once supported the structure's roof—a roof that had long since collapsed. Beneath the beam, the world dropped away into a stone-rimmed abyss—full of vertigo and darkness.

The worm was down there. Coiled. Waiting. She could smell its stink on the rising air. Holding her breath, she could hear the drone of its segmented heart somewhere in the darkness. But she still couldn't see it. Her gaze spiraled down along a stone staircase that vanished into a pool of stagnant shadows. She inched back along the beam, climbed onto the stone stairs, and began her descent.

Thirty feet down, she reached a ring of splintered planks—all that remained of the floor of the tower's uppermost chamber. Shadows deepened. She drew her sword and continued on, descending slowly, eyes adjusting to the deepening gloom as the stairs ran out and she stepped onto the tower's rocky floor.

Stone walls tapered above her now. Converging like the lining of a well. Beyond the broken beams and corbels that had once supported the roof, the sky hovered like a pool of blood. Then, in the darkness beside her, something stirred.

"I'm here," the worm said.

She turned, peering into darkness.

The voice hissed again, emanating from a mass of scaly darkness. "Do you see me?"

"Barely."

The beast inhaled, drawing a massive breath. Wind whistled, stirring the shadows. And then, with an echoing roar, the worm exhaled. Flames spewed from its nostrils, illuminating the ridges of its segmented neck as it raised its head like a flaming wick. And then, with another blast of inrushing air, the beast inhaled . . . and the fire went out. "Now?" the beast said. "Do you see me *now?*"

Yes. She saw it. The fire had burned the beast's image into her vision. Standing in the darkness, trying not to choke on the fumes, Gwythurn studied the afterglow that waxed and waned as she blinked her eyes. She saw forked flames and flared nostrils, smoke billowing from massive jaws, teeth as long as swords, a blistered tongue covered with barbs and bristles, and the endless folds of a coiled body. And just in front of the coils, she saw a trapdoor.

The image faded with each blink.

Cautiously, holding her sword in front of her, she eased forward.

"You're wasting your time," the worm said. "My prisoner doesn't want your help. She likes being locked away with her books and papers. She's safe and happy. Trust me."

Gwythurn kept walking, boots rustled through the fragments of the tower's fallen roof.

"I'm telling you," the worm said. "You're wasting your time."

Gwythurn knelt, brushed away the debris of the shattered roof until her fingers found the curved handle of the trapdoor. And it was then, as she gripped the handle, that she heard the monster's jaws race toward her. She turned, saw the worm's head blurred against the rusty glow of the sky, and raised her sword. The beast feinted left. Gwythurn moved with it, swinging her sword, driving the blade deep into the segmented neck.

The beast jerked away. Too late. Its head slammed the ground, jaws stretched in a breathless gasp. Vomit and blood spewed from the severed neck, slamming back against the walls as the coiled body beat against the floor.

Gwythurn scrambled away, cowering by the steps until the worm collapsed into stillness. Then, once again, she advanced to the door in the floor.

Gwyn was home, back in her tiny apartment—the bohemian niche in the ground floor of a place called University Towers. She had only the vaguest recollections of leaving Carol's office.

She remembered standing to leave while Carol's son stood in the doorway. "I have to go," she said. "Really, I'll be fine. I shouldn't have bothered you with any of this." Those words echoed in her now as she stood in her cramped living room . . . her solitary prison . . . only this time she wasn't alone.

Someone stood beside her.

Gwyn turned.

The figure beside her did the same.

Only a mirror, Gwyn thought, realizing what she was seeing. *Just the living-room mirror.*

But the woman reflected in the glass wasn't her, and the reflected room was certainly not part of Gwyn's apartment.

Gwyn stumbled forward, catching herself on her desk. Her hand skidded, scattering the pages of her dissertation. The pages rattled to the floor as the figure in the mirror drew nearer: green eyes, slender nose, high cheeks, tapered jaw. The mousy face was her own . . . but the resolute stare of the eyes was straight out of her dreams. She realized she was looking into the face of Gwythurn, and as she did, her attention turned again to the strange room in the mirror: dirt floor, stone walls, and a staircase that spiraled up through the splintered halo of a fallen roof. And she saw other things, too: the dead coils of a monstrous serpent, a severed head, and the rectangular darkness of an open trapdoor.

Her doorbell rang.

Gwyn turned from the mirror. "Who is it?"

A muffled voice.

"I can't hear you," Gwyn said. "Hold on a second!" She turned back to face the mirror.

The woman in the glass was dressed in leather and bronze. Her hair lay across her shoulder in a dusty braid. She held a sword. Blood stained the blade with a crusty glaze. "You're free," the woman said.

Once again, the doorbell rang.

Gwyn crossed the room, stumbled over something dark that lay in her path, and opened the door.

"Ms. Hurt?" It was a man in a denim vest and a plaid shirt. A short cigar smoldered in the corner of his mouth. "You Ms. Hurt? I got a time call for a Gwyn Hurt. That you?"

Behind the man, a yellow taxi rumbled at the curb.

"If it ain't you, I'm outta here," the man said. "I can't blow rush hour waiting for no-shows."

Gwyn looked back into the apartment.

In the mirror, the last rays of evening spilled through an open door in the castle wall. Beyond the castle's door, the leather and bronze woman heaved herself onto the back of a waiting mare.

"So you Ms. Hurt, or what?" the driver asked again.

He doesn't see it, she thought. *He doesn't see what's in the mirror.* "Yes," Gwyn said, surprised at the calmness in her voice. "I'm Gwyn Hurt."

"Good thing," the man said.

"But when did I call a cab?"

"Jeez, lady. I dunno. It's a time order. Scheduled through dispatch. Could've been yesterday for all I know." He pointed at something in her room. "You want me to get that?" At first he seemed to be pointing at the serpent's severed head in the mirror, but then Gwyn noticed the packed suitcase—the dark thing that she had tripped over while walking toward the door.

"No," she said. "I'll get it myself." The memories came flooding back. Everything fell together. "Give me a minute, okay?"

"Yeah, sure! But the meter's running." He turned and walked back to his rumbling cab.

Gwyn closed the door. She turned. The mirror was back to normal. She watched herself move to the center of the room and pick up her suitcase. She remembered packing it now. She had done it yesterday, after receiving the letter from Virg and before calling the cab. She crossed to her desk where the scattered pages of her dissertation stretched across the floor like the cast off skin of a snake. In her desk's top drawer she found the plane ticket to Philadelphia.

Gwyn looked out the cab's side window as the door of her apartment receded into the deepening night. Then the light changed, and she found herself staring at her reflection in glass. The face was strong, resolute. "Stay close," she said.

"Wassat?" the driver asked.

"Nothing," she said. "Just talking to myself."

Tires clattered like hooves over the cobbles of Academic Drive.

MERCENARY OF DREAMS

The Cara in this story is in some ways the precursor to the protagonist in "Daughters of Prime," just as the story's environmental theme anticipates those of the later works Veins *and "Great Heart Rising."*

The similarities, which never occurred to me as I was working on the stories, only become clear with the distance of hindsight. We will consider such things in more detail in the afterword. But first, let's slay another dragon.

Tell me again," Cara said, looking back at the human boy and pointing to a double-bladed ax in the center of the table. "Who is that?"

The human gave an awkward, half-faced smile. The colored plastic of his tooth-straighteners flashed in the firelight. "*Who?*" he muttered. He gave his head a bemused shake.

His name was Jason. He was twelve in human years, which gave him an intelligence roughly equal to that of an iron knife. Still, he had the qualities that Cara needed. He was small. His body and hands were the right size for elfin armor and weapons. But more importantly, the blood in his veins was human and could be spilled without upsetting the clan elders.

"It's weird," Jason said. He waved a slender hand over the weapons that lay in neat rows across the top of the table. "I can't get used to you talking about these things like they're people." He picked up the double-bladed ax. Cara watched his tendons bulge in his arms as his shoulders adjusted to the weapon's balance. "You should ask me *what* this is, not *who*."

"Look," Cara said. "You either show me that you know this stuff, or I'll find someone else to kill the dragon."

Jason shrugged. His face clenched with an expression that showed he was willing to play along, and then he said, "All right. *Who* is it? It's *Trom-tua*, the heavy ax."

"Show me how she fights."

Jason gripped the polished handle and stepped away from the table.

"Remember," Cara said. "Hold the stock tightly, but relax your arms. Let *Trom-tua* do the work."

"All right," Jason said.

Trom-tua hissed right and then left, moving so swiftly that the double blades on her polished head were little more than a glowing mist. Then, as quickly as she flew into motion, *Trom-tua* stopped and came to rest, standing straight and tall in Jason's white-knuckled grip. "That was cool!" he said. He set the ax back on the table. "You could cut a lot of trees with that!" he said.

"You could," Cara said. "But you won't." She leaned back across the table. "Now tell me," she said, pointing to a hooked dagger. "*Who* is that?"

Jason picked up the blade, studying it. Filaments of reinforcing iron spiraled down the length of the curved shaft, giving the weapon a cruel, serrated edge. "It's *Olc-fiacail*."

"Show me what she does."

His arms blurred as the dagger cut the air.

"All right," Cara said. "Now tell me who you're going to wear?"

He turned, looking back at the armored suit that hung behind him. The suit was made of leather and reinforcing plates of iron. "*Cogadh-garda*," Jason said. "The war guard. The iron skin."

Cara and Jason left the burrow and stepped out into the green light of evening. Jason walked ahead of her, moving toward the ravaged land on the mountain's east slope. *Trom-tua*, the two-headed ax, hung from a leather sheath between his shoulders. *Olc-fiacail*, the hooked dagger, hung from his belt. All around him, *Cogadh-garda*, the massive suit of skin and iron, clattered and creaked. Cara noticed the confidence of his gait. It was clear that he had given himself over to the suit's will, just as moments before he had given his arms to *Trom-tua* and *Olc-fiacail*.

He walked like an elfin warrior.

The forest opened before them as they reached the end of the trail, and suddenly they were standing on a barren slope, the ground parched and brittle. A few hundred feet down, a dirt road snaked around a pile of uprooted trees. Beside the road stood a row of partially constructed homes. Between the homes lay skids of cinder blocks, bricks, plastic-wrapped wallboard, and a numbing assortment of prefabricated wooden frames. Farther down, a herd of earth-moving vehicles slept in the leafy shadows at the clearing's edge.

"Where's the dragon?" Jason asked.

"Be here soon."

Jason sat on the edge of a felled tree and scanned the slope. "It's weird," he said.

She expected him to go on. But instead he slipped into a pensive silence. He looked almost thoughtful, sitting with an elbow on a leather-clad knee and his fist clenched beneath his chin. The weapons and the armor had begun to change him. He looked heroic.

"What's weird?" she asked.

"That a dragon would get pissed about a few mountainside homes."

"Not so weird," Cara said. "The dragon's not the only one who's . . . what's that word?"

"What word? Pissed?"

"Yes," Cara said. "The dragon's not the only one who's pissed."

The clan elders had sent for Cara the moment human surveyors began staking off portions of the east slope of their forest.

"We can't abandon another forest!" Teanga said. He was the speaker for the clan. "We can't continue to flee the moment humans arrive!"

"But it's not just the humans," Saoi said. He was one of the oldest and wisest of the clan. His eyes were smooth and shiny, like stones in an ancient stream. "The dragon has complicated things."

"*Pah!*" This came from Madra. He had the temper and build of a ferret—all spit and sinew. "When we first came to these woods, you said the dragon would sleep forever."

"The humans roused it," Saoi said. "It was their machines—all that digging and blasting."

"So," Cara said. "You've got a double problem."

"Which is why we sent for you." Teanga sat forward. "The Sidhe spoke well of you. They said you were a problem solver."

"I try."

"Can you solve this problem?"

"Depends on what you mean by solve."

Teanga glanced at the others, then at Cara. "Can you get rid of the human dwellings and the dragon without causing trouble?"

"Without trouble?" Cara said. "No."

"What Saoi means," Madra said, "is can you get rid of them without spilling elfin blood?"

"That's very important," Saoi said. "Our clan can't live where elves have bled."

Cara nodded. "I can take care of those things." She sat back. "Everything will be as you've requested."

"And your fee?" Teanga asked.

"The usual." She glanced at the others. "Payable when you're satisfied that I've done what you've asked."

"In the meantime," Saoi said, "we'll supply you with anything you need. Although . . ." He cast a smooth glance toward the satchel of weapons and armor that Cara had brought with her. "You seem to have come prepared." He leaned closer, noting a glint of cold iron. "Unconventional," he muttered.

"Times change," she said. "But there is one thing I didn't bring. If you could supply it, I'd be grateful."

"Name it," Madra said.

"If it's not asking too much," Cara said. "I should like to be supplied with a human boy."

As Jason stared at the slope's partially built homes, Cara gave voice to the spell that would draw the dragon from its lair. It was a simple song, sung in a high pitch that the boy could not hear. The song assured the dragon that the humans were nowhere in sight. The song goaded the dragon by claiming that the new structures being built on the mountain were intended to mock its clan. And the song challenged the dragon to come destroy the mockery before the humans took over the mountain.

She sang the song twice. Then she flattened her toes and felt the earth for dragon tremors.

At her side, Jason continued to stare down at the row of partially built homes.

"That's going to be our house," he said, pointing to a cinder block foundation near the edge of the road. "I was down there with my dad when your friends found me." His voice trailed off.

Cara got the impression that the boy was having trouble remembering what had happened . . . how it was that he had been with his father one moment and with Madra and Teanga the next. "It's weird," he muttered. Then he looked up at Cara. "Are you guys really elves?"

Cara nodded. "That's one of our names."

"Where're you from?"

"From a time when the whole world was forest," Cara said.

"When was that?"

"Long ago," Cara said. "Far away. In another part of the dream."

"What dream?"

"Earth."

"Earth isn't a dream."

"It is," Cara said. "It's many dreams. Human dreams, elf dreams, dragon dreams—all competing for control." The earth shivered beneath Cara's toes. "Get ready," she said. "The dragon's coming."

Jason stood. He reached behind him and pulled *Trom-tua* from the harness between his shoulders. Holding the double-headed ax in front of him, he stepped away from the fallen tree. Then he turned in place, scanning the air for signs of the dragon. "Where is it?" he asked.

"Close," Cara said. She stroked the ground with her toes. "I can feel it."

Jason kept turning. "Why can't I see it?"

"Because you're looking the wrong way."

He stopped turning. "The wrong way?" His voice cracked. "I'm looking *everywhere!*"

"Look there!" She pointed.

He followed the line of her finger, his breath hitching as he realized what she meant. He glanced up at her, giving her a look that seemed to say: *You're kidding, right?*

She was pointing at the ground . . . less than twenty feet from the scuffed toes of his armored boots.

"There's nothing there!" he said.

The tremors in the ground grew more pronounced. "It's a big one," she said. "Bigger than I thought." She reached for Jason. "We'd better get back." She tugged his arm, pulling him toward the woods as the slope exploded.

The force of the blast threw them into the trees as a black-veined fireball billowed from the shattered ground. And within the flame, looking like the twitching wick of a living candle, the dragon's neck unfurled.

This was the moment that would tell all. Either the spells and the weapons and the power of the armor would transform the boy into a warrior . . . or all would be lost.

She turned to look at Jason, but it was too late. He was gone. Already the iron will of *Cogadh-garda* had taken control. His leather-clad legs were hurtling toward the slope. She saw him silhouetted against the dissipating fireball. Arms rising, ax swinging, voice cutting the air with the shrill cry of battle—the child lunged forward to face the dragon.

Flaming ash spewed from the shattered slope as the dragon splayed its talons upon the ground. Then, with a motion that was surprisingly lithe for a creature its size, the beast pulled its ropy body free of the crevice. With its forked tail cracking like a whip, the monster turned, unfurled its wings, and soared down toward the base of the slope.

Cara looked for signs of the boy as she stumbled through the ashy air. But now all that she could see was the distant silhouette of the dragon. It had alighted atop one of the earthmovers near the bottom of the slope, and it was spewing flames over a row of partially constructed homes. The beast's head turned slowly as it panned its flaming breath . . . and it was then, as the skeletal homes exploded into flame, that Cara saw the boy.

He was climbing the dragon's neck, using the sharp spines of its dorsal fins as if they were the rungs of a jagged ladder. He had returned the double-faced ax to the leather sheath, and the heavy weapon twitched against his back as he inched toward the creature's head. Cara watched him, and even though she knew that the iron skin was doing the climbing . . . even though she knew that the spells she had worked were giving him courage . . . and even though she knew that when he wielded the ax it would be the weapon and not his arms that would guide the blow, she could not help feeling admiration for the human boy.

He perched atop the beast's head, straddled the peaked ridge in the center of its skull, pulled the ax from its harness, and brought the blade down between the beast's eyes. Cara heard the blade clang deep, wincing at the muffled crack of bone. The monster screamed. It arched its neck, throwing its head back until Jason, still clinging to the polished stock of the double-bladed ax, fell and slammed against the scaly body.

And then, slowly—so slowly that Cara was certain that her eyes were tricking her—Jason floated down along the monster's side. It was not until she saw the waves of molten blood surging from the serpent's flanks that she realized what she was seeing. *Trom-tua* had plunged her double-bladed head deep into the monster's thoracic cavity. The beast stood, frozen in a moment of mortal shock, while the ax, pulled by Jason's weight and the weight of the armor, cleaved the creature's side.

By the time Jason reached the ground, the leather of his suit was aflame with the heat of the dragon's blood. Cara ran to him, pulled the barbed dagger from his belt, and slashed the stays that bound the front of his smoldering armor.

The iron skin fell away. Sooty, bleeding, and nearly naked, Jason emerged from the burning heap of leather and iron. Cara grabbed his arm and pulled him up the slope. They scrambled around the shattered mouth of the dragon's lair, and then, as she was pulling the boy into the woods, a thundering roar exploded behind her.

She turned. The dragon had regained its senses and was shooting toward them. Its jaws gaped, expanding until they seemed ready to swallow the entire world.

She grabbed the boy's head and covered his eyes. And then, with a terrible crash, the creature dipped its shattered head and plunged into its burrow.

A moment of silence followed.

And then, deep beneath the mountain, the dragon threw its flanks against the walls of its lair. It thrashed and writhed until the east slope imploded, and the work of the humans—the skids of wood, the stone-lined foundations, the skeletal homes, and even the earth movers—all vanished beneath an avalanche of collapsing rock and clay.

The boy was dazed. His eyes stared silently inward as the elfin healers attended him.

"What now?" Teanga asked.

"Put him back where you found him," Cara said.

"*Pah!* We found him by the foundation of his home. That's a place that doesn't exist anymore. The quake swallowed it!"

The burrow's door swung wide. Rith, the clan's runner, raced in. He skidded to a stop in the center of the room, whirled about, and looked at Cara. "The boy's father has returned." His cheeks reddened with the pressure of his smile. "State troopers stopped him at the base of the slope. He looked dazed. The spells were leaving his mind, and he was babbling like a madman. I heard him telling the troopers that he had driven away without his son. He kept apologizing, as if the troopers cared. He kept saying, 'How could I forget my boy? What was I thinking?'"

"So there are troopers in the forest?" Teanga asked.

"Yes!" Rith said. "Troopers, land developers, gawkers—all kinds of people, and they all want to know what happened!"

"They'll leave soon," Saoi said. "They'll see the destruction, and they'll leave." He beamed at Cara with his smooth, stone eyes.

Cara turned away. She picked up her satchel of weapons, collected her pay, and then took the dazed boy by his arm. "I'll return him to his father," she said, guiding him toward the leafy door. Then she turned, glanced back at the elders, and said, "May your magic be strong."

They seemed not to notice the hollow ring of her words.

She put her lips to the boy's ear and whispered the poem of forgetfulness. Then she released him and watched from the shadows as he stumbled toward his father.

"Dad!"

The father turned, ran forward, and embraced the boy. The boy wept like a baby in the father's broad arms.

Watching the scene, Cara caught a precognitive flash of the future. She saw the boy emerging into brooding adolescence. She saw the father perplexed by his son's fascination with knives, blades, leather, and flames. She saw the summer home finally being built on another slope a mile away—a slope that the land developers insisted was safe, but that the boy sensed was teetering on the edge of something half remembered.

The boy would never feel secure on the slope. Within three years, the father would sell to another family. By then, the slope would be teeming with homes, and half the forest would be under development. . . .

Eventually, all of the world's old-growth forests would be gone, and lands that had always been in the stewardship of nature and elves would vanish beneath asphalt, concrete, chemical-enhanced lawns, mulched gardens, monocrop farms. . . .

But all of that lay in the future. For now, Cara watched as the father led the boy away. From the forest behind her came the slow, brittle chirps of the first crickets of August.

Cara listened to the crickets.

It was a painful sound—like the slow, inexorable shattering of an ancient dream.

BEERWULF

Here we revisit the story of Beowulf once again, this time in a humorous tale from the point of view of the monster's older brother.

The humans had gathered at the shore by the time Kalb and Schaf reached the far side of the lake. Schaf crouched, keeping his furry hump below the reeds while Kalb hid in the shadows. "That's him," Kalb said. "The big one. That's Wulf."

Wulf wore an iron breastplate over a vest of steel mail. Bossed metal covered his forearms and shins. At his feet lay a helmet studded with decorative brass.

Schaf asked, "What's he doing?"

"Getting ready."

"For what?"

Wulf slipped the helmet over his head, securing it with a heavy clasp that crossed beneath his chin.

"Swimming," Kalb said.

"In all that armor?" Schaf frowned. "He must have *scitte* for brains."

"Yeah. He's got that. But the big problem is his mouth. Last night he told the warriors about a swimming race he was in. He claimed he swam in full battle gear."

"Did he say he did well in this race?"

"No, but he said he would have if monsters hadn't stopped him."

"Did he kill these monsters?"

"Yeah. He said that's why there're no more monsters in the ocean. He killed them all."

"And the warriors, they believed these lies?"

"Yes. Completely. And now they want him to go into the lake and kill Modor and Grenja."

One of the warriors handed Wulf a sword with a heavy iron blade. Wulf accepted it, holding it high as he advanced toward the lake's edge. The water was dark, stained with the shadows of surrounding cliffs. Looking down at his reflection, Wulf probably assumed that the bottom fell away gradually, that he could just wade in and maybe put his head beneath the water for a quick look around. Certainly he had no idea what was really there, that the flooded crater plunged straight down to a depth of four rods. Ten men standing one atop the other wouldn't break the surface.

"I thought you'd want to know about this," Kalb said. "You told me to let you know if the humans ever got too close . . . and I guess this is pretty close."

Schaf watched, tensing as Wulf stepped toward the water line. Then, at shore's end, the big man turned and saluted the warriors. He seemed poised to deliver a heroic speech, an oath of fealty to the local king, a promise to slaughter any hell spawns that met him among the depths. And all the while he kept walking, stepping backward until—PLUNK!—he vanished into a ring of ripples, leaving the shore-bound warriors staring in mute amazement.

Schaf said, "This could be bad." He moved toward the water.

Kalb followed. "Where're you going?"

"To the bottom." Schaf looked back. "Stay close. You're going to help."

"Help with what?"

"Scitte-for-Brains wants to find Grenja and Modor. We're going to help him."

"Why?"

Schaf didn't answer. Instead, he slipped beneath the dark waters, leaving Kalb no choice but to follow.

They found Wulf embedded to his knees in the muddy bottom. Bubbles rose from his armored head. Schaf grabbed him from behind, hooking him under the shoulder and motioning for Kalb to do the same. Then, swimming together, the brothers carried Wulf toward the cave, through its entrance, and up into a fire-lit chamber.

Modor was there. So was Grenja.

Wulf gasped, choking as water drained from his helmet.

"Schaf?" Modor had been squatting by the fire, leaning on the stone hearth that vented through a natural chimney in the cave wall. Three large sacks hung from the mantel, each filled with the dark beer that Modor brewed from honey and peat.

"Is that you Schaf?" Modor had been doing something to Grenja, apparently reattaching his arm at the shoulder. She was a master at such things, a wizard with needle and string, but now she stood, wiping her hands on her furry loins, calling out to her eldest son. "Min Schaf has come back to visit!" She looked older than Schaf remembered, her beard grayer, her breasts limp and sagging to the ledge of her gut. But her eyes were as bright as ever, beaming as she looked from Schaf, to Kalb, and then to the man who knelt between them. "And what's this?" Her brow buckled. "A human friend?"

"Na!" Grenja turned, his reattached limb jerking in its socket as he tried pointing at Wulf. "That's the man what took min arm!" The limb spasmed, jerking at the elbow, swinging back to strike Grenja's face. It was often this way. A reattached arm took days to settle down, and even then it was never completely right. Grenja tried controlling it, pushing it down to his lap, holding it there while the bandaged elbow twitched against his side.

"Then he naegled it to the manhouse wall! Put an iron spike right through the joint!"

"And it would have been a fine lesson for you if I hadn't brought it back," Modor said. "I told you to leave the humans alone. Stay away, I said. And what did you do?"

Schaf knew what had happened. Kalb had told him how Wulf had attacked Grenja.

And for what? It wasn't as if Grenja had been bothering anyone, just hanging around the manhouse, pressing his ear to the wall, listening to the warriors tell their tales.

Modor leaned toward Wulf. "So you're the one?" She frowned, then turned to leer at Schaf. "So what's the idea? You don't visit all winter, now you're back with the human that naegls your brother's arm to a manhouse wall."

Schaf said, "The man was coming here on his own."

"By himself?" Modor looked at Wulf, focusing on the armor. "Dressed like that?"

"It's my wargear," Wulf said.

"You wear wargear when you swim?"

"Yeah, he does!" Grenja said. "He told a story. I heard it. He was swimming with a sword in each hand, fighting sea monsters!"

Modor tugged her beard. "Sword in each hand?"

Wulf shrugged. "Was just a story. It wasn't like anyone had to believe it."

"But everyone did," Grenja said. "They all started cheering, chanting his name. 'Wulf! Wulf!' And he liked it so much that he asked them if they had any monsters of their own that needed killing." Grenja looked at Schaf. "So they all start talking about me! 'Oh yeah!' one of them says. 'There's the stalker of the night! He's probably outside right now.' Next thing I know—" Grenja turned, glaring at Wulf. "You've got me cornered!"

"Was a good fight," Wulf said. "I grabbed your arm, a fearful death grip, broke the bone latches, ripped the sinew—"

"Like hell! It's not like a human arm! It comes off."

"Defense mechanism," Schaf said

"Like a crabba claw," Kalb said.

"Except it don't grow back on its own," Schaf said.

"Which is why Modor had to go back for it," Grenja said.

Modor studied Wulf, frowning as if she were looking at a foolish child. "And then you followed me back here, looking for another fight. Is that it? Is that what happened?"

Wulf didn't answer. He seemed to be having trouble accepting the sudden turn of events, as if part of him still wanted to be the great hero who had led an entourage of admiring thanes to the shore of a haunted lake. "They gave me their best armor," Wulf said. "They wanted me to wear it when I entered the water."

"And you didn't think you'd sink like a stone?"

He shrugged. "I didn't know it was deep. I figured . . . maybe I'd just walk around, stab the water. You know, make a show of it." His voice trailed off as he surveyed the chamber, firelight reflecting from his breastplate, illuminating the walls.

A pile of junk caught his eye. It was Grenja's stuff, things that the cub had found lying along the manroads. Much of it was rusting: pitted helmets, broken shields, sword blades corroded to blackened stumps.

"So what're you going to do with me?" Wulf asked, turning to look at another wall, this one piled with animal carcasses. "You should know that I'll be avenged if I don't return. I'm an honored guest. The king will keep the lake surrounded. You'll be prisoners in this cave, afraid to leave."

"Which is why I didn't let you drown." Schaf leaned forward, undid the clasp around Wulf's chin, and removed the helmet so he could make eye contact with the man inside.

"I've got a proposition that'll make you a hero and restore my family's privacy. Interested?"

"What're you talking about?"

"I'm talking about you going back to the surface and telling the humans that you slew the monsters in the lake. You tell them there's no more danger here, nothing of interest." He turned toward Grenja. "And you—you stay away from the manhouse. No more listening to stories."

"But I like listening to them!"

"He's been like this since you left," Kalb said. "Now that you aren't around to tell him stories, he goes and listens to the men tell theirs."

"He doesn't like the ones I tell him," Modor said.

Schaf's eyes flashed at Grenja. "All right then," he said. "Get ready for a good one."

"What one?"

"The one I'm going to make up right here." He turned back to Wulf. "Take off some of that armor. The breastplate and helmet can stay, but the mail and shin guards got to go."

"Why?"

"Too heavy. You'll never get to the surface with them on. And this sword—" he lifted the long blade from the floor. "Too heavy. It stays here."

"But it's not mine!"

"Tell the owner it failed in battle. Tell him no human sword can slay the creatures of the lake."

"Is that true?"

"What does it matter? It's a good story." Schaf walked to the pile of gear that sat rusting against the far wall. He grabbed the wooden hilt of an ancient sword and pulled it free.

"Hwaet!" Grenja said. "That's my stuff!"

"And it's about time it served a purpose," Schaf said, inspecting the sword he had pulled from the pile. The blade was little more than a rusted stump, pitted like volcanic rock. Schaf turned and handed it to Wulf. "Tell them you had to use this. Tell them this is the weapon that killed the monsters no human sword could kill."

"This?" Wulf frowned at the broken blade.

"Yes, but tell them it was a magnificent weapon when you found it, a blade of the gods that rusted in your hands when it drew monster blood."

Wulf frowned. "Think they'll believe that?"

"They believed you could swim in armor—"

"All right!" Wulf paused a moment, lips moving as he practiced the story. "But how do I get to the surface? I can't—" He tugged his beard, swallowing hard, looking around. "I can't really swim."

Schaf turned away again, this time crossing to the hearth and the three sacks that hung upon the mantle.

Grenja sat up. "We going to drink beer now?"

"No. No drinking. Consider this the price you pay for bringing humans to our shore."

Schaf walked to the pool at the far end of the chamber, the jagged sink that connected with the flooded portion of the cave, and there he uncorked the sacks and emptied the beer.

Protests erupted in the chamber. The loudest coming from Grenja, but the most serious coming from Modor who roared, "Have you lost your mind, Schaf?"

"No, Modor." He squeezed the last of the beer from the sacks, then pressed each to his lips, inflating the bladders with his breath before replacing the corks. "Put the straps around your arms," he said, handing the empties to Wulf. "Pull them tight. Like this."

He gave each a firm tug then backed away, inspecting the results.

Kalb snorted. "He looks like a beer merchant!"

Grenja laughed.

"The sacks will lift you to the surface," Schaf said.

"But what do I tell the warriors? They'll see the sacks and think I'm bringing beer."

"Don't worry about it," Schaf said. "They'll forget the sacks after you show them the head."

"What head?"

"The one you cut off. Remember, you cut off the monster's head, and its blood melted the sword of the gods."

"But I don't have a head."

Grenja snorted.

"Hey!" Wulf turned, glaring at Grenja. "You know what I mean."

"Relax," Schaf said. "A head will be provided." He turned to the pile of animal carcasses. "We got plenty."

Modor watched him rummage through the offal. "Now what're you taking?"

Schaf pulled a hog's head from the pile, grasping it by the bristles.

"That's for pie!" Modor said.

Schaf held onto the pig's head and reached back into the pile, coming out this time with a goat horn. To Wulf, he said, "Tell them it was a horned horror." He rammed the base of the horn into the hog's snout, twisting until it squeaked against bone. "Tell them you killed the mother, then you cut off the head of the son."

Grenja snorted. "What? Is that supposed to be me?"

Schaf passed the head to Wulf. "Tell them it's a better trophy than an arm. Tell them they need never fear monsters as long as they keep this head mounted over their manhouse door."

"But I don't look like that!" Grenja said.

Schaf turned. "Should we let him take your real head?"

"No! But if I'm going to be in a story, I want to look good."

"Looks good to me," Wulf said, turning the head in the firelight. "A fatherless fiend!" he said, lowering his voice to test the resonance of the phrase. "Hell spawn of the haunted mere!" He seemed pleased.

Schaf left the cave first, shooting to the surface and into a cover of reeds. A moment later, Kalb and Modor joined him. Grenja stayed in the cave with his unruly arm, brooding about being portrayed as a pig-headed hell spawn.

The thanes stood watch on the far side of the lake, looking at the water, awaiting their hero's return. And then, near the shore, the water started to churn.

Schaf tensed. "Scitte!"

"What's happening?" Kalb asked.

"One of the sacks must be leaking."

"He probably poked it with that goat horn," Modor said.

By now the thanes were pointing at the roiling water, the color of which seemed to have darkened with the residue of honey beer. "Blood!" one of them shouted.

And then, amid the roiling waves, two beer sacks broke the surface.

The call went out at once—"Beer!"—and echoed along the shore until Wulf surfaced between two inflated bladders. "Wulf!" the warriors shouted, their voices colliding with those who were shouting about the sacks. "Beer! Wulf! Beer! Wulf!" And through it all, Wulf thrashed and kicked, swallowing water, gagging and calling for help.

Kalb said, "This isn't going well."

"Give it time," Schaf said. "I have a feeling this is going to be one of those stories that gets better with the retelling."

Modor went back to the cave to finish sewing Grenja's arm, but Kalb stayed with Schaf, walking with him to the forest trail, a deer road so narrow and overgrown that no man could ever follow it. "Do you think we'll be in the story?" Kalb asked. "The story that Wulf tells, do you think we'll be part of it?"

Schaf paused, looking back along the way they had come—toward the human settlement that lay half a league beyond the flooded crater. It was still the budding season, too early in the year for cricket songs, and the night was cool and still. Cocking his head, Schaf made out the voice of a triumphant warrior singing his tale to a packed hall.

Schaf frowned. "He won't want to talk about us," he said. "We're the part he'll keep to himself."

For a moment the brothers stood in silence, brooding in the forest that no longer seemed as deep and vast as it had when they were young, before the humans had come with their ships, weapons, and stories.

"At least we know the truth," Kalb said, laughing as he remembered the warriors shouting along the shore. "Beerwulf! It's a good story."

Schaf reached out, cupping his little brother's head. "We'll remember that part if no one else does." He nuzzled Kalb's neck.

"I don't see why you can't live with us," Kalb said. "Like you used to."

"I'm too old for that, Kalb. And the cave's too small. One day, you'll understand."

"Maybe one day I'll come live with you, in the wild holt. We could tell the story of how we fooled the humans."

"And who would we tell it to, little brother?"

Kalb didn't answer, and Schaf held him close a moment longer, savoring the scent of his furry nape—the scent of home. Then he let him go, turned, and headed down the trail, leaving the cub to return to the flooded crater, the high-walled lake that was this very night becoming the place of legend.

ON THE BRINK

The following story, originally commissioned by Margaret Weis for the anthology New Amazons, *represents an attempt to move away from the traditional fantasy tropes of dragons, elves, changelings, and trolls. The monster depicted here is at once new and timeless, and the warrior who confronts it may well be the bravest of them all.*

Bitterness lingered. Kate swallowed again, forcing down the taste that clung to her tongue, and it was then that she felt her grief stirring in the shadows behind her. "It's not really there," she told herself. But still she felt the atavistic tingles along the back of her neck, the icy prickling that she always felt when things stirred behind her.

"Ignore it," she whispered. "There's nothing there." She closed her eyes and tried filling her mind with things that she knew to be true. She was alone in the kitchen, alone in the house, and more alone in her life than she had been for a very long time. The tingles on her neck were from the tea. The stuff had evidently been full of caffeine.

She opened her eyes and looked at the empty cup on the table in front of her. The chipped surface still bore the faded imprint of Canada's Niagara Falls, the place where she and Terry had spent what she remembered as being a perfect honeymoon. Inside the cup, black leaves lay like sludge. She had swallowed the tea in a single gulp, just as the tea lady had told her to do. She had thought that the stuff would calm her, but here it was giving her a case of nerves that were even worse than the ones she had been getting from her usual seven to ten cups of coffee.

Again, the grief shifted behind her. She tried ignoring it. Her imagination could do crazy things if she gave in to it. So she sat quietly with her racing heart. "I should never have done it," she told herself. "I should never have let that crazy woman talk me into drinking the tea."

"Tea," the woman said.

Kate stood beside the open door, looking out as the woman leaned forward from a veil of afternoon flurries.

"I have your tea," the woman said.

Kate hesitated. "My tea?"

The woman held up a sample case, presenting it with a white-gloved hand. "For you," she said. "May I come in?"

"Are you sure you have the right house?"

The woman produced a card, flipping it over so Kate could read the name and address scrawled across the back. The name, address, and handwriting were all Kate's.

"But I just mailed that card this morning," Kate said, realizing as soon as she'd said it that she might be getting her days confused again. Lately everything had been swirling together like churning mist.

"I wouldn't know about when you mailed it," the woman said.

Kate decided that she could use the company. "Would you like to come in?"

"Yes." The woman smiled. "That's the way this usually works."

At the woman's request, Kate filled the kettle and set it on the stove to boil.

"And we'll need a cup," the woman said.

Kate rinsed the coffee dregs from her Niagara Falls cup while the woman set her sample case on the kitchen table. Clasps rattled. She raised the lid. Inside, tea tins stood in satin-lined shelves, each labeled with hand-painted names: Generosi, Respectabili, Hones, Digni, Tenaci. . . .

"Looks like Italian," Kate said, scanning the words. "Are these Italian teas?"

"No," the woman said. "Not Italian."

The kettle clicked as it heated.

The woman removed a large, slender package from the bottom of the case.

"What's that?" Kate asked.

"A gift," the woman said. "Something you'll put to good use." The package clunked heavily as the woman set it on the table.

"What kind of gift?" Kate asked. "What is it?"

"You'll see," the woman said. "But first we'll brew your tea." She opened one of the tins. Kate caught a whiff of sweetness and musk. The woman picked up the cup and looked at the picture on its side. "Niagara Falls?" She ran a crooked thumb across the image. "Honeymoon?"

"Yes."

"How long ago?"

"Eighteen years."

The kettle screamed.

"Tea," Sara said.

Kate hesitated. "Tea?" It wasn't that she hadn't heard, but everything seemed so uncertain these days.

Kate raised her Niagara Falls cup, sipping her coffee while Sara slid a postcard across the kitchen table. "I got this for you," Sara said.

Kate studied the card. The address on the front was for a company called T Leaves. A scripted slogan in the lower left corner read: *Tea Lends Enchantment and Vitality to Every Season.*

"You want me to send away for tea?" Kate didn't pick up the card . "What do I want with tea?"

"You're drinking too much coffee," Sara said. "You have enough things agitating you right now. You don't need to add to it with caffeine."

"I'm not agitated," Kate said. "I'm grieving. There's a difference."

Sara sat back. Winter sun streamed through the window, filling her hair with tangled light. At fifty-one, Sara projected a natural, effortless confidence. Looking at her now, Kate found it hard to believe that five years ago Sara's life had been in ruin.

"It's funny," Sara said. "After Bryan left, I hated you for still having the kinds of things that I'd lost. Now here I am, on the other side, trying to convince you that life doesn't end when a husband leaves."

"Terry didn't leave me."

"Dying is leaving, Kate. It's not voluntary, but it's still leaving."

Kate picked up the tea card. Anything to change the subject. She looked once again at the printed slogan: *Tea Lends Enchantment and Vitality to Every Season.* Her gaze lingered on the line. She had always been a painfully slow reader, but sometimes that slowness caused her to notice things that more facile readers missed. "T Leaves," Kate said.

"Excuse me?"

"The initials in the slogan spell out the company name—T Leaves."

"Oh." Sara glanced at the card. "I didn't see that. Cute!"

"So what do you know about this company?" Kate asked.

"Nothing. I saw the card in a health food store. It was part of a display for caffeine alternatives. I thought of you."

"Really?"

"Throw it in the trash if you're not interested," Sara said. "But try cutting back on the caffeine. You've got enough to deal with without having to battle coffee nerves." She squeezed Kate's hand.

Kate felt the weight of things unsaid. . . .

The concern in Sara's eyes whispered the things that her lips had the kindness to keep silent. And the eyes said: *I'm worried. You're letting your grief carry you away. It's destroying your home. Destroying your life. You need to get rid of it before it washes you over the brink.*

Kate held Sara's gaze, trying to answer with her own eyes: *You think you know me, but you don't. There are secrets in me that only Terry knew, and if you knew them—if you knew even half of them—they would drive you mad with concern. If you knew one fourth of them you would be amazed that I have made it through two weeks without him. If you knew a fifth of them, you wouldn't waste your time talking to me about tea . . . and you would never dare leave me alone in this house!*

"What're you staring at?" Terry asked after he found her in the back of the gift shop.

She realized that he had already asked the question once before, but his words had gotten lost in the roar of the distant falls.

"What do you have there, Kate?"

She turned toward him. "A cup." She held it up, letting him see the image of the falls.

"Cute," Terry said.

"Can we buy it, T?" She always called him *T* whenever they were alone. In a group he was always *Terry*. Alone he was *T*. *T* for two, and *Terry* for three.

He slipped behind her, looking over her shoulder as she went back to studying the cup.

"Can you make it move?" he asked.

"Yes."

She had told him about the thing she could do with her eyes, how she could look at pictures and patterns and make them come alive. It was a secret that she had shared with no one but him.

He tucked his chin against her shoulder. "So what does it do?" he asked.

She touched the picture with her finger. "The water churns, the mist swirls, and this little boat—" She pointed to what for him must have been nothing more than a brass-colored speck among a tangle of painterly strokes. "This little boat sails out of the mist."

"Then we have to get it," he said. Just like that. No argument. No debate. He understood the pieces of her that no one else even knew existed, and for the eighteen years that followed he became the anchor that rooted her to the world in ways that no one could have understood. And sometimes, whenever she awoke at night and the darkness swirled into frightening shapes, she would listen to his breathing and feel his warmth, and the darkness would go back to being darkness. Terry made her whole. With him, the world developed a continuity that had never existed in the days before he had come into her life.

The woman lifted the whistling kettle from the stove. Water spilled into the Niagara Falls cup. The musky smell grew stronger, filling the kitchen.

"Let it steep for at least five minutes." The woman set the kettle back on the stove. "Anything less, and you won't get the full effect." She closed her case, secured the latches, and turned toward the living room.

"That's it?" Kate said.

The woman walked out of the kitchen.

Kate heard the front door swinging inward. "Wait a minute!" Kate hurried into the living room to find the woman standing in the doorway. Outside, the snow had stopped falling. The sun tossed low, winter beams against the front of the house. Days were so capricious this time of year; it was hard to know what to expect. The tea lady's slender body threw a twig-like shadow across the carpet as she turned to look back at Kate.

"Wait at least five minutes," the woman said. "Open your gift while you're waiting. When the five minutes are up, drink the tea. It's most effective when you drink it fast. One gulp is best. It might burn a bit, but it'll be a good burn. Trust me. You'll see. Tea has a way of making everything right."

The woman stepped outside; the door closed behind her, as if drawn shut by a gust of wind.

"Wait!" She dashed across the room. "There's something I need to know!" She pulled the door open and stepped onto the porch.

The wind whipped along the blanket of unbroken snow.

Kate returned to the kitchen. The water in the Niagara Falls cup had turned an opaque black, more like coffee than tea. Her reflection looked up at her through the wisp of surface clouds. She sat back and glanced at the clock. How much time had passed since the woman had added the water to the leaves? Thirty seconds? A minute? Kate had never been good with clocks. There was something about the shifting progression from left to right and then right to left that always confused her. And digital clocks with their segmented digits were even worse.

She took a pencil from the drawer beneath the sink and drew a line on the clock face beyond the tip of the minute hand. Then she counted ahead five lines and drew another line. God, what would people think if they ever knew about these things? She shoved the pencil back into the drawer. Then she sat down and reached for the narrow box, the gift from the T lady.

It felt heavy. She set it on her lap. Again, her own face looked back at her, this time reflected from the silver wrapping that covered the box. She ripped it open, cleaving her reflection and exposing a foot-long cardboard box embossed with the name T LEAVES. She opened the lid. Inside she found a sheath of neatly folded tissue paper. And inside the paper was something that looked like a wrought-iron *t*—a bold, lower-case letter with serifed arms and a curved stem. She tried picking it up, gripping it by the curve.

"Ow!"

She jerked her hand away. Blood flicked from her fingers, staining the white paper with a spatter of red stars. Raising her hand to the light, she saw that her palm, thumb, and index finger had been sliced nearly to the bone.

She moved the box back to the table and ran to the counter where she grabbed a handful of paper towels. Wrapping her bleeding hand, she looked back at the iron *t*.

"What are you?"

The *t* didn't answer. It only lay there, cold and silent in its bed of bloody paper, surrounded by a halo of torn reflections.

The kitchen had filled with shadows. Kate flicked on the light and returned to the table to take another look at the iron *t*. Now, in the ceiling's incandescent glow, Kate realized that what she had at first taken to be the curved stem of a *t* was actually a hooked blade. The thing was a dagger. "What kind of gift is this?" she asked the room.

The room, as it had for most of the past two weeks, refused to answer.

She glanced at the clock.

The minute hand had moved beyond the second pencil mark. She picked up the Niagara Falls cup and downed the tea. It had a pleasant taste, bitter but silky, not unlike coffee. But when she swallowed, a cruel aftertaste gripped her throat. She clamped her lips, set the cup on the table, and swallowed again. And it was then that she felt her grief stirring in the shadows behind her.

She sat still, trying to deny the atavistic tingle on the back of her neck. But then something happened that made the intruding presence impossible to deny.

Her grief screamed.

Kate turned.

A few feet behind her chair, the patterns in the kitchen carpet churned to life. Something was rising from the piles. A strange thing . . . amorphous . . . organic. It changed as she watched it. One moment it looked like a piece of twitching liver. Then it sprouted tendrils. The tendrils thickened, becoming arms. The arms sprouted claws. The claws dug into the carpet, and the nylon piles groaned as the thing pulled its haunches from the floor.

And then, with a jerk, it stood up. A head festered out from its twitching shoulders. Eyes formed. A mouth gaped. The thing coughed and gasped for air in the darkening room. Its rancid breath filled the kitchen. It looked at her, licking its lips with a blistered tongue. "Hurry!" it said. "Let's finish it!"

Then it ran from the room.

She followed it through the long hall, passing the rooms that made up the first floor of the large house: bathroom, game room, guest room, solarium, and finally the room for the child that she and T had never had. It raced past all of these rooms, heading straight for the master bedroom where it leaped onto the king-size bed and began driving its claws into the wall.

"What're you doing?" she screamed.

Its hooks snagged a beam. The wall buckled and split, collapsing around the headboard.

"Stop it!" she yelled.

But it kept on rending the wall, filling the room with squalls of flying plaster. She had to stop it.

She ran back into the kitchen to get a broom. The thing was strong, but it was no larger than a terrier. Perhaps she could shove it into the hall and out the door. But she had second thoughts as soon as she pulled the broom from the closet. It was too light, all plastic and aluminum. She tossed the broom aside. It gave a hollow clank as it toppled and fell against the stove. She needed something lethal. . . .

The hooked dagger was still on the table, sleeping in its bed of bloody paper. It might do the job, but to use it she would have to get close. "All right." She reached for it, this time gripping the hilt. The ribbed iron chilled her skin, and its heaviness fought her as she pulled it from its bed. But the iron warmed by the time she entered the hall, and the mass seemed to shift, finding balance in her hand.

The carpet churned beneath her as she raced back to the bedroom. The swirling patterns rose like river water, becoming a racing torrent by the time she reentered the bedroom.

The creature was still there, standing on the bed, rending the wall, opening a jagged hole that went clear through to the outside.

Beyond the shattered plaster and broken beams, a porch light flickered, streetlights blazed, evening stars peaked through gathering clouds . . . and beneath those points of light, a churning river spilled over the brink of a thundering precipice.

The view frightened her, not because she believed any of it was real, but because seeing such things marked a major regression in her life. Not since adolescence had she seen things so out of control. Now that she was seeing them, however, there was nothing to do but ride them out and play along.

She splashed into the room, raising the dagger and bringing it down so that its hook sank deep into the beast's pulpy hide.

The thing shrieked and looked up at her. Their faces nearly touched as she tried retracting the blade, but the barbed hook held fast. Pulling the blade only drew the beast closer.

"What did you expect?" it asked as it grabbed hold of her neck. "That dagger's made for gaffing, not for rending!" Its claws dug in, breaking her skin. "Work with me!" it said. "Help me ruin what's left of your life."

She twisted the hook. The thing shrieked as Kate climbed onto the bed. She set her foot on the beast's belly and yanked the hook out of its back. The barb came free in a shower of pasty blood.

"I was only helping," the grief shrieked as she brought the barb down again. This time she cleaved the thing from chest to groin. Its organs spilled out, running across the bed and diving into the rising currents that swirled toward the precipice beyond the shattered wall.

The beast stopped screaming. It lay motionless, drained. She drove the barbed dagger into its head and tossed it—dagger and all—toward the thundering cataract beyond the bed.

She had killed the beast, but the fantasy wasn't done with her yet. All around her the currents rose; the bed rocked from the floor and sailed forward until it wedged in the jagged break in the wall. Plaster crumbled. Beams shattered. The bed broke through into the foaming night.

Kate gripped the brass headboard, and the bed careened toward the thundering falls.

The bitterness lingered.

Kate swallowed again, forcing down the taste that clung to her tongue, and it was then that she felt the weight of Sara's concerned gaze. She realized that the two of them had been sitting in silence a long time. Sara was good that way. She gave a person time to think, time to wander the inner landscapes— no questions asked. Perhaps Sara understood a lot more than she let on.

"What're you staring at?" Sara asked.

"Nothing," Kate said. She put down her cup, setting it atop the T LEAVES card. "Just thinking."

"What're you thinking about?"

"About getting on with my life," Kate said.

She studied her cup. The little brass boat had faded, but it was still there, still afloat and sailing through the veil of churning mist.

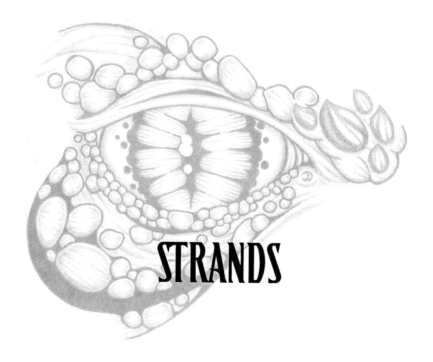

STRANDS

Our last story is entirely new, written specially for this collection, and yet it has been rattling around inside me for a very long time.

Fasten your seat belts, and enjoy the ride!

She was beautiful. They all were. That was Eddy's problem, and had been since he'd signed on as an adjunct instructor at the little college in the Pennsylvania highlands. The pay was lousy, but room and board were included. And the girls were stunning.

This afternoon he had found himself waylaid in the apartment of a red-haired teaching assistant named Helen. She'd invited him over for ironwort tea after his lecture on Epic Love: The Liaisons of Odysseus and Aeneas. But of course she didn't have any tea, and three hours later he was racing out the door, certain he would never make it to Pittsburgh in time for his 9:00 date with Penny.

"Take the short cut!" Helen said, calling from her second floor window. "You'll make it."

He paused beside his car. "You really think so?"

"Get you there in no time."

"But it's all back roads."

"And no traffic. You'll do it in less than an hour. She'll never suspect a thing."

That was another thing Eddy liked about his students. They had no illusions, no misconceived sense of self importance. They were all just passing through, casual encounters that were all about the moment.

"Turn left at the gates," Helen said. "Drive north till you hit the overpass. You can't miss it!"

So he drove north, speeding along a two-lane ribbon of yellow-lined road that dipped and curved through the Pennsylvania hills. After a while, as mountains rose around him and his view of the way ahead extended only a short distance beyond his racing hood, he began noticing the warning signs— yellow diamonds imprinted with silhouettes of swerving cars, leaping stags, and serpentine arrows. The latter were the most common, each marking a section of road that seemed more twisted than the one before.

Then came the shrines, handmade crosses rising above arrangements of dead flowers and framed portraits. The road had taken its share of lives, but this evening the weather was clear and dry. The car held the road. Eddy saw no need to cut his speed. He'd driven roads like this before. The dips and curves were always the same. Even the signs and shrines looked familiar.

He accelerated around the bend, past guardrail posts that had been dinged and scarred from collisions with less expert drivers. At one point the posts fell away completely, revealing a steep slope marked by a hand-lettered memorial:

Hamilton McKenna
beloved husband, father, friend.

A faded portrait showed a round-faced man with a flat nose and close-set eyes. The image fluttered in the wind, making fleeting eye contact with Eddy as he rounded the bend.

And that's when it happened.

With his windows raised and radio playing, Eddy never heard the roar of the approaching engine until the Plymouth Fury cleared the rise directly in front of him. He saw the glint of evening sun on its grill and a spattering of rust (or was it blood) on its hood. The Fury swerved, crossing the center line, screaming right into Eddy's path.

The image seemed to hover before him, filling his view as his car raced forward. Then he reacted, cut the wheel, and held on as his front tires roared onto the gravel shoulder. The Fury swerved too, clipping Eddy's sideview mirror before vanishing in a scream of burning rubber. . . .

Eddy hit the brakes, but his car kept moving. Gravel thundered beneath the floor, changing pitch as a post rose before him, splintered and scarred from where it had been sideswiped in a previous collision. But it was not going to be sideswiped this time. Eddy was going to hit the thing head on.

WHAM!

The world vanished, enveloped by billowing white. It was the airbag, slamming his face as his shoulder harness grabbed his torso.

And then it was over.

The bag deflated, sagging into his lap to reveal his hood crumpled against the shattered post. Steam rose from the grill. The car had stalled.

He sat back, turned his neck, flexed his shoulders. Everything moved as it should. No pain. He grabbed the rearview, twisting it until his reflection appeared in the glass. Airbag powder covered his face. Otherwise he looked fine. No blood. No contusions. But there were other things to consider. The Fury driver, for one.

"Jerk!" He turned in his seat, looking back through the settling dust. "Stupid idiot!" He wanted that guy caught. "Going to sue your ass!" He grabbed his cell phone, dialed 911, pressed it to his ear.

Silence.

He looked at the phone.

No signal.

That could change, of course. Country roads had a way of weaving in and out of range. A tenth of a mile could make all the difference. And there was something else to consider. A bigger issue. One that loomed all the larger now that he knew he wasn't hurt.

He checked the time: 7:24 PM. No way he'd make it now. He needed to get word to Penny before she left the house, tell her he'd been in an accident, play on her sympathies. But to do that he needed a working phone.

"So what now?"

He looked at the hood: caved in around the pole, bowed along the top. That was surface damage, right? What mattered was under the hood. He put the car in park and wrenched the key. The engine cranked and turned over. Something rattled. Maybe it was nothing.

"One way to find out."

He pushed the deflated airbag down between his knees and shifted into reverse. The rattling grew louder, but the car moved. He backed onto the road, shifted to forward, tried driving. The engine screamed, but he was moving, climbing onto a rise that descended down toward another hairpin turn.

That's when he saw the bodies.

The first lay across the center line, pressed flat and trailing a skid of blood. *Raccoon*, he thought, noting how the forepaws resembled hands.

But the raccoon wasn't the worst of it.

A short distance away, in a similar spread-eagle pose, a man in a plaid shirt and bib overalls lay facedown on the shoulder. Fresh blood pooled around his head.

"The Fury!" Eddy ran his hand along his dusty windshield, trying to get a better look as he approached the scene. "The jerk hit him and ran."

Something else lay in the road, a strangely incongruous detail that caught the light of the setting sun, reflecting it into Eddy's eyes as he came to a stop. It looked like a snow shovel.

"The hell?" Eddy shut off his car, opened the door, and stepped out into the hot August evening. "A snow shovel?"

The man shifted, clawing the gravel. He was still alive.

Eddy hurried toward him.

The man rolled onto his side, face bloody, eyes wide, pupils so dilated that they seemed to overrun his eyes. They looked almost like the eyes of an animal, an impression that was reinforced by the man's angled face and wooly beard. "No." The man blinked, looking at Eddy. "Go!"

"Don't move, Mister."

The man recoiled, falling back against the grill of Eddy's car.

"Lie down," Eddy said. "I'll get help."

"No!" The man kept moving, pulling himself up, slapping a hand against the dented hood. "Get away."

"I'm trying to help—"

"No help!" The man tried standing, kicking the ground with legs that bent backward at the knees.

"Your legs," Eddy said. "They're broken."

"No!"

Eddy grabbed the man by his overalls, pulling him away from the car, easing him back to the ground. "You need to take it easy, Mister."

The man said nothing.

Eddy backed away, checking his phone again. Still no signal. He looked around. There was a house on the hill, its upper floor visible beyond a grassy rise. "Is that your house?" Eddy asked.

"No," the man said, his voice strained, full of pain. "Go! Get out!" His voice tightened as he spoke, becoming low-pitched and feral, like the bleat of a wounded animal.

"I need to find a phone," Eddy said. "Call for help."

A blood bubble formed between the man's lips, bursting as he exhaled.

"I'll be right back," Eddy said.

The man trembled.

"Hang in there, Mister." Eddy removed his jacket, spread it over the man's chest, tucked it down against his shoulders. "I'll be back."

The man kept shaking.

Eddy turned and ran, heading for the house that seemed to stand just beyond the rise.

The house was built in the Greek Revival style of the early nineteenth century: round columns, Doric pediment, dentil cornice. It was also much larger and farther off than it had seemed from the road. He realized these things as he reached the crest and found the roof and upper floor standing behind yet another rise, this one capped with a wire fence.

He hurried on, down the slope to where a shallow stream muddied the ground, and then back up again to find the house looking even larger than before—more mansion than farmhouse. He shielded his eyes, blocking the setting sun's glare that reflected from the second-floor windows. There seemed to be someone up there, a woman silhouetted behind mullioned panes. He waved. "Hey!"

The silhouette moved.

He climbed over the wire fence and started down the slope. "Hey! There's been an accident!"

Part of the house sank below the rise as he descended, but the silhouette in the second floor remained in view, moving back and forth in slow, repetitive motion. He watched it move as the ground turned wet beneath his shoes. No stream here. Instead, a wide expanse of mud lay between him and the next rise. What now? He looked at the silhouette. "Hey!" He waved his arms. "Can you hear me?" The shadow leaned toward the window. Eddy made out a hand: palm up, fingers raised, gesturing for him to keep coming.

He looked at the muddy pool in front of him, too wide to walk around, but broken intermittently with curved rocks that might serve as a path to the other side. The trick would be getting to the first one, a rounded boulder that stood nearly four feet from the soggy bank. Eddy walked toward it, got into position, and glanced again at the house. The silhouette was still there. "I'm coming," he called. Then he leaped toward the boulder, falling forward as he landed, slapping his hands against a surface that felt more like flesh than stone.

And then the stone screamed.

Eddy leaped away, lost balance, and landed on his butt with a muddy splash. The screaming rock kept moving, turning around to regard Eddy with beady eyes and a flattened nose. It was a hog. A giant one. The biggest one Eddy had ever seen.

"Get away!" Eddy kicked mud at its face.

The animal raised its head, bore its tusks, and backed away.

Eddy got up and stumbled backward, climbed onto the shore, and kept backing away until he came to something that looked like a small rowboat. He glanced inside it. "Aw gross!"

He stumbled away.

The hog kept watching, joined now by a half dozen of his piggy friends—none of which looked like stones now that their heads were out of the muck.

Eddy's mud-soaked shoes made farting sounds as he rounded the little wooden structure that was no more a rowboat than the pigs were boulders. Instead, it was a wooden feed trough. And inside it, where a reasonable person might expect to see a smattering of hog slop, lay a jumbled collection of rodent bones. *Roadkill!* Eddy put it together. *The man on the road . . . he was harvesting roadkill . . . scraping it up with his snow shovel . . . that's what he was doing when the Fury nailed him . . . getting roadkill to feed his hogs.*

As if to confirm the suspicion, the closest hog let out a massive belch. The sound was oddly human. And the animal's face. . . .

Eddy did a double take, noting the flat nose and close-set eyes. The hog looked familiar.

"Hey!"

Eddy looked up.

"Hey, you!" It was the person in the window, leaning out now, her face shimmering in the evening light. She looked young and trim, classically beautiful. "You better quit fooling around and get up here!"

"Me?"

"Yes, you!" the woman said, her voice filling the ravine, incredibly clear in spite of the distance. "You ran into him, didn't you?"

"No," Eddy said. "It wasn't me. It was a Fury! A Plymouth!"

"Don't lie!" the woman said. "It was you. I saw the whole thing. And you're lucky he didn't take off your foot!"

"My foot."

"He could do it, too. Old Ham—he doesn't like people smacking into him, jumping on his back like he's some kind of boulder."

"Old Ham?" Eddy glanced at the wallowing hog. "You mean the pig?"

"Yes, the pig! Who else would I be talking about? I see everything from up here. Everything!"

"Everything?"

"Absolutely."

"What about the road? Did you see the accident?"

"The what?"

"The hit and run? Did you see—"

"You need to get up here if you want to talk."

"But there's—"

"There's a dry pass about five feet to your left," the woman said. "It's just beyond the feed trough."

He saw it.

"Don't just stand there," the woman said. "Get moving!"

"All right. But I'm going to need to use your phone!"

"Use my what?"

"Do you have a phone?"

"Yes, I'm alone. All alone. Just me and the animals. Now get up here before those hogs take a bite out of your ass!" She slammed the window.

Eddy pushed on.

The entire house came into view as he reached the top of the rise. It sat in the center of a flagstone courtyard, surrounded by trimmed shrubs, gardens of flowers, and miniature trees. And there were animals: cats and dogs mostly, but a few goats and sheep—all coexisting in a peaceable kingdom tableau that looked strangely staged, as if each piece had fallen into position moments before he cleared the rise.

He checked the window. The woman was still there, sitting behind the closed glass, rocking in the same repetitive manner he had noticed when he had first seen her. Although now the movements seemed more complex, almost like a dance.

A flight of limestone steps stretched down along the final rise. He paused before descending them, deciding to check his phone one last time. But now, instead of not having a signal, he found that his phone had no power. The fall in the mud had shorted the battery. Nothing to do now but continue on.

He started down the stairs, leaving muddy prints on the polished treads, continuing on when he reached the flagstone walk.

The animals moved closer, walking with him as he passed beneath the

Doric pediment. The front doors stood open. He stepped inside to find the place furnished with antiques, tapestries, paintings, and marble statues that glowed with the light of the setting sun. The interior seemed to have been designed to capture evening light, admitting it through west-facing windows and holding on to it with a thousand polished surfaces. The house glowed.

The woman called down to him. "Up here!"

He looked at his feet. "I'm all muddy."

"Up here!"

A fat tom cat rubbed his muddy cuffs, turned and made another pass before bounding onto the stairs. It paused, looked back, and meowed. *Now*, it said. *Now!* Then it turned and darted toward the second floor.

Eddy followed.

At last, he found her. Dressed in a chalk-white gown, sitting at a loom. At her side, a tall window looked out over the rolling ground that descended to the side of the road. Eddy's car was in plain view. So was the body.

"You saw it," he said. "You saw it all, didn't you?"

She worked her loom, the leavers clicking softly. "I see everything." She spoke without looking at him.

"Did you call for help?"

"No."

"We need to."

"You need to sit down."

He looked around. No chairs.

"On the bed." She gestured. "Sit on the bed."

"We have to—"

"Sit on the bed!" And now she turned, letting him see her face: long nose, full cheeks, polished eyes with barely a hint of iris and pupil. She looked like a statue, remarkably beautiful and cold.

The strength left his legs. He sat, skidding as his muddy pants struck the satin sheets.

"You didn't have an accident," she said.

"But I did. The Fury ran me into a pole, the same Fury that hit that man—"

"That was no accident either." She turned to face the loom, giving him the back of her head. She wore her hair pulled back, gathered in a sculpted bun above the nape of her neck. "No accidents." Her loom clicked. "I brought you here, Eddy." She turned, looking at him with one cold eye. "And I think I'll keep you."

He stood up.

"Please, Eddy." She reached back along the side of her head, probing her tightly gathered hair until she came away with a single strand. "I want you to stay."

"But I can't. I have to—"

She plucked the hair. "Do I have to make you?" She turned back to face her loom. "I can do that, you know. I can do anything I want." She threaded the hair onto the weave. The loom clicked.

Outside, tires squealed.

Eddy looked out the window to see a patrol car pulling to the shoulder.

"No need to call the police now," the woman said.

An officer stepped from the patrol car and knelt beside the body that was still covered with Eddy's jacket.

"Your wallet is in there, you know. In your breast pocket. And that blood on your car's grill and hood is most definitely the dead man's."

"He's dead?"

The loom clicked. "He is now." She looked back at him again. "It sure looks like you killed him, Eddy."

"How do you know my name?"

"Oh please, don't be droll. The fact that I know your name should be the least of your worries." She touched her hair again, selecting another strand. "Let's consider the big ones, the big worries—like what will happen to you if you go back down there now."

"What?" Eddy asked. "What will happen?"

"They'll arrest you."

"They?"

She threaded the new strand into the weave, clicked it into place, tamped it down.

Outside, a second cruiser raced over the hill, lights flashing, tires squealing.

"They," she said, making it clear the question had been answered. "But it's all right, Eddy. I can protect you. I can fix everything so no one will ever find you."

The large tom cat leaped onto the bed.

The woman frowned. "No, Brian. Get out of here. You had your time."

The cat meowed: *Please!*

"No. It's Eddy's turn. Get out of here."

The cat didn't move.

"Don't be a pig, Brian. You know what happens to cats who act like pigs?"

The cat leaped from the bed, dashed across the floor, but paused before leaving. It looked back at Eddy. *Circe*, it meowed. *Her name is Circe. Get it?*

"You're going to get it if you don't get out of here," Circe said. "Scram!"

The cat left.

Eddy frowned. "Circe?"

"I suppose it's his word against mine."

"The witch?"

"Please! I'm a nymph. Stick around. You'll learn to appreciate the difference."

"You mean—" Eddy collapsed back onto the bed. "You mean like in the Greek myths? That Circe?"

"You know another one?"

"But—"

"You're wondering what I'm doing here?" She grinned. "Well, wonder no more, Eddy. This is America. Everybody here is from somewhere else."

"You immigrated?"

"Had to. Was the only way to get any peace. Stupid Odysseus. I never should have let him go. I had to get out of there, relocate in a place where no one would come looking for me unless I were looking for them. So I came here, traded shipwrecks for car crashes. In all, it's worked out well."

He got up again, walked to the window, looked out at the dogs, cats, goats. "And all these animals?"

"Lovers. But that's not all of them. Just the ones that please me. The troublemakers have to spend time in the wallow. And the real rascals end up groundhogs and possums."

"Roadkill."

She shrugged. "Eventually." She took another strand from her hair. "After all, pigs must eat."

"I thought so."

"Thought what?"

"That guy with the snow shovel, he was harvesting roadkill, wasn't he?"

"No," she said. "Not really. That's what he was *supposed* to be doing, but the truth is he was making a run for it. I knew that even before he offered to do the day's roadkill duties. He thought he could outsmart me, so I brought the Fury to come take him out." She set the new strand into the loom.

"You made the Fury hit him?"

In the distance, an engine revved.

"*Made* the Fury hit him?" She shrugged again. "I suppose, although I'm sure the kid behind the wheel would call it an accident. He started refurbishing that car three months ago. Today he decided to put it through its paces . . .

put the pedal to the metal." She looked back at Eddy. "You're standing again. Please . . . sit on the bed. I'll be right with you."

Outside, the roar of the Fury's engine drew nearer, changing pitch as it neared the first hairpin turn.

"I know what you're thinking," she said. "You're thinking of running back to the road, getting the police to stop that car. If you can do that, they'll have their killer and you can go free."

"Is that true?"

"It's what you're thinking, isn't it?"

"But will I be free? Will you let me go?"

"One way to find out."

He turned and ran, racing from the room and descending the stairs three and four at a time. Brian the cat lay in the front hall. Eddy leaped over him, onto the porch, and down onto the flagstone courtyard. The Fury's engine raced louder, coming nearer—but Eddy was flying now, bounding up the limestone stairs to the top of the first rise.

The Fury was still rounding the hairpin turn, tires squealing, engine revving and falling back as it approached the scene of the accident.

"Hey!" Eddy waved at the troopers. "That car!" He pointed toward the bend. "Stop that car!"

One of the officers had retrieved Eddy's wallet from the jacket pocket. He opened it, glanced at something, then looked up at Eddy. *Checking my photo ID*, Eddy thought.

"Not me!" Eddy shouted. "You want him!" He pointed again. "Stop that car!" Then he started running again—down the slope, past the hog wallow, and then up the other side to see the Fury racing into view. Eddy wanted to yell once more, but he was out of breath, doubled over with exhaustion, watching helplessly as the Fury's driver lost control and slammed into the back of Eddy's car. The tank exploded. The Fury kept moving, flipping over as it plowed into the first patrol car . . . then the other.

KaBOOM!

The scene vanished in a black and orange fireball, and Eddy, having reached his limit, collapsed and slid backward down the slope, losing consciousness long before he reached the bottom.

He awoke to find a hog looking down at him.

"Forget about it." Old Ham grunted. "No one leaves." Then it turned and walked back into the wallow, bubbles rising from its haunches as it broke wind beneath the water line.

Circe appeared on the ridge, looking down at Eddy. "It's done," she said. "You're off the hook. Forensics will determine you died in the blast. You can move in with me, and no one will be the wiser."

Eddy closed his eyes, hoping the world would go back to normal when he opened them again.

"Look," Circe said. "You can lie there and become a pig like your friend Hamilton, or you can come home with me. Either choice is a gift, considering the life you've been leading. At least here, everyone knows the score."

He opened his eyes in time to see her turn back toward the house.

Eddy stayed put, lying on his back on the edge of the wallow, staring up into the wine-dark sky.

HINDSIGHT

LOOKING BACK

Western Pennsylvania, where I make my home, has few straight lines. It is a place where roads meander, dip, and rise through a landscape shaped by glaciers and industry. It is a world where neighborhoods hide in private hollows, wrong turns lead down strange roads, and a person can get lost in an instant.

The latter happened a few months back when a closed road forced me onto a street that I thought led toward home. Instead, I quickly found myself in *terra incognita*: an old train station, forgotten tracks, scrap yards piled with rust. When another turn came, I took it, emerging onto a street that led up a hill and into a neighborhood of peeling paint and hanging gutters. Totally lost, I continued on, steering by hunch, finally clearing a crest to emerge back into familiar territory.

Three minutes later I was home.

The incident didn't seem important at the time. An inconvenience, easily forgotten. But then, a few months later, something happened to bring it back.

I like writing at the end of the day, starting at sunset, settling into fiction as the world goes dim. When the muse is right, I don't notice the time until after 9:00. Then I stop, put the work away, and reenter the world with a walk through my neighborhood's familiar streets. Knowing the way, I navigate on muscle memory, barely noticing my surroundings. But one night, having gone perhaps a thousand feet from my home, I glimpsed something that made me pause.

It beckoned from a place I'd passed hundreds of times, a right-angled turn where one street ended and another began. Houses lined the way, close-set colonials with wooded backyards. But tonight the woods looked different. Perhaps the trees had been cut back, or maybe I was just being more attentive than usual. Whatever the case, on this night I caught what looked like a splash of light between two of the houses. It was there for a moment, then gone, hidden by the edge of a bay window. I paused, backtracked, and there it was again, a long swatch of incandescence extending into the distance: a dozen miles of glowing buildings, radio towers, streetlamps, and cars—all stretching away through the Ohio River valley, toward the neon-lit towers of downtown Pittsburgh.

I stepped from the sidewalk, trespassing now, moving past the bay window to stand on the edge of someone's backyard. Below me, in the middle distance beyond the precipice, lay a road that I sometimes followed when coming home from the city. I looked along it, discerning the place where I had been detoured a few weeks before. The train station was there, diminished by distance, toy-like beside its forgotten tracks. Farther on lay the scrap yards, and, beyond them, a dim road rose toward a neighborhood of rundown duplexes. It was the same route that had confounded me weeks earlier, but now it all made sense. Indeed, I wondered how I could have felt so lost while driving it.

That revelation occurred at the end of March. It's nearly May, now. Evenings are longer. Blossoms and leaves cover the trees. The warm sun is setting beyond my office window. And I am at my desk, looking over the manuscript of a book representing thirty years of writing: twenty-two stories of fantasy and science fiction written over the span of three decades. I also wrote horror and mystery stories in that time, but those (with the exception of a few that have been included here in the section labeled *Night Visions*) are for another volume.

I spent a lot of time getting lost during those three decades of writing. I made wrong turns, entered places I hadn't planned to go, and occasionally feared it was all for naught, that I would never get anywhere.

Yet here I am.

This collection contains my first story, the minor piece "Cockroaches" that sold to *Amazing Stories* in 1979. It also contains my relatively new novelette "The Others," which, by the time this book is released, will have appeared in the August/September issue of *The Magazine of Fantasy of Science Fiction*.

Thirty years.

It seemed like a maze while I lived it, but now—from the high ground—it looks orderly, logical, surprisingly close to home.

In the spring of 1978, after having walked away from an unfinished journalism degree to try my hand at a string of unfulfilling jobs, I decided to take a shot at becoming a science-fiction writer. I'd been reading the stuff voraciously and figured I knew enough to write some stories of my own.

I set a goal of writing something each month for one year. That seemed like a reasonable rate, one that would certainly yield at least one professional sale. Then, once I had my foot in the door, I figured I'd be only a step away from selling everything I wrote. Such are the dreams of youth.

In order to monitor my progress, I created a wallet card with twelve rows (one for each story I intended to write) and two columns (one for the date I started a story, the other for the date I finished it). Somehow this seemed important, carrying around a quantified record of my writing progress. Any newbie could claim to be a writer, but I had a document to prove it.

I also purchased a single-drawer file cabinet, hanging files, and manila folders. When I finished a story, its carbon copy (this was the 70s, after all) would be filed along with a record of where I had sent the original.

My first story was a character study of a man adrift in deep space. His ship's life support is fully functional, but the propulsion system is shot. He's not going anywhere. Needless to say, he begins losing his mind. I called the story "Adrift in the Ocean of Dreams." It took well over a month to write, but, in spite of that effort, you won't find that story in this book. Indeed, you won't find it anywhere, unless you feel like rooting through the old files that I keep in a shed behind my house. I sent "Adrift" to a few places: *Analog*, *F&SF*, and *Asimov's* (where editor George Scithers kindly told me that I had a flair for characterization), but I soon realized that the story was little more than a practice run. I haven't looked at it in years, but I'm pretty sure it's a mess. Still, writing it helped me get my bearings. In particular, it taught me how difficult it is to pull off single-character narratives.

The second story was "Cockroaches." I banged it out in a single sitting, put it in the mail the next day, and went to work on a third story. Then a fourth.

When a manuscript came back, I logged its return date in the file, wrote a new cover letter, and put the story back in the mail. All rejections, everything from the personally typed notes from George Scithers at *Asimov's* to the form letters from *Unearth Magazine* (which interestingly enough came with instructions on turning the printed rejections into origami swans), went into the files. No sales yet, but I was learning.

I should point out that none of my stories were being submitted blind. I didn't use market lists (except to learn about upcoming magazines), and nearly everything I sent out went to the addresses on the mastheads of magazines that I had read and studied, of which there were more than enough to keep a fledgling busy: *Amazing, Analog, Asimov's, Destinies, F&SF, Fantastic, Galaxy, Galileo, Omni, Questar, Unearth.*

I thought I knew what I was doing. But after a while I began wondering if I had missed something. What if my stories weren't selling because they were violating some secret code? Worse, what if the publications were really closed shops, and the kindly rejections I sometimes received merely schemes to keep me from dropping my subscriptions. Yes, those are crazy theories, but never underestimate the power of doubt.

I figured I had two choices. I could keep writing until something sold, or I could change course and cut my losses.

I opted for the former, feeling I'd already gone too far to turn back. Besides, my day job, which involved managing my father's small-town print shop, wasn't exactly the stuff dreams are made on.

So I kept writing and submitting.

But I also went back to school to finish that degree in journalism. Just in case.

Then, on April 25, 1979 (which by some strange coincidence is exactly thirty years from the day I sit writing this afterword), I put "Cockroaches" in the mail to *Amazing Stories.* This time I didn't even bother including a cover letter. I just sent it off, fully expecting it to come back.

But it didn't.

Instead, I soon received a small envelope from publisher Arthur Bernhard. Inside was a contract. He was purchasing the story.

And so after a year of producing a dozen manuscripts, my second story became my first professional sale. The door had opened, and I wasn't about to back away now.

More sales followed.

The introductions to the individual stories in this collection tell the rest.

Was it really that easy?

Perhaps not. But it looks that way from the high ground of thirty years.

I offer these memories in the hopes that they might encourage a new generation of not-yet-published writers, people who might sometimes feel there is more to life than collecting rejections. There is, of course, and although it may not seem like it at the time, the high ground is always there, waiting for you to discover how close it really is. If you believe that, then I encourage you to keep working. Write each day. Trust your instincts. And believe that the road ahead may yet carry you home.

Tomorrow I plan to get back to work on the manuscript for a new novel that takes up where last year's *Veins* left off. The new project, *Vipers*, is an ambitious book, and, although the writing was going well when I set it aside to work on this afterword, there have been setbacks.

On bad days I still worry about getting lost, for although I am aware of the symmetry of the route that has brought me here, I remain uncertain as ever of the road ahead.

Billy Wilder said that hindsight is twenty-twenty. That's true. But what is foresight if not a hopeful aberration, a movement away from the certainty of now, a journey into an as-yet-unformed world.

It's after 9:00. Time to push back from this desk, take a walk, reenter the world. The new project can wait until tomorrow. Tonight, I pause once more at the precipice, look into the valley, contemplate the roads that brought me here, and wonder at those that I've yet to travel.

ALSO FROM LAWRENCE C. CONNOLLY

Fleeing from what should have been a perfect crime, four crooks in a black Mustang race into the Pennsylvania highlands. On the backseat, a briefcase full of cash. On their tail, a tattooed madman who wants them dead.

The driver calls himself Axle. A local boy, he knows the landscape, the coal-hauling roads and steep trails that lead to the perfect hideout: the crater of an abandoned mine. But Axle fears the crater. Terrible things happened there. Things that he has spent years trying to forget.

Enter Kwetis, the nightflyer, a specter from Axle's ancestral past. Part memory, part nightmare, Kwetis has planned a heist of his own. And soon Axle, his partners in crime, and their pursuer will learn that their arrival at the mine was foretold long ago . . . and that each of them is a piece of a plan devised by the spirits of the Earth.

A finalist for the 2009 Eric Hoffer Award.

Nominated for the 2nd Annual Black Quill Award for Best Small-Press Chill.

Appeared on the Preliminary Ballot for the 2008 Bram Stoker Award for Superior Achievement in a First Novel.

Trade Paperback • 260 Pages • 8 Illustrations • $15.00
ISBN 13: 978-1-934571-00-2 • ISBN 10: 1-934571-00-8

www.VeinsTheNovel.com | www.FantasistEnt.com

Fasten your seatbelts and prepare to take your reading experience to a whole new level. With *Veins: The Soundtrack*, author and musician Lawrence C. Connolly provides a series of instrumental soundscapes inspired by themes and scenes from his critically acclaimed supernatural thriller *Veins*. Performing with his band, Connolly delivers a mix of trance, rock, and ambient compositions designed to complement the novel.

The CD also includes two music and spoken-word bonus tracks, each showcasing a complete story from *Visions*, "Aberrations" and "Echoes."

Packaged with Star E. Olson's distinctive cover art and including a synopsis and full production credits, *Veins: The Soundtrack* is a must for every dark fantasy reader.

Read the book. Hear the soundtrack. Enter a world where fantasy lives.

6 Tracks & 2 Bonus Tracks • Total Run Time: 38:13 • $10.00
UPC: 700261267371 • ID#: FE-934571-00-2

INCLUDES CONTRIBUTIONS FROM LAWRENCE C. CONNOLLY

Connolly opens *Sails & Sorcery* with a haunting introduction comparing the stories to the mysterious treasures he found during a scuba dive.

Featuring 28 stories of mermaids, pirates, and magic beyond your wildest dreams as well as an afterword by Mark Summers & John Baur, creators of International Talk Like a Pirate Day, *Sails & Sorcery* is beautifully illustrated by Julie Dillon.

Trade Paperback • 456 Pages
28 Stories • 42 Illustrations • $23.00
ISBN 13: 978-0-9713608-9-1 • ISBN 10: 0-9713608-9-8

www.FEBooks.net

You've read Connolly's "Beerwulf," now read 23 additional stories that will tickle your funny bone while quenching your thirst for adventure. *Bash Down the Door and Slice Open the Badguy* is a veritable chorus line of worthless warriors, simpleton sorcerers, and hapless henchmen, brought to quirky life by the art of Chris Chua.

Grab your giant axe or vorpal sword, and prepare to meet your destiny with a smile on your face.

Trade Paperback • 276 Pages
24 Stories • 29 Illustrations • $17.00
ISBN 13: 978-0-9713608-5-3 • ISBN 10: 0-9713608-5-5

LaVergne, TN USA
14 September 2009
157782LV00004B/92/P